Pirate

Pirate

A Sam and Remi Fargo Adventure

CLIVE CUSSLER
AND ROBIN BURCELL

MICHAEL JOSEPH
an imprint of
PENGUIN BOOKS

MICHAEL JOSEPH

UK | USA | Canada | Ireland | Australia
India | New Zealand | South Africa

Michael Joseph is part of the Penguin Random House group of companies
whose addresses can be found at global.penguinrandomhouse.com.

First published in the United States by G. P. Putnam's Sons 2016
First published in Great Britain by Michael Joseph 2016
001

Printed in Great Britain by Clays Ltd, St Ives plc

A CIP catalogue record for this book is available from the British Library

HARDBACK ISBN: 978–0–718–18290–8
OM PAPERBACK ISBN: 978–0–718–18291–5

www.greenpenguin.co.uk

Penguin Random House is committed to a
sustainable future for our business, our readers
and our planet. This book is made from Forest
Stewardship Council® certified paper.

Characters

1216

Norfolk, England

William the Marshal—Earl of Pembroke, served King John.

Robert de Braose—King John's knight-turned-traitor.

Hugh Fitz Hubert—William the Marshal's trusted knight.

John de Lacy—King John's guard.

King John—King of England.

PRESENT DAY

Descendants of William the Marshal and Their Adversaries

Grace Herbert—distant relative to Sir Edward Herbert.

Sir Edmund Herbert—(fictional) illegitimate son of Edmund Mortimer, Second Lord Mortimer.

Hugh le Despenser—rumored lover of Kind Edward II, adversary of Roger Mortimer.

Captain Bridgeman—an alias for the pirate Henry Every, connected through family lineage to Hugh le Despenser.

Henry McGregor—Grace Herbert's cousin, inherited Nottingham estate.

Pickering's Used & Rare Books

Gerald Pickering—San Francisco bookseller, uncle to Bree Marshall.

Mr. Wickham—Mr. Pickering's cat.

Bree Marshall—Remi Fargo's employee in charge of fund-raising.

Larayne Pickering-Smith—Bree's cousin, daughter of Gerald Pickering.

Robber—later identified as Jakob "Jak" Stanislav.

Fargo Team

Sam Fargo

Remi (Longstreet) Fargo

Zoltán—Remi's Hungarian-born German shepherd.

Selma Wondrash—the Fargos' research assistant and go-to person.

Sandra—flight attendant on the Fargo jet.

Professor Lazlo Kemp—assists Selma with research, from Great Britain.

Pete Jeffcoat—Selma's research assistant, Corden's boyfriend.

Wendy Corden—Selma's research assistant, Jeffcoat's girlfriend.

Former DARPA Members

Ruben "Rube" Hayward—case officer, CIA's Directorate of Operations.

Nicholas Archer—owner of Archer Worldwide Security.

Avery Company

Charles Avery—corporate raider and maritime salvager.

Colin Fisk—head of Avery's security team.

Martin Edwards—Avery's CFO.

Alexandra Avery—Avery's wife.

Kipp Rogers—Alexandra Avery's private investigator.

Winton Page—Charles Avery's attorney.

Jak Stanislav—one of Fisk's henchmen.

Marlowe—Fisk henchman.

Ivan—Fisk henchman.

Victor—Fisk's new henchman.

Rogen—Fisk's new henchman.

Scholars and Academics

Professor Ian Hopkins—Arizona, sixteenth- and seventeenth-century English literature.

Meryl Walsh, "Miss Walsh"—curator, British Museum.

Madge Crowley—librarian, King's Lynn.

Nigel Ridgewell—King's Lynn tour guide, former professor/expert in Old English.

Professor Cedric Aldridge—Nottingham University History Department.

Percival "Percy" Wendorf—retired professor, Nottingham University.

Agatha Wendorf—Wendorf's wife.

Restaurateurs, Hoteliers, and Travel Guides

SAN FRANCISCO

Mr. Bryant—on-duty manager for Ritz-Carlton Hotel, San Francisco.

ARIZONA

Chef Marcellino Verzino—owner of Marcellino Ristorante, Scottsdale.

Sima—Verzino's wife.

JAMAICA

Melia—waitress at restaurant, Jamaica.

Jay-Jay—owner of biker bar, Jamaica.

Kemar—car rental employee, Jamaica.

Antwan—biker at Jay-Jay's bar.

Billy—biker at Jay-Jay's bar.

BRAZIL

António Alves—hired driver, university student, São Paolo, Brazil.

Henrique Salazar—António Alves's uncle.

Captain Delgado—captain of the *Golfinho*.

Nuno—youngest crew member of the *Golfinho*.

Police Officers

Sergeant Fauth—detective, Robbery Detail, San Francisco PD.

Sergeant Trevino—Fauth's partner, SFPD.

Deputy Wagner—Carteret County sheriff's deputy.

Pirate

Prologue

Bishop's Lynn, Norfolk, England
October 9, 1216

The first flurries of snow fell from the gray sky, the temperature plummeting as twilight deepened. William the Marshal, Earl of Pembroke, reined his spirited stallion to a stop, the three knights behind him following suit. Around them, the forest turned into a menacing maze of rustling shadows, the path no longer clear.

When William failed to see the horsemen they'd broken away from earlier that evening, he wondered for a moment if they had taken a wrong turn. But no. There was the twisted oak on the left, as he remembered. He and the three knights with him had ridden ahead to scout the path for the others who would be following the next day, guarding the king's treasure. And though William had argued against the move, hoping to wait for more reinforcements, the king's advisers insisted that it was important to secure the treasure's safety—especially now that Prince Louis of France had taken London and was proclaiming himself King of England. With half of King John's barons siding with Louis against him, he wanted the royal treasure out of the usurper's reach.

Robert de Braose rode up beside him and William looked over. "My men should have been here by now."

"Perhaps the colder weather has delayed them."

William held up his hand, demanding silence. The faintest of sounds caught his attention, and he strained to hear. "Listen . . ."

"I hear nothing."

There it was again. A rustling that differed from the wind in the trees.

Beside him, a whisper of metal as Robert drew his sword from its leather scabbard. Then a cry as several horsemen emerged from the forest, their swords drawn. William's horse reared at the unexpected charge. He fought to stay seated. He heard the air swoosh as Robert's sword arced toward him.

Instinctively, he lifted his shield. Too late. The sharp edge of Robert's blade struck his rib cage. The tight chain mail of his body tunic absorbed most of the blow, though pain shot through him.

Had Robert mistaken him for the enemy?

Impossible, he thought as he drew his sword. He whirled about, then took out the horseman closest to him. The man's body landed near that of William's youngest knight, Arthur de Clare.

Anger surged through him as he turned to Robert. "Have you gone mad?" he asked, almost too stunned to believe he'd been ambushed by one of the king's handpicked men.

"On the contrary," Robert said. He urged his mount forward, swung again, but he no longer held the element of surprise. Their blades collided, metal ringing. "I have finally come to my senses."

"By attacking me, you commit treason against the king. To what end?"

"Not my king, yours. I swear fealty to Louis of France."

The betrayal struck deep. "You were my friend."

Robert kicked at his horse's flanks, sword lunging as he leaned forward, then pulled back at the last second.

William anticipated the feint, waited, then swung his shield, knocking Robert from his horse. The stallion ran off. Behind them, Hugh Fitz Hubert, also unhorsed, took down one rebel knight, then turned to find another riding off, leading the remaining horses away. Two-upon-two, and William the only remaining horseman. He liked these odds much better and he circled around, facing Robert. "I trained you. I know your weaknesses."

"And I, yours." The clouds parted, and a shaft of moonlight glinted off Robert's weapon of choice. A one-edged blade combined the power and weight of an axe with the versatility of a sword. The end curved slightly into a deadly point—one which William had seen penetrate tightly woven chain mail.

The heavier weight of the weapon gave Robert an advantage over the lighter two-edged longsword that William used. But Robert would tire easier, especially now that he'd been knocked from his mount. And no sooner had that thought crossed William's mind than Robert charged him, swinging his blade like a battle-axe, aiming for the horse's legs.

William retreated, realizing the greater threat. Take out their horses and, even if they did survive, they could never get back in time to warn the king.

A hard thing to do—giving up the advantage—but William knew it was his only chance. He dismounted, slapping his horse on its flank, sending it off. Fitz Hubert and the rebel knight squared off, swords clashing.

He faced Robert. The two men sidestepped, round and round. William examined Robert's metal tunic, hoping there might be some flaw in the mail. "Why?" he asked between blows. He needed answers. He intended to survive.

Robert eyed him, shifting the weight of his sword in his hand. "There is enough gold in the king's camp to fund an entire army—take back what was lost by *your* inept king's actions."

"His actions are his to make"—metal sparked against metal—"whether or not you find them to your liking."

"My family has lost everything," Robert said, circling William, searching for an opening, waiting for the right moment. "The king has lined his coffers with our gold—with our blood. Imprisoned my half brothers." He struck again and again. "That treasure belongs to us, and where it goes, we go."

William's muscles burned, he was tiring fast. Robert was a formidable enemy. Younger and stronger. The two men faced each other, their breath coming hard and fast. He lost track of Fitz Hubert and the other rebel knight but heard them somewhere in the dark. "You *will* fail," William said.

"Nay. The king is already dying."

Fear coursed through William. And, with it, the strength to lift his sword one last time. His blade arced. Robert parried—as

William knew he would. William's sword glanced upward, and he used the force to bring it farther, thrusting into the chain mail beneath Robert's arm. With both hands, he drove Robert to the ground.

William stood over Robert, noting the mixture of fear and loathing on his face as he stomped on Robert's sword arm. He pressed the point of his blade against Robert's throat. "What say you now?"

"We have still won."

"With your imminent demise?" It was a moment of glory. A heartbeat away from striking the deathblow to the traitor. Especially when he saw Fitz Hubert emerge from the trees unscathed.

But then Robert, his breathing labored, smiled at William. "Who do you think convinced the king to move his treasure for safekeeping, then set up this ambush? 'Twas I . . . Prince Louis, the true king, who sits now in London, will reap the benefits of your false king's greed . . . The treasure will be ours." He sucked in a lungful of air. "We have spies in every court . . . Every last jewel in his crown, every last bit of his gold, will finance Louis's campaign. England will be his . . . You and your ilk will swear fealty to Louis before this week is through."

"Not if I have aught to say about it."

William drove the sword home, twisting to make sure the final thrust brought death. He left the body where it was, then eyed Fitz Hubert. "Are you hurt?"

"A cracked rib, I fear."

"You heard?"

"Aye."

They managed to recover only one horse, William's, and they

decided because of Fitz Hubert's injury, William would ride to warn the king. When he reached the encampment in Bishop's Lynn, he saw it on the faces of the others. John de Lacy met him outside the king's tent, refusing him entry. "The king is ill. Dysentery. He wishes to see no one."

"He will see me. Make way or forfeit your life."

"What—"

William pushed past him and entered the tent, his nostrils flaring at the putrid air. The king's physician and two stewards were in attendance. Candles flickered in their stands around the king's pallet, casting a dim glow about the still form. Too still. William feared the king might be dead by now. But as he neared, he saw his chest rise and fall with each shallow breath. "My liege." William took to his knee at the king's bedside, bowing his head. "I have failed you."

The king's eyes opened slightly. A sheen of perspiration covered his brow. "How so?"

"What I have to say is best told in private."

King John said nothing at first, just stared at William. Then, a slight flick of his wrist. "Be gone. All."

William waited until the tent was cleared. And, even then, he was loath to impart the news. "I failed to recognize a traitor in your midst. Perhaps not the only one. Robert de Braose. He told me you were dying. Before he possibly could have heard."

"Dysentery."

"I fear not."

The king closed his eyes, and for a moment William worried that he would not waken. "Who would do this?"

"That, I do not know. But whoever has worked this evil, they know of the royal treasure you bring with you. It is meant to finance Prince Louis's claim on the English throne. They know you are moving it. Your illness was to be the distraction needed so that on the morrow they could take it."

"My son . . ." The king reached out, grasped at William's hand, his grip weak, feverish. "What of Henry?"

"He is safe. I will guard him with my life." The king's oldest son, a mere lad of nine, was innocent of the dishonesty and treachery of the last several kings—his father and all his relatives included. If there was to be any hope for England, it would be through a monarch who was untouched by greed and murder. "I fear that the temptation of such a treasure will be too much for the young prince's reign."

"He will need all of my treasure to finance his retribution. To win back our lands."

"My liege. If I may be frank. As long as that treasure exists, there will be those who want nothing more than to possess it. Louis of France is only the first of many. And lest you forget, the rebel barons you have fought against these past several months cannot be trusted. Not while the lure of gold and riches tempts them." He waited a moment to make sure his words were heard and understood. "A poor kingdom is far less desirable. Even more important, a young king barely old enough to rule a poor kingdom is no longer a threat . . ."

"What are you saying?"

"What if that treasure was lost this night while we were trying to move it through the quicksand of the fens? If you lose the treasure, you lose your son's enemies."

The king remained silent, his breathing shallow.

"You are dying, sire." Though he didn't want to believe, he knew the words were true. This was no dysentery. He'd seen it before. A slow poison that ate away at the gut. The king would last perhaps a week or more, his pain excruciating while he waited—nay, prayed for death. "This way, we know young Henry will be safe."

"And if my son should need the treasure? When he is older?"

"He won't. As long as it remains lost, he will be safe."

It was several long seconds before the king answered. "See that it is done."

One

San Francisco, California
Present day

Sam and Remi Fargo weaved their way around the tourists crowding the sidewalk. Once they were through the green pagoda-style gateway of Chinatown, the throng much thinner, Remi checked the map on her cell phone. "I have a feeling we took a wrong turn somewhere."

"To that restaurant," Sam replied, removing his revered panama hat. "A tourist trap, if I ever saw one."

She glanced at her husband, watching as he ran his fingers through his sun-streaked brown hair. He stood over a head taller than Remi, with broad shoulders and an athletic build. "I didn't hear you complaining when they brought out the moo shu pork."

"Where did we go wrong?"

"Ordering the Mongolian beef. Definitely a mistake."

"On the map, Remi."

She zoomed in, reading the streets. "Perhaps the shortcut through Chinatown wasn't so short."

"Maybe if you'd at least tell me where we're going, I could help?"

"It's the only part of this trip," Remi said, "that's my surprise for you. You haven't even shared what you have planned."

"For a reason." Sam put on his hat, and Remi linked her arm through his while they walked. He'd arranged this trip because their last adventure to the Solomon Islands had not been the hoped-for quiet vacation they'd planned. "I promise you nothing but rest, relaxation, and a week of no one trying to kill us."

"A whole week of downtime," she said, sidling closer to him as a cloud drifted over the sun, taking with it all the warmth of the early-September afternoon. "Have we had anything like that in a while?"

"Not that I can remember."

"There it is," she said, spying the bookstore. The flaking gold-leafed lettering in the window read *Pickering's Used & Rare Books.* "Just to show how very much I appreciate you traipsing all this way with me, I won't make you come in." Remi was being facetious. Sam's late father, a NASA engineer, had collected rare books, and Sam, also an engineer, had inherited that same passion.

He eyed the bookstore, then his wife. "What sort of husband would I be if something happened to you in there?"

"Dangerous things, books."

"Look what they did to your brain."

The pair crossed the street to the bookstore. A Siamese cat, resting on a stack of volumes in the window, looked up in disdain when a bell tinkled as Sam opened the door for Remi. The place smelled of musk and old paper, and Remi scanned the shelves, at first seeing nothing but used hardcovers and current paperbacks. She hid her disappointment from Sam, hoping they hadn't made the trip for nothing.

A gray-haired man, wearing gold spectacles, wandered in from the back, wiping his hands on a dusty cloth. He saw them and smiled. "May I help you find something?"

Sam's phone rang. He took it from his pocket, telling Remi, "I'll take it outside."

"Perfect, since this was meant to be a surprise."

He stepped out, and Remi waited until the door closed firmly behind him before turning to the proprietor. "Mr. Pickering?"

He nodded.

"I was told you had a copy of *The History of Pyrates and Privateers*."

His smile faltered for the barest of instances. "Of course. Right over here."

Pickering led her to a shelf where several identical volumes of *Pyrates and Privateers* sat. And while they were clearly reproductions, their faux gold-tooled leather binding gave them the appearance of something that might be found in a library centuries before.

He slid a copy from the shelf, used his cloth to wipe the dust from the top of it, then handed it to her. "How did you know we carried this particular volume?"

She decided to keep it vague—not wanting there to be any hurt feelings now that she knew the book was merely a reproduction. "A woman I work with knew of my husband's interest in lost artifacts and rare books." She opened the cover, admiring the detail that gave it an antiqued appearance. "It's a beautiful copy . . . Just not what I was hoping for."

He pushed his spectacles up onto the bridge of his nose. "It's popular with interior designers. Less emphasis on lost artifacts and more on decorating a coffee table. I do, on occasion, run across old volumes of historical significance. Perhaps your friend meant the Charles Johnson volumes on *A General History of Pyrates*? That, I do have."

"As do we. I was hoping for *Pyrates and Privateers* to round out our collection. My friend, no doubt, confused the two titles."

"Who did you say referred you here?"

"Bree Marshall."

"Oh. Well, that's—" A whoosh of air and the tinkling of the bell seemed to startle him, and he and Remi turned toward the door at the same time. Remi, expecting Sam, saw a much shorter, broad-shouldered man silhouetted against the light from the shop's window.

The bookseller eyed the man, then smiled at Remi. "Let me get the dust off of it and wrap it for you." And before she could object, tell him she really had no interest in buying a reproduction, he swept the book from her hands. "I'll be right back."

Her friend Bree had clearly misunderstood which book her uncle had in his shop. No matter. It was a beautiful copy and would look nice in Sam's office. He'd certainly appreciate the sentiment, she decided as she turned to browse the shelves while waiting, spying a copy of Galeazzi's eighteenth-century music treatise. It appeared to be a first edition, and she couldn't imagine why it was sitting in a simple locked glass case at the front counter.

"Do you work here?" the man asked.

She turned, caught a glimpse of dark hair, brown eyes, and a square-set jaw, as he moved from the backlighting of the window. "I'm sorry. No. He's in the back. Wrapping a gift for me."

He nodded, then walked past the aisle out of sight. When Mr. Pickering emerged from the back room, he walked around the counter to the register. The man stood off to one side, his hands shoved into the pockets of his black leather coat. His presence bothered Remi, though for no reason she could determine except perhaps the way he seemed to be watching their every move— and that he never took his hands from his pockets. She didn't like it when she couldn't see someone's hands.

Mr. Pickering slid her brown paper parcel onto the counter, his gnarled fingers shaking slightly. Nerves or age? she wondered.

"Thank you," she said. "How much do I owe you?"

"Oh. Right. Forty-nine ninety-five. Plus tax. No charge for the gift wrapping."

Not quite the wrapping she would have chosen. Aloud, she said, "On the good-news front, it's definitely less than I'd anticipated."

"Printed in China," he said, offering her a nervous smile.

She paid him, then tucked the parcel beneath her arm. The Siamese, on its windowed perch by the door, peered over at her, its tail twitching. Remi reached down and petted it, the cat purring, as she stole a glance at the stranger, who hadn't moved.

He pulled a gun from his coat pocket and pointed it at them. "Lady, you should've left when you had a chance. Keep your hands where I can see them."

Two

Sam finished his phone call with the hotel manager, who confirmed that the champagne on ice and gift for Remi had been delivered to their suite as ordered. Sam checked his watch, then glanced over at the bookstore, wondering what was taking Remi so long. Knowing her, she was probably having a lively discussion on some obscure topic with the bookseller and that customer who'd walked in shortly after. She'd been excited about the prospect of searching for this mystery book—something she was certain he'd want to add to his collection. But, really, how long could it take to find the thing and pay for it?

Time to urge Remi to shop a little faster or that champagne was bound to be room temperature by the time they made it back. He peered into the window, seeing no one, not even the cat who'd been perched on the books by the door. What he did see was Remi's purse sitting atop a wrapped parcel on the counter.

Not like her to leave her purse, he thought, and opened the door, the bells jingling as he stepped in. "Remi?"

The shop appeared empty.

"Remi?"

He eyed her unattended purse, then walked through the store, looking down each aisle, finally finding her standing in the doorway of what appeared to be an office or storage area at the back of the shop. "There you are."

"You're supposed to wait outside. Remember?"

"Everything okay?"

"I found that cookbook I've been searching for. The owner's wrapping it up for me. Now, leave or you'll ruin your surprise."

He stared for a second or two, unable to read anything on her face, her green eyes about as expressive as a poker player's. "I'll wait outside," he said. "Don't be long."

She smiled sweetly at him, never moving from the doorway. "I won't."

He retraced his steps. The door bells jangled overhead as he opened, then shut, the door, remaining inside the store.

While Remi wasn't exactly a stranger in the kitchen, she often joked that *cook* was a noun, not a verb.

Come to think of it, he couldn't recall her *ever* buying a cookbook, much less searching for one. Definitely not while they were married.

She was in trouble.

Nice time to be without a gun.

Typically, he carried a Smith & Wesson .357 Magnum, but they were in San Francisco for fun and so he'd left it on their plane.

Now what? Call 911 and hope the police arrived in time?

Not about to risk his wife's life, he silenced the ringer on his phone, set his hat on the counter, then quietly began opening drawers, searching for something a little more substantial than his small pocketknife to use as a weapon. He found a folding knife with a four-inch blade. He pulled it open, felt it lock. Decent weight, nicely balanced, point intact, probably used to open boxes, judging by the gumminess on the blade's edge. Now to get back to that room without being discovered.

He slid his hand into his wife's purse, found a small makeup bag, and took out a compact mirror. Flipping it open, he wiped the powder residue from the mirror with his pants, then edged his way down the aisle, making sure a row of bookshelves was between him and the door to that storeroom.

"You!" a deep voice shouted.

Sam froze.

"Forget the combination again and you die."

"Forgive me." Pickering, the bookseller, Sam figured, as he continued down the aisle. "I'm nervous."

"Please," Remi said. "There's no need to wave that gun around."

"Shut up! You, old man. Get that safe open."

"I—I'm trying."

Sam forced himself to breathe evenly. His wife was in that room, and all he wanted to do was rush in there, save her. But his haste could mean her death. A folding knife against a gunman. It was moments like this he was glad for the weapons-and-security training he'd received during his years at DARPA.

When he reached the end of the aisle, he stopped, used the mirror to peer around the corner.

Light spilled from the doorway of the storeroom onto the gray linoleum floor. Sam kept to the edge, careful not to cast a shadow. Holding the mirror out, he angled it to get a visual into the room.

Relief at the sight of his auburn-haired wife, now seated by a cluttered desk, was short-lived as he angled the compact farther and saw the short, swarthy fellow holding a semiauto to the shopkeeper's back. The two men stood in front of a large floor safe, the shopkeeper turning the dial. If Sam approached from this position, it put Remi between him and the gunman.

He didn't like the odds. At the moment, he had no other choice.

C'mon, Remi. Turn. See me . . .

He rocked the tiny mirror back and forth so that the light caught her face. Unfortunately, she looked away, leaning toward the desk, as an audible click indicated the safe had unlocked. Pickering pulled open the door, revealing a smooth wooden box large enough to hold two bottles of wine.

The gunman stepped closer to it. "What's in the box?"

"An old book. Just an antique."

"Put it on the desk."

He complied, placing the box on the desk near Remi.

Sam grasped the handle-heavy knife by its blade, stepped into the doorway, aimed, and threw.

The timing couldn't have been worse.

At that very moment, Remi jumped from her chair and swung the brass desk lamp against the gunman's hand. Sam's knife struck the man's shoulder. A shot cracked the air as he twisted, his gun flying from his hand.

Sam rushed in. The gunman pushed Pickering onto Remi,

then grabbed the box. He slammed it into Sam's head as he ran past and out the door.

Sam wasn't sure if it was the jangling of bells as the front door opened or the blow to his head causing the ringing.

"Sam . . . ?"

It was a second before he realized his wife was speaking to him. "Everyone okay?" he asked.

"Are *you* okay?" she replied.

"Fine . . ." He reached up, touched his head, his fingers covered in blood. "Looks like I came in second."

Remi set the gun on the desk, then pushed him into the chair she'd been sitting in moments before. Placing both hands on his cheeks, her skin warm, soft, she leaned down, searched his eyes, as if to ensure that he really was okay. "You're always first in my book. Ambulance?"

"Not necessary."

She nodded, took a closer look at his head, then turned toward the bookseller, who was using the desk to pull himself to his feet. "Mr. Pickering. Let me help you."

"I'm fine," the old man said. "Where's Mr. Wickham?"

"Mr. Wickham?" Remi asked.

"My cat. Wickham . . . ? Here, kitty, kitty . . ." A moment later, the Siamese wandered into the storeroom, and Pickering scooped it up.

"Well, then," Remi said, "everyone accounted for. Time to call the police."

Pickering eyed the phone as she put the receiver to her ear. "Is that necessary?" he asked.

"Very," she replied, pressing 911 on the keypad.

The police arrived about five minutes later, sirens blaring, even though she told them the robber had left.

One of the officers drew Sam aside to take his statement. When he'd finished, the officer asked Sam to show him where the gunman had been standing when his weapon discharged. Sam positioned himself next to the desk, then demonstrated the man's movement as Remi bashed his hand with the lamp. The officer stood where Sam stood, looking around. "And where were you when you threw the knife?"

"In the doorway."

"Stand there, please."

Sam did so.

The officer walked over, placed his finger on the doorframe. "Here's where the bullet hit."

Sam looked over, realized it was just a few inches from his head. "My lucky day."

"Mr. Fargo. While I commend your actions, in the future might I suggest you call the police?"

"If this happens again, I'll make sure to do that."

More often than not, he knew Remi would take the proactive approach.

It was one of the many things he loved about her, he thought, glancing toward the front of the store. She had already given her statement and was waiting patiently by the door.

A plainclothes investigator, Sergeant Fauth from the Robbery Detail, arrived and was questioning Mr. Pickering, who seemed distracted—understandable, considering his age and the circumstances. He opened the still-unlocked safe as the investigator asked, "Was anything else taken?"

"No. Just the box with the book in it. There's really nothing else of value in there. A few old coins. Spanish gold, but nothing that—well, nothing. The coins are still there."

"What sort of book was this?"

Pickering shrugged. "Just a reproduction of an old book on pirates. The book itself is of little value. I have several on the floor. I can show you." He walked out, retrieved one from the bookshelf, and set it on the desk.

"The box it was kept in, then? Did that have any value?"

"Not much. No."

"Why was it locked up, then?"

"I suppose in hopes that if someone thinks something is valuable, he'll ignore what really is?"

"Mr. Pickering," Sergeant Fauth said, looking at his notebook, then at the bookseller. "Any reason at all you can think of that this man targeted your store?"

He wiped a sheen of perspiration from his brow, his hand shaking slightly. The robbery had clearly taken its toll on him. "It may have something to do with a rumor that started about an original of this book being here. Why or who, I don't know. But really, page for page, the book that was stolen is the same book as this copy. A reproduction only." He patted the volume of *The History of Pyrates and Privateers* that he'd taken from the shelf.

The sergeant thanked him, then tucked his notebook into the breast pocket of his suit coat. CSIs arrived to dust for prints and photos. Once that process had started, the investigator handed his business card to both men. "If anything comes up—questions, something you remember—you have my number." He started to walk out, then turned toward Pickering. "Anyone you want me to call? Family member? Friend? Maybe come by, help you out?"

"No one. I'll be fine now."

He left, nodding at Remi on his way out the door.

Sam glanced over at the CSIs, then at Mr. Pickering, concerned about his being here by himself. "Are you sure we can't do anything for you?"

"No. Thank you, Mr. Fargo. I think after they're done here, I may just go upstairs and take a long nap."

Remi walked up to Pickering, giving him a hug. "I'm very sorry for what happened."

He took a deep breath and smiled at her. "I can't thank you enough. Your bold action may have saved our lives."

Sam picked up Remi's purse and handed it to her, wanting to speed their departure. "Ready?" he said, holding the door.

"Definitely."

"Wait," Mr. Pickering called out. "Your package. It would be a shame to have gone through all that and leave it behind."

"Thank you," she said, taking the parcel from him, then handing it to Sam as soon as they were outside.

"I take it this isn't a cookbook?" Sam asked.

"It's not even the book I came for. It's more a didn't-want-to-go-home-empty-handed book. I think it'll look nice on the table in your office."

"We'll certainly appreciate the backstory."

They crossed the street, walking uphill toward the Ritz-Carlton Hotel. They'd been in tough scrapes before—and they would be again. And even though he had every confidence in his wife's ability to take care of herself, he was never going to stop worrying about her.

It was this last thought that caught him each and every time. He reached over, took her hand in his, and she leaned her head into his shoulder. "You okay?" Sam asked after a bit.

"Me? Fine. I'm not the one bleeding."

"Superficial cut. It's already stopped."

She looked over at him. "We'll see when we're back at the hotel."

"Did you notice those gold coins in Pickering's safe?"

"Odd, isn't it? That the robber ignored the gold for a book in a box that he hadn't even seen?"

"A book that's supposed to be nothing but a reproduction."

"Definitely odd," she said as they turned onto Stockton Street by their hotel. "It was almost as if Mr. Pickering was downplaying the stolen book's value. Which doesn't make sense. I'd hate to have been shot over a reprint. Which brings me to my next point. What happened to that promised week of no one trying to kill us?"

"You didn't think I meant today, did you? Tomorrow. The week starts tomorrow."

"Well, then. Glad *that's* cleared up."

Inside the lobby, they stopped at the concierge desk, where Remi asked the woman working there to mail the book to their home with the other item she'd purchased earlier that morning—a large ceramic rooster from an antique shop—a gift for their researcher, Selma Wondrash, who said she'd always wanted a rooster for her kitchen.

"Insurance?" the woman asked. "Or special packing instructions?"

"No," Remi said. "It's just a book. It'll be fine."

"Same address as the rooster?"

"The same."

"I'll take care of it for you, Mrs. Fargo."

"Thank you."

At the door of their suite, Sam swiped the key card in the lock, then took a quick look inside before allowing Remi to enter. "Good to go," he said, holding the door for her.

She stepped into the room, and on a table in front of the sofa found a plate of sliced green apples, cheese, and a bottle of Billecart-Salmon Brut Rosé champagne on ice. He was pleased to see that someone from Guest Services had noticed they were later than expected and so refilled the ice bucket. The champagne was chilled to perfection, and the gift he'd arranged to have waiting there was next to the two fluted glasses. He handed the small, distinctively blue Tiffany box to Remi.

"And I didn't get you a thing."

"You got me a book."

"A copy, as it turns out."

He uncorked the champagne. "You'll make up for it later."

"Maybe," she said, untying the ribbon and lifting the lid to find a gold chain with a vintage-looking diamond-studded oval key charm. "The key to your heart?"

"No key needed there."

"Let's hope it's not to my new front door." She slipped the necklace over her head. "Imagine the cost to replace it every time we had to rekey."

"With all the security features we have recently added, diamond-studded keys would be the least of our expenses." In fact, they'd spent a small fortune turning their house into a veritable fortress after it had nearly been destroyed during a massive home invasion. Peace of mind, he thought, handing her a glass. Then, raising his own, he said, "New promise. Starting tomorrow, nothing but rest, relaxation, and a week of no one trying to kill us. Ah, yes . . . and my undivided attention."

"I'm holding you to your promise on that last part, Fargo."

"No one trying to kill us? Or my undivided attention?"

"Both would be nice," she said, touching her glass to his.

"Indeed."

Remi was still asleep when Sam awoke the next morning. He quietly rose from the bed and ordered their breakfast from room service. By the time it arrived, Remi emerged from the bedroom, her lithe form wrapped in a cream silk robe, her long auburn hair still damp from the shower. She kissed him, then took a seat at the table.

He poured her coffee and slid it across the table toward her, then resumed reading his paper. "Sleep well?"

"I did," she said, spooning fresh fruit into a small bowl of Greek yogurt. "Where are we off to today?"

"And spoil the surprise? Not saying." Sam turned the page of the *Chronicle*, scanning the articles, when his gaze caught on the headline *Robbery Victim Dies from Apparent Heart Attack*. "This changes things . . ."

"What?"

He lowered the paper and looked at her. "The bookseller, Gerald Pickering. He's dead."

Three

Charles Avery sat back in his seat, drinking coffee as he turned the page of the *San Francisco Chronicle*. In his late fifties, his dark hair salted with gray at the temples, he was—in his opinion—fit for a man of his age. Even so, he'd needed a second cup of coffee to get it together this morning, having flown in late last night on his jet from the East Coast to his San Francisco offices.

When he read about the death of the bookseller Gerald Pickering, he smiled. The news wasn't all that surprising. Not after yesterday's events.

Of course, all of that meant nothing if his men failed to recover the book and confirm it was the one he'd specifically been searching for.

Good riddance, Pickering, he thought as the head of his security team, Colin Fisk, walked into the room carrying a large, polished wooden box. Finally. "You found it," Avery said.

"The bookstore, yes. The book, no."

Avery took a deep breath, containing his anger. "What do you mean no?"

Fisk placed the box onto the table, lifting the lid, revealing a leather-bound volume. "Fake. We went back after the police left. Pickering said he sold it to another collector before my man got there."

"Did your man explain to him who I was?"

"Yes."

"And what I'd do to him if he didn't hand it over?"

"Yes."

"Did you at least find out who he sold it to?"

"I'm afraid he expired before we were able to obtain that info."

Avery lowered his coffee cup to the mahogany table, then forced himself to take yet another deep breath as he pinned his stare on Fisk, wondering if it had been a mistake to hire this team Fisk had suggested. They were supposed to be the best—and, in some respects, they were. They followed orders without question, and they'd certainly found Pickering easily enough, even after Avery's own men had failed to do so. Was it possible that Pickering had guessed Avery's intentions? Somehow known that the knowledge of the original book's existence in his shop meant his days were numbered?

For twenty years, Avery had been searching . . .

How was it that he'd gotten so close only to miss?

He lifted the book from the box, opening it to the first page.

Clearly, it was taken from a first edition, maybe even the one stolen from his family more than two centuries before. How else could someone so accurately reproduce the maps and wording? What this mere copy didn't have, and what he was sure he'd find in the volume Pickering had been hiding, was the key to deciphering the code on the maps printed within. What good is a map without a way to read the ciphered notations?

"You're sure you searched the place thoroughly?" Avery asked.

"Positive. We do have one possible lead, though. The names of the two who were listed as a victim and witness in the original police report. I did some checking on them. Apparently they're treasure hunters."

"Treasure hunters? Who's financing their operation? Go after the money and stop them in their tracks."

"They finance themselves," Fisk said. "And from what I've heard, others who have tried to go after them have failed. The Fargos aren't your average husband-and-wife hobbyists out searching for a quick buck. They're self-made multimillionaires who donate their proceeds to charity."

"Regular Robin Hoods? They should be easy to deal with."

"Highly trained Robin Hoods."

Avery reached for his coffee. "They haven't come up against me yet, have they?"

"No, sir. But forewarned is forearmed."

Four

No luck?" Sam asked as Remi called Bree Marshall's number again. They had just arrived by taxi at the new San Francisco Police Headquarters, at Mission Bay, after being contacted by Sergeant Fauth, who wanted to ask a few more questions.

"Her phone must be off," Remi replied, disconnecting. She didn't bother leaving a voice mail. She'd left one last night after the robbery, and this morning as well, telling Bree to call them at the Ritz-Carlton or call her cell as soon as possible. The last thing she wanted was for her friend to learn what happened to her uncle from a phone message. "I feel so bad. Between the robbery and—now this . . ."

"I'm sure she'll call soon. Let's see what the investigators have learned since yesterday."

"Hope it's good news. We could use some." The salt-tinged

wind gusted at them, and she wrapped her jacket tight to ward off the chill. "What on earth am I going to tell her when she calls?"

"Maybe she already knows and that's why she's not answering."

Sam held open the glass door, and the two walked inside the lobby to the left, where a few security guards waited to screen those entering.

Once through security, they checked in with an officer who was sitting behind a glass window, Sam saying, "Mr. and Mrs. Fargo to see Sergeant Fauth."

"Is he expecting you?"

"He is. Regarding yesterday's bookstore robbery."

She picked up the phone, repeated the information to whoever answered, then told Sam, "Sergeant Fauth's not here. But his partner, Sergeant Trevino, will be right down."

A dark-haired man stepped off the elevator about two minutes later, introducing himself. "Have to apologize for my partner's absence. Something came up," he said, escorting them to an interview room. "And, naturally, we're sorry for making you come all the way down here. But after Gerald Pickering's death, we're upgrading the case to a homicide."

Sam held the chair for Remi, then took the seat beside her. "The paper led us to believe his death was possibly due to a heart attack."

"And it may very well have been. Of course, we won't know until the findings of the autopsy are complete. But in our minds, the timing is suspect. We're looking at all angles. Either way, the crime was violent, and we'd like to catch the suspect." He opened his notebook, turned a page, saying, "I believe you told my partner yesterday that you were in Chinatown specifically to look for a book? Can you tell me why this particular shop?"

"A personal recommendation," Remi said. "I'd been searching for a specific book as a gift for my husband. I found out about it through Mr. Pickering's niece, Bree Marshall."

"And how do you know her?"

"She's done some volunteer work for the Fargo Foundation."

"Family business?"

"Family charitable organization," she said. After Sam had left DARPA, the Defense Advanced Research Projects Agency, to start his own business, he met and married Remi. With her encouragement, he invented the argon laser scanner, a device that at a distance could detect and identify mixed metals and alloys. There was an instant market. Four years later, they sold the Fargo Group to the highest bidder, securing the future for the rest of their lives. From there, they started the Fargo Foundation.

"Bree Marshall," she continued, "helped us on our last fundraiser for a new branch at the La Jolla Library. She's the one who mentioned that her uncle was trying to find a good home for an early-eighteenth-century book on pirates and maritime maps."

He looked up from his notes. "This would be the book we believe was stolen from the safe?"

"I never actually saw the book taken from the safe. Only the box. But I was definitely under the impression she was referring to a first edition."

"Because . . . ?"

"Mostly the way she talked about how her uncle would be so

pleased to find someone who would appreciate it for its historical value."

Sergeant Trevino eyed them, his pen poised over his note-book. "I understand you're professional treasure hunters?"

"We are," Sam said. "With the proceeds going to charity through the Fargo Foundation."

"I'll admit to knowing very little about rare books. But, see-ing as how it was a book of pirates and maps, is it possible that someone stole this book because they thought it would lead them to some long-forgotten pirate treasure?"

Remi laughed. "I suppose anything's possible. Honestly, though, had it not been for Mr. Pickering's niece saying he had a first edition for sale and us being in the area around the same time, I doubt I would have sought it out."

"Assuming the stolen book *was* a first edition, how much are we talking?"

"Depending on the condition . . ." Remi had researched the book when she'd first considered buying it for Sam. "I've seen copies for sale from several hundred dollars to a couple thou-sand. It's not a particularly valuable book because it was popular in its day. There are still a lot of first editions out there. For us, it was more sentimental," she said, placing her hand on Sam's.

"Exactly," Sam said. "We enjoy maritime history."

Sergeant Trevino closed his notebook. "That's about all I have for now. Unless either of you can think of anything we might've overlooked?"

"Not at the moment," Sam replied.

And Remi added, "We'll call if we think of anything else."

"Thanks again for coming all the way out here."

He escorted them back to the lobby.

Remi, about to follow Sam out the door, asked, "What's going to happen to Mr. Wickham?"

Sergeant Trevino's brows went up.

"The bookseller's cat."

"Right. I believe Pickering's next-door neighbor came by to pick it up. He'll be well cared for until we hear from Pickering's niece or his daughter and find out what she wants to do with it."

"Have you been in touch with either of them?" she asked.

"Not yet. I think his daughter lives on the East Coast. As for his niece, we have the number you provided. We'll try to reach her through that." He thanked them again, then headed back toward the elevator.

Back at the hotel, Sam handed his keys to the valet. "Not quite the relaxing diversion I'd hoped San Francisco would be."

She sighed. "I suppose that's my fault for suggesting we go to the bookstore to begin with. I thought the book would add to the nautical theme of your new office."

"I'll enjoy the reproduction as much, if not more. Especially with its checkered past."

"And where is it we're off to?" she asked as they walked into the lobby.

"First to get our luggage. Then a drive down the coast to Monterey."

"Dinner and key lime pie at Roy's?"

Before he had a chance to answer, they were met by the on-duty manager, his face etched with concern. "Mr. and Mrs. Fargo. I can't tell you how *very* sorry I am. And if there's anything I can do, I—nothing like this has *ever* happened before. At least not as long as I've worked here."

"What's never happened before?" Sam asked.

"The police. They came with a warrant to search through your things."

"A warrant?" Remi asked, certain she'd misunderstood. For the life of her, she couldn't imagine anything they might've done that would result in a police investigation.

"We tried to call you, but it went straight to voice mail."

They'd both turned off the ringers on their cell phones while being interviewed by Sergeant Trevino.

Sam asked, "You have a copy of the warrant?"

"A copy?"

"The police are required to leave a copy of the warrant."

"Perhaps you could ask them yourself. They're up in your room now."

"Good idea," he said. He and Remi started toward the elevator, the manager trailing behind them. "No wonder Sergeant Fauth wasn't there this morning," Sam said to Remi. "He was busy searching our rooms while his partner kept us distracted at the police station, asking superficial questions about the robbery."

"Search for what?" Remi asked as Sam jabbed at the up button. "We were just as much a victim as poor Mr. Pickering. And, really, they could simply have asked. Far less embarrassing that way." She turned a brittle smile on the manager, who seemed to be listening to every word. In truth, she was surprised Sam hadn't asked the manager to wait behind, but then realized if the police were searching their room—something she found hard to be-lieve, never mind extremely humiliating—having a witness was probably not a bad thing.

The manager inserted his key into the elevator, allowing it access to the concierge level. When it opened onto their floor, and the manager let them into their suite, Remi saw two men in dark suits, both wearing latex gloves, one going through her suit-case on the bed, his hand in the lining feeling about for whatever he thought might be hidden there. The other was opening the cabinets by the bar.

Remi whispered to Sam. "I don't see Sergeant Fauth."

The man near the bar moved toward them, his gaze narrowed and menacing. "This is official police business. You'll need to leave."

Sam stepped in front of Remi, shielding her. "That's not going to happen. I'd like to see some ID," he demanded. "And a copy of the warrant."

"Here's your warrant." He pulled out a sheaf of folded papers from his breast pocket as he and his partner advanced toward them.

The detective shoved the papers into Sam, pushing him into the entryway table. Sam grabbed the man's shoulder, then swung him around, slamming him into the wall. They struggled in the doorway. Suddenly, his partner jumped into the fray, coming at Sam from behind. Sam rammed his fist into the first guy's jaw, then spun around, kicking the second guy, who went flying into the manager, knocking them both to the ground. Remi jumped back, looked around for a weapon, grabbing a vase from a nearby table. She lifted it, ready to strike. The second guy saw her, took one look at Sam and his partner, then scrambled from the room.

Sam grappled with the first detective. The man swung. Sam blocked the blow with his left arm, brought his right fist into the guy's gut. The detective dropped to his knees, saw Sam coming at him again, then dove through the door after his partner. Sam started after them but thought better of it, returning and locking the door instead. He eyed Remi holding the vase. "That for me or for them?"

"I hadn't decided yet."

She gave a slight nod toward the manager on the floor.

Sam reached down, helping him to his feet. "You okay?"

"More startled than anything." He brushed at his clothing. "This is an outrage. I assure you, we'll contact the Police Department and register a complaint."

"Trust me," Sam said, "they weren't cops."

"But I saw the warrant."

Sam picked up the so-called warrant from the ground, looking at the papers. "Forged. There's no signed affidavit. Probably pulled off the Internet from some old case." He handed them to Remi.

She quickly looked them over. "What do you think they were searching for?"

"Whatever it was they hoped to find in Mr. Pickering's safe, would be my guess."

A quick call to the police verified that the two men were not, in fact, law enforcement, and within minutes uniformed officers flooded the area in hopes of finding the suspects.

The missing Sergeant Fauth arrived shortly thereafter, apologizing for not being at that morning's interview, having only just returned from the morgue. Apparently he was there for Pickering's autopsy. "You have no idea what they were looking for?" he asked Remi and Sam.

"None," Sam replied. "Honestly, we wrongly assumed you and your partner had set up this interview in order to come up here and search."

"Illegal searches aside, I'd like to think we'd have done a better job with a fake warrant. More than likely they were watching your hotel, waiting for you to leave. Which means that whatever they were trying to get from Mr. Pickering, they think you now have."

Remi, who was going through her suitcase checking to see if anything was missing, said, "Whatever it was couldn't have been all that big. They were searching in the lining of my suitcase. And the small zipper compartments. The book I bought would not have fit there."

"Where is this book?"

"Assuming the concierge did as asked, it'll be arriving on my front porch anytime this afternoon."

"Is there anyone who can check it when it arrives?"

"Our researcher, Selma. I'll give her a call."

"Appreciate it."

Remi took her cell phone from her purse, then called Selma's office number. There was no answer, and she left a voice mail.

She disconnected as Sergeant Fauth said, "So let me get this straight. You get back from the PD, walk into the hotel, and the Guest Services manager says the police are here searching?"

"That's right," Sam replied. "He was watching for us the moment we walked in the door."

The manager, still shaken, nodded in agreement. "I tried calling the Fargos as soon as they served me with the warrant. I wasn't able to get through. And, well, what was I supposed to do? Between the official-looking papers and their guns, I—"

"Guns?" Sergeant Fauth said.

He nodded. "I suppose I should have asked for ID, but . . ."

"Mr. . . . ?"

"Bryant."

"Mr. Bryant," Sergeant Fauth said. "Did either man say what they were looking for?"

"Yes. They wanted to know if the Fargos had said anything about a key. Maybe asked to put it in a safe. Finding one, hiding one. I—I don't remember. Just—they definitely said they were looking for a key."

"A key?"

"Yes. I thought maybe they were talking about the necklace Mrs. Fargo was wearing when she left this morning."

Remi fingered the diamond-studded charm, asking Sam, "Something about this you're not telling me?"

"An expensive trinket but a trinket nonetheless."

She smiled at the sergeant, trying to keep her tone pleasant. "I think we can all agree that whatever these people think we have, we don't. So if there's nothing else . . . ? We were on our way to check out. Or, rather, we were supposed to be."

He eyed their suitcases. "What I need to do is take a look at any surveillance video in the lobby. I expect Mr. Bryant can help me."

Sam closed Remi's suitcase and his own. "You have our cell numbers, should anything come up." He ushered her out of there without waiting to hear the sergeant's response. The manager started to follow, but Sam stopped him. "We'll see ourselves out."

"Of course." He backed off, and Sam escorted Remi onto the elevator with their luggage.

The moment the door closed, she asked, "What day was this relaxing vacation supposed to start?"

"Did I say today? I meant tomorrow."

"Hmm . . ."

"For the record, no one actually tried to kill us."

"But they *did* have guns." Remi eyed Sam. "And we left *ours* on the plane."

"Is this a good time to point out that it was your idea to stop off at that bookstore?"

"Pretty sure it's never going to be a good time to mention that."

Five

S am decided that their overnight trip to the Inn at Spanish Bay and dinner at Roy's on the Monterey Peninsula would have to wait for another day. He contacted his flight crew and had them fly back to San Francisco from the airport in Monterey. Remi was too worried over not being able to get in touch with Bree. That, along with this morning's events, had put a damper on Sam's plans for the week. Within a few hours, they were at cruising altitude aboard their G650, relaxing to the soothing allegretto of Beethoven's Seventh. Remi had received a text from Selma that the book arrived this morning in "fairly good shape," and other than some minor damage to the inside cover, possibly from being jostled during shipping, there was nothing that stood out. No keys or anything else packed with it.

Even with Selma's text, Remi seemed restless. Sam saw her check her phone, then return it to the table, a look of frustration on her face, no doubt hoping to hear from her friend. He wished he could ease her worry. He didn't know Bree Marshall well, but Remi had worked quite closely with her these last few weeks and had grown fond of the young woman.

When they arrived at the San Diego Airport, they drove straight to Bree's apartment in La Jolla. She lived on the second story in a complex about two miles inland. Palm trees lined the parking lot, the offshore breeze rustling the fronds above them. Sam and Remi climbed the stairs, Remi ringing the doorbell, waiting a few seconds, then trying again. When no one answered, Sam knocked sharply. The door behind them opened, and a blond-haired woman poked her head out. "No one's home."

"Any chance you know how to reach Bree?" Remi asked.

"You are . . . ?"

"Remi Fargo. My husband, Sam. We work—"

"That Foundation. I've heard her mention her job there," she said, opening the door wider, eyeing both of them. "Just wanted to make sure you weren't some random strangers. She took off suddenly."

"When?" Remi asked.

"Late last night. I was just getting home, and she was running down the stairs, saying something about her uncle. Going to see him, I think."

Sam pulled out his wallet, took a business card from it, and handed it to her. "If you hear from her, ask her to give us a call? It's very important."

"Of course. Sorry I couldn't be of more help."

In the car, Sam glanced over at his wife. "She's probably already in San Francisco."

"I'm sure you're right. I just hate to think how awful this must be for her."

"She has our number. She'll call. In the meantime, let's go home, check in with Selma, and take a look at this book Mr. Pickering wrapped up for you."

They lived just a few miles away in the hills of La Jolla's Goldfish Point, overlooking the ocean. The moment they stepped inside from the garage, their massive German shepherd, Zoltán, bounded down the hallway toward them, his nails clicking on the tumbled-marble tile floor as he skidded to a stop in front of Remi and Sam.

Remi kneeled down, scratching him behind his ears as he pressed himself closer to her. She'd acquired the dog in Hungary when they were searching for Attila the Hun's tomb, and the two had bonded so well, she brought Zoltán home. There was one slight drawback. Zoltán knew only Hungarian commands. Fortunately, their researcher Selma, a former Hungarian citizen—still retaining a slight accent—set about teaching the dog English commands to go along with the Hungarian. Zoltán was, Selma liked to say, the only Eastern European bilingual dog in the neighborhood.

"Good boy," Remi told the dog. "Let's get you a treat."

Treat was one of the first English words he picked up, and his tail thumped on hearing it. Remi gave him one last scratch, then walked toward the kitchen, the dog heeling by her side. He sat in front of the cupboard where the dog biscuits were kept, his eyes solely on Remi.

Selma walked into the kitchen a moment later, dressed in black yoga pants and her usual tie-dyed shirt, this one teal blue and hot pink. Her close-cropped brown hair seemed spikier than usual, and the reading glasses she usually wore on a chain around her neck had been replaced with wide-framed sunglasses.

"Mr. and Mrs. Fargo. Welcome home."

And here Sam had thought he'd convinced her that they were on a first-name basis. "Back to formalities?" he asked. "What happened to calling us Sam and Remi?"

"I tried it, Mr. Fargo. But I work for you. This makes me happy."

"Then it makes us happy," Remi said.

Selma eyed Remi, who was feeding a second biscuit to Zoltán. "You're going to make that dog fat, Mrs. Fargo."

"He's as fit as ever."

"Only because I walk him twice as far when you're home feeding him all those treats. *Someone* has to look after that poor dog's health." Selma opened the cupboard near the hallway and pulled out the leash. Zoltán heard the jingle and rushed over, almost too excited to sit as she leaned down and hooked the leash to his collar. "We'll be at the beach if anyone's looking for us."

"The book?" Remi asked Selma. "You didn't notice anything unusual?"

"Not right off. But Lazlo was impressed," she said, referring to Lazlo Kemp. They'd taken him on to help Selma with some of the research, during the time he needed to recuperate from an injury that occurred while they were searching for Quetzalcoatl's tomb in Mexico. Both were surprised when the man had become smitten with Selma, whose husband, a test pilot, had died over a decade ago. What they weren't sure about was exactly how Selma felt about Lazlo and so they were content to simply let the relationship run its course. Assuming it had a course to run.

Remi returned the dog biscuit box to the cupboard, asking Selma, "And what was Lazlo's take on it?"

"That he didn't know enough about the book to say what, if anything, was worth killing over. It's not his specialty. But he's arranged for you to meet with Ian Hopkins so that he can see the book. According to Lazlo, he's the nearest expert on the subject available on such a short notice. Unfortunately, Hopkins is in Phoenix, Arizona. Retired professor."

"No worries," Remi said. "I love Arizona in the autumn." She turned toward Sam. "This isn't going to interrupt your plans too much, is it?"

"The beauty of my plans is their flexibility."

"You don't have any, do you?"

"Playing it by ear, Remi. So where is this mysterious book?" he asked Selma.

"Locked in your safe."

"I'll go have a look."

"Bring it up," Remi said. "We can look at it together."

He retrieved the book, still in its FedEx box. He wasn't sure why Selma bothered locking it up except, perhaps, because it was connected to the robbery and then the death of Mr. Pickering, the bookseller.

When he returned with the package, Remi was looking out the window—apparently at Selma as she and Zoltán walked down the drive. "Now that she's in the sun, I do believe her hair matches her shirt. Pink and blue streaks."

He glanced out the window and saw Remi was right. A very subtle highlighting that hadn't been there before. "Not like the old Selma to fuss over her appearance. You think—?"

"Lazlo?" Remi finished.

They watched her until she and the dog disappeared from sight. Returning his attention to the book, he slipped it from the FedEx box onto the kitchen table, then unwrapped the brown paper, exposing the leather cover with the gold-tooled title. He could see why Remi had been drawn to it. "This is quite the find."

She opened the refrigerator and took out a bottle of sparkling water. "They went to a lot of trouble to make it look like an antique. They're printed in China to keep the cost down."

"Mr. Pickering said this was a copy?"

She poured two glasses. "One of several. Why?"

He looked over at her, saying, "You might want to rethink that."

"I'm thirsty."

"I mean, around the book." He stood aside so that she could see. "No way is this some made in China copy, Remi. It's the real deal."

Six

R emi stared for several seconds, noticing the worn leather binding, the gold-tooled markings, gilded pages,
and the inked typeset lettering that could never be
mistaken for modern-day laser print. "This is not the same book
he showed me."

"Then how did you end up with it?"

"I don't know. I only paid forty-nine dollars plus tax. I—"
Remi reached out and touched it, then pulled her hand back. "We
should be wearing gloves."

"Back up there, Remi. What do you mean you only paid forty-
nine dollars for this? Or did you forget a few zeroes before that
decimal point?"

"No. But when that gunman walked in, Mr. Pickering grabbed
the reproduction from me and said he'd wrap it up. The book he
took from me was *not* this one."

"Do you think he switched it with the book from the safe?"

"He must have. He must have known that man's intent when he saw him walk into the store." She glanced down at the volume on the table, still unable to believe what she was seeing. "We should probably let the police know about this."

"Undoubtedly. But if we do that, they're going to want to see it. And, right now, I'd like to know what's so important about this particular volume."

"So we take it to the expert in Phoenix first?"

"Definitely. Then we inform the police."

They flew to Phoenix the following morning, meeting with Professor Ian Hopkins, whose studies focused on sixteenth- and seventeenth-century English literature. He also repaired antique books, a hobby he'd taken up after his retirement, and was working on one when they walked in. He looked at them over the rims of his dark-framed glasses. "You must be Mr. and Mrs. Fargo."

"We are," Sam replied. "But call us Sam and Remi."

"Ian," he said, standing. He reached out and shook hands with them both. "So. My friend Lazlo tells me you have a decent copy of *The History of Pyrates and Privateers*."

Remi pulled the carefully wrapped book from her tote and set it on the counter. "We weren't aware that it was supposed to be particularly valuable, but it seems someone believes it is."

"Let's have a look." He donned white gloves, then examined the book, turning it over in his hands. "Full leather binding and spine in good shape. The gold-tooled geometric pattern on front and back still visible . . . Gilding on the page edges apparent, not worn . . ." He set the book on the table, then opened the cover.

"This," he said, running his gloved hand on the front endpaper, illustrated with a map, then flipping the book over and opening the back of the cover, also illustrated with a map, "is where the value lies in copies of this particular book. The endpapers have been removed from most of the copies I've seen. You'll notice that the maps aren't the same? The front differs from the back? No one realized that for quite some time."

"Why," Remi asked, "would someone remove them?"

"I believe they're copies of actual pirate maps that are described in the book. But since the same maps appear in the endpapers of later editions, including current reproductions, it's more likely that someone thought the older illustrated endpapers would make a nice framed decoration. That's the speculation from the author of an article on the recent endpaper theft from a copy contained at the British Library last year. A rather daring burglary, considering the cameras and such." He touched the edge of the back map along the bottom of the cover and the endpaper lifted slightly. "Not that they would have been all that difficult to remove. You can see the glue is no longer holding on to this copy."

Sam figured that was the minor damage Selma and Lazlo had mentioned. "With the endpapers intact," Sam said, "would that increase the value so much that someone would be willing to kill over it?"

The professor looked over at Sam, a bit surprised. "Not in my opinion. There are certainly far more valuable books out there. That being said, this is an excellent copy. I suppose it's possible someone would want it to add to a collection."

"How much?" Remi asked. "Assuming you were a collector and wanted this?"

"Assuming the rest of the book is in pristine condition and nothing is missing . . . four, five thousand."

"That's it?" Sam asked.

"It's not a particularly rare book. Just old, and with a subject matter that makes it highly appealing to the maritime collector and anyone interested in pirates. So, yes. No more than five thousand, I'd think. And that's due to the endpapers being intact."

"Still," Remi said, her brows arching, "that's a pretty penny, considering I paid less than fifty dollars for it. Unfortunately, I think we need to turn this volume over to the police."

"For what reason?" he asked her. "If you paid for it, legally it's yours."

She explained how the book came into her possession.

Professor Hopkins ran his gloved fingers along the leather cover. "Quite the interesting history for this little volume."

"Exactly," Remi said. "Which makes me wonder if we're not overlooking something."

"We are," Sam replied. "The two thugs in our hotel room who were asking if we'd found a key of some sort."

The professor glanced up from the page he'd been examining. "A key? For what?"

"That," Sam said, "is part of what we're hoping you might discover. Is there something different about this book in comparison to the others? Invisible writing? Pages that might differ from other copies?"

"I'd be glad to take a closer look for you. Examine it under different lighting. Photograph each page so that you can make the comparisons later. Of course, there is a fee. And one other appraisal ahead of yours."

Sam pulled out his wallet. "And what's your standard fee?"

"One twenty-five an hour. With only the one small volume, I don't expect it will take much over an hour, maybe two at the most."

Sam took five hundred-dollar bills from his wallet. "Would that cover moving it to the head of the line?"

"I'll give my client a call and let him know his appraisal will be late."

"We'd appreciate it." Sam looked at his watch, saw it was half past eleven, and asked Remi, "Lunch while we're waiting?"

"Definitely," she said. Then to Professor Hopkins, "Any recommendations?"

"There's an excellent Italian restaurant a couple of miles from here. Marcellino Ristorante. Highly recommended. In fact, if you prefer, I can bring the book to you there when I finish looking it over. The client I have to visit is actually very near there."

"Perfect," Remi said. "We'll see you then."

The restaurant was located in an open-air plaza that backed up to the waterfront in Old Town Scottsdale. Sam opened the wrought-iron gate for Remi and then the glass door. The sound—and scent—of sizzling garlic and fresh herbs wafted toward them as a charming woman introduced herself as Sima, warmly welcomed them and led them to their seats, wishing them a *"Buon appetito."*

There were two empty tables near the window overlooking the patio. She sat them at the table to the right, since the one in the corner on the left held a small placard stating it was *Reserved for Authors and Muses.* After looking at the menu, Remi started with *insalata caprese* of fresh mozzarella, garden tomatoes, red pepper, and basil, followed by *cozze in bianco*—mussels sautéed in white wine. Sam opted for the *carpaccio*, with raw ahi tuna on a bed of arugula, and grilled salmon, and, for the table, a bottle of sparkling white wine, Falanghina Nudo Eroico.

When the wine was served, Remi lifted her glass to Sam's. "Here's to hoping Professor Hopkins finds this mysterious key."

"Agreed."

They had just finished their meal when Chef Marcellino approached their table, greeting them, his Italian accent very evident. "You have met my beautiful wife," he said as he nodded to Sima. "I hope you enjoyed your lunch. And perhaps saved room for dessert?"

"The food," Remi said, "was wonderful. Dessert . . . ?" She looked over at Sam.

"I'm always a sucker for sharing tiramisu with a beautiful woman."

"Well, then," she said, turning toward Chef Marcellino, "I believe we'll be sharing an order."

"At once," he replied with a slight bow, his dark eyes sparkling. He returned shortly with the tiramisu, telling them to enjoy it.

Remi took the first bite, deciding it was the perfect balance of espresso-soaked savoiardi, creamy marscarpone, and a dusting of unsweetened cocoa. "This is the next-best thing to being in Italy."

"It can't possibly be as good as the tiramisu we had in Rome last month at Domus Magnanimi." He slipped the spoonful into his mouth, closed his eyes as though tasting a fine wine. After a moment, he said, "Then again, maybe we should have ordered two servings."

Remi was about to take a second bite when she saw Professor Hopkins enter the restaurant, the wrapped book tucked under his arm. He looked around, saw them, and walked over. "My apologies for interrupting your lunch."

"Sit, please," Sam said. "We're actually done, but couldn't resist trying the tiramisu."

"Exquisite here, isn't it?" He pulled out a chair and sat.

"Very. So . . ." Sam eyed the package that the professor had set on the table in front of them. "Did you find anything?"

"At first, nothing. The volume is in amazing shape. Of course I examined each page, looking at it under oblique lighting, black lights, various wavelengths. Nothing on any of the pages that would make me think of this key. That's what you said they were looking for?"

Remi and Sam nodded.

"I have a friend with a metal detector and he stopped by and placed it over the book, my thought being that perhaps if there were some key hidden in the binding, we might detect it that way. Nothing. And then it occurred to me that perhaps we weren't talking about a metal key at all. It is a book on pirates and their maps. Why not a key to the map?"

Remi said, "Makes perfect sense."

"So I went back over each page. And, as you asked, photographed each for direct comparison to another copy. Unfortunately, I don't have a copy on hand. I thought you might compare them yourself later using the digital copy I made for you. You might find something written in this edition that doesn't appear in the others. Especially the pages that have maps on them. I also examined the ink to see if something had been added later . . ." He patted the box, taking a deep breath. "But, back to the key search. Once I realized what was right in front of me, I couldn't believe it hadn't occurred to me sooner." He looked first at Remi, then Sam, saying nothing.

Remi wanted to reach out and shake him. "Exactly *what* hadn't occurred to you sooner?"

"The reason why the endpapers were missing from all the other volumes. I know what they were looking for."

Seven

Professor Hopkins opened the manila folder. "This," he said. "It was hidden behind the endpapers."

"May I?" Sam asked, reaching for the folder.

"Of course."

Sam took it in hand, holding it so that he and Remi could view it together. Inside was a piece of yellowed parchment almost as large as the book cover with something illustrated in black ink. A map of an island and, next to it, a circle with symbols, atop a square with letters beneath. The complete alphabet, he realized. "A cipher wheel?" he asked the professor.

"An illustration of one," Hopkins replied. "It has to be what they were searching for. Had it not been for all those thefts and reported damage to the endpapers, it might have gone unnoticed. Honestly, I was about to call to ask if you wanted me to glue the endpaper that had come loose. That's when I saw it."

Remi leaned in for a closer look. "I wonder if Mr. Pickering was aware that this was in there when he gave it to me?"

A very good question, Sam thought. But not one he wanted to go into right now. "We can't thank you enough," he told Professor Hopkins.

"Since you've paid me twice over what I normally charge, I think you have. You've definitely got a fascinating mystery here."

The screen to Remi's cell phone lit up. She glanced at it, then turned it facedown on the cloth. "We do appreciate your time."

The professor slid his chair back. "And I really do need to get to that next appointment." He stood, shook hands with Sam, and smiled at Remi. "Enjoy the rest of your lunch."

The moment he left, Remi picked up her phone. "It's a text from Bree."

"Saying what?" Sam asked.

"To call her as soon as I can."

Sam asked for the check, and they finished their dessert while they waited. Once it came, he paid and left a generous tip, then they hurriedly walked to the rental car.

Remi called, placing it on speakerphone. "Bree? Are you okay? We were so worried when we couldn't get ahold of you."

"I'm fine. Now. I'm—I'm in North Carolina."

"North Carolina?"

"To visit my cousin. To tell her about her father."

"We're so very sorry."

"I know. Listen, I was wondering if—did my uncle give you the book when you were there? *Pyrates and Privateers*?"

Remi glanced at Sam, hesitating the slightest of instances as she said, "I bought a copy from him. Why?"

"My cousin—um, she's pretty devastated. Apparently he promised it to her, and—and I was hoping I could give it to her. Something to remember her father by."

"After what happened to your uncle, Sam and I thought maybe we should turn it over to the police."

"No! Please . . ."

"Bree? Are you sure you're okay?"

"I'm—yes. It's just—you can imagine how devastating this has all been. And it would mean so much for her to have it. If you turn it in, it'll only be tied up in probate. She's too ill to travel, and—" Bree broke down crying. After several seconds, she said, "I'm sorry. This has all been so hard."

"What can we do to help?" Remi asked.

"I was hoping you wouldn't mind mailing the book to her. To remember her father by."

"Of course we wouldn't mind. But Sam and I will deliver it in person."

"No. I couldn't ask that of you. It's too much."

"We insist," she said, eyeing Sam, who nodded in encouragement. "This book is too valuable to trust to the post office. Just text me the address and we'll deliver it tomorrow."

"I will. Thank you . . ."

They heard a quiet sob as Remi said, "We'll see you tomorrow. And pass on our condolences to your cousin."

Sam pulled out of the parking garage and on into traffic. "She sounded pretty upset."

"Understandably," Remi said. "First the robbery, then the heart attack. I can't imagine what Pickering's daughter must be going through. Not being able to travel. At least Bree's there for her."

"About the book . . . ?"

"I thought about that. And I think at the very least we should show it to Pickering's daughter and let her make that decision. She is the next of kin, after all. At least this way we can explain in person why we feel it best to turn it in to the authorities."

He stopped at a red light, looked over at his wife, then back at the road. "I guess we'll be filing a change in flight plans to North Carolina."

The advantage of having a private jet meant they could change plans at a moment's notice. Selma made the arrangements for a hotel and rental car on their arrival, and after a decent night's sleep and a hot breakfast, they drove to the location Bree had texted. Remi, of course, asked Selma to look into the address on the off chance something was wrong. Much to her relief, it came back to a Larayne Pickering-Smith, who Selma had determined was, in fact, Gerald Pickering's daughter.

She lived in rural Harlowe, and as they drove east through miles of tobacco farms, the sky darkened with a gathering storm. Sam parked in front, eyeing the property, a white clapboard farmhouse, with a black SUV in the gravel drive. Someone pulled the drape slightly from an upstairs window, then dropped it.

Remi, the book in her lap, patted the front cover, saying, "Let's get this thing delivered."

"You sure you want to give it to her?"

"Yes. It has to be better than tying it up in evidence or even probate for who knows how long. Maybe his daughter can tell us what's so important about the book."

Together, they walked up the path, and Sam knocked on the front door. It opened a moment later a few inches, and Bree looked out at them. Her eyes were red and slightly swollen, no doubt from crying. "Mr. and Mrs. Fargo . . ." She gave a faltering smile. "You have the book?"

Remi handed her the brown-wrapped parcel. "How is your cousin?"

"She's . . . not well." Bree hugged the book to her chest. "I'd invite you in, but . . ."

"No worries," Remi said. "We were wondering, though, if you know what was so important about this volume. Why someone might be looking for it?"

"No." She gave a slight shrug. "But thank you. For bringing it all this way."

"You're sure you're okay?"

Bree nodded.

When the silence became awkward, Remi took a step back and smiled. "Let us know if you need anything."

"There is one thing I was wondering. How is Mr. Wickham? He wasn't hurt in the robbery, was he?"

"No."

Bree looked down at the book, then at Remi. "Tell him I miss him and that I'll try to write to him. Would you?"

"I'll be glad to." Remi linked her arm through Sam's, saying, "We should get going. It's a long flight home."

Sam gave a polite nod. "Bye."

"Good-bye," Bree said, then closed the door as he and Remi returned to the car.

Remi said, "She's in trouble. You heard what she said? Asking me to pass a message to Mr. Wickham? Pickering's cat? We need to go in there and rescue her."

"Not a good idea, Remi."

"But you've got a gun this time."

"One against how many? We don't even know who's in there. If you had yours, we might stand a chance."

She frowned at him, then took out her cell phone. "Then we call the cops and up our odds."

"Not in front of the house," he said. "If she's being held, they'll be watching us." He pulled away from the curb, then drove down the street.

Remi phoned the moment they were out of sight, and the dispatcher directed them to wait at a market that was located off the highway about a mile inland. A few minutes after they pulled into the parking lot, her phone buzzed, and she saw she had a text from Selma to call home ASAP.

Remi called, putting the phone on speaker. "You found something on the digital photos we sent?" she asked.

"Not yet, Mrs. Fargo. But that's not why I needed to talk. An officer stopped by a few minutes ago asking for you. They found Bree Marshall's car abandoned on the side of the road not too far from the airport. There were several boxes of fund-raiser tickets and an envelope with checks made out to the Fargo Foundation in the vehicle. The officer was wondering if we wanted to pick them up from the tow yard."

Remi looked at Sam, who said, "Was there any indication of a struggle?"

"He didn't say, Mr. Fargo. But I expect if there was, he might have mentioned it."

"Thanks, Selma," Sam told her. "We've just called a deputy to check on her. We'll let him know."

About ten minutes later, a Carteret County sheriff's deputy pulled up. The offshore wind whipped at him as he stepped out of his car, nearly blowing his hat from his head, and he directed them to the front of the store, where they'd be somewhat sheltered. Remi gave a brief explanation.

The deputy's expression turned dubious. "Is it possible her car broke down on her way to the airport? Maybe she called for a cab or something."

"Maybe," Remi said. "But there's also the matter of her telling us to pass a message on to her late uncle's cat."

"A lot of people talk to their animals."

Sam, realizing the deputy failed to appreciate that bit of evidence, took a step forward, leveling his gaze at the officer. "Is it possible to ignore the reason we think our friend is in trouble and just check on her and see if she's okay?"

"Sure. Not that I don't believe you," he replied, sounding exactly as if he didn't. "Just like to get the facts. I'm the only deputy in the area here, so if it's something that I can handle myself, I will. Otherwise, we're looking at waiting a good twenty minutes for backup."

"Of course," Sam said. He took a card from his wallet, handed it to the deputy, saying, "Our cell phone numbers. Should anything come up in between here and there."

The deputy took the card, got into his patrol car, and drove off in the direction of the farmhouse.

They were about to follow him over when Remi pointed toward a vehicle driving in the opposite direction as the deputy. "That's the SUV that was parked at the farmhouse."

"You're sure?"

"Definitely."

He started the car. "You see who was inside?"

"Two men. I can't say for sure, except the passenger's profile reminded me of that gunman who robbed Pickering's shop," she said as he took off after the SUV. "What about Bree?"

"The only deputy in a twenty-minute radius is checking on her. And judging from his reaction to your cat story, I highly doubt he's going to drop everything and follow a car that we have absolutely no evidence is doing anything wrong even if we could get ahold of him."

"Good point."

The two-lane rural road wasn't exactly one on which a person could drive unnoticed for too long. Even so, Sam did his best to keep plenty of distance between him and the SUV, figuring it was en route to Beaufort. Apparently it was headed to an industrial area near the water, and Sam followed as it made a right turn down a street that dead-ended into a dock with several large warehouses on one side. Sam slowed but didn't stop as they passed the street. If the car was there, he saw no sign of it. "See anything?" he asked Remi.

"No. It must have driven onto the dock or it's between the warehouses out of sight."

Sam's phone rang. He dug it from his pocket and handed it to

Remi, who pressed the speaker function and held it up for Sam to answer.

"Deputy Wagner," came the voice on the other end. "Just wanted you to know that I checked the house. There was no answer."

"Sam . . ." Remi whispered.

He glanced at his wife, then back at the road. "We appreciate you checking. We followed the car we saw parked at the house. My wife thought one of the men looked like the man who robbed us in San Francisco."

"Your friend wasn't in the car?"

"Didn't see her."

"Where are you?"

"Near the water about ten to fifteen minutes south of Beaufort."

"Do me a favor. Don't do anything rash. I'll try to get backup from Beaufort and meet you out there."

He disconnected, and Sam pulled over to the side of the road. "Guess all we can do now is wait."

Remi reached for the door handle. "We might not have fifteen minutes."

"Remi," he said, reaching out, grabbing her arm.

She stopped, looked over at him.

He leaned in, kissed her, and said, "You didn't think I was going to let you go out there alone, did you?"

"Of course not." She smiled at him and opened the door. "Now let's go find my friend."

Eight

Sam slipped his revolver from its case clipped to his belt, then popped the trunk. Remi stood watch, ready to warn him if there was any movement. And though he hoped that they wouldn't need any weapon, his instincts told him otherwise. There was only one vehicle seen on that roadway. If Bree wasn't at the beach house, then she had to be in the SUV as it drove past. And, since they couldn't see her, chances were good that she was either injured or dead.

They both turned their cell phones on vibrate. Remi kept hers in hand—just in case—and Sam shoved his into his pocket. Sam gave Remi his Smith & Wesson, then took a tire iron from the trunk. "Ready?" he asked.

"Ready."

He peered around the corner. "Clear."

The wind gusted as they walked to the dock just beyond the first warehouse, the only sounds their footsteps on the wooden planks and the cry of the gulls as the water lapped against the pilings.

There were no boats at the dock nor anyone working nearby. On closer inspection, the warehouses appeared abandoned, the windows broken, the doors padlocked shut from the outside.

The perfect place to take a kidnap victim, Sam thought as he and Remi made their way, keeping close to the side of the warehouse.

A faint sound caught his attention. He stopped, signaling for Remi to do the same. "Listen," he whispered.

"Sort of a rusty, squeaking sound."

He nodded toward the end of the warehouse they stood against. A gull cried out overhead, startling Remi as it dove down into the water just a few feet away.

Sam gave her a thumbs-up signal.

She nodded, then trailed him as he started forward again, following his lead as he ducked beneath a window to keep from being seen—on the chance someone was watching from within that particular warehouse. Unfortunately, the dock was long, and they didn't know which warehouse they might have gone into.

When they reached the end of the building, Sam peered around the corner, saw the SUV parked between buildings. A door of the warehouse on the far side of the vehicle stood slightly ajar. He stepped back. "It's there."

"Anyone in it?"

"Doesn't look like it," he said. "The door is open on the next building. I'm taking a stab that's where they are."

Remi nodded, then glanced back in the direction they'd come, hoping to see the deputy's car speeding their way. Sam didn't bother mentioning that he was at least ten minutes behind them. They were on their own.

He watched the warehouse a few moments, wishing he had something beside a tire iron.

His gaze strayed to the SUV, realizing they'd only seen the two men in the front. No other passengers.

Sam motioned for Remi to stay put. He crouched down and moved over to the SUV, rising just enough to peer into the tinted back windows.

Bree was there on the floorboard, her hands bound behind her, a gag over her mouth, her feet tied.

He tapped on the window, relieved when she looked up at him. He put his finger to his lips to let her know that they weren't going to leave her there.

Bree nodded, and Sam tried to open the vehicle's door. Locked, of course. He gave her a smile of encouragement, then checked to make sure it was clear before returning to Remi. "She's in the car."

"Is she okay?"

"Tied-up, but appears okay," Sam said. "We need to get a look into that warehouse first. Find out what we're up against."

They made their way to the warehouse near the open door.

Sam put his ear against the side of the building, but couldn't hear anything. "What I wouldn't give for that mirror from your purse right now."

"For what?"

"To see inside that door without breaking cover."

She held up her phone. "How about a camera lens?"

"As brilliant as you are beautiful."

"Flattery will get you—"

"Everywhere?"

"A cell phone," she whispered as she accessed the camera feature, then handed it to him.

Sam set the tire iron on the ground, then squatted down as he held the camera close to the floor. He angled it about, using the lens to see in, as he took a movie of the interior. After about a minute, he rose, stepped back, and played the recording.

"There," he said, pointing. They saw three men leaning on a workbench, at least two with guns in hand, looking down at something—probably the map book that Remi had turned over to Bree. The picture was small but clear.

"Our two fake cops from the hotel," Remi said.

"And our robber from the bookshop."

Wait? Or move in? He weighed the risks. One gun and a tire iron against three armed men. So the odds sucked. But Sam had Remi, and when it came to capable partners, he'd take her over some brainless thug any day. He grabbed the tire iron and pulled Remi away from the doorway to the other side of the vehicle. "First thing," he whispered, "is we get Bree out of this car."

His thought was simply to smash the car window—until he glanced over and saw the red light flashing on the dash.

"Plan B?" Remi asked.

Actually, his initial plan might still work. The vehicle looked like a base model, one he hoped didn't come with what was often an added feature to the standard motion alarm—a glass-breakage alarm. He dug out his little knife and gave it to Remi and she put it in her pocket. "You cover me while I break the window. If the alarm doesn't go off, wait until I'm at the back of the SUV before you unlock it. If it does go off, they're going to run right toward us. You may only have seconds to cut her ties and get out of here while I rip off a few shots to slow them down."

She moved by the front fender, aiming his gun toward the warehouse door.

Sam stood in front of the driver's window, hefting the tire iron. Vehicle safety glass was designed to shatter yet hold together under impact—which meant he had to hit it in the right spot to get it to break. He'd have one chance. The alarm would definitely be set off by movement. He pulled back, then rammed the tip of the iron into the lower right corner. It shattered, diamond-like bits raining down onto the driver's seat.

Silence. So far, so good. He set down the tire iron, took the gun from Remi, and hurried to the back of the SUV. When he was in position, his aim on the door, he nodded at her.

She reached in, popped the locks. The moment she opened the back door, a deafening wail filled the air. From the corner of his eye, he saw Remi ducking down, trying to cut Bree's ties.

Sam braced himself. The warehouse door swung open. A figure burst out, his gun aimed at the SUV and Remi.

"Hey!" Sam cried. His .357 revolver barked. The shot struck the man in the face and he went down. Something flew from his hand. The car keys.

Sam dove, scooped them up, then stood, shouting, "Remi. Keys!"

He flung them over the top of the car.

She caught them, then pushed the back door shut, opened the driver's door, and slid in. The engine revved to life. Sam jumped into the passenger seat. He slammed his door shut just as the other two men raced out of the building, firing at the SUV.

Remi hit the gas. The tires screeched as she backed perilously close to the edge of the dock.

"Remi!" he snapped, bracing himself.

"I see it." She turned the wheel, braking hard as she threw it into drive.

Sam looked back. The second man was aiming at them. Sam shot first and saw the third man fall and clutch his left knee.

Remi jabbed the gas pedal to the stop The sharp report of bullets hitting metal pierced their eardrums. "Come on," she said as though urging the SUV to move faster.

The tailgate window shattered. "Stay down." He fired through the broken rear window. The two men dove for cover.

Remi slid as low as she could, not slowing until she reached the end of the street. She turned the corner, racing down the same road they'd arrived on, the first, fat drops of rain splatting against the windshield.

In the distance, they saw the flashing lights of the deputy's patrol car, then heard the faint sound of the siren as he sped toward them.

Remi pulled over, and they got out of the SUV, waving at the deputy.

He stopped beside them, cutting his siren.

"We found our friend," Remi said, then opened the passenger door.

The deputy looked in, saw Bree still tied up, his mouth dropping open slightly. Then, recovering, asked, "Anyone hurt?"

Remi removed the gag from Bree's mouth. "How are you?" she asked.

"Fi—" Bree stopped, took a deep breath. "Fine. My cousin? Where is she? Is she okay?"

"I don't know," Sam said.

Remi used Sam's pocketknife to cut her ties as the deputy drew Sam to the back of the car out of the roadway. "What's going on?"

He gave a brief explanation, showing him the video on Remi's phone, shielding the screen from the scattered rain.

"Where did this happen?"

Sam pointed north. "About five miles up. Some old warehouses on that first street near the docks. Second warehouse in."

The deputy glanced at the bullet holes along the right rear fender of the SUV and the missing rear window, then keyed his radio, reporting shots fired at one of the abandoned warehouses outside Beaufort. "Three suspects. Description: white male adults, dark clothing."

The dispatcher copied.

The deputy started for his car, but Bree called out, "What about my cousin?"

"What about her?" he asked.

"Did you talk to her?"

"At the house?"

She nodded.

"I'm sorry, ma'am. No one answered the door. It was locked."

Bree turned toward Remi, her face pale. "We have to go there and check! What if something's happened to her?"

Nine

Bree grasped Remi's arm. "Please. Larayne might be in trouble."

"She's right," Sam said. "We have to check on her."

"Sir," Deputy Wagner said to Sam. "I'm going to have to trust you know what you're doing. I have no idea what sort of backup Beaufort's sending, and I've just sent the only other deputy within driving distance to deal with three armed men. I'm not about to leave him without backup."

"We understand."

The deputy turned a stern gaze to Bree. "I want the three of you—four, if your cousin is there—at the sheriff's office for statements when this is done."

He hurried to his patrol car, then sped off, the engine roaring.

"Let's go," Sam said, opening the driver's door.

"What about our car?" Remi asked, climbing in the front passenger seat.

"We can pick it up on the way back," Sam said.

Bree slid into the seat behind Remi, telling Sam, "Please hurry."

"Buckle up," Sam said as he took off toward Harlowe, turning on the windshield wipers. Wind roared through the shattered back window, and rain sluiced in through the driver's window, striking him in the face and shoulder. Even Remi felt it in the passenger seat. She turned to check on Bree. The young woman looking shell-shocked. "I'm so sorry about your uncle," Remi called out over the rush of wind.

"I know. I—I can't believe this all happened." After a moment, Bree leaned forward, placing her hand on Remi's shoulder. "Thank you for coming."

Sam leaned in toward the center of the car as he drove, the rain coming down harder. He looked back at Bree. "We're just glad you're okay," he said, before turning his attention back to the road.

Remi said, "Last we heard, you were on your way to the airport. We assumed to San Francisco."

"I was. They ran my car off the road and I never made it."

"Selma called us," Remi said. "The police found your car. I was beside myself until your call."

"They were holding a gun to me. I never would have put you in danger."

The wind and rain rushing through the broken windows made it difficult to carry on a conversation. "Let's check on your cousin and we'll talk after."

It took about ten minutes to reach the farmhouse. The moment Sam pulled to a stop, Bree dashed out of the SUV, then up the front steps. She tried to open the door, then started pounding on it, crying, "Larayne! Larayne!"

Remi and Sam followed. At the steps, Sam said, "I'll see if there's any other way in."

Remi and Bree dashed through the rain to follow him around to the back.

Sam tried that door, also locked, and Bree asked, "Can't you kick it in?"

"Might not need to," he said, eyeing the lock. Slipping his wallet from his pocket, he removed a credit card, then shoved it between the doorframe and the lock, jiggling until it popped open. "Your cousin should get a dead bolt for this thing," he said, opening the door.

Bree rushed past him, through the kitchen. "Larayne! Where are you?"

Remi and Sam hurried after her as she ran down the hallway opening doors, looking behind them.

Remi, brushing the wet hair from her face, was just starting up the front stairs when she thought she heard something beneath them. She stopped and listened. Sure enough, there was a thump below her. "In here!" she called out, spying a storage door below the stairs. She opened it as Bree came running down the hall.

Bree almost dove inside to get her cousin out. "Larayne!" she said, helping her to her feet.

Like Bree, the woman had been bound and gagged. Bree yanked the gag from her mouth. "Are you okay?"

Larayne nodded.

Sam cut the ties around her hands and feet, then helped her to stand.

Bree wrapped her in a hug, then drew her to the couch. "I was so worried about you."

"How'd you get here?" Larayne asked.

"My friends," she said. "The Fargos. They're the ones who brought the book."

Larayne eyed them, saying, "I can't believe this. I—" Thunder rumbled in the distance, and the sky let loose, rain drumming down on the rooftop. She stood suddenly, her hands shaking. "I need something to drink."

"Sit," Remi said. "I can get it. Water?"

"I think I need something stronger. But thanks."

They followed her down the hall and into the kitchen. She took a glass from the dishwasher, then opened the freezer, pulled out a bottle of vodka, and poured several fingers into the glass.

Bree gave a tremulous smile. "Are you sure that's a good idea? We still have to talk to the police."

"It's a very good idea. Do you have any idea what it's like to be shoved in the cupboard and not know if anyone was going to come looking for you?"

Remi, acknowledging Bree's discomfort, put her arm around her. "I can't imagine what either of you must have been going through, not knowing where the other was. It must have been terrible."

"It was," Bree said, meeting her cousin's gaze.

Larayne lowered her glass, seemingly surprised by that statement. "Oh, Bree . . . I'm sorry. Can you forgive me?"

"For what?"

"You're the one who was kidnapped. It must have been horrible what happened to you."

"You have nothing to be sorry for. I'm only glad that Mr. and Mrs. Fargo found me right away."

"Yes. Very lucky."

"The phone?" Remi asked Larayne. "We should probably call the sheriff's office. They're going to want to know if you're okay."

"There's a couple of portable handsets around. Should be one in the hallway by the stairs."

Sam left to find it. He was speaking with the dispatcher when he returned to the kitchen. "Yes," he said into the phone. "I understand. We'll be here."

He disconnected, then set the phone on the counter. "They're sending someone from investigations out here."

Bree nodded, and Remi asked, "What about the suspects? Any word on if they caught them?"

"Maybe we'll find out more when the investigator gets here."

Larayne eyed the vodka bottle, then asked Sam, "Why are they sending them here?"

"The police? To take our statements and to gather evidence."

She seemed shocked at his answer. "What sort of evidence?"

"Prints, I expect."

Larayne downed her vodka, then set the glass on the counter. "What a nightmare this has turned out to be."

Bree reached out and grasped her cousin's hand. "They'll find who did this. Maybe they even have them now."

Her cousin's response was to pour more vodka into her glass. Not that Remi could blame her. After all, she'd just lost her father, and now this. Remi pulled out a chair at the kitchen table, saying, "Maybe we should all sit down. Try to relax."

"Good idea," Larayne said, bringing the bottle with her. "Bree, get yourself a glass and join me."

"I'm fine."

"No you're not. They almost killed you. Have a shot."

Bree filled a glass with water instead, then took a seat next to her cousin. "I don't know how you can drink that stuff."

"It grows on you," Larayne said, taking a long sip.

Remi, worried that the woman would be in no condition to speak to the police by the time they showed up, decided it couldn't hurt to ask a few questions of her own. "I hope you don't mind my prying, but what exactly is going on here?"

Larayne shook her head. "I wish I knew."

"Something to do with your father's map book?"

Larayne exchanged glances with Bree. "Maybe if my father had sold it to the buyer I found, none of this would have happened."

Remi asked, "You found him a buyer?"

"I did," Larayne said. "Someone who was willing to pay way more than he could have gotten for that book."

"Who?" Remi asked, trying to ignore Sam's pacing as he went from window to window, then down the hall to the front of the house.

"I don't remember his name."

"I do," Bree said. "Someone named Charles Avery."

"Whoever." Larayne eyed her drink. "All I know is, my father suddenly backed out and he wouldn't say why."

"He was worried," Bree replied. "He'd received those phone calls asking about his copy. And then that strange visit from someone asking about it. I think it was the timing of it all."

Sam had returned to the kitchen and was peering out the window down the long drive. "Timing?" he asked, turning toward them.

Bree nodded. "My uncle learned about the theft of the endpapers from other first edition copies. I think he started to suspect that someone might be trying to target him for the same reason."

"Reasonable assumption," Sam said. "How was it we became involved?"

"When I started working for your wife, I told him about the Fargo Foundation and the charities that benefited from your treasure hunting. That's when he suggested that if his book could go to someone like the two of you, it would take a great weight off his shoulders."

"That explains it," Larayne said, sounding none too happy. "He wouldn't sell to the collector because he was looking to sell it to you."

Remi thought about the circumstances leading to her visit at the store, telling Bree, "He didn't seem to be expecting us when we arrived."

"Sorry about that," Bree replied. "I called the morning you left for San Francisco, but he was so distracted when I told him you were coming. He'd received another call, this one threatening." She gave an apologetic smile. "I guess I thought once the book was out of his store that everything would be fine."

"Right," Larayne said. "And now he's dead."

Bree laid her hand on top of her cousin's. "I tried to go see him that night after I found out about the robbery." Her eyes shimmered. "I'm so sorry. I never made it. They ran me off the road on the way to the airport. Next thing I knew, I ended up here at Larayne's." She brushed the tears from her cheeks, trying to smile at Remi. "They said they were going to kill us if we didn't get the book. I thought they meant it. I would never have—"

"Bree," Remi said. "I don't doubt for an instant that you did what you had to do."

Sam started pacing past each window again, looking out. And each time he neared them, both Bree and Larayne turned worried glances his way. Remi smiled at the two women and stood. "I think I'll get a glass of water."

She walked over to the cupboard, found a glass, then filled it, moving to Sam's side. "What are you doing? You're making them nervous."

He turned his back to the women, lowering his voice. "With only one gun, we're easy targets out here in the middle of no-where."

Lightning flashed so brilliant, it lit the kitchen, followed by the rumbling of thunder overhead that shook the windows. Bree's hand flew to her chest. When the handset on the table rang right after that, the cousins stared at it in shock.

Larayne finally reached for it, answering, "Hello? . . . Hello?" She disconnected and dropped it to the table. "Maybe it was a wrong number."

Remi and Sam looked at each other. Apparently he was thinking the same thing she was. The bad guys were calling to see if they'd returned to the house. Remi checked the back door to make sure it was locked.

Sam drew his gun, then turned to Larayne and asked, "Do you have any other weapons in the house?"

Ten

Every creak in the house seemed magnified. The rain lashed against the windows, the crack of thunder made Bree and Larayne jump.

The police were just a few minutes away, but Sam wasn't about to relax until they arrived. The odd phone call had rattled the two women, and while it could have been a coincidence, the timing set everyone's nerves on edge.

Armed with a rusty shotgun that belonged to Larayne's late husband, Sam gave Remi his revolver, then had everyone sit in the front room while he stood where he could see out the window to the road beyond.

Remi was doing a great job keeping their minds off the interminable wait by peppering them with questions about the map book. And when Larayne was ready to flee the house—an idea that Sam was against—Remi distracted her by asking, "Why is everyone after this book?"

Larayne looked at Bree, saying, "I—I heard them talking about it. These—these people who showed up at my house. It was right before they brought Bree here. Before they forced her to call you about sending us the book."

"What exactly did they say?"

"That once they got this map from it, they'd have everything they needed to find the key. If it was there, they'd get their money and they'd let me go."

Bree nodded. "That's what they told me, too. That they were going to let us go when they got the book and their money. But they were going to have to find the key somewhere. Honestly, my heart was beating so fast, I may have misunderstood."

"The book," Remi said to Larayne. "What made them think it was *the* book?"

"Bree knows more than I do about that."

Clearly, Sam thought, they were missing some important detail regarding this book's history. And the one man who might know what that could be was now dead. "What did your uncle have to say about it?"

"He said more research needed to be done. He was in the midst of doing that when Larayne first approached him about selling the book to Charles Avery."

Charles Avery . . . The name seemed familiar to Sam, but he couldn't place why. There were other factors that bothered him as well. The timing and location of this kidnapping. Why drag Bree all the way across the nation to get this book? Maybe it had more to do with the isolation of Larayne's house, but that was another point that bothered him. "Larayne," he said. "Is there any reason you can think of that you were singled out for this?"

"Of course. My father owned the book."

"Beyond that, even. Did you speak with this Charles Avery personally?"

"I've never met him. He sent someone here to the house."

"Has anyone else come to the house or contacted you about the book?"

She shook her head. "Why?"

"I just think it's strange that all this happened here, of all places."

"You don't think that Charles Avery's behind this?"

"Honestly, I have no idea. But it's worth looking into."

Larayne leaned back in her chair, then glanced at Bree. "Couldn't it have been someone else that my father may have contacted? You were closer to him, Bree. Did he say anything to you?"

"Not about anyone in particular. He did mention that he'd found something. But he said he wanted to check into it some more."

Sam looked out the window, saw headlights in the distance coming their direction. He glanced at Bree, then back out the window. "When was this?"

"Around the time those articles came out about the theft of the endpapers from other first editions." She looked down at the water glass in her hand, turning it in her fingers. "But then the robbery happened, and—" She turned an apologetic smile toward Remi, saying, "I never meant for any of this to happen. Not to you. I would never have mentioned the book to you if I'd known. I swear."

"Do not," Remi said, "blame yourself for what happened."

The detective arrived and took their statements. He seemed particularly interested in the man Sam had shot. Probably because the body was gone by the time they got to the warehouse. "You're sure you shot someone?" he asked Sam.

"Positive."

"Whoever's involved in this didn't want him identified."

In the midst of all this, a CSI arrived, and Larayne, more nervous than ever, sipped at her vodka while she watched the woman dusting for prints. In Remi's opinion, Larayne had had far too much to drink—not that anyone could blame her.

It was nearly five in the evening when the detective completed his investigation, then offered to give Sam and Remi a ride to their rental car since they were going to tow the SUV for evidence.

Sam accepted, and Remi turned to Bree, asking, "Would you like to fly back to California with us?"

Bree seemed torn as she eyed her cousin. "I don't want to leave Larayne alone."

"Don't worry about me," Larayne said. "I'm gonna have a friend come get me. Go. I'll be fine."

"You're sure?"

"I'm not alone," she said, nodding to the woman dusting for prints. "If my friend doesn't get here by then, I'll get a ride to his place with the CSI. If that's okay. He's just a mile up the road."

The CSI agreed, saying it wouldn't be a problem.

"Then, yes," Bree said to Remi. "I'll go with you."

Two hours later, they arrived at the hangar where the jet awaited.

Sam and Remi changed out of their damp clothes that were covered in glass dust from the SUV's broken window. While Sam was up front in the cockpit discussing their travel plans with the crew, Remi sat with Bree at the table in the main cabin.

Bree was talking on the phone. "Why don't you try to get some rest. I'll call as soon as I get home . . . Talk to you then."

When Bree disconnected, Remi asked, "Everything okay?"

"I just wanted to check in with Larayne to see if her friend had picked her up. He did. She'd had quite a bit to drink by the time we got out of there."

"I noticed. Speaking of, would *you* like something to drink before dinner?"

"Yes," Bree said. "If it's not too much trouble."

"What would you like? Coffee, tea, or something stronger?"

"You know . . ." Bree took a deep breath. "I think something stronger. As long as it's not vodka. Maybe a little sherry."

Their flight attendant, Sandra, appeared with a tray bearing cheese and crackers. Remi thanked her. "Two glasses of sherry will do nicely," she said. "Actually, pour a scotch, too. Sam will undoubtedly join us."

Sandra returned shortly with the sherry and scotch, then faded into the background. Remi lifted her glass. "So glad to have you back."

"Thank you." Bree gave a tired smile, then sipped, catching her breath as the alcohol hit her mouth. "That's . . . more than I'm used to."

Remi smiled as Sam joined them at the table, taking a seat next to her. "So," he asked, "how is Larayne doing?"

"Fine, I guess. She was pretty upset, apologizing for what happened, saying it was her fault, that she brought Charles Avery into all this."

Sam picked up a couple of crackers from the tray. "We don't know yet if he's behind this."

"Larayne seems to think he is. She said she remembered one of them talking to someone named Charlie on the phone about looking for these markers."

"Markers?" Sam said.

"Something to do with the map book. I have to assume it was related to this key or something."

"Did she say where?" he asked.

"Something about some pit or oak on some island? Larayne was pretty blitzed," she said as Sandra walked back from the cockpit.

Sandra smiled at Sam. "Excuse me for interrupting, Mr. Fargo. We've received clearance for takeoff."

"Hold up a sec," Sam said, then looked at Bree. "Is it possible your cousin was talking about the Money Pit at Oak Island?"

"It could have been. It was hard to understand her."

"What do you think, Remi?" Sam asked.

"Nova Scotia?" She wanted to get to the bottom of this mystery, but she was worried about Bree's well-being. "Only if Bree is up to the trip."

"I'll be fine. I promise."

He turned to Sandra. "Inform the pilots we'll need a change in flight plans. Halifax International. We'll arrange to get Bree home from there."

"Very good."

When she left, Bree said, "What if they're still out there? I'm not even sure I want to go home."

Remi gave her a sympathetic smile. "You can stay at our place in La Jolla until this is all over."

"Trust me," Sam said. "That house is a fortress. You'll be safe there."

Bree shook her head. "I can't possibly impose—"

"You won't be," Remi replied. "Between you and Selma, we may very well get to the bottom of this mystery. Speaking of, Larayne was saying you knew more about the history of this book . . . ?"

"A bit. I know that Uncle Gerald bought it during an estate sale from a distant cousin on my father's side. The so-called family history that was guarded by the male line of the Marshal family since the time of King John." She gave a cynical laugh. "Of course, that can't possibly be true because the book was written in the late seventeen hundreds. And, really, a book on pirates and privateers being passed down from generation to generation?"

"Unless," Remi asked Bree, "the value had something to do with this key everyone seems so interested in?"

"Even that is historically questionable. After all, the key is to the maps in the book, maps that are related to pirates and privateers who came several centuries *after* King John. So you see, I don't know how that could help much."

Remi smiled at her. "An interesting history nonetheless."

"You both have been so nice to me. After everything that's happened—" She stopped, tried to smile, then broke down in tears.

Remi waved at Sam to vacate his seat. Sliding out, she walked over to Bree, put her arms around the girl, then drew her from the table. "Maybe you'd like to wash up, then lie down for a bit? A good nap might be just the thing. There's plenty of time to go over this later."

Bree nodded. "Yes. I'd like that."

Remi walked the young woman to their sleeping quarters at the back of the plane, then returned a few minutes later. "Poor thing," she said to Sam. "I feel horrible about what happened."

"She has a right to be upset. Imagine losing your uncle, then being kidnapped like that."

"She's safe now and that's what counts." Remi lifted her glass, about to take a sip, then stopped, eyeing Sam. "So when did you say this week of rest and relaxation was going to start?"

"Remi, why ruin a perfectly good moment? It's not every day we get to sip twenty-five-year-old scotch while parked on a tarmac in North Carolina."

"Not trying to ruin it at all." She sipped her drink, enjoying the moment. It was one of the things she loved about Sam. Being able to laugh in the face of adversity. "Just wondering if I should block out more time on my calendar."

"Day after tomorrow, then."

"*Not* tomorrow?" she asked.

"We have a lot to do before we even get to Oak Island. Never mind that once we get there—assuming Bree understood her cousin's intoxicated ramblings—there's bound to be two or three angry mobsters who want to use us for target practice."

"We did get trip insurance, didn't we?"

"I knew there was something I forgot," he said, snapping his fingers.

"What do you think about this Charles Avery character?"

He eyed his glass of scotch, swirling the liquid, thinking about everything they'd been through these last few days. Clearly, the man was dangerous, with no regard for human life. Of course, one had to look at all the facts, not just make opinions based on a few events. "Timing is everything, isn't it?"

"My thoughts exactly. He suddenly finds out he's not going to be able to acquire this book and then the robbery and kidnapping occur?"

Sam drained his glass, then reached for a pad of paper and a pen at the side of the table. "I'll add his name to Selma's research list. It might be a good time to find out not only who this Charles Avery is but what's his interest in the map book."

Eleven

Charles Avery examined the list of assets of his newest possible acquisition. Salvaging ran in his blood, and when he couldn't be involved in the stealing of rare and valuable treasures, he whetted his appetite by searching for companies on the brink of bankruptcy. He'd buy them for a pittance, rip them apart, parcel out the remains, and make a tidy profit. Granted, there were a lot of casualties in the form of jobless employees when he finished, but collateral damage was the price one paid to succeed, he thought, turning the page, as his CFO sat across the desk from him waiting for his input.

The numbers satisfied him and he closed the folder. "Has anyone else shown an interest?"

"Not yet, sir."

His CFO, Martin Edwards, had been with his company since its inception. When it came to finances, Charles trusted him implicitly. "Your recommendation?"

"Considering the basis—" Edwards stopped as Colin Fisk walked into the room.

"My apologies for the interruption," Fisk said, his tone sounding anything but sorry, "but I have news that can't wait."

Charles eyed him, trying to determine if the news was good or bad. The man's face was a blank slate, he thought, turning to Edwards and saying, "The figures speak for themselves. Unless there's something I'm not seeing?"

"No, sir. My opinion is, we should proceed."

"Do so. Now, if you'll excuse us, apparently I have some pressing business that needs dealing with."

Edwards gathered his papers, then left.

Charles waited until the door had closed behind him before addressing Fisk. "Is it done?"

"We have the book and the key. On the way here as we speak."

He leaned back in his chair, relieved, and very much pleased with the outcome. "And the Fargos? They believed the story?"

"Not exactly. They followed my men to the warehouse."

"Tell me they were dealt with."

"They escaped. But then, so did two of my men, so all was not lost."

Charles gripped the arms of his chair, wanting to lash out, break something. These Fargos had already cost him considerable time and money. "I want these treasure-hunting socialites dealt with."

"At the moment, they're no more trouble than a thorn in our side."

"Thorns have a way of becoming infected. If they so much as appear on the fringes of any of my operations, kill them."

"I have a plan in the works."

"What sort of plan?"

"Involving the two women. Pickering's niece and daughter. Let's just say they've been very useful up to this point. If things proceed as expected, we should hear good news within the next day or so."

Twelve

S am and Remi sat across from each other in the cabin of their jet, both enjoying the relative solitude of each other's company. Remi was refreshing her memory about the history of Oak Island and the hunt for treasure in the so-called Money Pit while he read the report on Charles Avery that Selma had put together and forwarded.

After a while, Sam sat back, then looked up at Remi. "I thought this guy's name seemed familiar. I remembered reading about him in *Forbes*," he said. "Made his millions raiding corporations. When he's not buying cash-strapped companies, he fancies himself an expert in maritime salvaging."

"How is it we've never heard of him beyond that?"

"We don't run in the same circles. And judging from the number of people he's put out of business, I wouldn't want to."

Remi smiled as Bree wandered in, looking somewhat more refreshed from having had a nap. "Feeling better?" Remi asked her.

"Much."

Sam nodded at a light dinner laid out on the sideboard. "Help yourself. Selma's made arrangements for you to fly home tomorrow afternoon."

"Thank you." She looked over the paperwork Remi had spread all over the table. "Oak Island? You really think that's what Larayne was talking about?"

"It's a logical assumption based on the information given. And the map found in the endpaper certainly resembles the island. Do you know anything about it?"

"The basics. The constant hunt for a seemingly nonexistent treasure after a couple of teenagers dug up some stones and oak logs in the late seventeen hundreds."

"Seventeen ninety-five," Remi said. "In fact, starting right around the time *Pyrates and Privateers* hit the market."

"Coincidence?" Bree asked.

Sam glanced up from what he was reading to answer. "My opinion? Yes. Personally, I've never believed there was any treasure on Oak Island. And the various reports from scientists and engineers who've studied it over the years seem to confirm that."

Bree picked up one of the printouts on the island. "Then why would Avery's men be headed there? Assuming Charles Avery *is* behind this."

"Judging from this," Sam replied, holding up the papers Selma had sent, "I think we can safely assume he is behind it. As for why they'd go there in search of treasure? Not everyone believes the evidence."

Remi searched through the many photos on her tablet downloaded from the *Pyrates* book. When she found the illustration of the map hidden behind the endpaper, she held up the screen for Bree to see, then showed her the actual map of Oak Island. "My opinion, which is not based on any scientific background whatsoever, is that they believe this map in the book bears a strong resemblance to Oak Island." She glanced at Sam. "You have to admit, this particular map *does* look like it."

"It also looks like a lot of other small islands dotting the Atlantic. It would be nice if they had satellite photos back then."

Remi wasn't about to be dissuaded. "What about that mysterious cipher stone found in the pit at Oak Island declaring that two million pounds were buried forty feet below?"

"You mean the mysterious stone *supposedly* found in the pit? One that's never been seen—never mind the message on it is thought to have been a hoax."

Remi knew Sam's dim opinion of any treasure being on Oak Island. "Be that as it may," she said, "our kidnappers seem to think there's some reason to head in that direction and so we should brush up on the lore of the island. And if that's not enough to pique your curiosity, there are several known shipwrecks in the area. The one we're looking for could very well be there."

Bree eyed all the papers scattered about on the table, telling Remi, "I'd be glad to help."

"And we're glad to accept. Aren't we Sam?"

"We are." He smiled at Bree. "Remi's right. It doesn't matter what she or I believe. If they're heading there, there has to be a reason. And considering what they've recently put us all through—you especially—I'm making a point to find out what that is."

Of course, by the time they landed in Nova Scotia, they were no closer to discovering whatever secrets the island held. All they knew for certain was that millions of dollars had been sunk into the Money Pit by numerous groups over the last couple of centuries in the belief that a treasure was buried there. Remi hoped they'd learn something more by actually visiting the island.

The following morning, Bree remained with the crew, insisting that she felt much safer there, while Remi and Sam rented a car and drove the hour from Halifax down to the western shore of Mahone Bay and across the causeway to Oak Island. Selma managed to reserve two spots for them on the tour of the famous Money Pit.

Remi looked over at Sam as they got out of the car. "Do you think this is a good idea with all the tourists?"

He put his arm around her, giving her a reassuring hug. "Those men who came after Bree and Larayne were careful to make sure there were no witnesses. Think about it. If they're here on this tour—something I find unlikely—I seriously doubt they'll do anything with so many others around. Safety in numbers."

And there were certainly a lot of potential witnesses here. Remi knew the island was popular, but she never expected the number of people on the two-hour walking tour. The weather was perfect, the sky blue and cloudless, a soft breeze rustled the evergreens on the outskirts of the parking lot near the tourist center.

Men, women, and children gathered round as one of the guides, a young man in his twenties, called out to get everyone's attention. Remi and Sam moved to the back of the crowd, Remi searching to see if Avery's men had joined the group of about thirty tourists. "Quite the popular attraction," she said.

"No kidding. See any familiar faces?"

"No. So what is it we're looking for?"

"That's the question."

They pretended interest as the guide detailed the island's history, moving them in the southerly direction of the famed pit, the depression in the earth near the sole oak tree. "If history is to be believed," their guide said, "the two boys who found and first dug into the pit discovered layers of non-indigenous rock as well as oak logs every ten feet. They finally gave up after digging through about thirty feet. And there it remained, untouched, until one of them remembered it early in the nineteenth century." He stopped to face the crowd. "Neither boy could have foretold the man-hours and the amount of money poured into the aptly named Money Pit in search of whatever secrets it might reveal. Templar treasure? Burial crypt of a long-forgotten high priest?" He took a dramatic pause. "No one knows. But the new owners of Oak Island intend to find out, and we'll let you make up your own mind. So if you'll follow me this way . . ."

He led them inland toward the pit, relating more history as they walked. There seemed to be nothing that stood out beyond the known history: the pit, the rocks with symbols carved on them, the reported tunnels that flooded the pit every time someone dug deep enough.

In fact, it was beginning to look as though they'd wasted two hours. After being led to the outer shore where another cryptic formation of carved rock supposedly pointed to the Money Pit—thereby strengthening the legend—Sam said, "Hear that?"

The loud revving of a motorboat out on the water.

"Over there," he said. He nodded toward the small island just east of them, where Remi saw two men motoring toward it in a boat.

"Is it them?" she asked as he lifted his binoculars for a better view.

"Sure looks like it," he said and handed the glasses to her.

She adjusted the focus and watched as the boat maneuvered into the cove at the south shore of the island. One of the men got out, waded toward the shore with a shovel and a backpack, searching for something on the rocks. She recognized one of the two from the warehouse and their hotel in San Francisco. "Our book robber and one of the faux cops."

"Clearly, they know something we don't."

After several minutes, Sam drew Remi from the crowd, not heading toward the pit but toward the outer bank through a stand of trees. He continued watching the men on the other island.

"They found something," he said. "They're digging behind that boulder."

"Excuse me," came a voice from behind them. "You're not supposed to be over here."

They turned and saw one of the tour guides standing a few feet away, his arms crossed.

"Sorry," Sam said. "We didn't realize . . ."

"You'll need to rejoin the others."

She and Sam followed the man back to the group.

Sam caught up with the guide. "That island back there?" he asked. "What's the name of it?"

"That?" he said, glancing behind him. "Frog Island."

Sam nodded, and Remi asked, "Is it part of the Oak Island mystery?"

"Find me something around here that isn't."

"Anything specific?"

He glanced over at her and she gave him her most charming smile. "Actually," he said, "there *were* some claims that at one time there was some sort of connection between Frog Island to Oak Island. An underwater tunnel, though how anyone could have built one without it flooding is beyond me. Probably someone was digging there for treasure and a new rumor started." He stopped and pointed toward the shoreline. "See that little cove where the boat is? By all accounts, that's where the tunnel was built."

Remi and Sam watched as the two men on shore waded back to the boat, tossing in their shovels and packs. "Do you think there's any truth to the legends?" she asked.

He laughed. "I certainly hope so. I'd hate to think how many people have spent millions of dollars digging a hole in the same spot looking for something that isn't there."

"Good point," she said as he left them to join the group again. Through the trees, she saw the boat speeding away, and she looked over at Sam. "What now?"

"Come back tonight and figure out what they found so interesting on that other island."

Thirteen

Sam skyped Selma on Remi's tablet when they returned to their hotel.

"Good morning, Mr. Fargo," she said from her desk. "You'll be pleased to know that Bree is safely on her flight and will be landing in just a few hours."

"Good," Sam replied.

Remi took a seat on the sofa next to him, asking, "What fascinating theories have you discovered so far?"

"Lazlo believes the cipher wheel is for a simple substitution code."

Lazlo's face appeared on the screen behind Selma. "Good show, you two," he said, his British accent evident. "Miss Marshall informed us of your timely rescue. That must have been frightful."

"It was," Sam said. "About the cipher . . . ?"

"Right-o. Actually, what I believe is that you're looking for a shipwreck off the southern tip of the island, according to the hidden map." He shuffled through some papers, then held up the photo of the map Professor Hopkins had found behind the endpaper. "I was able to translate part of the text," he said, "but not all of it. To do that, I need to have the key. Unfortunately, the drawing of the cipher wheel on the map the professor found is merely an illustration of what we're looking for. If I had to guess, an actual instrument. One hopes it wasn't on paper because that supposedly was lost in said shipwreck."

Remi sighed. "Never easy, is it?"

Sam asked, "Do we have this shipwreck narrowed down?"

"I'm assuming the map of the island is either where it was buried or perhaps even where the ship was wrecked. There is one word that has popped up twice—assuming I have translated it properly. *Serpens*. Being that it's Latin, it could be *snake*, *dragon*, or *serpent*."

"That narrows it down," Sam said.

"Quite." Lazlo turned Selma's tablet so that he was once again in the frame. "One other thing that has popped up is a reference that whatever it is will be found on or near the southern tip of the island."

Remi and Sam exchanged glances, Remi saying, "That has to be why they were digging there."

"Who?" Lazlo asked her.

"Avery's men. We spotted them on the island across from Oak Island." She gave a brief description of what they'd witnessed.

"Ah," Lazlo said. "It appears they're one step ahead of us in the translation of the ciphers. Let's hope they haven't found the actual cipher wheel. I certainly haven't found any specific location. But if they're digging there, at least we know we're on the right track."

Selma poked her head into view. "We'll update you as soon as we know more."

Remi said, "We have every confidence."

"In the meantime," Sam told Selma, "we're going to need a motorboat for this evening. Something small enough to maneuver ourselves."

"On it," she said. "Any other equipment?"

"I don't think so," Sam replied. "We have wetsuits and dive gear. I think that's about it."

Sam was about to end the call when Remi added, "Don't forget insurance."

Selma's brows raised slightly. "As hard as you two are on equipment? That goes without saying. Along with detailed plans so we know where to find you in case anything happens."

Sam gave her a mock look of offense. "I'm shocked you'd have so little confidence in us."

"Not you, Mr. Fargo. It's the type of people you tend to run into on these ventures of yours. Greed brings out all sorts of evil."

Two hours before sunrise, Sam and Remi donned their wetsuits, then set out for Frog Island from the Gold River Marina at the north end of Mahone Bay in their seventeen-foot Boston Whaler. It wasn't the fastest of vessels, but it would blend in with any other boats that left before dawn.

Even though the Oak Island guide had made mention of an underwater passage between there and Frog Island, neither Sam nor Remi believed anyone from the seventeenth or eighteenth century had the skills to build something of that nature.

Then again, the attention to Frog Island intrigued Sam for a different reason. In past centuries, the area surrounding Nova Scotia had certainly been frequented by seamen, from French and English warships to pirates. The rumors of buried treasure in the area had always been bandied about—Oak Island happened to be the most popular location.

But Frog Island? Like many of these small islands in the area, it was privately owned. This one boasted a large house on the southeast side, probably a vacation home, and one Sam hoped wasn't occupied at the moment—not that they expected to be there for that long.

He cruised toward the small cove at the southernmost tip of the island. They wanted to see the area where Avery's men had been seen. What they were doing there was anyone's guess, but the way they were digging made Sam wonder if they weren't looking for this cipher wheel that Lazlo had mentioned.

"Look," Remi said, pointing to the sky. "The aurora borealis."

Sam glanced up. Through a parting of the clouds, he saw a faint greenish glow that seemed to pulsate. "Too bad it's not a clearer night."

"A glimpse is better than nothing. Right now, the cloud cover's a good thing. No moon to give us away."

"Pragmatically said." He slowed as they approached the cove.

Remi shined a light along the shoreline. "That looks like the area they were poking around," she said. "I remember that heart-shaped boulder."

"That's a heart?" he said, eyeing the massive boulder near the water's edge. He let up on the throttle. The boat slowed and bobbed in the surf. "It looks more like a two-humped camel-back."

"No sense of romance, Fargo."

"What if I said I ordered the aurora borealis just for you?"

"It seems someone lost their line."

"I thought it was a pretty good line."

"Not you. *Fishing* line." She aimed the beam of her flashlight near the base of the boulder.

Sam saw nothing other than rocks and water lapping against them in the growing wake of their boat. "Where?"

"About a foot to the left of the, uh, camel-humped boulder. A bit of moss or something stuck on it."

There it was, the wisp of moss or seaweed hanging from a nylon line about six inches above the waterline, possibly secured to something on the land behind the boulder. His gaze followed the glint of light on the line before it disappeared into the dark to his left, and the same to the right.

Whatever that line was caught on, it was tight. Their boat moved up and down with the current, but the line remained still.

"Call me paranoid," he said, maneuvering the boat to one side of the boulder for a better view, careful not to move in too close, "but that has all the markings of a trip wire."

"Do you really think they wired explosives?"

"They certainly had enough time. An even better question is, if they wired them because they knew we'd be coming here to investigate?"

"You think they set us up?" Remi aimed the beam near the boulder and a pile of small rocks behind it.

Sam saw the light reflecting off copper wiring disappearing into the midst of the pile.

"We're idiots," she said. "Of course they did. Otherwise, why make such a big show? That boat engine was the loudest in the bay. Making sure we would hear them and see them. Knowing we'd probably investigate . . ."

"How far does it go?" he asked, his gaze following Remi's light.

She pointed the beam to the left of the cove where a dead fir had fallen into the water, the fishing line barely visible wrapped around a branch of the tree. "I seem to remember them getting out there."

He turned the boat south, passing the boulder to the right. The fishing line continued on past it, swept across the water onto the shoreline, and was secured to a stump. If anyone tripped that line trying to get to shore . . . "Investigation over. We go back, notify the authorities. Let the experts deal with the explosives."

"Agreed," Remi said, shutting off the light.

Sam turned the boat, heading northwest. As he neared the northern tip of Oak Island, he noticed another craft heading right for them.

"Sam . . ."

"I see it." He turned the boat south at full throttle only to see a second vessel coming toward them from the south side of Oak Island.

He glanced over at the Money Pit's brightly lit visitor center, then back at the approaching boats, trying to decide if they should make a run for it.

The rapid muzzle flash from an automatic weapon changed his mind.

They'd never make it in time. Not against that sort of fire-power, and certainly not in a fishing boat.

Remi gripped the side of their craft. "This is where you're supposed to tell me you have a brilliant plan in the works."

"Sorry."

"*Not* what I was hoping to hear."

He glanced back toward the boats, then at Frog Island, realizing they were meant to be herded right toward the cove and the explosives. So be it, he thought, turning the Whaler that direction.

"Remi, get the boat hook," Sam said as he turned the wheel, aiming the vessel in the direction of the boulder.

"Sam—"

"I'm going to send this boat right through that trip wire."

"The pressure wave . . ."

If the bomb was in the water with them, the pressure wave would kill them. In this case, he was hoping the bomb was planted out of the water and *behind* the boulder to hide it from view, since the fishing line disappeared there. That way, any explosion was going up, back, and out the sides. A gamble, since there was always the possibility that there were more explosives hidden.

Only one way to find out—not that he was about to voice his concerns to Remi. If they were going to die, better to go fast and not know it. "You think you can hold your breath until we get to that fallen tree?"

She looked over and nodded.

Sam jammed the handle of the boat hook through the wheel to keep it on course.

"Get ready to jump."

Fourteen

Sam glanced at the approaching boats, saw the flash of more gunfire. He hoped they wouldn't notice two dark forms dropping from the side. "Ready?"

"Ready."

They sat on the edge, turned, and pushed off. The boat sped on.

Sam dove down into the cold depths, sensing Remi beside him as they swam. A few seconds later, the water lit up as the explosion rocked the air above them, sending a shock wave through the cove. Flaming debris rained down on the water. Sam and Remi kicked harder, Sam hoping the hull of the boat wasn't going to follow. He had no idea how far they'd swam, only hoped they'd arrive at the safety of the tree. After several more hard kicks, Sam reached out, feeling his hand brush up against the trunk.

He turned in the water, grabbed Remi's hand, and pulled her

beneath the trunk to the other side. They broke the surface, both sucking in air as they treaded water behind the trunk. Just beyond, they heard the crackle and roar of a giant fire, the air glowing above it. The sound of boat engines grew closer.

He used one of the branches to lift himself slightly so that he could peer over the trunk.

Their little fishing boat had overturned and what was left of it was burning in a blinding fire fueled by the spilled gasoline. The two craft carrying the gunmen neared, one moving in close to the vessel. One of the gunmen aimed his weapon toward the cove and fired. Dozens of rounds peppered the burning boat and the water around it.

Finally, the man stopped, looked around, then signaled to the driver. The vessel veered toward them, and Sam quietly dropped into the water, watching as both boats sped off toward the north.

Neither he nor Remi made a move until the engines had faded in the distance. When Sam felt it was safe, he and Remi swam beneath the tree trunk to the other side.

The blast of the explosion had blown their rental boat to the middle of the cove. Beyond it, not much was left of the boulder that had shielded the explosives. It was split down the middle, one half broken into several pieces from the force of the blast, the other half sitting in a deep hole on the shore.

Sam's gaze returned to the boat. He didn't want to think about what might have happened if Remi hadn't seen the trip wire and they'd gotten out to see what those men had been digging for.

Even Remi couldn't tear her gaze from the sight.

"Let's go," he said.

"Where?"

"We can swim over to Oak Island. There's got to be a phone at the visitor center. At the very least, we can walk to the mainland from the causeway."

They had covered about half the distance, nearly a thousand feet, when Sam heard the rumble of a large sea vessel coming from the south.

He glanced in that direction, worried Avery's men were returning. But as the boat sped into view, its emergency lights flashing atop and spotlights sweeping the water before it, he realized help had arrived.

They both shouted, waving their hands, relieved when the spotlight swung their direction, blinding them momentarily as their rescuers steered toward them.

They were pulled aboard the Royal Canadian Mounted Police vessel, where Sam related what had happened to the captain, who said, "You're telling me you survived an underwater explosion?"

"No. I am saying we went underwater to survive an aboveground explosion. That boulder," he said, pointing at it, "or, rather, what's left of it—directed most of the force away from the water."

"Darn lucky," the captain said.

"That's putting it mildly."

"What makes you think they were targeting you specifically?"

Sam glanced over at Remi, who sat in the chair across the table from him, holding a blanket tightly about her. "Sort of a long story."

"And I get paid by the hour. So tell away."

Sam gave as brief a version as he could, starting with the San Francisco trip, Bree's abduction, and then what she overheard her kidnappers discussing.

"Quite the story, Mr. Fargo," the captain said. "Any chance it can be verified?"

"Easily. San Francisco PD and Carteret County in North Carolina."

"We'll check it out. This employee of yours. Bree Marshall. You're sure you can trust her? You don't think she set you up, do you?"

"What do you mean?" Sam asked.

"She's the only one who heard this alleged discussion about Oak Island."

Remi seemed to bristle at the idea. "I trust her implicitly."

"And I," Sam said, "trust my wife's judgment."

"Just throwing it out there. Wouldn't be the first time someone was betrayed from inside." He looked down at his notes, then back at Sam. "Guess that's about all the questions I have for now."

"I have one," Sam said. "What are the chances of publicly ignoring that you found us?"

"Not sure I get what you're saying."

"If you hadn't found us, what would your impression of the crime scene have been?"

"On first glance? The boat on fire after an explosion? A recovery operation. Search for survivors."

"So if you have to make a press release, can't you say that?"

The captain held Sam's gaze as if contemplating the pros and cons. After a moment, he gave a nod. "Sure. Assuming your story checks out with those other agencies, we could probably work with that."

"We'd appreciate it," he said, ignoring Remi's menacing glance.

Sam looked over at Remi as he drove back to their hotel. Even though he couldn't see her facial expression in the dawn of the new day, he sensed her tension. "What?"

"You're actually going to let everyone think we're dead?"

"It's a brilliant plan."

"It's a horrible plan. After everything that Bree has been through, you honestly believe she could possibly survive more emotional trauma by thinking we're dead? And thinking it's her fault?"

"It would only be for a day or so."

"And what about Selma? And the rest of our staff?"

"We'd tell them, of course."

"But not Bree?"

"You heard what the captain said. Inside job."

"It was a suggestion, Sam. It doesn't mean it was."

"Everything that has happened to us happened *after* Bree set it up."

"She was also a victim."

He looked at her, then back to the road. "Are you sure?"

"How can you think otherwise?"

"You said her uncle wasn't even expecting you. And you were robbed at gunpoint. You left a message for her that we were staying at the Ritz-Carlton, and the gunmen appeared there. Then she's supposedly kidnapped—"

"Supposedly?"

"—and she asks us to bring the book to her cousin's. The book's taken, we're almost shot trying to rescue her. And then she tells us this story about Oak Island, and we're nearly killed there."

"I refuse to believe it."

"Remi . . . You heard what that officer said."

"Coincidence. All of it. And bad luck. How many times have you told me that the lure of treasure brings out the worst in people?"

"And you don't think it can bring out the worst in someone like Bree?"

"No," she said, crossing her arms. "And I refuse to let you think so. So come up with a different plan."

"I think we're making a mistake."

"Fine," she said, her voice terse. "It won't be the first time."

He checked the rearview mirror for the headlights that had been steadily behind them for several miles, making him suddenly wonder if someone was following them. But when he slowed, the vehicle sped up and passed them.

Maybe he was being paranoid. But he had every right to be, after their close encounter. Right now, they'd have to agree to disagree—even if it meant letting her believe she'd won this argument. When it came to Remi's safety, he wasn't about to take any chances. "We'll come up with Plan B at the hotel."

Of course his Plan B and her Plan B differed vastly. Remi

wanted to call Selma the moment they got back to the hotel to let her know that they were okay—Sam opted for the not-saying-anything approach.

"How is that different from your first plan?"

"Nobody's contacting her to say we're dead or that our boat was even found."

He followed her into the bedroom of their suite. She stopped him in the doorway. "I'm not going to be able to sleep until we settle this."

"What's there to settle?"

"That I'm right and you're wrong."

The woman was as stubborn as she was beautiful, he thought, taking her into his arms and kissing her. "You know I'm right."

"Are you? How about a little rock-paper-scissors?"

"That's how you want to decide this? With a game?"

"It's worked before."

He fell into bed, exhausted. "Fine," he said, closing his eyes. "I just need to rest for a minute . . ."

After falling into a deep but fitful sleep, he awoke to the phone ringing. Momentarily confused by the surroundings, he sat up, eyed the phone extension on the nightstand, and, without thinking, picked it up. "Hello?"

"Mr. Fargo." Selma's voice cut through the fog in his head. "I was worried when I didn't hear from you."

"We're fine," he said, hearing the bedroom door open and seeing Remi standing there, a vision in her off-white silk robe. "It's Selma," he said.

She walked over to the extension at the desk and picked up the receiver there. "Hello, Selma," she said.

"Mrs. Fargo. Good to hear from you. Just wondering how it went last night?"

Remi eyed Sam through the doorway, saying, "Perhaps you'd like to answer?"

Apparently she wasn't quite over their disagreement. "We ran into a bit of an issue when our boat blew up."

"I'll contact the insurance company."

"Actually," he said, "if you could hold off on that."

"I'm not sure I understand."

"The RCMP have agreed to keep our rescue quiet for now. To buy us a little time."

"Time for what?" Selma asked.

"My question exactly," Remi added.

"If whoever set us up last night thinks we're dead, maybe they won't be in such a hurry to come after us. I'm hoping we can make some progress on the maps and finding that cipher wheel."

"Except," Remi said, "we're checked into our hotel under our real names."

Good point, Sam thought. "Let's hope the explosion was convincing enough that they're not calling the area hotels to find out if we survived. Now, about that cipher wheel," he said to Selma.

"That's the reason I wanted to call you," she said. "Bree told us about your idea of taking the outline of the maps to see if there are any similarities to other islands."

"My idea?"

"She said you mentioned it on the plane. That the maps were similar in shape to a number of other islands in the Atlantic. Her suggestion was to rule out those that weren't frequented by pirates and compare the map to the shape of those with rumors of treasure, such as the Oak Island legend."

"That one didn't end well."

Selma cleared her throat. "Anyway, while we were working on the cipher code last night—and not having much luck—Bree took the illustration of the map from the *Pyrates* book that was thought to be that of Oak Island and started comparing it, shape-wise, to islands in the Atlantic. She found one that we think is a pretty close match off the coast of Brazil. Ilha da Queimada Grande. It fits with the Latin *serpens* Lazlo found in the text."

Sam noticed that Remi's I-told-you-so look faded into one of concern. Though neither had actually been to the island, they were well familiar with the area. They had studied it in the past, due to rumors of Incan treasure being buried there. Ilha da Queimada Grande, aptly nicknamed Snake Island, was home to the golden lancehead, a species of pit viper so venomous that the Brazilian Navy had forbidden all public access. According to the island's geological history, the rising sea had separated Ilha da Queimada Grande from the mainland more than eleven thousand years ago. The isolation was the reason the vipers on the island had evolved into the most venomous snakes on earth. With only seabirds landing on the island and no other prey, the snakes needed a fast-acting venom that would incapacitate a bird before it could fly away. Snakes aside, there were several documented shipwrecks in the area around the island.

"And what is it we're searching for?"

"If the map is legit, a shipwreck off the southern tip of the island."

"Even if we spent years searching, the odds would still be astronomical that we'd find the cipher wheel."

"*If,*" Selma said, "we were actually *looking* for the wheel itself. I'm hoping for the next-best thing. Identify the ship."

Remi's brows went up. "Am I missing something here?"

Even Sam was stumped. "How does that help us?"

"Lazlo thinks the stolen cipher wheel was a copy and that the ship's captain scuttled his vessel to keep the wheel from being captured. Which means the original cipher wheel's still out there. Narrow down where and when that ship was made, we might be able to identify its owner through manifests. We find its owner—"

"—We find the original cipher wheel," Sam said. "Send us what you have."

"It should be waiting in your in-box. Along with travel information that I'll be passing on to your flight crew for the trip to Brazil."

He dropped the phone into the cradle, got out of bed, and joined Remi in the other room. "That sounds promising."

"Is that an apology?" she asked, walking toward him.

"I can't apologize for wanting to keep you safe."

"You're wrong about Bree. She's not sitting there with Charles Avery on speed dial, relating our every move."

Something was going on. He just didn't know what—not that he was about to ruin the moment with his suspicions. "I apologize for making it seem I didn't believe in you. That was never the case."

She draped her arms over his shoulders. "Apology accepted."

"Off to Brazil, then?" he asked.

"I love Brazil this time of year."

Fifteen

S am and Remi flew in to Miami first, where they picked up the supplies that Selma had requisitioned for them, as well as clothing more suited to tropical weather. After spending the night, they flew to São Paolo, Brazil, landing around seven that evening.

The following morning, Sam left to meet with government officials for the necessary permits to search around Snake Island. Remi remained behind at the hotel, using her tablet to skype with Selma about the boat and crew Selma had found for them at the Port of Santos.

"All considering," Selma said, "they appear very capable."

"That sounds ominous."

"There must be something going on. Maybe because it's a weekend. Every charter is booked. But their references checked out. And it was, *literally*, the last vessel available in that area that had the minimum requirements you requested and could accommodate an overnight stay on the water."

Remi, seated at the desk with her tablet propped up on its stand, smiled at the screen, knowing that Selma had done her best. She went over her equipment list one more time, among the items a portable side-scan sonar system, metal detectors, underwater camera and lights. "It looks like you've sent everything we need."

"Then I'll send word that you'll be contacting the boat owner this evening or tomorrow. I'm assuming you both looked over the papers Lazlo sent last night?"

Remi had them on the table. "We did. The coordinates of the two known wrecks off the southern tip and their documentation." Or, as Sam put it, a "crapshoot." While the mysterious map may have been hidden for the last couple of centuries behind the endpaper of the *Pyrates and Privateers* book, the two documented wrecks had been found and looted long ago. Based on the few artifacts recently discovered, the first wreck was most likely of Spanish origin. Selma was certain that they were looking for a ship with English ties. That was the main reason Sam decided they should be searching the second wreck in the shallower waters at the very southern tip of Snake Island. Very little had been documented beyond its location—at the end of a rockslide at the island's tip. "Lazlo's certain of the translation to the key on the map?"

"He feels confident that the words *sea* and *serpent* are in the mix."

"Too bad it couldn't have been something like *sea* and *dolphins*. I'd much prefer that to *pit vipers*."

"It does, however, strengthen Bree's suggestion of Snake Island as a possible location. I was looking over the map again this morning and it's . . ." Selma lifted the transparency she made, holding it over the map of Snake Island. "Well, it's definitely a stretch. But who am I to say that it is or isn't the right location? That's something that you and Mr. Fargo will have to determine once you get out there."

"How is Bree?" Remi asked, glad that Sam wasn't there. She knew in her heart that Bree would never betray them, but she also understood Sam's position and was still hurt that he was angry over the matter.

"She seems fine," Selma replied. "At the moment, she's helping Lazlo research the illustration of the cipher wheel next to the map. She seems fairly knowledgeable about that period of history."

"Glad to hear it. Did Sam talk to you about her?"

"Just to find out how she's getting on."

"Nothing else?"

Selma paused a second. "Is there something I should know, Mrs. Fargo?"

"No. But do me a favor. Keep an eye on her, would you? Sam . . . worries about her."

"I'll do that."

They ended the connection. Remi had never known Sam to throw an accusation out if there wasn't something to base it on— not that he had actually *accused* Bree, merely pointed out the possibility after that RCMP captain had suggested it. And even though she was almost certain that her friend wasn't conspiring with the enemy, now that the seed was planted, she couldn't shake the thought that there were a few too many near-fatal coincidences.

If she was wrong about Bree, it put both her and Sam in danger. Not about to take a chance, she picked up her cell phone and called Selma back. "Are you somewhere you can talk in private?"

"In my office, yes. Let me close the door." A moment later, Selma was back. "Is something wrong?"

"It's about Bree." Remi explained Sam's concern. "Personally, I don't think it can be true, but Sam's right. There are just too many things that can't be explained away. If he's wrong, I don't want Bree to be hurt. But if he's right . . ."

"I understand, Mrs. Fargo. She hasn't acted unusual, but I'll certainly keep an eye on her."

Having informed Selma about Sam's concerns lifted a weight from Remi's shoulders and she was able to concentrate on preparations for the next leg of their journey. By the time Sam called to say he was heading back to the hotel with the proper permits in hand, she had the entire trip mapped out.

Sam walked into their hotel room about an hour later, handing her a bouquet of bright sunflowers. "Apparently it's good luck to start a trip with yellow flowers."

"Is it?"

"Today it is. It was that or purple iris. It's all I could find for the girl who has everything including a husband who comes up with some not-too-brilliant plans every now and then."

She took the flowers, laid them on the table, then put her arms around Sam. "You're always brilliant."

"Then I'm forgiven?"

She kissed him, then leaned back and studied his face. "Would this be the right time to mention that I passed on your concerns about Bree to Selma?"

"Are you saying I'm right?"

"I'm saying your concerns are valid enough to let her know— which is not the same as making everyone think we were dead."

"So that makes me *almost* right?" His brown eyes sparkled.

"Don't push it, Fargo."

Remi hired a car to take them to the Port of Santos to meet with the captain and the crew of the *Golfinho*. They stepped out of the hotel at dawn, the sky a mixture of vermillion red brushed across bright turquoise.

Red sky at morning, sailors take warning.

The old adage popped into her head even though she'd dou-ble- and triple-checked the weather. Light showers were pre-dicted for later the next evening, surely nothing to be concerned about.

Their vehicle was waiting out in front, their dark-haired driver, tall and reed-thin, leaned against the front fender—like most youth, absorbed in whatever was on his phone screen. He saw them approaching and hurriedly shoved his phone in his pocket. "Mr. and Mrs. Fargo?"

"We are," Remi said, figuring he was perhaps eighteen or nineteen. "You must be António Alves?"

His smile broadened. "Thank you for hiring me. You are my first big fare. I won't disappoint you," he said in a thick accent, carefully pronouncing each word.

Sam, tipping the bellman who had wheeled their gear out on a cart, looked up at that statement. "I was under the impression that you were an experienced driver."

"A good driver, yes," he said as he took the gear from the luggage cart and loaded it into his trunk. "I make this drive all the time, even if *you* are my first fare to Santos. My cousin, who is concierge, will vouch for me."

Which explained the recommendation, Remi thought.

António opened the door for her. "Please. Get in and buckle up for safety."

Sam wasn't convinced at the young man's professed driving skills. "You're sure about the drive to the coast?"

António nodded. "I used to work on my uncle's fishing boat to earn money for school. Now that I am at university, it's easier to work in town. But no classes today, so you're in luck!"

Remi said, "Your cousin *did* mention that we would need you to stand by—overnight, even—to give us a ride back?"

"Yes. I practice my English on the way and I study while you dive. A win-win, right?"

Remi liked him and his enthusiasm. "Definitely."

Even Sam seemed to warm to him, asking, "So what're you studying?"

"This is only my first year, so there is everything. Math and history and science and politics. One day I hope to be a doctor. But that is a long time from now." And for the remainder of the winding mountain drive, in between pointing out scenic areas of interest, he talked about his school, his seven brothers and sisters, his uncle the fisherman, and his cousin the concierge, who was also putting himself through school because, unlike the rest of their family, he did not inherit a fondness for boating. And before Remi knew it, they'd arrived at the port.

António unloaded their gear that filled his trunk. "Where is it you're diving?" he asked.

"Out by the southern end of Snake Island."

His smile faded. "Keep watch. My uncle tells of pirates. What sort of boat have you hired?"

"That," Sam said, "is a good question. The *Golfinho*, is all we know."

António seemed to perk up at the name. "Captain Delgado. My uncle speaks highly of him."

"Good to hear," Sam replied. "So how do we get in touch with you when we're back in port?"

He pointed into town. "My uncle's house is not that far. I can see the docks from there. It is good it is a weekend and I can stay overnight. When I see the *Golfinho* return tomorrow night, I will come." He looked up at the sky and, though there wasn't a cloud in sight, said, "Let us hope it is before the storm rolls in."

Captain Delgado seemed to be the polar opposite of António. In his mid-forties, he was short, stocky, with permanent frown lines across his brow. He and two of his men had been waiting there, watching for them, only approaching after António drove off. "Fargo?"

"Sam and Remi," Sam replied. "So where's this vessel of yours?"

"Right there," Delgado said, pointing toward the end of the closest dock.

Remi was pleased to see a fairly new catamaran research vessel. "That should do nicely." But he continued past the gleaming forty-eight-foot boat, not stopping until they reached a dilapidated forty-two-foot fishing charter, its faded green hull having seen better days probably decades ago. "That's the . . . *Golfinho*?"

The man grinned, his teeth yellowed from tobacco. "A bit rusty around the edges, but very seaworthy."

Sam eyed the vessel. "You're sure about that?"

"A good boat. Fast. Pirates, they leave us alone. No money, right?" He laughed.

Remi and Sam laughed with him, but with less enthusiasm. Remi, recalling António's warning, asked, "Are there many pirates around here?"

"Some. But we have guns. We protect you." He nodded to his men to gather the Fargo gear. "If you are ready, we load up your things and get started. We want to be on our way back tomorrow before the rain starts."

At the second mention of weather, Remi accessed her phone just to make sure the chance of light showers hadn't been upgraded. The symbol now showed a lightning bolt through it. Even so, it still wasn't expected to hit until later the next evening. If they didn't find what they were looking for tomorrow, they'd have to come back after the rain.

Once they were in deep water, Remi let her fears about the weather and the boat's storm-worthiness rest. Aside from the occasional creaking and moaning of the ship's hull as they cruised toward Snake Island, towing a fairly new-looking Zodiac behind them, nothing seemed amiss. Selma had vetted the captain, his crew, and his references and had assured Remi that they were reliable. Besides, António had mentioned that his uncle spoke highly of the *Golfinho*'s captain. That had to mean something, even though Captain Delgado and three of his four crew members looked more like pirates than fishermen. The fourth and youngest, Nuno, reminded her a bit of António, both in age and build. Unlike António, he seemed nervous, glancing over at her, then looking away whenever she made eye contact.

Remi couldn't decide if it was her presence on board or something else bothering him and so she did her best not to look at him.

Sam noticed also, moving beside her and whispering, "Quite the motley crew, eh?"

"I'll say. As long as the *Golfinho* gets us there and back in one piece, I'll have nothing to complain about."

As they neared the island that evening, the captain turned the helm over to one of his older crew members, then walked back toward Sam and Remi, leaning over the side next to Sam. "What brings you to the Ilha da Queimada Grande?"

"Looking for evidence of a shipwreck," Sam said.

"Treasure?" The captain smiled. "I hear that is your specialty."

"In this case, no. We're here to document possible artifacts."

"*You* are braver than I," the captain said. "Too many snakes."

"Lucky for us," Sam said, "we only need to search the water."

"Good thing. They could have the winning Mega-Sena lottery ticket on that rock and I would not go. Better to die an old pauper than a rich snakebite victim."

His smile sent a shiver down Remi's spine, and she was glad when they were interrupted by the call to dinner. She and Sam took seats near Nuno, but when Remi tried to engage him in conversation, he politely excused himself and left the table.

The weather held up that night, and they slept peaceably, awaking early the next morning to begin the dive.

Sam suggested that they suit up and do a final check of their equipment. The captain asked if they needed help with anything, which they politely declined, and he returned to the helm.

The *Golfinho* eventually anchored well off the southern tip of the island—far enough away from the very rocks responsible for sending many a ship to the depths over the past few centuries. Whether one of those ships was the vessel they were searching for remained to be seen, Remi thought, watching as they readied the fifteen-foot Zodiac SeaRider.

Nuno climbed down the ladder, secured their gear in the boat, including the large case with the portable side-scan sonar unit. He helped Sam in first, and Sam, in turn, helped Remi. The young man still had difficulty making eye contact, but he seemed polite and willing to help. Soon they were speeding toward Ilha da Queimada Grande. The beauty of the island grew as they neared, the treacherous rocky shore giving way to lush jungle that climbed to a steep peak. Had it been anywhere else, Remi would have enjoyed hiking up to the top to look out over the water. Just thinking about the snakes made her very glad for the large body of water between her and them.

Sam set up the side-scan sonar unit, then directed Nuno on

the speed and direction to achieve the best scan of the ocean floor while he monitored the screen. At the moment, the water was fairly calm, but with the predicted rain later, that could change. Much depended on luck and the accuracy of their instruments for locating the wreck—and hoping it was the right one—or they'd be repeating the entire operation when the weather cleared.

If they were lucky, they'd find what they were looking for— not that she was naive enough to think they'd stumble across the actual cipher wheel. A lot of factors came into play when it came to salvaging wrecks, and quite often the contents of a ship weren't always found in the immediate area where it went down—never mind the possibility that the cipher wheel had already been re- covered and was lying in some private collection, its owner none the wiser as to its true purpose and worth.

Right now, all they needed was enough wreckage to figure out what sort of ship went down. That thought sent her gaze to the deadly island, wondering what it must have been like for the survivors, if there were any, thinking they could swim to shore and safety. Assuming they could avoid being smashed against the rocks in the storm-tossed waters and they managed to make it onto the island . . .

Sam sensed her concern and glanced up from the sonar screen. "Something wrong?"

"I was thinking about the shipwreck. Imagine being that close to land, thinking you were safe . . ."

His gaze followed hers to the island. "I think I'd prefer drown- ing over death by pit viper venom."

"I'd prefer neither."

He drew her toward him. "I can use your sharp eye," he said.

They sat next to each other, and Remi tried to concentrate on the sonar readings, feeling as if they'd been out there all day with nothing to show for it. Eventually the wind picked up and, with it, the water got rougher. She was about to suggest they call it a day when Sam pointed to the screen. "I think we've found it."

Sixteen

The area Sam had indicated looked like the remnants of a rockslide, as though some long-ago earthquake had turned the rocky southern end of the island into a pile of rubble that had swept down to the ocean floor. A few feet away was another long, narrow stretch of rubble that seemed far too neat to have been caused by any landslide. Undoubtedly ballast from a ship. The fact it wasn't scattered meant the ship went down right there either because it was too badly damaged or it was scuttled to prevent it from being captured.

Remi leaned in closer for a better look. "Do you think the rockslide came *after* the wreck?"

"Possibly," Sam replied. "Either way, that vessel was too close to navigate safely. Too many underwater rocks that could have done it in, especially in a storm."

"Maybe they did it on purpose. Keep it from falling into the wrong hands."

"Makes you wonder what that cipher wheel leads to."

After final instructions to Nuno, they gathered their metal detectors, put on their diving gear, and dropped into the water.

They descended into the depths. As always, the tranquillity and beauty of the sea amazed Remi. It didn't matter how many dives they made, each one was like a new world to be discovered, as the tropical fish scurried away and the bright colors muted into blues and greens the farther down they went.

The ballast pile she'd seen in the monitor seemed to be all that was left to indicate that a ship once rested there, a mere twenty-five feet below the surface, most of it having disintegrated long ago.

Before they explored what was left of the wreck, they scanned the water around them. The coast of Brazil was known for its higher-than-average fatal shark attacks. Granted, the majority occurred in the northeast coastal region around Recife. But the state of São Paolo due west of them had the second-highest concentration. For the most part, the victims had been swimmers and surfers, probably attacked by the aggressive bull sharks known to frequent the shallower waters off the beaches and estuaries. But the warmer equatorial coastal waters were also home to the equally dangerous and much larger tiger shark, but not as likely—Remi hoped—here in the shallows off Snake Island.

As she and Sam circled about back-to-back, they saw several barracuda, but no sharks, and so they started at the far end of the ballast pile, working their way inland toward the rockslide, moving their metal detectors along the ocean floor. Neither expected to find anything—although there was always hope—and the silence of their equipment confirmed their suspicions. The wreck's location was well documented and had undoubtedly been searched numerous times. Even so, as Remi and Sam well knew, the ocean floor was constantly shifting, revealing secrets one day, hiding them the next.

They examined the ballast stones. Sam moved a few, tossing them aside, each one raising a cloud of silt as it landed. The next one he picked up was different. Sharp, triangular, and yellow. He shined his light on the stones, and she saw more of the same. Broken pieces of yellow brick. Not your typical ballast. Maybe something that could be traced. She held open the dive bag, he dropped the piece in, and they continued their search.

After several minutes, he tapped her shoulder, pointing to his right, where a moray eel slithered out of its home in the rocks. For a moment, she thought he was teasing her about it being a seafaring pit viper, but then he shook his head and pointed back toward the dark enclosure where the sea snake had emerged in a cloud of silt and shined his light across the space. It was several seconds before the silt settled, but then she saw what caught his attention. Whether it was the way those large rocks landed or the eel that had enhanced the opening for a home, there was a shallow hollowing beneath it. Sam swam over and used his hand to fan the silt, revealing a barnacle-encrusted rib from the ship on the ocean floor that hadn't been visible before.

That confirmed that the rockslide had probably occurred after the ship went down, possibly covering part of the wreck.

Which meant that there could very well be something beneath those rocks. He signaled for her to check. She inserted her metal detector into the space, hearing nothing near the entrance, but a definite ping as she moved it farther in. She handed the metal detector to him, then aimed her light into the space, waving her hand over the floor, lifting the silt.

Something dark showed in the light a moment before the sand settled over it. She scooped her hand into the sand and pulled it out. At first she thought it was a coin, heavy and crudely stamped. A small tab jutting from one side almost made it look like a pendant from a necklace. On closer examination, she realized it was a lead seal, often used to secure bolts of fabric carried on merchant ships.

Sam photographed the front and back. Remi dropped it into her bag, then looked at her dive watch to make sure they hadn't lost track of time. But no, they had at least twenty more minutes, and so she and Sam continued their exploration. He pointed toward a shark swimming at the outer edge of their dive zone. The flat, edgy snout and stripes along its side told her it was a juvenile tiger shark. It looked about seven feet, and she nodded that she saw it, watching for a bit. The shark seemed uninterested in them, swimming calmly, apparently content from feeding elsewhere.

Sam swam over the top of the rockslide, getting a reading from his metal detector somewhere in the rock pile. It turned out to be a fishing weight. He changed his direction, swimming along the edge of the rocks.

Remi hadn't finished exploring the shallow rock cave and decided she'd better take advantage before the eel returned. Her metal detector pinged on the left side, toward the back, and she reached in, brushed at the sand, but didn't find anything. Something was in there, enough to send a strong signal.

Sam indicated that it was time to leave. Figuring it was probably some fishhook, she was about to give up, but then shined her light between the rocks on the left side, brushed at the sand, scooping it out of the cave mouth, excited when she felt something smooth beneath her gloved hand.

She waved Sam over, pointing down into the rocks.

Sam stopped her, pointing upward, clearly worried that if they weren't careful, they might possibly trigger a small landslide on their own. She nodded her understanding. She'd be careful. If she could just move a few of those rocks, she could get to the artifact. She managed to pull out one rock, moving it to the side. And then another, which rolled down to the bottom of the pile. Several rocks slid out beneath it but didn't seem to move anywhere else. When she turned on her light and aimed it into the area she'd been working, she saw it. A small cannonball. Disappointed, she reached down, picked it up.

She felt a slight punch on the back of her thigh and spun around—Sam was teasing her about her great find.

But it wasn't Sam.

A larger tiger shark circled around, this one about eight feet. It dropped to the ocean floor, zigzagging, turning from graceful swimmer to aggressive predator as it shot toward her.

Remi fell back toward the rocks, kicking out with her fins, striking the shark on its snout with her metal detector. It turned, then darted toward her again. She held the cannonball, hoping to smash it against the shark's face as it came at her. It hit the beast's flesh, then fell from her grasp. She kicked back, up against the rocks, sending several down the pile. The rocks beneath her shifted, then tumbled down, one after another, turning the clear water opaque.

Remi, lost in a cloud of silt and sand, kicked away from the rocks as she slid down, worried when she couldn't see the shark.

Heart pounding, she turned about, swinging her metal detector frantically. A dark form swam toward her. She gripped the metal detector, ready to ram it, when Sam emerged from the cloud of silt.

She reached out, grasped his hand, relief flooding through her as he pointed to the shark swimming off in search of easier prey.

They'd have to come back tomorrow and try again. She turned to survey the damage the rocks had done to what was left of the wreck site.

As the water cleared, her gaze lit on a dark circle about the size of a saucer. It was half buried in the silt and precariously positioned partway beneath the rocks and sand.

Sam saw it, too. He eyed the rocks, undoubtedly worrying that the slightest of movement could send them down farther, and he motioned for Remi to keep watch as he slowly worked the sand beneath the object until he was able to slip it out, the rock pile remaining intact.

He handed her the disk, and her thrill of excitement that it might be the missing cipher wheel died at the realization it was only a small tin plate. Sam photographed the front and back. She dropped it into the dive bag, then glanced at her watch. They were on the last few minutes of air. They needed to end the dive. He gave her a thumbs-up and they began their ascent.

As soon as they broke through to the surface, she pulled her mouthpiece out, turning to Sam. "Not bad, Fargo!"

Sam looked anything but excited.

"What's wrong?" she asked.

"Get behind me," he said, then nodded toward the boat.

When she turned, she saw Nuno leaning over the side, a gun in his hand. And it was pointed at them.

Seventeen

H and it over." The young man's dark eyes bored into Sam as he treaded water near the boat. "Now."

"Nuno," Sam said. "You don't want to do this."

"Yes. I do."

"Why?"

"It doesn't matter. Hand it to me."

"And what?"

"And you die a quick death instead of a slow one."

"Whatever they're paying you, I'll double it."

Nuno hesitated, his gaze moving from Sam to Remi, then back. "You do not understand. They have already killed Captain Delgado. They will kill my family if I do not do this."

Remi, disregarding Sam's advice to stay behind him, tried to swim closer.

Sam grabbed her arm, stopping her. "They'll murder you, too," he said to Nuno. "These men are cold-blooded killers."

"It is my family. Please . . . forgive me." He waved the revolver at them, his dark eyes shimmering as he recited something in Portuguese. A prayer, Sam thought.

Not a good sign.

"They watch even now," Nuno said. "To see that I kill you. Please. I do not want my family to die."

"Remi," Sam said. "Hand me the bag and swim away."

"I'm not leaving you, Sam."

"Yes. You are. Once my wife is safe, I'll give you the bag."

Nuno shoved the gun forward. "No! I do not trust you. You!" he said, pointing the gun at Remi. "You give it to me. Not him!"

"Remi . . ." Sam held tight to her arm.

"Now!" Nuno cried.

Remi smiled at Sam. "He's protecting his family."

Which is what made him so dangerous. The last thing he needed right now was to stir up any more anger and he reluctantly let go of Remi.

She swam toward the boat and held up the bag. The young man grasped it, but Remi held tight, saying, "Nuno, I pray that your family is safe. And that you will do what is right by them."

And then she let go.

Sam's heart thundered in his chest as he watched his wife treading water, far too close to the gunman and the barrel of that revolver.

Nuno opened the bag, peered inside, then dropped it into the bottom of the Zodiac. He looked at the gun, then Remi. "I am sorry." He pointed and fired.

Remi jerked in the water, then turned toward Sam, her face

pale, eyes wide, as she reached out. Her hand grasped his, and he pulled her toward him.

A second shot shattered the air, and Sam wrapped his arms around her, adrenaline racing through his veins. He turned, placing himself between Remi and the gunman. But a third shot never came. The Zodiac engine revved as it sped away, leaving the two of them there in the water.

"Remi?"

"I'm fine."

He looked into her eyes, unable to believe. "How? I saw—"

"He fired into the water. It scared me."

"Why?"

"I think he hopes they'll believe we're dead. What if—"

Sam kissed her hard, then let her go, as they both started slipping below the surface. He looked out toward the *Golfinho*, the growing whitecaps making it difficult to see clearly. If they were lucky, the same was true for anyone on the *Golfinho* looking out toward them. The Zodiac was halfway to it, and he hoped that Nuno was convincing in his part. If he wasn't . . . At least they'd have some warning—should anyone want to return to finish them off, they'd have to do it in the Zodiac.

Now their best bet for survival was to stay near the rocks, where the *Golfinho* couldn't navigate.

After what seemed like an eternity, the Zodiac arrived back at the *Golfinho*. Sam and Remi watched as the anchor on the boat was raised. Someone leaned over the side, pointing an assault rifle. Sam and Remi dove from sight as the Zodiac was peppered with gunfire.

The *Golfinho* motored away. Sam reached out and grasped Remi's hand.

"On the bright side," she said, calling out over the roar of the wind and the roiling ocean, "we're alive."

"There is that." What they didn't need was the extra weight of their near-empty air tanks sapping their energy as they treaded water. They removed and dropped them. Sam turned, taking in their situation. They'd drifted quite a ways from their dive location, the island looming close, and the waves crashing against the treacherous rocks. The strong current continued its relentless pull, and they swam farther out, away from the danger.

Sam glanced up at the sky, the dark clouds threatening imminent rain. "Looks like we have two choices. Try to make it to the mainland or wait it out here."

"In the water?"

"Or on the island," he called out. "Sharks or pit vipers?"

She took in the island, her gaze sweeping across the rocky shoreline. "What if I don't like either choice?"

"Sorry, Remi," he said. "Unless you can think of Plan B?"

"Wait for Selma to send help?"

The whitecaps grew higher and the wind picked up as the storm neared. All too soon, the first few raindrops fell. Trying to swim to the mainland in this would be near impossible even for the best of swimmers. And that was assuming they didn't get caught in a crosscurrent and get pulled out to deeper waters.

"The island," he said. Better to stay put. Wait for help. And hope the snakes didn't like the rain.

Remi nodded, undoubtedly realizing that was their safest course of action. They'd have to find a safe, rock-free place to get to shore—and together started swimming north parallel to the island, staying on the west side. Unfortunately, it was against the current, and after several minutes Sam realized they hadn't gone far.

They needed to reassess.

Remi treaded water next to him. "Sam . . ."

"Give me a minute," he said.

"Look!" She pointed south.

He turned, worried that the *Golfinho* was back, searching for them. "What?"

"There. Plan B."

He saw nothing but gray, choppy water.

"About two o'clock. I think that might be the Zodiac."

And there it was. A bit of red popping up over the swells, then dropping down again. If it wasn't the Zodiac, it was something bright. At this point, they had nothing to lose. "Let's go."

The upside was that they were moving with the current and not against it—the downside was that so was the object they were swimming toward. Eventually they made headway.

Definitely the Zodiac, but partially submerged. As they neared, he realized the stern with the outboard motor was beneath the surface. The bow was all that was left holding it above water.

More a life preserver than a boat, it wasn't going to get them home, but the bright red surface would certainly show up better than their black wetsuits if a search party happened to come for them.

Unfortunately, as they grabbed onto the front end, it didn't look as though it was going to stay above the water. Too much weight and not enough air left, the transom and stern were completely submerged. "Stay here," Sam said. "I'm going to check it out."

Remi nodded, holding on to the bow. Sam adjusted his mask, took his flashlight from his belt, and dropped below the surface. It was extremely hard to sink an inflatable boat. Delgado's men must have missed a few air tubes when they shot it up. A sickening feeling that young Nuno had met his fate in this boat swept through him as he loosened the motor's clamps, detaching it from the transom and letting it drop.

That, he hoped, would buy them more time, and he rose to the surface and joined Remi. "Let's hope it holds air long enough. Lot of bullet holes."

She said nothing for several seconds, then, "He saved our lives."

"Temporarily."

A crack of thunder in the distance brought them to attention, and Sam hoped that if lightning struck anywhere nearby, it would hit the island, not the water.

As the rain pelted down, dusk turned into dark. They clung to what was left of the Zodiac, the wind tossing them about. And just as it occurred to him that the tiger sharks they'd seen earlier were nocturnal hunters, Remi said, "I've been thinking . . ."

He looked over at his wife, grateful she was alert and calm. "About what?"

"That vacation you promised me."

"Oh?"

"We should hold off for a bit. Don't you think?"

It was moments like this that his love for Remi magnified.

Here they were, clinging to a sinking raft, and she found the absurdity in all of it. "Good idea. Let's say . . . day after tomorrow."

"*Not* tomorrow?"

"We should at least wait until we get back to the mainland. Figure out where we're going next."

She smiled at him, and he grasped her hand a moment, thinking about how they'd ended up in this predicament. There was only one way their whereabouts could have been revealed. Bree.

Now was not the time to bring up the obvious betrayal by his wife's friend. They needed to concentrate on surviving. But she must have read his mind because her next words were, "I'm sorry."

"Never, Remi. We're in this together, you and I. Always."

He wasn't sure, it was too dark to tell, but her smile this time looked pained. When she gave her heart, she gave all of it. It broke his to see her hurt, but there was nothing he could do or say to change their circumstances.

Except survive.

For the next several hours, that's what they concentrated on. The Zodiac was losing what was left of its buoyancy, and he feared they were being pulled out to sea, far from the island and where anyone might look for them.

They both were exhausted and hungry. The strangest thought came to Sam as he closed his eyes to rest a moment, the crazy idea of seeing a desert mirage on the water. A light nearing them as though they were drifting closer to shore. He blinked, then realized there really was a light and it *was* getting closer.

Eighteen

R emi . . ."

"I see it."

A boat heading toward Snake Island.

If it continued in that direction, it would miss them. They'd drifted too far.

Sam and Remi called out, waved their arms, but their voices were lost in the wind.

They watched for several minutes when suddenly the vessel turned away from the island, a beam of light sweeping the choppy waters as it moved toward them.

They shouted and waved again until their voices were hoarse. After what seemed to take forever, the most beautiful, ancient, rusty, hulking shrimper Sam had ever seen chugged toward them, its spotlight bouncing over the waves, then blinding them.

Sam and Remi waved as the boat pulled alongside and someone threw over a couple of life preservers on a rope. Sam reached out, caught the first one, slipped it over Remi, making sure she was safely assisted on board, before he grasped the offered hand.

António, their angel in disguise.

"Thank you," Sam said.

The young man smiled. "Not me. My uncle." He nodded toward the helm. "Come inside. Out of the rain."

He drew them into the cabin where his uncle, a grizzled man with salt-and-pepper hair, stood at the helm. He said something in Portuguese to another man, slightly younger, who took his place as he walked back toward Sam and Remi.

"This," António said, "is my uncle, Henrique Salazar."

Sam shook hands with the man. "We can't thank you enough."

Henrique reached over and gave António a playful push, saying something in Portuguese.

António grinned as he gave Remi and Sam blankets. "My uncle, he says that if he did not come out here, I would lose my first big fare. And then he would have to support me. His son already eats too much!"

Remi was about to hug António until she realized she was still dripping wet. "We owe you our lives."

"How'd you know to come looking for us?" Sam asked. "And so close to the island? We weren't due back until tomorrow."

"The men I saw leave on the *Golfinho* with you this morning, I do not know them. I do not see Captain Delgado. So I tell my uncle, who tells me that the captain would never have taken you out with a storm coming in. He suspects—is that how you say it?—something is wrong. As for finding you out here, he fishes these waters. The current, he tells me, the word is *shifts*? When we reach Snake Island, he knows this. And here we are."

They reached port early the next morning, both Sam and Remi sleeping soundly in their bunks on the ship. They waited for the police at Henrique's home, a two-bedroom bungalow overlooking the Atlantic. What remained of their gear and their personal items were found by the police on board the abandoned *Golfinho* and returned to them later that afternoon. Even though it was quite late in the evening when they were finished, António insisted on driving them back to the hotel in São Paolo.

"You and your uncle saved our lives," Sam said. "It's something we won't ever be able to repay. But we know where your uncle lives, and we'll be sending something to the both of you for your kindness."

They'd discussed what to do the night before. A scholarship would be set up for António to cover his university costs as well as his medical school. And his uncle would have a new boat, along with tuition for his cousin.

Remi hugged him. "You'll be hearing from us. We won't forget you, António."

Sam and Remi sat at the table in their hotel room in companionable silence. He knew they needed to discuss what had happened—especially the possibility of a leak in their camp—but for the moment Sam was content to ignore the subject.

Remi glanced up, saw him looking at her, and gave him a smile tinged with grief. "It's Bree, isn't it?" she said.

"I can't imagine how else anyone knew where we were. Unless Avery's men suddenly came to the same conclusion as we did, coincidentally knew *which* boat we'd hired, kidnapped the crew, let us find the shipwreck for them, then tried to kill us."

"I still have a hard time believing she'd do this. I trusted her. I—" She took a deep breath and let it out in a sigh of frustration. "I suppose we should check in with Selma and plan our next course of action."

Sam looked at his watch. Selma was probably up and about by now. "Definitely."

"What should we tell her?"

He took out his phone and opened the text messaging. "To call when she has the utmost privacy. She's smart. She's going to know what this is about."

Remi leaned her head back against her seat, closing her eyes. "Oh, Sam . . ."

"We'll get to the bottom of it."

"I suppose we'll have to go to the police."

"Not without conclusive proof." He sent the text.

Selma called about five minutes later.

"We have you on speakerphone," Sam told her. "Remi's here with me."

"Good morning," Selma said. "I assume you're calling about what happened yesterday."

"You're alone?"

"Secured in my office. Bree and Lazlo are having breakfast upstairs as we speak."

"Good," Sam said. "Then you're aware of our concerns."

"Very much so. I'm mystified, Mr. Fargo. I haven't seen her talking to anyone. And she seems genuinely concerned."

Sam felt Remi's gaze on him. There was no other way their whereabouts could have been known unless Selma or Lazlo had let the information out—something both he and Remi knew was not a possibility. And unless someone had bugged their newly renovated, high-security, near-impregnable, hack-proof house, it had to be Bree. "One possible way," he said, "some *dis*information that will prove where the leak is coming from." He dared a glance at Remi to see how she was taking this.

Remi kept her gaze on Sam's phone, placed in the middle of the table. "I think it's the best way."

"Unless you have a better idea," Sam told Selma.

"Let me get back to you on that. Once Lazlo has a chance to thoroughly study the photos of the artifacts you recovered from the shipwreck, he and I can come up with something plausible. I'll give you a call as soon as I know anything."

"We'll wait to hear from you."

After a long day of fact-checking on their own—finding little that helped—Sam and Remi broke for an early dinner at Esquina Mocoto, known for its northeastern Brazilian food. Instead of a main meal, they split several tapas—their favorite, the *dadinhos de tapioca*, fried cheese squares—and the *torresmo*, crackling bacon, along with roasted vegetables, and the recommended pairing of artisan beers instead of wine.

They were walking out of the restaurant when Selma called back.

"We have an update on the items you found at the shipwreck," she said. "Lazlo's here with me."

After she put Lazlo on the phone, Sam said, "I'll call back as soon as we return to the hotel. We're not in the greatest of locations to talk."

"Just as well," Lazlo said. "This is, I believe, what you Americans call a good news, bad news sort of thing."

Nineteen

Charles Avery was just stepping out the door of his Washington, D.C., office when his secretary informed him that he had a call. "Can it wait? I have a dinner meeting scheduled."

The other half of said meeting was currently sitting on the couch in the lobby just outside. A stunning twenty-something-year-old brunette named Suzette, who glanced up just then, saw him, and gave a flirty wave.

"It's Mr. Fisk," his secretary said.

He glanced at Suzette, tempted to blow off Fisk's call—except he wanted to hear that the Fargos were now lying on the bottom of the ocean floor as fish food. "Send it to my phone," he said, then strode into his office. He sat at his desk, then picked up. "I'm on my way to dinner. Is this important?"

"I've just met with the crew in São Paolo."

"And?"

It seemed a heartbeat before he answered. "Something that might lead us to the cipher wheel."

A feeling of elation swept through him. At long last, he thought. He glanced at the *Pyrates and Privateers* book he kept on his desk. For centuries, his family had been searching to recover what had been stolen from them. So close . . .

"Where is it?"

"Brazil. Near São Paolo. I'm headed to the airport as we speak."

Charles was tempted to fly out himself—and he might have if he thought it didn't show weakness on his part or just how important the wheel was. Fisk knew that it was a family heirloom he wanted to recover. What he didn't know was what it led to. That was a secret he intended to guard until the right time. "The Fargos? What of them?"

"It appears they either drowned in a storm or went ashore and were bitten by an island snake. Rest assured, the Fargos have been dealt with."

Finally. He leaned back in his seat, relaxing for the first time all week. He'd gone to great pains to hire out every charter boat once he learned the Fargos were en route to the Port of Santos. Did it really matter now that they were that much closer to finding the cipher wheel? Unless, of course— "How much of this can be traced back to me?"

"Not a thing. The crew has been dealt with. There are no paper trails. Every charter hired was through a shell account. Anyone looking into the Fargos' deaths won't find a thing. As of now, there is absolutely *nothing* that points to you."

"Good," Charles said. "Make sure it stays that way."

"I will."

He hung up, then sat there for several seconds, staring at the book, telling himself that soon all this money and trouble would pay off in a big way. So close, he thought, as his office door opened.

He looked up, surprised to see his wife, Alexandra, walk in.

Still beautiful, even at fifty, her blond hair cut in a short bob, she flipped the door closed, tossed her purse on the couch, then sat. "Who's the bimbo in the lobby?"

"A client."

"Is that what we're calling them nowadays? Clients? Exactly who is paying for whose service here?"

"What do you want, Alexandra?"

"There seems to be a chunk of money missing out of my household account. I'm wondering what it is I paid for."

"Nothing you need worry about."

"Does this have something to do with that map you've been chasing after? Because if it does, the money should be coming out of *your* account, not mine. Wouldn't you agree?"

She got up from the couch and walked over to the liquor cabinet, examining the labels on the bottles, then reached past them for the brandy she kept for herself. She poured a finger of amber liquid into a crystal glass, swirled it and sipped, then walked over to the desk, running her hand along the spine of *Pyrates and Privateers*. "For a man who's busy hiding assets due to our impending divorce, I think you'd be more worried about what you're spending money on."

Charles pushed his chair back, rose, then walked over to the liquor cabinet. He refused to let his wife bait him. The money from her account had been used for something entirely different. He needed access to ready cash for some other projects because Fisk was using the other accounts for this hunt. "I have no idea what you're talking about."

"Don't play dumb, Charles. You think I haven't known about this obsession of yours ever since the beginning? One, I've hired a forensic accountant. So any money you *thought* you could hide will be found in short order. I don't intend to get fleeced in this divorce. Two, if this treasure really does exist and you find it using *our* money, that makes half of everything mine. Or did you forget we were married in California? Fifty-fifty, darling. Right down the middle."

She held up her glass in a mock toast.

He poured his own and drank it down, then poured a second shot, before turning toward his wife. "The map would be an inheritance, something you're not entitled to."

"Inheritance?" She walked around the desk and opened the book, turning the pages. "If memory serves me correctly, this map or code or whatever it is you're so keen on recovering was stolen centuries ago by your ancestors from the rightful owners. That is what you told me, isn't it? Back when we still talked?" She looked up from the book, her blue eyes filled with venom. "Pirates, weren't they? Your relatives? Apparently the apple hasn't fallen far from the tree."

He walked over, closed the book, and pulled it away from her. "It was *stolen* from my family."

"Stolen or recovered? After all, wasn't it your family who stole it to begin with? Or did I miss something in the retelling?"

"Is there some reason you're here? Or is it just to torment me?"

"I see my skills have improved somewhat. I used to only annoy you." She finished her glass, then left it on the desk and walked over to the couch and picked up her purse. "Just wondering about the missing money. And when it's going to be replaced. I have expenses and I'd rather not drag this through court to get them paid."

"Fine. I'll have a deposit made in the morning."

"I appreciate it." She opened the door and peered out. "Looks like your, uh, client, left. Hope it wasn't something I said to her on the way in."

Charles resisted the urge to throw his glass at the door as she walked out. He wouldn't give her the satisfaction. Besides, she wasn't worth the waste of good scotch.

Everything she had was because of him. Once, he had loved her. But now? She was just another woman climbing the social ladder. Everything was about impressing someone else—even that charity she'd recently started.

Like that Fargo woman. It didn't matter he'd never met her. He knew she was just like his wife. Shallow, petty, and all about the money.

The thought angered him. If anything, it furthered his resolve to make sure *he* found the treasure. It belonged to him. Not his wife. Or anyone else. To him.

And he'd kill anyone who got in his way recovering it.

Twenty

S tart with the good news," Sam told Lazlo as he took a seat next to Remi.

"Your underwater photographs were top-notch," Lazlo said. "We were able to enhance the features—well, actually, Pete and Wendy get the credit for that," he said, referring to Selma's research assistants, Pete Jeffcoat and Wendy Corden. "Photo-shop or some such. Regardless, the artifacts you recovered allowed us to narrow down the countries of origin."

"That's great news."

"Yes. Except that it's *countries*, as in plural."

Remi sighed. "Always something, isn't it?"

"Quite," Lazlo replied. "But there is a bright side. The lead seal belonged to an English textile company that was only in business between the years of 1691 through 1696. The yellow brick you found in the ballast is Dutch."

"Then what's the bad news?" Remi asked.

"Selma and I are still trying to come up with a viable plan to pinpoint our information leak."

"Actually," Sam said, "I think I've come up with something that might work. We pretend we searched the wrong shipwreck and we *now* know the correct location—then we wait for the results." He gave a brief rundown of the idea.

Lazlo said, "You think this will work?"

"If Bree *is* leaking information, then I can't see how it'll fail. The men who stole the *Golfinho* want the cipher wheel, not some artifacts that may or may not lead to the ship's identity. What better way to lure them than to let them think *we* know where the cipher wheel is. Or, rather, that we're about to acquire it. Unless anyone has any objections, I think we should contact Ruben Hayward and arrange for assistance."

"Very good," Lazlo said. "We'll get started on it."

Sam disconnected the call, then eyed Remi. "You're okay with this?"

How could she not be? These men were murderers and they needed to be stopped. Besides, just hearing Hayward's name brought her some peace. Hayward, a case officer in the CIA's Directorate of Operations, trained with Sam in covert operations while Sam had worked for DARPA. Fast friends ever since, there was no way Hayward would let Sam get involved in anything he couldn't handle—even if that meant bringing in outside assistance on occasions.

She nodded. "It's the only way to know for sure."

"Then all we can do is wait."

They didn't have to wait for long. By the next morning, Selma called to report that they'd told Bree about searching the wrong shipwreck and the impending dive at the actual site, now that they'd found it. They figured they'd need to give it at least a day for Avery to ready his men, assuming he'd find a way to strike at the site or the dock. And to make sure the proper information was dispatched, Selma and Lazlo included Bree in their plans on setting up the dive: the boat chartered, when and where they'd leave, as well as the location—also off Snake Island but slightly north of the original dive site. "About security," Selma said. "Mr. Hayward made all the arrangements with a firm called Archer Worldwide Security. He said that you'd know who that was and to expect a call."

"Nicholas Archer," Sam replied. "He trained with us at DARPA."

"Very good. It looks like everything's in order. Good luck."

"Likewise," Sam said. "Let us know if anything comes up on your end with Bree."

With everything in place, Remi thought she might have been able to relax. But that night, after she and Sam went to bed, she tossed and turned, trying to reconcile the woman and friend she thought she knew. This sort of betrayal seemed so out of character, which made her wonder if someone had something on Bree— was perhaps forcing her hand somehow.

That had to be it, she decided, and the thought calmed her enough that she was finally able to sleep.

The next morning, with someone from Archer Security posing as their driver, they left for their dive.

Remi had met Nicholas Archer in the past. And even though she knew of his background with Sam and Rube at DARPA, she had only the vaguest of ideas of what any of them had actually done there. They'd always been very hush-hush over the matter. She'd gathered it had to do with Sam inventing something for the government—something that required travel to countries where they needed expertise in self-defense and weapons. Of course, one benefit of all Sam's training was that it had come in handy after his retirement. Many of their forays searching for treasure had put them in the path of some very dangerous sorts.

But where Sam had left DARPA for the private sector, Archer had remained in government service for a number of years, moving from DARPA to the FBI, before finally leaving to start his own international private security firm.

What made Archer a particularly good source was that he retained all his former government and law enforcement connections, like Rube Hayward, which gave him access to valuable intel should the need arise. More important, he could assemble a team at a moment's notice for international travel, drawing from former special ops types, all highly trained and extremely trustworthy. According to Sam, this group made anything he and Remi did look like the work of the high school junior varsity team.

Remi had a hard time believing *that* about her husband, but nonetheless she was glad to know they were in good hands. As expected, every aspect of this op was choreographed to the last detail, including a team standing by at their La Jolla house ready to move in. If Bree was their leak, they'd have her in custody by day's end.

So why, then, was her heart beating so hard as she, Sam, and Archer set out on the boat toward Snake Island?

Sam moved up beside her as they set off. "Are you okay?"

"I didn't sleep well last night."

"I know. I felt you tossing and turning all night."

"What if we're making a big mistake?"

"We're not," he said as Archer walked up and joined them. "There's only one way anyone could have known we were coming here to begin with. All we can do is hope that she takes the bait the second time and Avery's men show up."

Remi surveyed the boat. On the surface, it appeared to be a simple yacht converted to a research vessel. According to Archer, it was outfitted with a more powerful engine and a crew hiding inside with enough firepower to take down a cruise ship, should it be necessary. Archer had even supplied Sam with a fishing vest that looked innocent enough but had a hidden padded Velcro pocket that neatly holstered Sam's Smith & Wesson.

Sam and Remi wouldn't be diving, either. They had agents who were subbing for them.

Remi smiled at Archer. "I have to admit that your crew looks a bit more trustworthy than our last."

"Each one personally vetted, Mrs. Fargo."

"Remi—please," she insisted. Although she'd only met Archer a couple of times in the past, she liked him. He was similar in height and build to Sam, tall and broad-shouldered. And, like Sam, his appearance was deceptive. Tan, with a shock of blond hair, he looked more like a surfer than some highly trained operative. "I know you've talked to my husband at length about this but I'm still concerned. What if something goes wrong?"

"We've looked at every possible scenario. We have you covered, Mrs.—er—Remi. You'll be safe, and if all goes as planned, we'll make the dive, come up with the fake artifact, and then be able to take these men to local law enforcement."

"I hope so." She looked out to the horizon. Snake Island was a growing speck in the distance. The only things missing were any boats that seemed to be heading the same direction, something she pointed out to him.

He handed her a set of binoculars. "It's possible they'll wait until we return to port tomorrow before they make their move. Just in case. If you see a boat, you might recognize the suspects before we do."

She hung the binoculars around her neck. "I'll keep an eye out."

He left to oversee the rest of the operation, leaving her and Sam alone. She looked over at Sam. "Go," she said.

"I'm perfectly happy standing here with you."

"I know you are. But I also know you miss those days at DARPA and whatever missions you and Archer used to work."

He smiled. "It wouldn't hurt to get an update on what they have planned."

She held up the binoculars. "I'll let you know if I see any suspicious characters sailing about."

"That's what I love about you, Remi. *One* of the reasons I love you," he called out as he followed Archer into the cabin.

But in the time it took to sail out to Snake Island, spend the night, then allow for the two divers posing as Sam and Remi to make the dive the next morning, the few passing boats on the water never came close enough to pose a threat.

After eight hours, Archer called an end to the operation, stating that if anything was going to happen, it would have happened by now. No sooner had they pulled anchor, a trawler rounded the southern point of Snake Island. Everyone tensed, silently taking their places. It chugged past, no one on board paying them the slightest attention beyond a passing glance.

As the trawler continued westward, Remi sensed a feeling of disappointment among the crew.

Archer looked at his watch. "Time to head back. Keep a sharp eye. It's highly likely that they're waiting for us in the port."

But the danger never materialized.

No one was waiting in the port.

No one followed them along the winding mountain road to the airport.

"I don't get it," Sam said later that evening when they were on board their plane, seated at the table. "This should have worked."

Archer, who'd accompanied them to make sure they got off the ground safely, said, "It was a good plan. Maybe some of the intel wasn't as good as we thought."

Sam got up from the table and walked over to the bar. "Something to drink?"

"No thanks," Archer said. "I have to get back to my crew for debriefing."

"Remi?" Sam asked, lifting the bottle of Glenfiddich.

"Actually, a glass of port right now would suit me."

He set down the Glenfiddich and opened the temperature-controlled wine cabinet beneath, pulling out the port. "So," he said to Archer after he'd opened the fifty-year-old wine and poured it, "any ideas on what went wrong? Is it possible they knew it was a trap?"

"Anything's possible. From what I can see, there were no signs on the docks that anyone had been watching before or after your arrival. I'd call it a complete no-show."

Sam handed Remi a glass. "We should call Selma. She'll be wondering how it went."

Remi sipped the port, thinking that this operation they'd so meticulously set up should have worked. Had Bree somehow found out and warned Avery and his men? "Call."

Sam dug his cell phone from his pocket, called their house, and placed it on speaker function. "How goes it, Selma?"

"Mr. Fargo," she replied. "I take it the operation failed."

It wasn't a question, and Remi looked at Sam, who in turn looked at Archer. "Why would you say that?" Sam asked.

"Because—well, I'm afraid I have bad news."

Twenty-one

At Sam's request, Selma called back using Skype. He wanted to see her and the others to judge for himself just how bad this news was. Archer seconded this idea and stood off to one side, out of view of the lens, so that he could observe without being seen. A moment later, Remi's tablet lit up. But instead of Selma, they saw Bree standing in front of the camera, her gaze moving downward, undoubtedly sighting Sam and Remi on the screen. A look of relief seemed to cross her features and she reached for the desktop, leaning forward slightly as she said, "Thank goodness. I was worried."

"Worried?" Sam said, his tone cautious. How could he not be after hearing that Selma already knew about their failed operation? He eyed Selma and Lazlo, both standing behind Bree, their expressions neutral. Turning his attention back to Bree, he asked, "About what?"

"That something happened to you."

"Bree," Remi said. "What would make you think something happened?"

"Because of what occurred on your first dive. I think it was because of me."

That wasn't the response Sam had been expecting. Denial, yes. But this? "Please explain."

"I—I think my cousin may have been passing on information."

Remi shifted next to him. "Larayne?"

"Yes. I didn't realize what was happening, at first. They'd threatened us both. They tied us up. She was a victim just like I was. At least that's what I thought. So when she asked about you, it never occurred to me that I would be putting you in danger by saying anything. I—" She tried to compose herself, brushing the tears from her cheeks. "I'm so sorry. I never would have said anything had I known."

Sam studied her face. She seemed genuine, but he wasn't about to throw out caution and forgive her right away. "What made you think something was going on?" he asked.

"It was after I found out what—what had happened on your first dive. And then Larayne asking me afterward if I'd heard from you. It was . . ." She reached for something offscreen. A tissue apparently. "I—I started to get suspicious. So when Selma and Lazlo told me you were going to try to find this other piece of the cipher wheel, I lied to Larayne. I told her I didn't know where you were or what you were doing. I was worried." Her smile faltered. "If anything had happened to you . . ."

She broke down completely, and Selma picked up the tablet, then moved across the room. In the background they saw Lazlo taking Bree into his arms as she sobbed against his shoulder.

"There you have it," Selma said.

Sam turned toward Remi. "Thoughts?"

"I believe her."

"Selma?" he asked.

"I suppose it's possible that she's the best actress in the world. But like Mrs. Fargo, I believe her. It makes sense. And you weren't there when she came to us. She was near inconsolable. It took this long just to get her calm enough to talk to you."

"Great," Sam said. "The one time we need her to pass on the information, she suddenly grows a conscience—"

"Or," Remi said, giving him a dark look, "as Bree mentioned, she realized the danger she was putting us in."

"Well, at least we know the source of the leak."

"Unfortunately," Selma said, "it doesn't net you Charles Avery or his men."

"All in good time."

Selma lowered her voice. "Assuming she *is* telling the truth, then we have to assume that Avery and his crew are trying to discover the identity of that ship. And now they have a good couple of days head start."

"Where does that leave us?"

"Playing catch-up."

"We better get started, then," Sam said. "It'd be nice to find out whatever the map leads to. Treasure, we hope."

"Treasure? Tomb? Who knows? Whatever it is, someone went to a lot of trouble to make sure it was well hidden." Selma paused, looking behind her at Lazlo and Bree before turning back toward the screen. "That should about cover it. In the meantime, I've booked you a hotel in South Beach. Think of it as kick-starting that vacation you've been attempting to go on. That should give us time to do some further research and you and Mrs. Fargo some time to unwind after the last few days."

"Much appreciated, Selma. Keep us informed."

Sam ended the call and closed the cover on the tablet. "Not what I was expecting to hear."

"That," Archer said, "would explain why no one bit on our well-baited lure." He looked over at Remi. "I don't suppose you did any sort of background before you hired her?"

"The usual basic sort of thing," Remi said. "She was only working on fund-raising."

"What," Sam asked Archer, "would you recommend at this point?"

"A full background. Not just on her. I'd also look into her cousin, see what we can dig up there as well. If nothing else, it might verify Miss Marshall's story and you can at least rest easy."

"Remi?" Sam asked.

"I'd like to clear her name, so yes."

Archer nodded. "I'll get started on it, then." He leaned forward and shook Remi's hand. "Good to see you again. Sorry the op was a bust."

"Don't be."

Sam stood. "I'll walk you out."

At Archer's car, Sam said, "Remi has a real soft spot for that girl."

"I gathered. I'll do a thorough job on both women. Don't worry."

The following day as Sam was relaxing by the pool in South

Beach, Archer called with a preliminary report on the two background checks.

Remi was still swimming laps. Sam, stretched out on a chaise longue, watching her while he spoke with Archer on the phone, asked, "Anything we should be concerned about?"

"Your wife's instincts appear to be good. Nothing on Bree Marshall that stands out. Good credit, a solid work history, and, from what we could find on a first pass, she was close to her uncle."

"Exactly how did you determine that last part?"

"Sent a couple of guys from my San Francisco office out to canvass the area around the bookstore. There's a neighbor who took in the cat after the owner's death. Says Bree was a regular visitor up there. Not so with the daughter, Larayne."

"Perhaps because she lived on the East Coast?"

"Possibly, but my agent gathered that he was closer to his niece."

"Which doesn't make the daughter guilty of anything."

"No. But her financial health tells me she'd be more likely to take chances. Her husband's death left her in debt and her farm is in foreclosure."

"Criminal history?" Sam asked as Remi stopped at the far end of the pool, looked over, saw him on the phone, then swam toward him.

"None."

"What would you recommend?"

"That depends on how far you want to go with this and how much you want to spend."

"Don't worry about expenses," he said as Remi hoisted herself out of the pool, pearls of water raining down off her. An auburn-haired Aphrodite, one that he wanted to keep very safe. "Do whatever it takes to get the answers we need."

"Very good. I'll put a couple of agents on her house to start. We'll see what she's up to, and if anyone else pops up. In the meantime, you might want to keep it business as usual—at least when it comes to any conversations between Bree and her cousin. I'd like to keep that channel open without giving away that we're aware of the leak. That way, we're not telegraphing that we're on to how Avery's crew learned where you were."

"We'll take care of it. Anything else?"

"Just that I took the liberty of picking up copies of the police reports in San Francisco. No prints on the fake cops you found tossing your hotel room. But there was a match on a print from the man who robbed the bookstore. Jakob 'Jak' Stanislav."

"I take it he's well known in the system?"

"Definitely a vast criminal history. From a crime family suspected in a number of missing persons cases where the bodies have yet to be found."

"Duly noted."

"If I discover anything further, I'll let you know."

"Thanks." He disconnected.

Remi reached for her towel and wrapped it about her, then sat next to him on the longue. "Who was that?"

"Archer. Bree appears to check out."

"Hmm," she said, her tone very smug.

"He's doing some further digging into Larayne. Seems she's having financial issues and is literally about to lose the farm."

"But to set up her father?"

"People have done worse for less. The good news is that until Archer's done with his investigating and Selma's done with her research, we have *nothing* better to do than make headway on that vacation I promised you."

"A lovely thought, Fargo, but we did promise to visit your mother this afternoon."

His mother, Eunice, still going strong in her seventies, lived in Key West, where she ran a charter boat for snorkelers and deep-sea fishing. "Surely she'd understand."

Remi arched a fine brow at him. "And *what* would you be telling her as the reason we had to cancel?"

Before he could think of something suitable, his phone rang for a second time that morning. It was Selma, and Sam placed it on speaker. "Sorry to interrupt your vacation, Mr. Fargo, but Lazlo thinks he knows how to find that cipher wheel."

Twenty-two

"Tell us what you have," Sam said, then sat back as Selma talked about the history of the ship that sank near Snake Island.

"It was a part of a fleet that set sail from Jamaica. We were able to find some of the records of the other ships on the Internet but hit a dead end. We think you'll be able to find what you're looking for in Jamaica."

"Jamaica?" Remi said. "I love Jamaica this time of year."

"Unfortunately," Selma replied, "you're headed to Kingston, not the beaches. Definitely some areas you want to avoid."

"Kingston it is," Sam said. "So what is it we're looking for, Selma?"

"Records that trace the ownership of the fleet. Where it originated prior to the stop in Jamaica. That should give us a fair idea about where to start looking for that second wheel—or, rather, the original one. Just be careful. If we found the information this easily, chances are that Avery's men may very well be there chasing after the same lead."

The ever-efficient Selma made sure everything was ready the moment their plane touched down at Norman Manley International. A rental car employee greeted them at the office after they cleared customs. "Welcome to Jamaica, Mr. and Mrs. Fargo," he said with a lilting accent. He gave them a broad smile, his teeth gleaming white against dark skin, as he held out a map, the rental papers, and car keys.

Sam eyed the map. "The car has GPS?"

"Of course. A very nice one, I assure you. The map makes a good fan on a hot day."

"Thank you," Sam replied, signing the paperwork.

The employee walked them out to show them the car, a blue BMW 528i sedan. Once the inspection was done, he asked, "Will there be anything else you will be needing this fine afternoon?"

"Recommendations on a good restaurant," Sam replied. "We're headed to Kingston."

"Good as in expensive. Or good as in good?"

"The latter."

"I know just the place." He took out a pen, wrote down the name of a restaurant along with the address. "A lot of dangerous areas in Kingston. This area is not where I would normally send tourists, but not because it is dangerous. The people are very nice. Not like the bad parts. When you get there, you ask for Melia and tell her that Kemar sent you. It will be the best meal you have in Jamaica. I promise."

"Thanks," Sam said, tucking the address in his pocket.

"I forgot to ask. Were you meeting friends here?"

"No," Sam said, thinking the question odd. "Why?"

"Two men came by and asked if you had picked up your car."

"And what did you tell them?" Sam asked.

"The same as I tell all our other customers. We do not release that information."

"Any chance you know what they were driving?"

"Unfortunately, no. They came inside the building, and I was with another customer."

"Thanks," Sam said, giving Kemar a generous tip, before getting into the car.

"Great," Remi said, buckling her seat belt. "We've only just arrived and we're already being stalked?"

"Only, this time, they'll receive a hot reception." He patted the Smith & Wesson in the hidden Velcro holster of his fishing vest. "One way to look at it is, we're on the right track."

"Unfortunately, it also means so are they."

"At least we're forewarned," he said.

Due to the island's British roots, the driver sat on the right, and, as always, it took Sam a few minutes to settle in to driving on the so-called wrong side of the road, especially when it came to the first few turns. As they left the airport, he kept watch in the rearview mirror. After a couple of miles a white SUV caught his eye. Everyone leaving the airport by the same route meant they were bound to see the same cars for a while. The SUV started to pass the vehicle behind Sam, then suddenly braked and darted back into its original position. The opposing lane ahead

of Sam was wide open, with a large gap in traffic that would easily have allowed safe passing.

Whether a tourist deciding against making a lane change or
Avery's men trying to verify it was Sam and Remi in the car, he
didn't know. They were too far back for him to see who was
inside. "We may have company."

"Already?" Remi glanced out her window into the side mirror. "Which car?"

"White SUV. They were trying to pass the car behind us, then
changed their mind."

"Trying to see if we were here?"

"Possibly."

"Now what?"

"The scenic route to the restaurant to see if we're being followed."

As soon as they reached town, Sam made a quick left and was
glad to see the SUV continue straight. "Catch who was behind
the wheel?" he asked.

"Tinted windows."

He made another left, then pulled to the curb, parking about
a half block down in front of a large truck that would, he
hoped, block their view. He watched the intersection from his
side mirror. When the SUV didn't appear within what Sam
thought was a reasonable amount of time, he pulled out, keeping to side streets as they drove to the restaurant. As Kemar had
warned, they were in a part of town where tourists seemed to
be absent. They drove past shanties and corrugated-metal
shacks on streets crowded with pedestrians who darted into the

roads certain that any vehicles would stop in time. Eventually the smaller buildings were replaced by larger structures. When they reached the right neighborhood, he drove past the restaurant, a bright purple building, tucked in between other businesses and restaurants, each painted a different color of the rainbow, some clashing garishly with whatever was built next to it. Distinctly Jamaica.

"Did we lose them?" Remi asked.

"Looks like it. Just in case, we'll park away from the restaurant. No sense making it easy for them."

He drove around the corner, reasoning that there were a dozen or more restaurants in the area and someone would have to pop into a lot of doors to locate them. That at least would give them time to eat in peace.

The walk to the restaurant took about three minutes. If anything, it seemed even hotter now than it had when they left the rental lot. The high humidity level didn't help.

Remi wiped a sheen of perspiration from her forehead, then ran her fingers through her hair, pulling it back into a ponytail, the sunlight bringing out the vibrant auburn color. "What are the chances this place is air-conditioned?"

"In this part of town? I'll be happy with a good working ceiling fan." But when they entered the purple, stuccoed building, the lone ceiling fan didn't seem to move much air.

A woman greeted them as they entered. Tall, with short dark curls cropped close to her head, she picked up two menus from the counter.

As suggested, Sam asked for Melia.

"I am Melia."

When he mentioned Kemar's name, it brought a smile to her face.

"Kemar?" she said in the same lilting accent. "A good man to send you here. Please, come this way. Our special guests sit on the patio. Much cooler, with the breeze that comes in from the ocean."

Melia led them through the stifling dining room to a side door, then up a creaking, narrow staircase that led to a rooftop patio overlooking the street below. As promised, a cooling breeze swept in from the south.

She set out the two menus, both on the same side of the table facing out toward the rooftops of the neighboring buildings. "Much cooler beneath the umbrella."

"Lovely," Remi said, taking a seat.

Sam walked over to the edge of the second-story rooftop, eyeing the cars driving below. No sign of any white SUV or any suspicious-looking pedestrians milling about. Satisfied that they hadn't been followed, he returned to the table, grateful that they were far enough back where they wouldn't be seen by anyone walking on the street below.

Of course, that wouldn't stop Avery's men from doing a door-to-door search, should they happen to notice their rental car parked around the corner. Just in case, he took out a hundred-dollar bill. "Melia. Is it possible to warn us if anyone should come in and ask if we're here?"

She pushed his hand away. "That is far too much for such a small favor. Keep your money, and I will be glad to tell you should anyone come looking. Now, what is it you'd like to eat?"

Sam picked up the menu. "What do you recommend?"

Melia smiled. "On the menu or off? You tell me what it is you like and I will see it done."

Exactly the sort of restaurant they preferred. In short order, they were dining on jerk chicken—smooth, moist, and served with a fiery Scotch bonnet pepper marinade.

Melia returned before they finished, her dark brows etched with worry. "You said to warn you should someone come asking?"

"Yes," Sam said, his gaze moving to the doorway. "What happened?"

"It is as you said. A white man walked in, asking if we have seen a man who would be with a beautiful woman with red hair." She smiled apologetically. "We told them no. You can see for yourself." She motioned for Sam to approach the balustrade, pointing down to the street. "There on the corner?"

Sam looked out, saw a short, broad-shouldered man, his back to them, talking on a cell phone. Unlike everyone else in the vicinity, who seemed to be wearing shorts or khakis and short-sleeved shirts, this person wore dark slacks and a leather coat. Jak. The same thing he'd been wearing when he robbed Pickering's bookstore. A second man stepped out of a restaurant across the street, looked around, then made eye contact with Jak.

Sam stepped back out of view. "Any chance you have another way out of here?"

"The fire escape," she said, pointing to the opposite side of the roof. "A ladder leading down into the alley."

"Works for me," Sam said. "Remi?"

"I'm in."

He left several hundred dollars on the table, and Melia started to protest.

"Worth every penny," Sam said. "Trust me."

He walked toward the ladder, Remi right behind him. The alley looked clear. Even better, there were two large dumpsters, one on either side of the ladder, and he climbed over the edge, then waited for Remi. Once she was safely on the ladder, they started down. "Sorry about lunch," he said as they descended.

"You realize that chicken was to die for?"

"But not worth dying for."

"We'll simply have to go back."

"Let's lose our tail before we start making plans."

The ladder stopped about four feet off the ground. An easy jump for him. At the bottom, he waited for Remi—very much enjoying the view as she climbed down.

She noticed. "We're running for our lives and you're watching me?"

He grinned as he took her by the waist, helping her to drop the last few feet. "At least I'll die happy."

They stepped from the relative cover of the dumpsters. Remi looked both directions. "Which way?"

Good question. If Avery's men just started their search from where they saw the rental car parked, they'd be heading to their left. "Right."

At the end of the alley, he poked his head around the corner, then ducked back just as the white SUV turned onto that street. They'd be caught in seconds. On the other side of the alley, he saw several doors, the second one closed only with a screen, undoubtedly to let the breeze flow through the shop. "This way," Sam said, running across the alley, hoping the screen door wasn't latched.

Twenty-three

Remi followed Sam into the building, the screen door clattering shut behind them. It took a moment for her eyes to adjust to the dim interior as they rushed down a hallway, its dingy white walls covered with a mix of graffiti and scrawled names and cities from past visitors. The beat of reggae music thrummed louder as they emerged into a barroom. Judging from the look of the rough clientele—Jamaica's equivalent of a biker bar, Remi presumed—it was not the sort of establishment she and Sam tended to frequent. At least eight men and two women eyed them over the tops of their beer bottles. Most wore leather vests over sleeveless black T-shirts, their burly arms covered with tattoos, though some were hard to see against their dark skin. Remi smiled, hoping they weren't being sized up as an easy mark.

Sam dug some money from his pocket, slapped it on the bar.

"Drinks for the house, Mr . . . ?" He gave a questioning look toward the bartender.

"Jay-Jay to my friends," he replied in a melodious accented voice. "That amount of money, my good man, makes you one of them."

Sam introduced himself, then extended his hand. The bartender shook it. "My wife will be safe here? I won't be gone long."

"Very safe. You have my word."

Sam turned to Remi. "I'm going to see if I can get to our car. Back in a flash." He walked to the front door, peered out, then left.

Remi glanced at the bartender, then his customers, who regarded her as they drank, and she told herself that Sam was very good at reading people—he wouldn't leave her anywhere he didn't think was safe.

Even so, she found it hard to sit and wait.

Alone.

Jay-Jay smiled at her. "Who are you running from, pretty lady?"

She swiveled around on the stool and faced him. His long dreadlocks were pulled back in a ponytail, and he wore a black T-shirt with a Harley-Davidson logo on the front. His dark eyes held no malice, and she realized this was probably what Sam had noticed. "A couple of men who apparently think we're better off dead."

"Those would be the white men who came in here earlier asking if we had seen two Americans—one a woman with red hair?"

That feeling of vulnerability increased, and Remi suddenly

wished that women's head scarves were back in fashion. "They were here?"

"About twenty minutes ago, but not to worry. As I promised your husband, you will be safe here, pretty lady. What will you have to drink?"

"Water, please," she said. Serious alcohol would have to wait.

He poured her a glass, slid it toward her, then took a rag and started wiping down the bar.

Remi sipped her drink. But as the seconds ticked past into minutes, her gaze kept returning to the door, hoping Sam would appear. At one point, she walked over, cracked open the door, noticed a number of motorcycles parked out front but no sign of Sam.

The bartender joined her. "Perhaps you should let me have a look instead. No one will notice a man like me. But you're a different story." He stepped out to the sidewalk, wiping his hands on his towel as if merely taking a break from bartending. When he returned inside, he guided her back toward her stool. "Your husband will be here soon. He is good at hiding, but I am better at finding."

Less than a minute later, Sam rushed in. He crossed the room toward Remi, somewhat out of breath. "Big problem."

Jay-Jay poured Sam a glass of water. "What problem, my friend?"

He took a drink, nodding toward the door. "Avery's men . . . Saw their car parking just up the street . . . One walked into the business at the far end."

Jay-Jay nodded at the bikers sitting at the tables closest to the bar. They rose from their seats, two moving to the front door, two heading down the hall to the back. "The second time they have been on this street," he said. "That would worry me."

Remi grabbed her purse from the counter beside her. "Should we go out the back?"

Sam shook his head. "No way to get to our car without being seen." He looked around the room, eyeing the men and women who remained. "Then again, there actually may be a way . . ." He leaned toward the bartender, disclosing his idea in a voice too low for Remi to hear over the music.

Twenty-four

Jay-Jay nodded in agreement as Sam went over the details, asking a few questions in return. At the conclusion, the man gave a deep laugh, saying, "A good plan, my friend. Hide in plain sight. *If* we can find some volunteers." His gaze landed on a couple sitting near the jukebox. "Antwan, bring your lady here."

The pair walked up to the bar, and Jay-Jay asked, "How would you like to earn free drinks for a week?"

"For what?" Antwan asked.

Sam said, "Lend us your gear for a few minutes."

An agreement was struck. Antwan and his girlfriend turned over their leather vests and motorcycle helmets, and Jay-Jay slid a set of keys across the counter toward Sam. "You'll take very good care of my bike."

"Like it was my own."

"You're sure you know how to ride?"

Sam picked up the keys. "Anything happens to it, there'll be a new one waiting before the day is through."

"The old one is fine. It's the black Harley with the license frame advertising my bar."

Sam glanced at Remi's expensive-looking purse—talk about a beacon announcing their presence. Jay-Jay, however, solved the problem by providing a backpack to hide it in. And just in time, as one of the bikers standing watch at the front door announced that the two men had just emerged from the shop across the street and were eyeing the bar.

Jay-Jay nodded. "Who wants to ride?"

Everyone in the room stood, ready to roll.

"You see?" Jay-Jay told Sam. "My friends are your friends."

"One problem," Sam replied. "These men are armed."

"No worries," Jay-Jay said. "Billy here will make sure you're well protected."

A towering biker stepped forward and lifted both sides of his vest. On the left, Sam saw a handgun in a shoulder holster, and, on the right, a trench knife with a handle that doubled as metal knuckles. Suspecting that Billy wasn't the only armed man in the room, he was grateful that everyone here had decided he and Remi were the good guys.

Turning back to the bartender, Sam shook hands with him one last time. "We'll make it worth everyone's while."

"Which will be very much appreciated. But not necessary. Be safe, my friend."

Sam and Remi put on the helmets, Remi tucking her hair beneath. Both lowered their visors before stepping outside, surrounded by the other bikers. They mounted their motorcycles,

Remi sitting behind Sam, wrapping her arms around his waist, as he started the Harley, then shifted into gear.

They took off, engines roaring. Sam glanced in the rearview mirror and saw Avery's men crossing the road toward the bar. One of them looked their direction.

Suddenly, both men started running down the street.

So much for that deception. And any advantage they had in getting to their car. They'd have to lose them on the motor-cycles—not part of Sam's plan.

Unless . . .

He stopped his bike alongside the white SUV. Billy circled back around and pulled up alongside him, Sam asking, "Mind if I borrow that trench knife?"

Billy drew it from its sheath, handing it to Sam. As hoped, the two-edged dagger was razor sharp.

Remi's grip around his waist tightened. "They're coming," she said. "Wouldn't the gun be better?"

"Don't worry." He leaned down, punched the sidewall of the right front tire, yanked it out, then repeated the process, widen-ing the hole.

The tire flattened in a whoosh of air.

"That should buy us some time," he shouted as he returned the knife to Billy. They took off again.

Just before they turned the corner, Sam looked back, saw Av-ery's men stopping by the SUV, one of them punching the hood in anger.

He smiled. Finally, something was going their way, and he relaxed, enjoying the short remainder of the ride to the rental car.

"That was close," Remi said, waving to the bikers once they were safely in their own car.

Sam pulled out, angry over the turn of events. "Too close. I don't know what I was thinking, bringing you here."

Remi had just started plugging in their route to the hotel and looked up from her phone. "What do you mean by that?"

"It was foolish to come to lunch when we knew they were out here."

"I was just as much to blame. You certainly didn't see me protesting."

"But I know better."

"You mean, I don't?" Remi sighed. "First of all, we had no reason to think they'd be going door-to-door looking for us. It would have been far more expedient and efficient to stake out our car. That's what we would have done. Second of all, it turned out fine, so quit blaming yourself."

She was right about the door-to-door thing. Which made him wonder just how intelligent Avery's men were—not that it made them any less dangerous. Though this trip was much less eventful, he and Remi kept their gaze glued to the mirrors. No sign of the white SUV or any other car that seemed to be following them. Even so, when they reached the hotel, Sam checked out, drove to a new hotel where they checked in under a different name, then made arrangements to have the rental car returned and a new one sent. No sense giving Avery's men the advantage of knowing where they were and what car they were driving.

Settled in their new hotel room, Sam placed his phone on the glass-topped coffee table, turned on the speaker, then relaxed on the couch.

Selma answered on the first ring. "I was hoping you'd call. I figured you might be at dinner and didn't want to interrupt."

"Room service," Sam said. "We opted for low-key after our attempt to dine out at lunch."

"Oh?"

"Avery's men are already here. They followed us from the car rental lot. I'm assuming that whatever it is, they haven't found it yet."

"What makes you say that?" Selma asked.

"It's the only explanation that fits why they'd waste time coming after us. They've had a full day or more to search before we even got here. If they'd found what they needed, they would have left."

"Maybe," Remi said, taking a seat next to Sam, "Avery's men like to hold a grudge."

"Undoubtedly." Sam leaned back, asking Selma, "What, exactly, are we looking for?"

"Ship manifests and court records. While we've been trying to decipher the code on the map, Pete and Wendy have been searching for information on that ship that went down off Snake Island. As I mentioned before, some of what we deciphered made us suspect it was part of a larger fleet that left from Jamaica. We have it narrowed down even further. I need you to look through the manifests from between 1694 and 1696. If we find out who owned the fleet, we're that much closer to discovering where to find the original cipher wheel. And if we're really lucky, it's right there in Jamaica."

"Where is it we'll find this information?" Sam asked.

"The Jamaica Archives and Records Department in Kingston. I'll send you all the pertinent information."

"Thanks, Selma. Give our best to everyone at home."

He disconnected, then held up his wineglass. "Here's to a productive search come morning."

Remi touched the rim of her glass to his. "At least it's a public building. There's bound to be all sorts of security."

Lightning flashed just outside, lighting up the balcony in stark relief. Within seconds, thunder rumbled overhead, as the center of the storm raged above them.

"A warning or an omen?" Remi asked.

Twenty-five

Charles Avery's attorney, Winton Page, sat across from him, sliding documents over for his review, as the man detailed the figures on each. The hour was late, but Charles had been tied up all day and this was the first opportunity they'd had to meet. He wanted this divorce over and done with. "What's the bottom line?"

"Bottom line," Winton said. "You're better off paying your wife what she wants. It'll be cheaper in the long run."

"I'll be damned if I give her a penny of anything she's asking for. I built this empire from the ground up. All she did was spend the money I made."

"And she bore two of your children."

"Who followed in her footsteps. Spoiled, predatory brats."

"Which is what wills are for. Your wife is the more immediate problem."

Problem was right. If there was some way he could do away

with her and not bring any attention to himself, he would have done it by now. That was certainly an option down the line. For now, her nosing around his banking was the more pressing threat. "What about this forensic accountant she says she hired?"

"It's one of those 'It depends' answers. If your wife somehow gained access to records you weren't aware of, the possibility exists they might discover some of your hidden assets. In other words, it's a gamble."

One he was willing to make. He'd been careful over the years, and while he knew Alexandra was aware he'd been hiding assets, she didn't know the half of it. In fact, she might not have even been aware of any recent activity had it not been for the Fargos' untimely arrival in the middle of his search for the map. Their interference had caused him to make several rash decisions that led to a sudden shortage of liquid assets—hence the need to dig into his wife's accounts.

He glanced at the clock, wondering why it was that Fisk had failed to call with an update on their Jamaica search. The information that was supposed to lead to the cipher wheel. He should have heard something by now, and so as Winton droned on about the legalities of what he was doing, his gaze kept turning to the phone.

Finally, it lit up. He grabbed the receiver, his secretary saying, "Your wife—"

The office door burst open. "—is here," Alexandra said. "I don't know why she bothers with the announcements. As if I need permission to walk into a building in which I'm half owner."

"Half owner, my—"

"Tsk, tsk, dear. You know what the doctor said about your

blood pressure." She opened her purse, pulled out an envelope, then tossed the handbag on the couch. "Winton," she said, walking up to him. "So good to see you diligently on the job. You did get the subpoena for the accounting records?"

"What subpoena?"

"Oh, silly me. This one." She waved the envelope at him, then handed it over. "Of course, this is just a copy. I'm sure the process server will turn over the original. I'm just trying to be a good sport by giving you a heads-up."

He opened it, then slid it across the desk toward Charles, who merely glanced at the document, not wanting to give Alexandra the satisfaction of seeing him lose his temper. "Is this becoming a nightly ritual of yours? Coming to my office to goad me? Or is your social calendar suddenly empty?"

"On the contrary, it's actually fuller than ever, now that news of the divorce is out." She put both hands on the desk and leaned in toward him, her smile icy. "Had I realized how much you hindered my social standing, I might have filed much earlier."

"A shame you didn't."

She looked down at the papers on his desk, and he immediately turned them over so that she couldn't read them. Instead, her gaze landed on the yellow scratch pad covered with notes, phone numbers, and figures from various phone calls he'd taken throughout the day. She reached over, turning it her direction. "Fargo?" she said, reading the name circled and underlined on the pad. "A new business acquisition in North Dakota? Something I should let my lawyer know about?"

He pulled the pad away from her and turned it upside down as well. "You've served your subpoena, now go."

"Oh, I wasn't here to serve that. It's not *legal* if I do it. I just wanted to let you know that my lawyer's asked for the accounts to be frozen. In case you're wondering why your ATM card suddenly stops working." This time, her smile positively dripped acid. She patted the notepad he still held, then turned and walked to the couch to retrieve her purse. "Do take care, Charles. Winton, always so good to see you."

Charles, his teeth clenched, waited until the door shut after her. "Do you *see* what I've had to put up with all these years?"

"She's only trying to goad you on."

"Well, it's working." He got up, poured himself a drink, finally relaxing enough to think about what she said. "Can she do that? Freeze my money?"

"We'll find out come morning when the banks open. But assuming her attorney could convince a judge you've been hiding assets, then yes she can. If I had to guess, this forensic accountant of hers suggested it. Trying to force your hand to see where your money is moving from."

Charles carried his glass and the bottle of whiskey to his desk, then sat. "She wants to start a war? I'm willing to dig in for as long as it takes."

"Or you could pay her what she's asking and end it."

"No." Charles took a swig of his drink. It would be a cold day in hell before he allowed that, he thought.

His phone rang. It was Fisk. Finally.

"I have an update from Jamaica," Fisk said. "You may not like what you hear, but, I assure you, it'll work out."

He clenched his glass in his hand. "Work out? Are you telling me you failed to get the documents?"

"About that . . . Turns out, the Fargos may have survived after all."

Anger surged through him. "What the— How is it those two keep slipping through your fingers?"

"I told you, they aren't your average couple. Sam Fargo has extensive training at DARPA and possibly even the CIA. The wife was a Boston College graduate . . ." Avery heard him shuffling papers as he checked his notes. ". . . with a master's in anthropology and history with a focus on ancient trade routes."

"Which explains her interest in treasure. What it doesn't explain is *how* she escaped."

"Unless you factor in that she's extremely intelligent—and an expert marksman."

"And what? Somebody handed her a gun on board the *Golfinho*? I don't want to hear excuses for your failures. I pay you for confirmed results."

"Mistakes were made. They're being addressed."

"I was under the impression that the crew you hired to take over the *Golfinho* was more than capable of dealing with a couple of spoiled jet-setters who keep sticking their noses where they don't belong."

"As mentioned, they've been dealt with. In the meantime, we have a lead on the Fargos. My men were able to follow them from the car rental to Kingston. Unfortunately, the Fargos managed to evade them. But they won't for long."

"I thought you said that these men were capable of getting the job done."

"They are."

"Then how is it that these two meddlesome socialites have

managed to elude them thus far? To me, that sounds as though your men are anything *but* capable."

"I warned you the Fargos were resourceful."

Charles slammed his glass to the desk, whiskey sloshing over the rim. "You *told* me that you could handle this. That your men could handle this."

"They can. And they will."

"They better. I want those documents and then the Fargos eliminated. Period. If you can't trust them to get the job done, then handle it yourself. I want results, not incompetence."

"Understood. We do have a plan. I'll call you once the details are firmed up."

Charles dropped the phone into the cradle, grabbed his glass, then took a long drink.

"I take it," Winton said, "the news isn't good?"

"How about you concentrate on keeping my wife from getting her hands on my fortune. I'll worry about my extracurricular activities."

"As long as you're aware that any money you're moving toward those activities might be discovered."

"I'm well aware of the risks."

Winton nodded, then stood. "If there's nothing else, I'll see myself out."

He left, and Charles poured himself another drink, his eye moving to the scratch pad. The Fargo name glared up at him. He ripped it from the pad, crumpled it, then tossed it to the ground. At the moment, he wasn't sure what angered him more—the Fargos inserting themselves into his business or his wife trying to steal his fortune.

Death was too good for all of them.

Which made him wonder, did he really want Alexandra dead?

Actually, he did. She might be the mother of his children, but neither of them had anything to do with him. They were definitely their mother's spawn. What he needed to do was make sure his wife was dealt with in the most expedient manner possible. The question was, how? How to make it look like her death had nothing to do with him?

First things first, he thought. Deal with the Fargos. An hour later, Fisk called him back.

"I have good news . . ."

Twenty-six

S am and Remi rose early the next morning and drove to the archives, making sure they were there the moment the doors opened for business. Sam left Remi at the front entrance, deciding he wanted to take a quick look around before following her in.

She entered the building, checked the directory, and found the Records Department, noting a flurry of activity in the halls as employees hurried about, clearly too busy to take notice of her. A woman in bright yellow, wearing a turquoise scarf tied around her dark hair, dropped a thick stack of manila folders on the counter, then started to walk away.

"Excuse me," Remi said. "Do you work in Records?"

The woman looked up. "Yes. Have you not been helped?"

Remi smiled at her. "Not yet."

"My apologies. The unexpected storm damage caught us by

surprise. Alarms going off all night, water getting in. As you can guess, we're all quite busy. But what can I do for you?"

"We were hoping to have a look at some old shipping manifests."

"We?"

"My husband. When he gets here."

She reached below the counter and pulled out a form. "Researchers, are you?"

"Yes."

"If you can fill out the information, I'll get to you as soon as possible."

"Thank you."

By the time Remi filled out the form, Sam had joined her.

"Looks clear out there," he said. "How's it going in here?"

"Slow. Storm damage apparently."

"At least the air conditioner works. All that rainwater from last night is turning the island into a sauna."

When the woman returned, she looked over the paper. "Shipping manifests, you say?"

"Yes," Remi said. "I don't suppose you know if anyone else has been here asking about this particular time period?"

"No. You're the first," she said, then led them to the archives, pointing out the row where they'd need to start their search. "Everything's by year. I'd say it shouldn't be too difficult to locate, but sometimes things get misfiled."

"Thanks," Remi said, hoping that wasn't the case. There were hundreds of volumes, which meant if something was misfiled, it would be difficult to find.

Sam moved to the far end of the row, Remi started at the beginning, and they worked their way toward each other. Eventually they met in the middle, Sam saying, "Come here often?"

"It's a good thing that's not the pickup line you used when we first met at the Lighthouse."

"I thought that *was* the line I'd used."

"Glad I didn't hear or we might not have had a second date." She maneuvered around him. "I'm having no luck."

He returned his attention to the shelves. "What're the chances the one book we need—"

"Exactly what I was thinking."

"I'll go over what you covered. You go over my half."

But the results were the same.

Sam started on the next row, even if the years were way off. Remi looked over the volumes they'd already checked, pulling them from the shelf and looking inside just to make sure the bindings hadn't been mismarked.

"Nothing," Sam said. "Makes you wonder, doesn't it?"

"Definitely." She returned a book to the shelf and pulled out another. Although she'd gone through several centuries, none matched up to the time period in question. About an hour into their search, a thought wormed its way into Remi's head. "Sam . . . Why aren't Avery's minions here, looking?"

"Waiting for us to find the information so they can steal it again."

"What if—"

She stopped when the clerk who had first helped them entered, pushing a cart before her. The woman looked up, surprised to see them. "Still at it?" she asked.

"It's not here," Remi said.

"That's hard to believe. What year?"

"Sixteen ninety-four through sixteen ninety-six."

The woman walked up to the same shelves they'd searched. "I hope the volumes weren't misfiled . . ." After a few moments, she straightened. "Wait. I noticed a stack of books on the research table. I assumed someone was in the midst of a project, so left them alone. Maybe it's there."

She pointed them in that direction. Sure enough, there were several volumes on the table. One was sitting well away from the others.

Sam walked over, examined the cover, then the spine. "This looks like the one."

"Finally." Remi moved to his side, watching as he turned the pages, not daring to voice her concern as to why *this* particular book happened to be singled out. But after a few moments, he found the records in question.

"There was an inquest."

"For what?"

"Claims that the *Mirabel* was stolen in June 1696."

"Good. Then that should tell us who the owner was."

"If we can wade through the testimony." He slid the book her way.

The flowery script was hard to read. "Makes you appreciate modern type."

"Look at this," Sam said, pointing to a paragraph lower on the page. "Testimony from a crew member who claims that he was captured in Madagascar and taken aboard the *Fancy* by Captain Henry Bridgeman, arriving first in Jamaica, before setting sail for New Providence . . . On arriving at Nassau, they claimed to be interlopers pursued by the East India Company and were allowed into port."

"Interlopers?"

"If I remember my history," Sam said, "that would be *unlicensed slavers*. It was a way of getting past the slave monopoly held by the East India Company."

"Bridgeman was a slaver."

"As well as a pirate."

"So he's the owner that we're looking for?"

"No," he said, scanning the page. "Bridgeman turned the *Fancy* over to Governor Trott as part of a bribe for safe harbor. Trott denied all knowledge of the ship and Bridgeman, but this crew member claims that part of its cargo was stolen before Trott could lay claim to it—and the thief fled in the *Mirabel* just before it sank off Snake Island." He paused as he read further. "This is interesting . . ."

"What is?"

"Bridgeman was being pursued by the Royal Navy . . . Commander . . ." He turned the page. "Gone," he said after a moment.

"Commander Gone? Or *gone* as in *not there*?" she asked, leaning in for a closer look. "This *is* the right book, isn't it?"

"Several pages are missing."

He ran his finger down the center. Jagged edges were all that was left where the pages had once been.

Remi looked at Sam, that seed of suspicion growing. "Didn't she say something about alarms going off last night?"

"Undoubtedly it had *nothing* to do with the storm."

"All this time wasted."

"Let's take it up front. See if anyone remembers anything about this book or who might have come to look at it."

When they arrived at the office, the counter clerk looked up from her paperwork. "Something wrong?"

Sam slid the book toward her. "It's the book, all right. Except the pages we need are missing."

"Missing?" She eyed the volume. "I don't understand."

"Someone tore them out."

"Why would anyone do that?" she asked. "They can photocopy them."

"You're sure no one came in and asked for this particular volume?"

"Not in the recent past," she said as her phone started ringing. "A historian came looking over the manifests for inclusion in the museum at the King's Royal Naval Dockyard, but that was years ago. One moment, please." She answered her phone. "Archives . . . Of course." Then to Sam and Remi, "Is there anything else? I have to take this call."

"No. Thanks again."

They left, Sam pushing open the front door. He stopped suddenly, and Remi nearly ran into the back of him.

"Company," he said, nodding toward the parking lot. She looked out, saw the white SUV and, near it, one of the men from the warehouse. He was looking at the screen of his phone as he walked with a noticeable limp toward the driver's door.

Sam pulled Remi to one side of the lobby, out of sight.

"Now what?" she asked.

"Let's see if there's another exit." There was, at the side of the building. Sam opened the door. "Looks clear."

They headed the opposite direction of the parking lot, rounded the corner, and came face-to-face with Jak Stanislav, the man who robbed the bookstore. He stood with his hands in the pockets of his leather coat, a leering smile on his face.

Sam stopped short, positioning himself between Jak and Remi. "Fancy meeting you here."

"Fancy," Jak said. He pulled a gun from his right pocket and pointed it at Sam. "How about we do an about-face and return to the car, where my friends are waiting."

"Or not," Sam said.

"Hands up or I'll kill you right here."

Sam slowly raised his hands, then punched his right hand at Jak's face and his left at the gun, knocking it upward. In a flash, he took the gun, slammed Jak into the building, then shoved the barrel of the gun into Jak's head.

Remi barely had time to react when she felt the sharp barrel of a weapon against her back. She looked behind her. A towering man glared down at her, saying, "Call your husband off."

They'd brought in reinforcements.

"Sam . . ."

Sam turned, saw the man holding a gun on Remi. He lowered the weapon, handing it back to Jak, then put his hands up over his head.

Jak sneered at him. "Thought you might see it my way. And, word to the wise—Ivan's trigger happy."

A moment later, the white SUV pulled up, parking at the curb next to them. Jak nodded toward the vehicle. "Get in."

The odds had risen, but Sam refused to move.

Ivan said, "I have no problem shooting you right here in public. Beginning with your wife." He aimed his weapon at Remi, stepping in close. "Backseat, Fargo. Now."

"All the way over," Jak said, and Sam slid to the far side. He pointed his gun at Remi. "Now you. Middle seat."

She climbed in. Jak climbed in next to her, shoving the gun into her side. "Buckle up."

She pulled her seat belt around her, Sam doing the same, saying, "Worried your insurance rates will go up if anything happens to us?"

The new guy climbed into the front passenger seat and looked back at them. "What insurance?"

"Where are you taking us?" Sam asked.

"A little ride."

Remi slid her hand toward Sam, felt his fingers entwine hers.

The road forked up ahead, and the driver headed left, clearly a less traveled route. Soon the steep road was one switchback turn after another, and the driver slowed to a crawl, navigating the wide SUV up the narrow road.

Jak craned his neck. "Good enough," he said. "Stop here."

The silent driver pulled into a narrow turnout at the side of the road. He got out, opened Sam's door, and motioned with his gun for Sam and Remi to get out.

Remi waited for Sam to exit, then slid over, swinging her feet out. The heat of the jungle enveloped her the moment she stepped her foot on the ground. Lush green foliage dripped with moisture from last night's rain, the humidity too thick to allow it to evaporate. Instead, it all seemed to drip down, running together, forming a rivulet that ran across the road, then on down the hillside.

Jak pointed with his gun. "On the side of the road, both of you."

"Look," Sam said. "If you're going to kill us, at least let me kiss my wife good-bye."

"Hurry up."

Sam stepped in close to Remi, reaching beneath his fishing vest. "Guess that vacation will have to wait."

She tried to laugh.

Sam pivoted. With a quick, two-handed aim, he shot the driver in the middle of his forehead.

Twenty-seven

rack! Crack!

Sam snapped off two more rounds but missed the other killers as he suddenly felt nothing but air beneath his feet.

Unaware, he and Remi had stepped back, causing the muddy ground at the edge of the hill to crumble under their weight. They both lost their balance and toppled over the edge of the steep hill.

Sam crashed into a maze of greens and browns swirling in front of him as he slid at breakneck speed down the hill.

He lost his grip on Remi's arm and she vanished from his sight as he grabbed at tree branches and fern fronds, trying to slow his descent.

Crack! Crack! Crack!

The volley of return gunfire sent birds screeching from their roosts. Sam spotted a fallen tree coming up on his left. He twisted sideways and tensed as he slammed into what felt like a big pile of mush that stopped his momentum. Stunned, and covered with slime from a tree trunk that had rotted from years in the damp forest, he wiped the muck off his face. He moved slowly, feeling for injury. It took a minute before pain began to register, but, fortunately, the decayed tree had softened his impact. Nothing was broken.

"You fool!" Ivan's voice carried down. "You let them get away."

"No way they could survive that fall," Jak replied. "Or this."

Each gunshot sent Sam's heart thundering.

Remi . . .

The firing finally stopped when Jak ran out of shells.

"You see anything?" Ivan asked.

"Nothing. Climb down. Make sure they're dead."

"And what?" Ivan growled. "Break my neck? Better we drive down and check the hill from the lower road."

"What about Lorenzo?" Jak asked. "Just gonna leave him here?"

"Dump him down the hill. Let him rot with the Fargos."

They rolled the body off the road, and Sam heard it crashing through the underbrush. Finally, the SUV's engine started. The vehicle was heading up hill, not down. They'd have to drive until they found a wider turnout for the large SUV before it could change directions.

"Remi?" he called softly.

"Down here."

It sounded like she was about fifteen feet below him. He let out a sigh of relief, only then realizing he'd been holding his breath until that moment. "You're okay?"

"Bruised but still in one piece."

"They're looking for a place to turn around."

"I can see the road below us. It's pretty close."

"I'll come to you. Let's see if we can't get across the road before they get here. They'll be searching up, not down."

He moved away from the thick growth of rotted tree that had stopped him, then looked around for his gun. He saw it about eight feet up the hill, half buried in the mud. The slick ground made the climb up difficult. He had to dig in his heels several times, while using the plants like steps, as he maneuvered upward to retrieve it. The descent was even more treacherous as he made his way to Remi. When he reached her side, he brushed some of the mud from her face. Like him, she was covered in debris from the forest floor.

"Let's not do that again," she said.

"Not too soon anyway."

Looking up from where they'd fallen, Sam saw the trails they'd left as they slid down—a clear indicator of where they'd been. "We're going to have to be careful not to leave tracks."

Her gaze followed his. "Any ideas?"

They had at least twenty feet to get to the road below. "Let me go first. Step where I do."

He eyed a tree trunk about five feet down. The slope wasn't as steep as above them. He jumped, landed on the roots, then turned. "Ready?"

"Ready." Remi leaped.

He caught her at her waist, lowering her down. They repeated the process, using trees, ferns, and anything that covered their tracks. About five feet from the road, Sam stopped. The SUV's engine rumbled above them.

"They're coming," Remi said.

He and Remi reached the road. Taking her by the hand, they ran across it, then stopped, looking down the mountain, nearly as steep as the slope they'd just come down. They'd have to be cautious and not leave a trail. He found an area about ten feet down where a large growth of ferns offered a hiding place. Hopping from the roots of one tree down to the roots of the next tree, they'd barely reached the copse of ferns when the SUV rumbled past, then stopped just a few feet above them.

They ducked behind the fronds as they heard the vehicle doors opening, then the sound of booted feet on the pavement.

"You see them?" Ivan asked.

"There," Jak said.

"I don't see anything."

"At the top of the hillside near the road. You can see where they fell. Like bobsled trails."

"Yeah. Now I see it. Doesn't go any farther. You think they're hiding up there?"

"Or they're dead. Maybe I managed to hit them after all."

Sam parted the leaves, just able to make out the two figures on the road about ten feet away. Both men, gripping their handguns, stood with their backs to Sam and Remi, searching the area above them on the mountainside. The SUV was parked, its front doors standing open.

So temptingly close.

The odds were not in their favor. Even if they could climb up to the edge of the road without making any noise, there was no cover once they got up there. Had the men not been armed, he might have considered it—a thought brought home when Jak raised his weapon, aiming right where Sam and Remi had been hiding only moments before.

He felt Remi stiffen beside him and looked back. A thick boa was slithering across her leg. "Don't . . . move . . ." he whispered, watching as it slithered off.

"Nothing up there," Jak said as he turned, then looked downhill. Suddenly, he fired again and again. Bullets whistled overhead. The rush of adrenaline sent Sam's pulse into overdrive. "Something down there. I saw it."

A few seconds of silence, then Sam heard the sound of the two men walking, their feet crunching on the loose gravel as they scoured the edge of the roadway.

"What's that?" Ivan said. "I heard something."

Sam heard it, too. A tap-tapping noise. At first it was behind him, then all over. The rain, he realized. The drops came down harder, splatting against them as they lay hidden.

"I don't see anything," Jak said after a moment. "Let's get out of here."

"What about the Fargos?"

"If they're not dead, it'll take them days to get back. No one takes this road."

The men retreated to their SUV. Sam kept his arm over Remi, holding her long after Avery's men got in, then drove off, the sound of their engine fading in the distance.

Remi shifted beside him. "Did I mention I hate snakes?"

"At least it wasn't hungry." He got up on his elbow, looking down the mountain, the drop to the road below steeper than the one they'd just climbed down. He waited until he caught a glimpse of the SUV, wanting to make sure it continued on without stopping.

He sank back, staring up at the tops of the trees, reveling in the feel of the rain as it splashed his face. "Wasn't sure we were going to make it this time."

Remi leaned back against the hillside, her shoulder next to his. "Of course we were. I never doubted it."

"Except when the snake showed?"

She sat up, looked around as if worried another one might appear. "Not funny."

Remi started shivering—probably more from the adrenaline leaving her body than the cool rain. He knew it would be best to keep moving. "We should go," he said, helping her to her feet.

Together, they climbed up to the pavement. At the top, Sam pulled out his cell phone and looked at the screen. "Too much to hope we'd have a signal up here?"

"Imagine if someone had called us when we were hiding."

"Good point."

Remi linked her arm through his, and they began walking. "How long do you think it'll take to get back?"

"Not sure," he said. "But at least it's downhill."

"That's what I like about you, Fargo. Always seeing the bright side." She sighed. "We were so close . . . A long way to come for nothing."

"But the company's good."

She smiled, then leaned her head against his shoulder as they walked.

After about an hour, the rain had lightened to a sprinkle. Too late, because they were soaked through, their wet clothing chafing against the skin. Even though they'd covered about three or four miles, they hadn't descended all that far down the steep, winding road.

When they finally reached the fork that merged into the main road, Sam stopped, worried that Avery's men might be parked farther up, lying in wait.

"Wait here," he said while he took a quick look. Not seeing anything, he waved to her and she joined him. "Let's stay close to the side in case they're parked there, watching."

After a few minutes, Sam checked his phone again. Still no signal. Frustrated, he shoved it in his pocket, then stopped when he heard a faint but growing sound coming from somewhere up the hill. "Listen," he said. The sound of tires rolling across wet pavement. "Someone's got their car in neutral."

There were two reasons he could think of that a car might be heading downhill in neutral. Someone was having car troubles or they didn't want the vehicle's engine to be heard.

The latter worried him.

He grabbed Remi's hand and pulled her into the bushes.

Twenty-eight

S am hoped they hadn't been seen. As much as he'd been glad when the rain stopped, he found himself hoping for a sudden deluge, the better to limit visibility.

But the only water was that dripping off the trees and foliage. Within seconds, the car was upon them. He looked through the leaves just as a 1970s era, mud-covered yellow Jeep CJ5 came rumbling down the hill, still in neutral. Sam wasn't about to move until he knew who was at the wheel—he wouldn't put it past Avery's men to hijack another car. As the Jeep neared them, the engine sputtered to life and the vehicle jerked forward.

Not one of Avery's men.

Sam scrambled to his feet, slipping in the mud as he raced into the road waving his hands. "Help!" he shouted. "Over here!"

Remi raced to his side, waving and shouting herself, but the Jeep reached the bend in the road, brake lights coming on as it entered the turn. Too late, Sam thought, wondering if the driver had even heard or seen them. But then it stopped. And backed up the hill.

The driver, a tall, white-haired man with a goatee, his green eyes alight with curiosity, rolled down the window. "Need a ride?"

"We do," Sam said.

Remi added, "If you don't mind the mud?"

The man laughed. "Hardly a classic I'm driving here. A little dirt won't hurt it any. But you might want to hurry. Rain's coming back in."

They walked around to the other side of the car, Remi opting to sit in the back. Sam opened the door for her, then climbed into the front seat. "Thanks. We really appreciate this."

"No worries. My engine stalled when I had to slam on the brakes. Darn boa in the middle of the road. Good thing I was headed downhill." He looked over at Sam, then back to the street. "Don't see a lot of tourists way out here."

"We didn't start off that way. Forced by a couple of gunmen in Kingston."

"Robbed you, did they? What part of Kingston were you in?"

"The Records Department. That's where our car is."

The man looked over at Sam. "Tourists aren't usually kidnapped from public buildings."

"It doesn't matter now. They got what they wanted. And—well, we got away. That's what counts."

Remi reached over, putting her hand on Sam's shoulder. "Exactly."

"So," Sam asked when the silence took over, "you live in Jamaica? Or just visiting."

"Visiting. My friend owns a coffee plantation. I keep this old Jeep just to drive up to his place. Muddy roads get pretty deep during the rainy season."

For the remainder of the trip, they discussed the complexities of coffee growing, and, from there, the best places to fish around the island.

When he pulled into the parking lot next to their rental car, Sam checked for Avery's men, relaxing when it was clear they were nowhere in the vicinity. He and Remi thanked him again, asking if they could pay for his gas or trouble.

"No need. Coming down here anyway to get a new alternator. I am curious, though. What sort of information were they after?"

"Ship manifests," Sam said. "From the seventeenth century. The one we were looking for was missing."

"Well, good luck." He put it in gear and started to drive off, then stopped suddenly, leaning out the window. "Not sure if it'll help. But it just occurred to me. You might check at the Fort Charles Maritime Museum in Port Royal. Quite a collection of artifacts."

"Appreciate the tip," Sam said. They thanked him again, only realizing after he left that they hadn't gotten his name.

Any trip to Port Royal would have to wait until morning. Right now, they needed a long shower, some warm food, and a good night's rest. And even though Sam took enough evasive maneuvers to ensure they weren't followed, he didn't relax until they were safely in their room.

Good thing the hotel minibar had a nice bottle of Argentinian

Merlot. Sam poured two glasses of wine, handing one to Remi as she sat. He held his up. "Here's to narrow escapes and Good Samaritans."

Remi touched her glass to his. "And to finding what we need tomorrow in Port Royal."

Port Royal, a quiet fishing village once known as the wickedest city on earth, was originally colonized by the Spanish. Captured by the English in 1655, the heavily fortified town became one of the wealthiest trade centers in the world due to its notorious association with pirates and buccaneers. And it might have remained so had it not been obliterated by a massive earthquake in 1692, which sank more than half the town into the sea, its remains now underwater and buried by three centuries of silt and sand.

One of the few structures that remained standing was Fort Charles, which now housed the maritime museum. Sam and Remi paid their fee, then entered the brick fortress, the salt-tinged offshore wind whipping at them. Dozens of cast-iron cannons lined the arched battlements, at one time used to protect the city. The grounds were nearly deserted, and their footsteps echoed across the vast courtyard as they walked toward the old naval hospital that housed the museum.

Inside were display cases of pewter and dishes, showing items from everyday life, as well as fine jade carvings from China, giving evidence to the wealth that had graced Port Royal.

"Look at this, Sam." Remi pointed to a photograph of a pocket watch, the time showing eleven forty-three, recovered from the water and supposedly stopped the moment the earth-quake struck.

"Amazing find. Imagine what else is still down there."

"If only we can get the Jamaican government to grant us permission to dive."

"One thing at a time, Remi. Starting with finding someone who can help us."

Help found them. Two women walked into the room from a side door, the taller stopping to greet them. "Good morning. Welcome to the Maritime Museum."

"Good morning," Remi said. "We were hoping you might help us with some research."

The woman smiled.

"We were told you might have copies of old ship manifests. Particularly one from 1694 to 1696."

"No. So sorry. Have you tried the Archives in Kingston?"

"Unfortunately, the book was damaged. Someone mentioned that you might have copies."

"I don't know of any. Again, I am so sorry."

They thanked her as she left.

"Good try," Sam said. "Maybe Selma's dug up something by now."

Empty words. They both knew it. Selma would've called if she'd found anything.

"Silver lining," Sam said.

"Is there?"

"We can take that vacation now."

She gave a sigh, then smiled, disappointment evident in her eyes. "Let's go home."

As they started out, the second woman walked up to them, her voice low but pleasant. "I couldn't help overhearing that you were looking for old ship manifests?"

"We are," Sam replied.

"The Archives Department in Kingston was going to make them all digital, but the budget ran out. Lucky for us, we actually scanned a few before the money disappeared. One of the directors hoped to make some reproductions for the museum. Unfortunately, it's only the copies right after the big quake."

Remi looked hopeful. "*After* the quake? What years?"

"Sixteen ninety-three to sixteen ninety-six."

"Please," Remi said. "We'd love to have a look."

Twenty-nine

Alexandra Avery and her hired PI, Kipp Rogers, watched across the street, waiting until they saw her husband's car pull up to the front of his office building. About time, she thought, as he stepped out the door with his latest so-called client on his arm into the waiting car.

Kipp snapped a few photos. "Quite the looker, that one."

"They always are." How it was that Charles could date someone the same age as his daughter was beyond her. Then again, he'd never been close to his children, always preferring to leave them in the care of nannies when young, then boarding school when they were older. Alexandra always made a point to visit on weekends and talk on the phone. Charles embraced the distance, saying it built character.

And he wondered why it was they never spoke to him.

His loss, not hers.

"Better get to it," Kipp said once the car drove off, then turned the corner.

She nodded. "I'll call when I get into his office."

"I'll be here."

She crossed the street and walked into the building. If Charles had the faintest idea of what she was about to do, he'd have her forcibly removed from the building. As it was, she'd made enough innocuous visits this last week to put them all off guard.

Everyone had come to think of her as an interfering, obnoxious, soon-to-be ex—which she was. In this instance, however, she had a perfectly good reason. Although she couldn't put her finger on it, she knew her husband was up to something beyond his usual buying and stripping companies. Sure, he'd made his fortune from the practice, but the last decade or so she'd noticed he did it not only to stroke his ego but because he enjoyed seeing the lives destroyed after these onetime-thriving businesses were shredded to ruins.

It wasn't that she was much better than he—after all, she married him for his money way back when. It was more that she'd grown somewhat of a conscience since then. Maybe because she'd seen what this lifestyle had done to her own children.

It would be nice to think that was her only motive, the children, but she knew better. There was also the threat of being completely cut off from the fortune he'd built during the time they were married—which is why she hired Kipp in addition to her legal team.

Fair was fair, and as long as she had a breath in her body, she was not about to let Charles get away with what rightfully belonged to her.

The challenge was making sure she still had a breath in her body, because the way he'd been acting lately, she wouldn't put it past him to find some way to get rid of her just so he could keep his empire intact.

The first step, however, was finding proof that he was hiding something, and she knew without a doubt if anything was to be found it would be in his office.

She walked through the lobby, smiling at the security guard working the desk. He looked up, saw her, saying, "Your husband just left, Mrs. Avery."

"He didn't drop off my cell phone at the desk, did he?"

"No, ma'am."

"I think I might have left it in his office. I'm just going to run up and have a look around. I might be a while. I have a few phone calls to make."

He gave a polite nod, then went back to monitoring his screens.

That should keep him from wondering why she wasn't coming right back down, she thought, taking the elevator to the penthouse.

Charles's secretary was gone, and the lobby in front of his office empty. Perfect. His door, however, was locked, and she dug out a set of keys, duplicates for about every important room he felt needed to be secured from her.

If only he knew . . .

She found the key, unlocked the door, then slipped inside, only then wondering if he had any cameras set up.

Not that it mattered. Last she heard, prosecuting half an owner for theft was near impossible.

She set to work, going through his desk drawers first. The man was anal, everything neat, in its place. Doubting he'd keep something he didn't want seen in so obvious a location, she sat back in his desk chair and looked around. The only thing that caught her eye was that map book he'd been so obsessed about. It sat on a table in the corner of his office, and she walked over, opened it, taking a closer look.

What was it about this thing that had him so fired up? Nothing that she could see. It looked just like the reproduction sitting in their library. She turned the pages, aware of how brittle they were in comparison to the copy at home. Her attention waning, she was just about to close it when she realized that someone had taken a pencil and drawn small circles in various spots around the intricate border design of . . .

Were those letters?

That's exactly what they were. Archaic-looking letters that seemed more decorative, since they didn't spell out any real words.

So why circle them?

She leaned in closer, about to take a better look, when her cell phone rang.

She walked over to the couch and dug it out of her purse, saw it was Kipp. "Glad you didn't call when I was downstairs," she said.

"Your ringer's not off?"

"Who thinks of that stuff?"

"You should, if you're sneaking around in your husband's office. You were supposed to call me when you got up there."

"If you were up here doing what I'm paying you for, I wouldn't need to worry about that."

"Right. Because no one would suspect a total stranger digging through your husband's office. Who better to know what belongs and what doesn't than you? So what've you found?"

"Nothing yet. Except that pirate book that he claims was stolen from some ancient relative of his."

"The original book?"

"Yeah. Interesting thing, though," she said, returning to the table and eyeing the yellowed pages. "Someone went to the trouble of circling letters all over it. Like a code."

"Might explain his obsession. Take photos while you're there. I'll check into it. Have you looked at his computer yet?"

"No. Not yet."

"Hurry up. You've already been there too long as it is."

"You did see the number on his arm when he left? I doubt he'll be coming back anytime soon."

"Not worth chancing. Get moving."

She took her cell phone, snapped pictures of each page of the book, her instincts telling her that whatever Charles was up to, it had something to do with this.

Photos done, she opened up his laptop, typed in the password he used for nearly everything—Pirate—then scanned the folders.

Nothing on there stood out.

She leaned back in his chair, looking around the office, certain she was missing something . . .

Her gaze strayed to the notepad. He'd ripped off the top sheet, but she recalled the town Fargo written across it and she entered that in the search bar, wondering what his interest in North Dakota was.

But it wasn't the state that popped up in his Internet search history.

Fargo Group, Sam Fargo, Remi Fargo.

What the . . . ?

A little more digging and she realized his fascination with this couple.

They were treasure hunters.

She glanced at the map book just as her phone started ringing. Kipp, of course. "You're never going to believe this," she said. "I know what he's after."

"You need to get out of there. He's on his way up."

Thirty

The digital copy of the manifest was exactly what Selma had been hoping for and she got to work researching the fleet of ships that had set sail from Jamaica right after Sam and Remi emailed the pages they'd found in Port Royal. She called them back the next morning with what she'd learned.

"Good news, I hope," Sam said.

"Mostly," Selma replied. "I was able to link the vessel that sank off Snake Island to the theft of cargo from Captain Bridgeman during his time in Jamaica. More important, connecting that name to the sunken ship fills in a lot of the blanks. Especially now that we know the cipher wheel sank with it."

"How so?" Sam asked.

"Bridgeman was an alias for the pirate Henry Every."

"Every?" Remi asked. "Is it coincidental that Every and Avery sound similar?"

"No," Selma said. "It may have started off as a misspelling, but they're used interchangeably throughout most of the documentation I've located about Every's history. Henry Every, or Avery, is none other than Captain Henry Bridgeman. Started off as a slaver, then apparently turned pirate. Not much difference between the two, in my opinion."

"So what happened to him?" Sam asked.

"Disappeared. Last seen in the Bahamas, supposedly set sail for England, to live and die in obscurity. He was very much a wanted man at that point. The interesting thing is that until you found those missing pages, there were no official records showing that Bridgeman or the *Fancy* had ever sailed into Jamaica. Clearly, that's part of what Avery was trying to hide from you."

"What else was he trying to hide?"

"Two things. One, this wasn't the first time Every attacked the *Mirabel*. Two, the identity of the English investors who had an interest in the *Mirabel*."

"Investors. As in, more than one owner?"

"There could still be one owner. But multiple investors could mean that the ship was under the control of others. What we do know from the testimony of this crew member is that this item— we're assuming it was the cipher wheel—was taken during Every's first contact with the *Mirabel* off the coast of Spain a few years before. He specifically sought out this ship, which could mean that he knew the wheel was there. He also spared the ship, and the lives of the captain and crew, instead of scuttling it or bringing it into his fleet of pirate ships."

"He wanted out of there fast," Sam said. "The second contact was in Jamaica?"

"The *Mirabel* followed him there. According to the testimony, something of extreme value was stolen from Every in Jamaica. The *Mirabel* fled, we assume with the cipher wheel. He pursued in the *Fancy* to Snake Island. The rest, as you know, is history. Once the *Mirabel* sank, the wheel was lost to him—which may be why he suddenly gave up piracy."

"If," Sam said, "there's no record of his being seen after that point, is it possible that he captured the *Mirabel* but went down with the ship when it struck the rocks?"

"A logical assumption," Selma replied. "Except for the map detailing *where* to find the cipher wheel off Snake Island. It seems to me that Every made sure to document where the wheel was located in case he was ever able to get back to recover it. Unfortunately for him, his Bridgeman alias had been discovered by this time, and the Royal Navy had joined in with the East India Company in their pursuit of him. Probably prevented him from getting back to Snake Island. Some historians show him returning to England and dying a pauper, forced to live in obscurity without access to his treasure. Lazlo believes he returned to England and spent what was left of his treasure in search of the original cipher wheel."

"We're sure," Remi said, "that he never recovered the original wheel? Or that it even exists?"

"Definitely," Selma replied. "One, Charles Avery wouldn't be after it if he had—and he seems to know his family history. Two, Lazlo's research confirms that the original exists. Every-Bridgeman either died or was captured before he could go after it. Unfortunately, he failed to record *where* it was or *who* was in possession—assuming he had this knowledge to begin with. Either way, Charles Avery has the shipping manifest information. He's no doubt hot on the trail."

Sam reached over, spreading out their copy of the digitized transcripts they'd gathered from the maritime museum, looking them over. There were just a few pages of the court testimony they'd read in the Kingston Archives. "So, right now, we're still looking at who he originally stole the cipher wheel from?"

"We have it narrowed down, we think, to a couple of the *Mirabel* investors. Both happen to be in England, which makes it convenient. So that's where you're headed next."

Sam looked at Remi. "What do you say to a trip to the British Isles?"

"I love Great Britain this time of year."

Late the next afternoon, they touched down at the London City Airport, and the next morning they were up early. Selma had given them two names and addresses. One was for a Grace Herbert, just outside of Bristol, the other for Harry McGregor, farther north near Nottingham. Unfortunately, Selma couldn't narrow the odds any further, and so Sam flipped a coin while they waited for their car at the valet stand. "Heads, Herbert. Tails, McGregor," he called as he caught the coin and covered it with his hand.

"Heads," Remi said. "I have a good feeling about Bristol."

"If we don't find what we're looking for there, it's a long drive up to Nottingham."

"Call it women's intuition. Heads, Bristol."

Sam peeked at the coin. Tails. He pocketed it, then smiled at Remi. "Why leave something to chance. I trust your intuition."

"Tails, was it?"

"It was." When the car arrived, Sam looked at Remi. "You drive, and I'll navigate?"

"Ha! And trust that you'll pay attention to the map?"

"Have I ever gotten us lost?"

"There was that time in—"

"Never mind." He tipped the valet, then took the keys. Eventually they left London behind, the houses growing fewer, farms beginning to dot the landscape. A light mist came down, and Sam switched on the windshield wipers. It stayed that way for the next two hours.

Remi sighed at the green, rolling hills. "Beautiful out here."

"If you like the damp."

She glanced over at him. "You'd prefer the hot humidity of Jamaica over this?"

"I was thinking more of the warm breezes of La Jolla."

"All in good time." She eyed the directions on her phone. "About ten miles farther. Right turn at the next intersection."

They continued down a two-lane paved road that wound through pastures and farmland. Eventually they found the dirt road that led to the Herbert farmhouse and saw it in the distance. White smoke swirled up from the chimney of a large cottage with several outbuildings behind it. Geese honked as they drove up to the house, and the chickens scattered, then returned to pecking the ground, looking for grubs.

Sam parked, and they got out, crossed the gravel drive to the front door, and knocked. A woman in her late fifties answered, her short brown hair graying at the temples, her gray eyes serious as she took them in. "You must be the Fargos?"

"We are," Sam said. "Mrs. Herbert?"

"Actually, Herbert-Miller. But call me Grace. Come in, please. I have a kettle on, if you'd care for some tea?"

"Please," Remi said.

She led them into the parlor, and Sam had to duck to walk through the low doorway. As soon as they were settled, Grace returned a few minutes later with a silver tray carrying a porcelain tea service. Sam, still tired from the transatlantic flight, would have preferred a robust cup of coffee, as he accepted the tea, declined the offer of milk or sugar, and sat back in his chair, listening as Mrs. Herbert-Miller discussed her surprise at inheriting the collection of artifacts.

"The call came out of the blue," she said, stirring the sugar into her cup. "A solicitor from London, no less. Wanting to know if I was Grace Herbert of the Milford Herberts." She set the spoon onto the saucer, lifted the teacup, and took a sip. "Naturally, we put up the property for sale. I can't imagine living in an old, drafty castle, although Milford is a lovely place—or so I've heard. I don't think I could convince my husband to move even if I wanted to."

"It's a beautiful area," Remi said. "I passed through there once a long time ago."

Sam, wanting to move things along at a far quicker pace, said, "Was there anything . . . historically significant in what you saw? Besides the castle, of course."

"To be sure, I couldn't say. It's all being dealt with. I inherited the castle, and my cousin in Nottingham, Harry McGregor, inherited a small estate up there. It's possible he knows of something, though, like me, he sent everything that seemed historic to the museum. They were very interested, even though Sir Edmund Herbert, it turns out, was an illegitimate son." She lifted a plate of cookies. "Biscuit?"

Remi declined. Sam took one. "Thank you."

She returned the plate to the center of the table. "The only proof I have that my cousin and I are actually related is an old family bible that was among the items given to me. If I've read the lineage correctly, he and I are the second cousins of the last-known male heir."

"These historical items," Sam said. "Is there some sort of list of what they are?"

"There is. Would you like to see it?"

"We would."

She rose from the table, crossed the room, and picked up a manila envelope from a secretary in the corner that was cluttered with bills and paperwork for the farm. She pulled a sheaf of papers from the envelope and handed it to Sam as she took a seat. "Not that you can tell much. It's all up for auction, and I believe they're going to have photos of everything. I don't yet have them."

Remi leaned over, glanced at the papers as Sam looked them over. "That's quite the list," Remi said.

"Imagine someone like me putting a harpsichord in this parlor. Or a suit of armor. Even if I had room. Better to sell it and provide for the farm. I did keep a few items, however."

"Oh?" Remi said.

"This tea set, for one. It's quite lovely."

Remi ran her finger over the delicate edge of her saucer. "It is."

"There were also a few paintings." She pointed toward two small pastoral landscapes on the wall hung on either side of a coat of arms. "They didn't seem too outlandish for a simple farmhouse. The family crest, however. Vanity, plain and simple. It's not every day you find out you're distantly related to the illegitimate son of some lord, even if that son's father *was* only a minor land baron. And then just below it on the wall is the leather shield that dates back to Sir Herbert's time. I kept it mainly because that engraving of the Celtic knot in the center is so pretty."

Remi lowered her teacup to the table. "Would you mind if I took a closer look?"

"Help yourself."

Remi wandered over as Sam turned the page, noting there were several cartons of miscellaneous items listed. "These boxes," he said. "Any idea what was in them?"

"Just odds and ends. A lot of papers, books, and one box looked like someone had dismantled a suit of armor into it. The appraiser thought some of it might be historically significant. Which is why my cousin and I decided to lend the entire collection to the British Museum in London. Whether or not anything there is of any real value, I couldn't say . . . More tea?" she said, noting that Sam's cup was nearly empty.

"No thank you."

She refilled her own cup. "Not that we're rich. We just have no need of anything. We'd rather see the artifacts go to the museum than end up in private collections. They're having some gala fund-raiser there this coming weekend and they wanted to include it in their display."

"A fund-raiser?" Remi asked, returning to her seat. "We should go."

"Sold out, I'm afraid," Grace said. "Has been for weeks."

"Too bad," Sam said. "Any chance you'd allow us to look at those items prior to the event?"

"Of course. I'll give you the name of the person at the museum."

She read off the name and number for the contact information, which Sam entered into his phone. They spoke a few minutes longer, then, when it was clear there was nothing more to be learned, they thanked her for her hospitality.

On their way out, Sam paused by the paintings hanging on the wall near the door. He didn't recognize the name of the artists. The coat of arms, however, intrigued him, and he turned to her, asking, "You wouldn't mind if we took a photo of this, would you?"

"Not at all."

Sam used his phone to snap a couple of shots, checking to make sure he had a clear photo to forward to Selma, both of the family crest and the round leather shield hanging below it. The interlacing Celtic knot engraved on the convex brass boss at the center of the shield seemed at odds with the definite English heritage on the family crest hanging above it, but if anyone could make sense of that, Selma could. Some of the symbols engraved on the shield boss were worn from age, and the flash washed out what could be seen, and so he tried without the flash. Unfortunately, the room was too dark, but he could read the heraldry on the crest to some extent. Enough for Selma to work from, at least. "Thanks again," Sam said as he slipped his phone into his pocket.

She opened the door for them, smiling. "It was a pleasure. I'm sorry my husband wasn't here to meet you. Suddenly discovering a fence that needed mending, don't you know. I think he was a bit put off by our visitors yesterday."

"Visitors?" Remi asked.

"Like you, they were inquiring about the inheritance. Honestly, I can't see what all the fuss is about. If you saw that castle, you'd understand. A pile of stones, my husband calls it."

Sam paused in the doorway. "Do you recall their names? Or what they were interested in?"

"I'm afraid I didn't quite catch them. But, like you, they were interested in those boxes that went to the museum."

In the car, Sam handed his phone to Remi. "Do me a favor," he said as he turned the key in the ignition. "Forward those photos I took to Selma."

"Quite the interesting coat of arms. Considering that her long-lost ancestor was the illegitimate son of some minor baron, there's an awful lot of heraldry painted on it."

"Exactly what I was thinking." He turned down the graveled drive toward the country road, then checked his rearview mirror. The sun broke through the clouds, reflecting off the hood of a car heading down the hill toward them. He put on his sunglasses.

"Done," Remi said, then placed the phone in the center console. "I suppose we shouldn't be surprised that we weren't here first?"

Sam slowed as he entered a turn. "I'm tired of being one step behind these guys."

"Let's hope the museum sees these crooks for who they are, or at least asks for ID before they let anyone in for a personal look at the artifacts."

"I'd like to think the British Museum has some security protocols in place. Just the same, maybe give them a call. Let them know we'll be heading out their way in the morning."

Thirty-one

The following morning, Remi called the contact at the British Museum to view the historical artifacts on loan by Grace Herbert-Miller and her cousin. A young woman with barely a trace of a British accent informed her that Miss Walsh was not expected in until the reception that weekend.

Remi asked who else might help. Apparently there was no one there with the power to give them an early view of the display or to look at the storeroom where the remaining items were kept. Everything was scheduled for the grand opening, and, unless they had a ticket for the event, they'd have to wait until the following week.

"Great," Remi said, sliding her phone across the tabletop in frustration. "That was a dead end."

"Maybe Selma can work some magic," Sam suggested. "Or Lazlo. He's got to have contacts left here."

"We can only hope." She glanced at her watch, subtracted the eight-hour time difference. Remi emailed the details to Selma. "So now we wait."

Sam grabbed their coats. "Or we take a walk and do a little recon of the museum. See what we're up against."

"I like your way of thinking, Mr. Fargo."

The museum was slightly over a half mile from their hotel, and, within the hour, they were milling about, moving from one display to another. They wandered into the gallery and stood near the Rosetta stone, an artifact that had always intrigued Remi. "Wouldn't it be nice if the key to our cipher wheel was right here?"

Sam, watching for signs of Avery's men, drew his gaze from the crowds and eyed the massive stone. "Where's the challenge in that?"

"Asks the man who doesn't have to do the deciphering." She looked around.

"Different gallery entirely." She waved her map. "This room is Egyptian sculpture."

He took her arm, leading her away from the Rosetta stone. "The drawback, if his men *were* seriously injured in that accident, is that Avery would just send someone else."

"Good point. At least we know what those guys look like."

"Does that map of yours tell you where this special event is going to be held?"

"No. But I expect we can find a helpful docent to point us in the right direction."

They did. A gray-haired woman who told them the display

was currently housed in Room 3. "Once you enter the Great Court," she added, "you'll cross through it and see the entrance to your right."

They thanked her, then walked through the vast atrium, its glass-and-steel-checkered ceiling giving the area a brightly lit space-age appearance. Eventually they found the room in question.

Blocked off, with a guard present.

He, however, had little information to add or was unwilling to discuss it.

Sam and Remi stared at the closed-off area.

"Ideas?" Remi asked.

"Not a one." He looked at his watch. "If we're lucky, Selma's found out something by now."

Sam retrieved their raincoats from the coat check. Outside, they found a quiet spot to call Selma. Sam held up his phone so that he and Remi could hear. "Tell me you have some good news?" he asked her.

"Sorry, Mr. Fargo. This is a highly anticipated event, with a waiting list. And unless you can convince the organizers that you're more important than some of the various celebrities on said list, I don't think you're getting in."

"Lazlo? Surely he still has contacts here."

"Academia isn't the sort of profession that is able to break through the ranks of royals. Neither is simply being a multimillionaire. I do, however, have some good news."

"And that would be . . . ?"

"That academia is good for researching the coat of arms. How much do you know about heraldry?"

Remi replied, "Enough to know it'll put you to sleep slogging through the archaic language."

"Exactly," Selma said. "According to Lazlo, it appears your farmer's wife and her cousin up in Nottingham aren't related to just any illegitimate son of a minor land baron. It would be a minor land baron who appears to be the illegitimate son of Edmund Mortimer, Second Lord Mortimer."

"And Mortimer's significance would be . . . ?" Sam asked.

"The father of Roger de Mortimer, Third Lord Mortimer, who happened to have an affair with Queen Isabella. Undoubtedly one of the reasons he was executed by her son, Edward III."

"Got it. Any connection to this cipher wheel business?"

"Hard to say. Still working on it, as well as the rest of the coat of arms. It's like a foreign language. Everything means something."

"You know where to find us." He disconnected.

"What now?" Remi asked.

"I say we find a decent pub, have lunch, and figure out our next plan of action."

They started down the street and hadn't gone more than a half a block when a Rolls-Royce pulled up alongside them. The rear passenger window rolled down, revealing a man with dark hair salted with gray at the temples. He smiled at them, though his dark eyes looked anything but friendly, Remi thought.

"You must be the Fargos."

Sam took Remi's hand, pulled her back, then stepped between her and the car. "Let me guess. Charles Avery?"

"Sorry to disappoint. Colin Fisk. It seems you and my employer are after the same little bauble. The original cipher wheel."

"Not sure what you're talking about."

"By the way, my men survived their car accident yesterday."

"Don't recall asking," Sam said.

"I take it you weren't able to get tickets to the festivities tonight at the museum?"

Sam gave a casual shrug. "There'll be other displays and other events."

"A shame. As I *will* be there."

Remi, curious, asked, "And how was it you managed to get tickets?"

"Connections. It's all about who you know. It's a not-to-be-missed event. Unless your name is Fargo. I understand you're on the blacklist. Enjoy your stay in London. You're at the Savoy, correct?"

"And where is it you're staying?"

"Somewhere else." He gave a cold smile again, then rolled up his window as the car took off.

Remi moved to Sam's side, watching until the car was out of sight. "That was a bit unsettling," she said.

"I'm sure that was the purpose."

"How do you think he found out where we were staying? We're not registered under our names."

"Picked out the various five-star hotels and made a lucky guess?"

"Maybe we should have stayed someplace a little less refined." She linked her arm through his. "Now, what were you saying about lunch and a battle plan? I have a feeling we're going to need it."

They found a nearby pub and ordered fish-and-chips with

mushy peas and a pint of Guinness each. Sam carried the beer to a table, where they could keep their backs to the wall and watch the windows and entrance—just in case.

He handed Remi a pint.

She took a sip of the dark, room-temperature brew, then leaned back in her seat, thinking about their encounter. "How is it," she asked, "that Fisk, of all people, managed to get tickets and we couldn't?"

"Because he's willing to break the law."

"We have to find a way in there."

"I'm open to suggestions."

"Same," she said as a waitress brought their lunch. They finished eating. Sam ordered another beer while Remi sat back, watching two women walk past their table on the way out, one of them saying, "Don't know what you're so upset about. Especially since your ex will be there. It's just going to be a bunch of blighters singing happy birthday. I'm not going if that makes you feel any better. Unless you want to crash it?"

"Remi . . . ? Did you hear anything I just said?"

She looked at Sam. "Sorry. No."

"If you want to walk away from this, I'll do it. We've cleared Bree's name, and—"

"What? No. The last thing I want is to let a man like Charles Avery win."

"It's not a game."

"He tried to kill us."

"Remi—"

"We crash it."

"What?"

"Those women who just left were discussing crashing a birth-day party. *We* could do that."

He waited for her to explain.

"How many fund-raisers have we been invited to over the years where someone didn't show? And how many of those where someone who *wasn't* invited ended up attending?"

"Plenty."

"Exactly. The worst that can happen? We're turned away at the door. The best? We get in and find what we're looking for."

Thirty-two

From the backseat of their hired Mercedes, Sam watched the entrance where the luxury sedans dropped off the formally dressed guests, then departed. Slipping into a tightly controlled and heavily guarded event unnoticed wasn't going to be easy. Liveried personnel stood at the doors checking invitations before allowing entry.

"Ideas?" he asked Remi.

"Waltz in like we own the place?"

"Don't think that's going to work. What we need is some sort of distraction. A bottleneck of some sort. Something creative . . ."

"The royals are always good for a distraction."

"You happen to know any who are coming?" Sam asked as the Maybach pulled to a stop.

"It's called *A Royal Night at the Museum.* Surely one or two will be attending."

"Or it's just a theme, which explains the liveried servants."

A footman approached and opened their car door. A moment later, Sam and Remi stood waiting behind a number of other people near the entrance.

Sam noticed a few admiring glances turned their way, undoubtedly directed at Remi, who wore a sleeveless black silk gown and a diamond pendant at the neckline that drew the eye to the hint of cleavage. Some designer. Chanel? Armani? The moment she rattled the name off, he put it from his mind, not that it mattered. What did was that his wife looked amazing.

Remi nodded at the footmen. "They're announcing names at the door."

"That presents a slight problem. At least if we want to stay low-key."

"So what's the plan?"

"I'm working on it." The truth was, he hadn't yet come up with anything. Within seconds, they'd be at the door, only two more couples ahead of them.

He glanced around him, hoping something would come up, as he heard the footman announce, "Sir John Kimball, Lady Kimball."

"Sam," Remi whispered, a smile pasted on her face. "We're almost up."

"Isn't that Charles Avery's Rolls-Royce?" he asked. "Or, rather, his hired henchman Fisk?"

She looked back. "It would seem so."

"What are the chances he or his driver has a gun in the car?"

"About a hundred percent."

Sam leaned toward her, whispering, "And what would happen if a beautiful, frightened woman were to make that fact known?"

"You know any?"

"Beautiful? Yes. Frightened? Never."

"One way to find out . . ."

As they reached the doors, the so-called footman asked for their invitation. Remi placed her hand on her throat, her beautiful green eyes turning all doe-like, as she said, "Thank heavens." She moved in closer, lowering her voice. "I've never been more frightened in my life. There's a man with a gun."

The footman, his shoulders tensing, scanned the crowd behind her. "Where?"

"Standing near that Rolls-Royce. He's tall, dark hair, graying at the temples. You see the way he keeps looking at us? It's like he knows."

"Wait right here, please."

He left them to go talk to a couple of men in dark business suits standing about ten feet to their right, undoubtedly part of the security detail.

Sam used that moment to take Remi's arm and lead her in. They were stopped by another footman, who asked for their invitation. "I gave it to that other gentleman," Sam said, pointing to one of the three men who were now walking toward Fisk and the Rolls.

The guard eyed them, slightly confused. "What names to announce?"

Remi stepped forward. "Longstreet," she said, giving her maiden name.

Sam added, "Mr. and Mrs."

"Mr. and Mrs. Longstreet," he intoned, and he waved them through.

Sam moved Remi quickly from the door, planning to get lost in the crowd before anyone realized what had happened. Especially if Fisk connected the contact by security to them. "That worked out well," he said once they were safely inside and there didn't seem to be anyone coming after them.

A liveried waiter passed by carrying champagne flutes and Sam took two, handing one to Remi. "Here's to beautiful women who are good actresses."

"And handsome men who can think on their feet." She touched her glass to his and sipped as they strolled through the atrium, neither of them wanting to waste any time mingling.

Sam glanced back as they exited toward the gallery with the display.

Remi asked, "Something wrong?"

"We probably stirred a hornet's nest by siccing those guards on Avery's man."

"If we're lucky, we can get in and out before we get stung."

"Let's hope so," he said as they neared the gathering of guests just outside the new exhibit. He took in their surroundings, searching for anyone who looked the least bit suspicious. He noticed a few undercover security guards, something to be expected. He dismissed them as a threat, instead looking for anyone who might be working for Avery or Fisk.

So far, so good.

A woman at the entrance of the gallery handed them a colored, tri-fold pamphlet.

Remi looked over hers. Sam took the moment to examine the

guests milling about inside the long room. No one seemed to be paying them the least bit of attention.

"Fascinating," Remi said.

"What is?"

She pointed to the pamphlet. "Considering what this display is focusing on, you'd think they would've come up with a different name for the event. It's formally called the *Illegitimate Royal Children of England*."

"Somehow I don't think that would have the same cachet as *A Royal Night at the Museum*." He looked around the room and noted a large number of older patrons. "Some of these people might have a hard time writing the official version in their checkbooks."

Remi laughed. "Good point, Fargo. Shall we see what all the fuss is about?"

He took her arm, and they strolled through the exhibit, set out chronologically by year and by the family associated with it.

About midway through, they reached the display that contained the items donated by Grace Herbert-Miller and her cousin and they stopped, took their time giving everything a thorough examination. There were paintings, a suit of armor, weaponry, and jewelry, just to name a few of the many items. If the cipher wheel was there, it wasn't in plain view.

"You take photos," Sam said. "I'll watch for Fisk."

She used her phone and snapped pictures of every item. "Done," she said after a couple of minutes.

A woman in a business suit approached, her ID tag clipped to her pocket identifying her as a museum employee. "Interesting, isn't it?"

Sam's first inclination was to agree with her, but he decided that action would elicit less information. "What is?" he asked instead.

"The Mortimer Collection. Our newest. I helped put it together."

Sam and Remi exchanged quick glances, and Remi moved closer, smiling. "What a fascinating job you must have, Ms . . . ?"

"Walsh. Meryl. And, yes, it most certainly is fascinating."

Sam asked, "What can you tell us about the collection? Edmund Mortimer, Second Lord Mortimer—where does he fit in?"

"It's Mortimer's grandmother, Maud de Braose, who generated our interest in this display as well as giving us the idea for our event name, *A Royal Night at the Museum*. Through her children, Maud de Braose is related not only to the last Plantagenet kings, Edward IV through Richard III, but all English monarchs from Henry VIII on. When Grace Herbert-Miller offered the artifacts for display, we couldn't resist."

"Impressive," Sam said. "Anything about Mortimer's illegitimate son that makes him stand out in history besides a distant link to royalty?"

"Unlike his ancestors, who certainly have their share of skeletons in their closets—massacres, plots to dethrone the king—Sir Edmund Herbert and his descendants appear to have led rather boring and exemplary lives—as long as you overlook his half brother's feud with this notable character."

She moved to the adjacent display. "Here we have the illegitimate grandson of Hugh le Despenser, a man who was reputed to be having an affair with King Edward II. Queen Isabella hated him and managed to convince her husband to force Hugh into exile, during which Despenser was said to have turned to piracy."

A pen-and-ink illustration of a single-masted ship was posted on Despenser's time line in 1321, with a paragraph below noting that Despenser was "the monster of the sea."

Remi leaned in for a closer look. "I'm assuming this feud is the reason these two sons were placed next to each other?"

"It is," the woman said. "When Despenser took to the seas, he attacked a ship belonging to the Mortimer family, which was carrying a fortune belonging to Queen Isabella. Roger Mortimer, who helped Queen Isabella depose her husband, Edward II, from the throne, was eventually executed, and some say it may have been due to the loss of Isabella's fortune."

"Despenser?" Remi said. "If I recall my history, Mortimer was executed several years *after* Despenser."

"True," she continued. "But there was also the matter of family honor. For generations, Mortimer and his ancestors had sworn an oath of fealty to the kings they served. Edward III could forgive Mortimer for participating in the deposing of his father, whose relations with Despenser had endangered all of England. But once Edward II had abdicated, Mortimer's duty was to step aside. He failed to do so."

Sam, who had always been a history buff, took it all in while examining the artifacts laid out in the cases. "How do these illegitimate sons play into this? Beyond simply being born on the wrong side of the blanket?"

"Sir Edmund Herbert, Mortimer's half brother, managed to recover part of Isabella's treasure stolen by Despenser, which in turn brought the Mortimers back into the good graces of Edward III. In contrast, Despenser's illegitimate son, Roger Bridgeman, carried on the new family tradition of piracy."

Bridgeman? Sam thought. That certainly explained Avery's interest.

"Fascinating," Remi said. "But is this everything?"

"I'm sorry?"

"I mean, all the artifacts from the Mortimer side? We were fortunate enough to run into Grace Herbert-Miller, who mentioned that she'd recently turned everything over to you. Naturally, that made us wonder if this was everything or were there some items that didn't make it to the display?"

"Well, naturally, not everything would fit, and so we picked the most relevant pieces or those that we thought would tie into our theme. Was there something in particular you were interested in seeing? I might be able to arrange a private viewing at a later date."

"That," Remi said, "would be appreciated. Do you have a detailed inventory list of what was turned over?"

The woman hesitated when she noted Remi typing into her phone. "May I ask what your interest is?"

"Writers," Sam said. "We're hoping to complete a history on the Mortimer family. And now that we know there's a Mortimer-Herbert on the wrong side of the blanket, we'd like to add him."

Remi nodded, holding up her phone. "Notes."

"Oh," Miss Walsh said. "Then you've come to the right person. Let me get your name and number and I'll be glad to give you a call." She pulled a small notepad and pen from her pocket.

"Longstreet," Remi said. "Mr. and Mrs." She recited her cell phone number.

"I'll give you a call."

As she walked off to speak with other guests, Sam asked Remi, "You get all that?"

"Texting to Selma and committing it to memory as we speak."

Since Remi had a near-photographic memory, he didn't doubt it for a second. "Let's see what else we can find." He looked up and saw Colin Fisk approaching, in his hand a black cane with a wide brass handle—not that he seemed to walk with any noticeable limp. "Guess who just arrived."

"Lovely. And here we were having such a good time."

"How original," Fisk said. "Man with a gun? That's all you could think of?"

Sam gave a casual shrug as he scanned the room for any more of Avery's cronies. "Did the job." He was surprised to see Fisk without one of his henchmen. "No 'plus one'?"

"Some of us have the good sense to leave our stunning wives at home when danger lurks."

Sam felt Remi bristle beside him at the veiled threat. "I'd ask what brings you here, but we know the answer to that."

"Or do you? I see you've found the Mortimer Collection. A shame they put it next to the Despenser display."

"Seems the perfect location, considering their background."

"If you only knew." He gave a cold smile, his gaze flicking to Remi, then back. "Now, if you'll be so kind as to precede me out the hall toward the back."

"You think we'd go anywhere with you?"

"Naturally, no. Which is why I've taken the liberty of ensuring your cooperation. That young curator . . . Walsh, I believe her name is? On the far side of the gallery?"

Sam looked that direction. She seemed to be watching them, her face pale. Two of Fisk's goons, Ivan and some new guy, stood behind her—too close, Sam realized.

"And if we choose not to cooperate?" Sam said.

"Then you'll have the lovely Miss Walsh's death on your conscience."

"You really think you can get away with that here? In the middle of the British Museum?"

"It's already in motion. The question is, how many people do you want to see hurt?"

"What's in motion?" Sam asked.

"In less than sixty seconds, the fire alarms will go off. The museum staff, being well drilled, will usher everyone out in an orderly fashion. What they won't realize is that there is an ambulance loaded with enough explosives to take off the front of this building. It's about to pull up as we speak—to care for a man complaining of chest pains. So your choices are these. When the alarm sounds, you're ushered out with the hundreds of others to the front, putting your lovely wife in danger of a blast that will undoubtedly have a very high body count. Or you save dozens of lives, your wife's included, by accompanying me and the frightened curator, who is undoubtedly feeling the very sharp point of Marlowe's dagger at her back." He held up his cane as if to imply that's how the knife was smuggled in. "And for all your wasted efforts in sending security after us, Ivan managed to bring a gun in after all."

Sam looked over at the two men. Ivan, his right hand in his

jacket pocket, smiled at him as though he knew he was the sub-ject of their conversation. And then, as though to prove Fisk's point, he lifted his jacket, his hand, and the concealed weapon aimed in their direction. A moment later, the fire alarms went off.

"Your decision, Mr. Fargo. Make it quick."

Thirty-three

Remi gripped Sam's arm as the fire alarms blared throughout the gallery. "I'm not leaving my husband."

"The choice is not yours, Mrs. Fargo."

Sam asked, "What happens to my wife if I cooperate?"

"When she dutifully shows up alone out front, they'll know not to set off the explosives—as long as no police arrive. The better question is for her to ask what happens to you." He pinned his gaze on Remi. "Stay in sight of the entrance, don't use your phone, and your husband will be safe."

"Sam . . ."

"I'll be fine, Remi. Go." He looked toward the exit, where museum employees were guiding the guests out.

She stopped before Fisk, looking him in the eye with a cold stare. The last thing she wanted was to anger him and so she turned to Sam, saying, "Be careful."

He gave a quick nod, and she forced herself to walk away,

finally glancing back as she neared the exit, willing Sam to look at her.

They'd reached the far end of the gallery, and Fisk's man forced Miss Walsh around, plucking a white key card that was clipped to her pocket, using it to open the door. Finally, Sam looked toward Remi. He crossed his fingers, touched his temple near his eye, then pointed at her.

She did the same. Their own little signal for *Don't worry, I love you.*

Forcing herself to walk calmly among the other evacuees, she tried to regulate her breathing, get her fear under control. Sam was very capable, and if anyone could defeat Fisk, he could.

The cool air hit her as she stepped out, and she looked around, hearing sirens in the distance. Guests milled about near the entrance, the sequins and jewels on the women's gowns sparkling in the lights.

Laughter and quiet conversation filled the air. No one seemed to be panicking.

She saw no ambulance—nor any guest who seemed to be suffering from a heart attack, fake or otherwise.

Fisk had lied to them.

Idiot. Of course he had.

She turned on her heel, walked to the door where security was still ushering other guests out due to the fire alarms.

When she tried to enter, one of the guards put out his hand. "I'm sorry, ma'am. You'll need to stay outside until the fire department clears the building."

"My husband," she said, her hand to her throat, attempting to look as panicked as she felt. "He's . . . diabetic. He needed his insulin and said he was going to the restroom to give himself an injection. He hasn't come out. I—I don't see him anywhere. Please. It's the first-floor restrooms in the atrium. If I could just go check . . . ?" Pleading with her eyes. "I'll come right out as soon as I find him."

He considered her for a moment, then nodded. "In and out," he said.

"Thank you! I'll be quick!"

She walked straight toward the atrium. Glancing back, she saw the guard was no longer paying her any attention. Perfect. She continued on, saw perhaps fifty or so guests coming down the grand curved staircase on the left. Two young women, both museum employees, stood on either side at the base of the stairs, repeating, "Please head to the nearest exit. Thank you."

Remi wandered up, smiled at the employee closest to her. "Excuse me. I'm worried about my husband. I can't find him and I'm hoping he's upstairs."

"Just wait here, ma'am. They're clearing everyone from upper levels."

"Thank you." Stepping back, Remi stumbled against someone, lost her balance, fell forward against the woman, her purse flying from her grasp to the floor, its chain strap rattling as it slid across the surface. "Oh no," she said, trying to right herself as the woman helped to catch her. "I'm so sorry!"

"Are you okay?"

"Fine," Remi said. "More embarrassed than anything. I didn't hurt you, did I?"

"No. Here. Let me get your purse."

"I can get it," Remi said, moving past her, scooping up the

chain, then holding the purse against her as she strung the chain over her shoulder. "I can't believe I did that. Darn high heels." She glanced upstairs. "I don't see him. I guess I can wait at the front."

Remi moved with the crowd toward the exit, hiding the stolen key card behind her purse as she quickly sidelined toward the gallery. After a quick glance back to make sure no one was watching, she made a beeline toward the door leading to, she hoped, Sam. She slid the key card against the lock, hearing it click as the light turned green. Opening the door, she slipped inside, entering a stairwell, then dropped the key card into her purse. She looked up, dismissed that direction, and descended, cracking open the door at the bottom. She saw it was clear, stepped in, and quietly closed the door behind her.

Remi pulled off her shoes before starting down the hallway. She passed several doorways, all closed, following the corridor to a T intersection at the end. An EXIT sign on the wall pointed to the left. Doubting they'd leave the museum—unless they'd already found what they were looking for—she peered around the corner to the right. About ten feet in, she heard the faint sound of voices, floating down the corridor.

Remi stilled, tried to listen. She couldn't tell who was talking or what they were saying.

At least she was heading in the right direction.

Pressing herself close to the wall, she continued on, the voices growing louder.

"Keep looking." This voice sounded like Fisk.

"Maybe," came a woman's voice, "if you told me what you're trying to find?"

"I did tell you. Something round with symbols on it."

Remi edged her way toward the room, her back against the wall. The door was closed, but not tight. Fisk stood with his back to the door, watching Miss Walsh sort through items on a table. Marlowe, his dagger in hand, stood next to them. What Remi didn't see was Sam or Ivan. She eyed the door. A slight push would be all it would take. She reached out, pressed her fingers against it. A quarter inch more allowed her to see into what was apparently the workroom where they'd been cataloguing the Herbert Collection. Several weapons scattered on the table clearly didn't make the cut for the upstairs display: a mace detached from the handle, a maul, an old leather shield, and pieces of body armor. Unfortunately, nothing that could readily be used as a weapon on her part—except, perhaps, a brass star that appeared to have been attached to the leather shield at one time, its points possibly sharp enough to do some damage if thrown with enough force.

The door swung open. Ivan shoved the barrel of a small pistol right toward her. "Don't move."

Remi glanced into the room, seeing Sam off to one side, seated in a chair, his hands zip-tied in front of him, but otherwise unharmed. "No need for violence," she said, giving a glance at the gun.

"You should've stayed outside."

"I'd be glad to return."

"Too late," he said and yanked her into the room.

Thirty-four

S am forced himself to remain still when he saw Remi stumble past the door, landing against the table of artifacts. As much as he wanted to blast his fist through Ivan's face, then break his neck, he knew their best bet was to wait. Ivan might only have two shots in that small-caliber handgun that he'd managed to smuggle into the museum, but that was two shots too many.

"What's this?" Fisk said, watching Ivan take hold of Remi.

"Visitor."

The older man took a frustrated breath. "Does no one listen around here?" Then, realizing Miss Walsh was distracted from her search, he turned back to her. "Keep looking."

She nodded, hurriedly searching through stacks of folders and papers.

Remi leaned over the table, reaching for one of her shoes that had slid across the tabletop when she fell.

Ivan grabbed her arm and pulled her away.

"Leave my wife alone."

"Or what?"

Sam started to rise from his chair until Marlowe rushed over and shoved him back in his seat. "Stay there or I'll slit your throat."

Remi, clutching her shoes and her purse to her chest, turned a stern eye on Sam. "I'm fine."

If there was one thing that he and Remi excelled at, it was coming up with alternative plans. They were definitely going to need one now, he thought, watching as Ivan led Remi to Sam's side.

"Sit," he ordered, shoving Remi into a chair next to Sam.

She stole a glance Sam's way. "Come here often?"

"Shut up, you two," Ivan said, then crossed the room, standing where he could keep an eye on them.

Miss Walsh, who was currently dumping the contents of yet another box on top of the table, looked over at the dagger in Marlowe's hand. "Must you stand so close with that thing?"

He said nothing, just stared at her. She turned back to the box, her hands shaking as she sorted through the papers.

Fisk glanced at his watch, then at Miss Walsh. "You're sure you don't remember seeing anything like that in the artifacts?"

"If there was, I'd know. There wasn't."

Fisk narrowed his gaze, stepping in closer to her. "Then what are you digging around for? Because those don't look like artifacts in that envelope."

"You said it was round, with symbols? I remember a drawing of something similar." She shoved the box toward him. "You're certainly welcome to look yourself."

He picked up a stack of papers from the box, then nodded at Ivan and Marlowe. "Keep an eye on those two."

Sam turned his attention to his wife. "You okay?"

"I'm fine. Really."

"You shouldn't have come back."

"I was worried. The ambulance that was supposed to be filled with explosives never showed."

"A needed ruse," Fisk said without looking up from the papers he was shuffling through. "It worked."

"So," Remi said, ignoring the man, her gaze moving to Sam's wrists and the zip tie around them, "I was a tad worried about *your* safety."

Sam smiled at her, then glanced at Miss Walsh, who was going through the papers, but with a bit more care than Fisk, undoubtedly because she was more worried about preserving history. Or maybe she realized once this item was found, their lives were forfeit.

Fisk held up a yellowed document, then took a step back. "This is it."

Miss Walsh froze.

Sam had been trying to loosen the plastic tie around his wrists as he kept his eye on Ivan, who was watching Fisk for further instructions. Fisk, though, seemed in awe of his discovery, almost forgetting the others were there. Then, suddenly, he looked up. His gaze met Ivan's, then Marlowe's. "Meet me upstairs when you're done. I'll send Jak down to help."

He walked out.

Not good, Sam thought. "You only have two bullets in that gun," he told Ivan.

"No worries. Got more in my pocket. And Marlowe's itching to try out his new dagger."

Marlowe held up the gleaming blade and smiled at Miss Walsh.

She took a step back, her face paling.

Remi took a frustrated breath. "For heaven's sake, if you're going to kill us, at least let me put my shoes on and die with dignity. Here," she said to Sam, holding her clutch almost to his chest so that he had no choice but to reach up with his bound hands and take it from her. She bent over, making a show of putting her high heels on her feet.

Ivan sneered at her as if he couldn't believe she had the audacity to worry about her appearance at a moment like this. Sam gripped the purse, only then realizing what was hidden under the flap. The brass star. And here he'd been hoping for a knife to cut the zip tie.

Suddenly, Marlowe grabbed Miss Walsh, pushing the dagger against her carotid.

Sam let go of the purse as he rose, then hurled the star. It struck Marlowe's neck. The man's eyes widened as he dropped the dagger, then grasped at his throat, unable to breath. He staggered back, crumpling to the ground next to Ivan, who'd just leveled his gun at Remi. Sam rushed forward, shoving Ivan's gun hand upward as he fired. He struggled with Ivan, straining against the zip tie while trying to get ahold of the gun. Ivan fired again, the shot so close to Sam's head, he felt the sting of gunpowder on his cheek. Ivan gripped the empty weapon, swung at Sam, then blindly reached behind him, grabbing the maul from the table. Sam jumped back as the sledgehammer narrowly missed him. He ducked as it came down again, then rammed Ivan in the chest with his shoulder. The maul fell from Ivan's grasp and he tripped, stumbling into the table behind him.

"Run!" Sam said.

Remi pulled Miss Walsh from the room. Ivan grabbed the broken mace, holding the spiked ball in his fist, then came at Sam. Hands still tied, Sam dove for the leather shield on the table. He swung around, bringing it up. The mace skidded across the leather, piercing through it. Sam shoved the shield into Ivan's face, pushing him back.

Ivan tripped over Marlowe's body and crashed to the floor.

Sam threw the shield at him, then ran from the room. Remi and Miss Walsh were up ahead, racing down the hall.

They stopped at the intersection, one hall leading back to the museum, the other up toward the emergency exit. "Which way?" Remi asked.

Miss Walsh looked both directions, too shocked to make a decision.

"Exit," Sam said, hoping that the grounds would be filled with patrons who were waiting outside due to the alarm. Get lost in the crowd.

They raced up the stairs, bursting out the door, only to find they were far from the front entrance and any crowd. Instead, they stood in a dark passage between buildings, used only by maintenance.

They needed to get to the street outside the museum grounds. At the moment, their only choice was to turn left or right. Sam chose left, then stopped in the next doorway, where a shallow stairwell led down to another basement office. "Over here," he said, urging them into the darkened stairs just as they heard the squeak of the emergency exit door opening, then slamming shut.

Ivan's booted feet scraped the gravel on the pavement just

above them as he came to a stop, looking around, the small pistol in his hand.

Sam drew in a slow, steady breath, pressing tight against the wall, as Remi cut the zip tie from his wrists with his pocketknife. Suddenly, Ivan turned. They froze as he walked in their direction, then stopped, so close that Sam could almost have reached up and grabbed the man's ankles. Ivan pulled out his phone and made a call. "Marlowe's dead . . . No. Lost them. I'll check the grounds. You watch the streets . . . Do *not* leave here until you find them. The boss wants them—"

A power generator in the next building kicked on, covering the remainder of his conversation. Sam watched Ivan walk off in the other direction, disappearing around the corner.

Satisfied they were safe for the moment, he looked over at both women. "You okay?"

They nodded.

"Good. Let's get out of here." He eyed the door behind him. "Does this lead anywhere?"

Miss Walsh, having recovered somewhat, shook her head. "Just the maintenance office. No inside entrance. Shouldn't we just call the police?"

"I'd like to make sure we're alive to give our statements. How do we get back inside?"

"The easiest and quickest way," Miss Walsh said, "is back the way we came. But they took my key card."

"I have one," Remi said, holding up her purse. "Borrowed it from another employee."

"That's my girl." He climbed the stairs, then stopped at the top, waited to make sure it was clear, then motioned the others to come up. "Straight to the other door," he said, bringing up the rear.

They filed in, Sam not relaxing until the door was shut tight behind them.

"We'll head to the security offices," Miss Walsh said. "We'll be safe there until the police arrive."

"This document they took," Sam asked her as they walked, "did you happen to get a good look at it?"

"It was a pen-and-ink sketch."

"Of what?"

"A round object with symbols on it. I must have seen it back when I first started cataloguing the Herbert Collection because I knew right away what he was talking about when he described it."

"Any chance you might remember any of the symbols on it?"

"Unfortunately, no. Sorry."

Hours later, Sam and Remi finally returned to their hotel room, exhausted. Side by side on the bed, they stared up at the ceiling. Remi reached over, grasping Sam's fingers. "I can't believe we were that close."

"A good effort. Just not good enough."

"How is it that he's been one step ahead of us?"

A good question, Sam thought. They'd stopped the leak. Archer had assured him that Bree had not contacted her cousin since they confirmed she'd been the source. And still they were constantly behind with every step they took. "They did have several days' head start."

"Maybe Selma has some news for us."

"You want to call or should I?"

When Remi didn't answer, he looked over at her. She was fast asleep. He watched her for several moments, thinking about the mixed emotions of that night's events. He knew Fisk never intended to let them walk out of there, and while Sam wasn't about to simply give up and die without a fight, he'd been okay knowing that Remi was outside and safe. At least until Ivan dragged her into the room.

His lovely wife had risked her own life to rescue him. And she'd had the brains to grab a weapon in the process.

He listened to the sound of her even breathing as she slept next to him and he smiled in the dark, thinking about the way she'd insisted that she be allowed to put on her shoes.

"Good one, Remi," he whispered.

She stirred slightly but didn't waken.

When he woke, it was to the sound of the phone ringing. He opened his eyes, surprised to see sunlight through the window, his fog-filled brain trying to remember where they even were. Hotel, he realized as Remi blindly reached for her cell phone, then put it to her ear, her voice hoarse as she said, "Hello . . . ? Wait . . . What?"

"Who is it?" Sam asked.

"Miss Walsh." She propped herself on one elbow listening, then turned to Sam. "She knows where to find that circle with the symbols."

Thirty-five

"How could we have been so blind?" Remi asked.

"Easy," Sam said, hitting the gas harder. The long stretch of country road before them was empty, which made the getting there that much faster. He checked his mirrors, even though he was fairly confident that they weren't being followed. Why would they be? Fisk had gotten what he came for. "It was hidden in plain sight, and we weren't looking in the right place."

Or, rather, when they *were* looking, they didn't know what they were looking at. They did now, and he only hoped that they hadn't made a grave mistake by chasing after the false lead at the museum.

They made good time, and Sam relaxed slightly as he turned onto the dirt road that led to Grace Herbert-Miller's farm. As before, the chickens scattered as they pulled up in front, the geese honked, and the few goats that had wandered up to the split-rail fence bleated their arrival.

Sam and Remi walked across the graveled drive to the cottage, their footsteps crunching beneath them. No one was approaching this farm without being noticed, Sam thought as he knocked on the front door.

There was no answer.

He stepped back, glanced up at the chimney. No smoke. "Maybe we should have a look around. Make sure everything's okay."

Remi nodded but didn't comment. He knew she was thinking the same thing he was. Something had happened to the Herbert-Millers.

They walked around to the side, the brick path thick with moss, making it slippery in some areas. Diamond-paned windows reflected the sunlight as they passed, the white lace curtains inside preventing Sam from seeing in. Around back, a well-tended vegetable garden was fenced off, but a few chickens had found their way in, pecking for grubs between rows of carrots and celery.

Two steps led up to the back door, painted forest green, and Sam noticed fresh gouges in the wood near the lock as though someone had recently tried—or managed—to gain entry. "Not what I was hoping to see."

"Definitely not," Remi replied.

He was just reaching for the handle when he heard the loud chorus of chickens, geese, and goats out front, followed by the sound of a car's tires on the gravel drive.

"That," Remi said, "is one heck of an alarm. Maybe we should look into getting one ourselves."

"I'm not sure Zoltán could resist the temptation of fresh chicken for lunch."

"Good point."

They retraced their steps, Sam taking the lead. At the front of the house, he signaled for Remi to wait as he peaked around the corner. Grace Herbert-Miller was getting out of the front passenger seat of a late-model blue Fiat that had pulled up behind their rental car. Judging from her red and black flowered dress, black wool coat, and the small black hat with red buds decorating one side, she'd just returned from church.

What he didn't see was her husband.

Not wanting to alarm the woman, he waved Remi forward, and together they walked out to greet her as she said good-bye to the driver.

She saw them and smiled. "Mr. and Mrs. Fargo. I certainly wasn't expecting you today . . ."

"Mrs. Herbert-Miller," Sam said, smiling in return. "Sorry to drop in unexpectedly. I was hoping to have a word with you and your husband. Is he home?"

"Unfortunately, no. He left early this morning to visit his brother, who's been quite under the weather. But do come in."

She started for the front door. Sam reached out and touched her arm. "Actually," he said, "I'm a little worried that someone might have broken into your house."

Surprisingly, she laughed, then started forward again, pulling her keys from her purse. "I doubt that. We're so far out in the country, who would waste their time? It's not like there's anything of value in there."

"Even so, it looks like someone may have gone in through the back door."

Together, the three walked around to the back, and Sam pointed out the gouges in the wood by the lock.

"Oh dear."

He reached out, opened the door. "It was locked, I assume."

She nodded but said nothing.

"I'm sure they're gone," he said. "But, frankly, I'd rather not take any chances."

"It will take forever before the police arrive. We're so far out."

"I can check while you call from Remi's cell phone."

"Please."

He pushed the door open, listening a moment before entering. Behind him, he heard Remi saying, "Don't worry. He's very good at this."

Then Grace replying, "Why would anyone break in?"

The back door led into a mud porch, rain boots neatly placed on the floor beneath slickers that hung above them on the wall. He passed through the small kitchen, drawing his gun from its holster. Undoubtedly, they'd come for one thing only, and, sure enough, that's exactly what he found was missing. Regardless, he checked the rest of the house, then holstered his gun before joining the two outside. "They're gone."

Remi said, "The police are on their way."

Grace, her face pale, asked, "Is anything missing?"

"I'm afraid so," Sam said, leading them to the front of the house, then pointing to the wall near the front door.

She looked up at the empty space between the two paintings and below the family crest. "The shield? Why on earth would anyone steal that?"

"We believe," Sam said, "that the symbols on the shield boss were used in creating an old code to decipher a map."

"A shield boss? I'm not sure what that is."

"It's the round brass seal at the center of the shield. It's a decorative piece used to connect the handle to the shield itself."

She stared at the wall, then turned toward Sam. "You're certain it hides a code? It was just a pretty Celtic design."

"It's what was around the border of that design on the edge of the circle. Not the Celtic interlacing in the center."

"That's . . ." Grace put her hand on her chest, shaking her head. "I think I need to sit down."

"Here," Remi said, stepping forward and taking her by the arm, leading her into the parlor. "Can I get you something to drink?"

"Thank you, no. I'm fine."

Sam took a seat in the chair across from Grace. "You said something about two men who came by just before we did asking about the artifacts you'd inherited."

She nodded.

"Would you be able to describe them?"

"I think so . . . Do you think they . . . ?"

"If it's the same men we've run into, then yes."

"But why?"

"This code I mentioned. We're not sure, but it's possible the map it deciphers is to some treasure."

Her brows went up. "*That* old legend?"

"You've heard of it?"

"Well, yes. But it was just one of those stories told at bedtime. No one actually *believed*."

"This legend," Sam said, wanting to keep her on point before the police arrived. "Can you tell us the story?"

"It's been so long . . ." She leaned back in her seat, her glance straying to the empty space on the wall. "I couldn't have been more than ten or eleven. It was at my cousins' . . . They teased me because I was a girl, therefore couldn't be part of it."

"Part of what?"

"The protectorship. I remember my oldest cousin teasing me, saying, 'Don't you know anything? You have to be a boy. Girls can't be protectors.'" She gave a slight shrug. "Or something like that."

"Protector of what?"

"King John's Treasure, of course."

Thirty-six

Remi was certain she'd misunderstood Mrs. Herbert. "King John, as in King Richard's brother?"

"The same," Grace said.

"That's supposed to be quite the treasure," Remi said. "Over seventy million pounds, if I recall correctly."

"But the stories aren't real, are they? Why on earth would anyone believe them?"

"Hard to say," Sam said. "What exactly do you recall from the story you heard?"

"Well . . ." She looked at Sam. "They were more like fairy-tales than anything else. King John asked William the Marshal to hide the crown jewels to save England. The treasure being lost in the fens was all a ruse so that the young crown prince wouldn't be attacked. Or something along those lines. As I said, I never paid much attention. Just stories I heard my uncle telling my cousins when we were children."

"What happened to your cousins?" Remi asked.

"My older cousin died about ten years ago in a car accident, and his younger brother this last year of a heart attack."

"No other relatives?" Sam asked. "Anyone else who might have heard the stories?"

"Unfortunately, neither had children of their own, and my other cousin who inherited the estate up in Nottingham knows what I know." She furrowed her brows a moment, then brightened. "Actually, there is someone else. Madge Crowley, my cousin's ex-wife. I'd quite forgotten about her, mostly because I haven't spoken with her in years. Not since the divorce. She still sends round the occasional Christmas card. Lives in Norfolk somewhere. I could try to find her address if that will help."

"That would be great," Sam said.

She'd found the name and address, Madge Crowley in King's Lynn. The officer arrived and Sam gave a statement and the name of the investigator from Scotland Yard who was handling the case.

The officer looked up from his notebook. "You're sure this theft is related?" he asked Sam. "After all, you mentioned this Fisk found what he was looking for at the museum. Why come here?"

"To keep us from finding it."

The officer turned a dubious glance at the wall where the shield once hung. "So what's the value?" he asked Grace.

Remi piped in with, "Old relics. More museum pieces than anything else."

"History," the officer said. "Don't know why everyone gets so worked up about this stuff." He finished his notes, then stood. "I'll be in contact."

"Thank you," Grace replied, walking him to the door. She returned a moment later.

Remi said, "I hope you can forgive us for not being more up-front to begin with. We weren't exactly sure what we were dealing with."

"If I'd known any of this would happen," Grace said, "I'd have made sure the shield went to the museum with the rest of the items." She smiled, placing her hands on her hips. "I trust there's nothing more you need? I'd quite like to get back to my simple country life."

Sam and Remi stood at the obvious though polite dismissal, Sam telling Remi, "I can't think of anything. You?"

"Nothing," Remi said.

Grace saw them out. "If you do find anything, please send it to the museum. I've had enough excitement to last me a lifetime."

In the car, Sam handed Remi the address of Grace's cousin. "King's Lynn. That's a three-and-a-half-, four-hour drive. Makes for a long day."

"Don't know about you, but my schedule's wide open."

"Turns out, so is mine." He looked at his watch, then started the car. "Selma should be up by now. Give her a call. I'm hoping those photos we took of the shield boss can be enhanced."

Remi set the GPS directions, then called Selma, putting it on speakerphone. "We've had a few developments. First off, we're heading to King's Lynn, so we'll need a place to stay."

"I'll see to it. What about your suite at the Savoy?"

"We'll stay checked in. We shouldn't be gone that long." She related the information told to them by Grace about the family history and King John's Treasure.

"Right now," Sam said, "I'm more interested in the leather shield that Grace inherited. Particularly that metal circle in the middle. Any chance those photos we sent from our first visit are usable?"

"Let me pull them up."

While Selma was checking, Remi looked at the images they'd taken. One was washed out from the flash, the other too dark. But as before on that day she'd first seen the shield, her focus was drawn to the intricate Celtic knot engraved in the center of the shield boss. The small, rune-like symbols around the border had, on first glance, looked more like an extension of the Celtic design. Then again, maybe that was the reason for the interlacing in the center—to deflect attention from the ciphers decorating the border. Hide the cipher wheel in plain sight. After all, who would look for it on an old, battered leather shield?

"I have the photos here," Selma said.

"Check into it," Sam said. "We believe it's *the* cipher wheel."

There was a long pause. Then, "That certainly changes things."

"Unfortunately," Sam said, "it's now missing. And why we're calling. Can you enhance the photos enough to read the symbols around the border?"

"I'll have Pete and Wendy take a look. They're far more proficient with photo enhancement."

"Appreciate it," Sam said. "Let us know, ASAP."

It was well after four by the time they drove through the South Gates of King's Lynn to the city center. The low sun cast shadows across cobbled streets and centuries-old buildings, making it easy to imagine what it must have been like back when King's Lynn was still the most important seaport in Britain.

The Old World charm extended to Madge Crowley's neighborhood. Her address was one of several town houses that, according to the plaque on the building's brick front, had originally been a Benedictine priory built around 1100. Smoke swirled up from one of the chimney pots on the roof, and Remi hoped that meant she was home.

They walked through an archway into a cobbled courtyard. Sam knocked on the door. A stout, brown-haired woman about the same age as Grace opened it, her expression one of curiosity.

Sam smiled at her. "We're looking for Madge Crowley."

"I'm she."

"We were given your address by Grace Herbert-Miller. She said you might know something about an old family legend. Something to do with protecting King John's Treasure."

She was silent a moment as she searched Sam's face. And just when Remi thought she was going to send them off as the crackpots they surely must be, she stepped aside, waving them in. "I was wondering when someone might come around about that."

Thirty-seven

Might I inquire why you are asking about Grace and . . . ?" She smiled politely, waiting for them to fill in the blanks.

Remi deferred to Sam, who said, "Grace mentioned that you were familiar with the family legend. Regarding King John."

"I was. The bigger question is, why are you?"

"Someone broke into Grace's house and stole an heirloom she'd recently inherited. We believe it's connected to this legend."

"To the treasure, you mean?"

"Yes," Sam said.

Her expression remained neutral as she studied them both. "Perhaps if you explained why it is that *you're* interested, I might be more inclined to help."

"We're treasure hunters," Sam said.

"Treasure hunters?" she repeated in a disapproving voice.

"Not for profit," Remi said. "We either donate the proceeds

to charity or return what we find to the rightful owner. There's plenty of information about us on the Internet. What we do and the charities we support."

"Anyone can create a web page, Mrs. Fargo. How do I know I can trust you?"

"Because—" Remi realized right then she had nothing. "Just our word. I'm sorry, but that's all we have."

The woman was quiet a moment as she studied the two of them. "I like to think I'm a good judge of character. I hope you don't prove me wrong. What is it you need to know?"

Sam answered. "Anything at all you can remember that has to do with the Herbert legacy that might lead to the treasure. Or, at the very least, information on it."

"It might take me a moment to find it if you don't mind waiting." She excused herself, went up the stairs, and returned a few minutes later with a manila envelope that she handed to Sam.

"A syllabus?" Sam said as she sat across from them.

"And a detailed outline to a book I planned to write on it. I'm a librarian. We have a monthly history group that meets at the library where I work. Several years ago, I'd presented my research to the group, thinking it might be fun to look into. Unfortunately, one of the members, Nigel Ridgewell, a former history and linguist professor at the local college, refused to entertain what he condescendingly called my attempt at *revisionist* history. He quit in a huff."

"Too bad," Remi said. "When you think about it, it's no more revisionist than any of the other legends about the king's treasure."

"Exactly what I thought," Madge replied. "So imagine my

surprise when I later discovered that Nigel had used *my* work and self-published a book on it, claiming it for his own. And if that wasn't bad enough, he presented my syllabus to one of his classes as the course outline. Unfortunately, as soon as it got out, he lost his job at the college. I feel bad about that, but I wasn't about to let him steal my work."

"Understandable," Sam said.

"After he lost his teaching position, he took a job as a tour guide. I heard from one of the other members of our group that he was using *my* information in his dialogue during his walking tours, citing it as one of the *many* legends of what happened to the treasure."

"People do like legends," Remi said.

"That they do. I thought about asking him to stop, but how many times can you kick a man when he's down? He was young and impetuous."

Sam looked up from the papers. "Can you give us the abbreviated version of what's in here?"

"Quite simply, the Herberts are descended from William the Marshal, First Earl of Pembroke. Pembroke was entrusted to hide the Royal Treasure of King John in order to protect the crown prince from invaders looking to enrich their coffers. The story about the treasure being lost in the fens during the king's travels was a concoction to keep others from finding out what really happened to it."

Sam handed the papers to Remi, then asked, "And what do you think happened to it?"

"It's all right there. Hidden by William Pembroke, with each of his chosen descendants protecting the secret. Pembroke's sons died without issue and so the secret passed on through his daughter, Maud de Braose, who passed it on to her son, Edmund Mortimer, who apparently made a copy of this key and gave one to his legitimate son, Roger de Mortimer, and one to his illegitimate son, Sir Edmund Herbert—which turned out to be a wise move. Mortimer's legitimate son ended up having an affair with Queen Isabella and was executed as a result." She gave a half smile as she leaned back in her chair. "Perhaps Mortimer knew his children and realized his illegitimate child was far more loyal. What it doesn't tell you is *where* the treasure is. Only the history of it after it left Pembroke's hands."

Remi closed the envelope. "If you don't mind, could we borrow this? We would copy and return it."

"No need. As much as I wanted to follow up, it wasn't my story to tell. It belongs to my ex-husband, Henry McGregor, and his cousin, Grace, neither of who have any interest in the subject. There it has sat for years and years. It's yours. And clearly Grace has given you her blessing or she wouldn't have sent you here to begin with. The only thing I ask is that you let me know what you find."

They thanked her and left. In the car, Remi slid the papers from the envelope. "There's a *lot* of information here."

Sam glanced over. "I didn't see anything that stood out."

"Would have been nice if there was an actual *copy* of the cipher wheel." She flipped through the pages. "We need to get this to Selma. The more eyes on this, the better."

Once at the hotel Selma had found for them, they scanned and emailed the pages to her, after which they each took a stack and started looking over what they had.

Remi was reading over the time line that Madge had prepared. "If Edmund Mortimer divided the secret between his sons, that would seem to be a logical point where one of the cipher wheels was stolen."

Sam looked up from his pages. "Do you recall your notes from the display at the museum on Mortimer's illegitimate son?"

"I do."

"And the notes on the onetime-lover-turned-pirate of the king? Hugh Despenser."

Remi smiled. "And his illegitimate son, Bridgeman."

"Who could forget Avery's ancestor?" Sam eyed the paper in front of him. "Wasn't there something about the king being angry with the Mortimers due to something being stolen by Despenser?"

"That's got to be it," Remi said. "Despenser stole one copy of the cipher wheel, which somehow ended up in the bottom of the ocean several hundred years later."

"Which explains Avery's obsession with trying to get it back."

"*Part* of his obsession, you mean. I'm sure the other part has to do with finding the treasure for himself."

"Good point." He straightened the stack of papers, then returned them to the envelope. "Let's hope we locate it before he does."

Selma skyped them early the next morning. She was seated at her office desk. "Wendy and Pete were able to make some headway on enhancing the photos, and Lazlo's working on deciphering the map as we speak." She held up the improved copy of the photo, pointing to the side of it that was still too dark to make out clearly. "Not the best lighting, even with the enhancement. And there are a few symbols worn too smooth to read. We're not quite sure what they are."

"Bottom line . . . ?" Remi asked.

"Lazlo has enough to work with, but something could be lost in the translation."

Lazlo leaned into view. "Quite right. But I'm hopeful it's nothing too drastic. Like sending you to South America when you need to go to North America."

Sam and Remi looked at each other, then the tablet screen. Sam said, "We're headed to South America?"

"No," Lazlo said. "I was merely giving you an example of what could go wrong with a few letters missing. South versus North. That sort of thing."

"So where *are* we going?" Remi asked.

"Good question," he said. "If Miss Crowley's information is accurate—much is dependent on her research, and it seems that was done as a result of childhood tales, never a—"

"We get it," Sam said.

"Right-o. Anyway, it looks as though the person you need to contact next is Nigel Ridgewell."

"Ridgewell?" Sam said. "You're sure?"

"Quite. He's the resident expert in Old English. Former professor. We'll need his help to translate what I've deciphered on the map—unless, of course, you want to wait until we find another expert."

"This should be interesting," Sam said. "He happens to be the person who stole Madge Crowley's research."

Thirty-eight

olin Fisk hid his shock when he saw Alexandra Avery standing in the middle of his hotel lobby. He gave her a bland smile as he approached. "Mrs. Avery," he said. "I had no idea you were in London."

"I'm sure you didn't," she replied, her expression as neutral as his. "I like surprises, though. Don't you?"

"What are you doing here?"

"I expect the same thing you are. Searching for this mysterious treasure that my husband's so obsessed with. Any luck so far?"

"We're making progress."

"Hmm. And the Fargos? They're not getting in your way?"

"Not in the least." The fact she knew about the Fargos bothered him, although he told himself he shouldn't be surprised. During the time he'd been employed by Charles Avery, he'd come to realize that the man's wife wasn't quite the inept socialite that

Charles had made her out to be. "Does Mr. Avery know you're here?"

She laughed. "Hardly. The last thing I need is to have him looking over my shoulder. Actually, I've come to head you off. Include me in the hunt or expect that the funds my husband is using to finance your venture will suddenly disappear." She smiled sweetly. "I'm sure he mentioned that all his assets are frozen?"

"He did."

"He may have neglected to inform you that my forensic accountant has a *very* good lead on this income that Charles seems to be tapping into to pay your salary. Especially since it's coming from *my* hidden account. And *technically*, since I'm funding this venture, I'm willing to overlook it for now. That is, if you're willing to overlook my being here." Again, that sweet smile.

Fisk held out his hand. "Welcome to the party."

She shook hands with him. "So glad you could see it my way. So . . . what's next on your agenda?"

"Why don't we discuss this over a drink," he said. The interruption would give him time to gather his thoughts, because the last thing he needed or wanted was a socialite like Alexandra Avery underfoot.

"Lead the way."

"Exactly where are you staying?" he asked once they were seated at a table.

"Well, here, of course. But only for one night. Tomorrow we're off to King's Lynn."

Fisk stared in shock.

"That *is* where you're headed next?"

"How did you know?"

This time, her smile wasn't so innocent. "I pay good money to stay informed, Mr. Fisk. Something I learned from my husband." She reached out, gave his hand a pat. "No need to trouble yourself with such trivial details about where I get my information. I vote we compare plans. Maybe we'll find that we can actually be of use to each other."

An interesting thought. Maybe there *was* a way to capitalize on her presence. Ivan and Jak weren't exactly the sharpest pair. Another set of eyes on them might be what he needed to finally get ahead of the Fargos.

The more he thought about it, the more he liked the idea. Alexandra Avery was far more intelligent than Charles had ever given her credit for. Clearly, she was tapping into her husband's computer or phone. Or maybe she had his office bugged. How else would she have known about their plans? And while that worried him, there were ways to keep her in line. Besides, it wasn't like he had to keep Charles in the loop about her actions. At least not now.

This could actually work . . .

Thirty-nine

The following afternoon, Sam and Remi left their car at the car park, then walked to the town center along Purfleet Quay, to meet with Nigel Ridgewell at the information center where he worked. That was located in the Custom House, a stone building with a steep-pitched tile roof with dormers, crowned by a wooden bell tower.

Several tourists gathered outside the building, some of them snapping photos of the river. At the head of the group, a lanky, brown-haired man in his late thirties looked up, saw them, and asked, "Here for the tour? You can still buy tickets inside."

Sam said, "We're looking for Nigel Ridgewell."

"I'm Nigel." He said something to the group, then walked toward them. "You must be the Fargos."

Sam eyed the people waiting in front of the tourist center. "Maybe I got the time wrong. I was under the impression you asked us to meet here."

"Sorry about that. I was supposed to have the rest of the afternoon off, but one of the other guides called in. Any chance we can meet later this evening?"

"Shouldn't be a problem," Sam said. "What time?"

"Maybe around six? That'll give me a short break after my last tour before we meet up. Of course, you're welcome to come along. Or save yourself five pounds, pick up a map inside, and use that for your own tour."

"Thanks," Sam said. "Maybe we'll take a look around."

Nigel returned to his tour group. "If you'll follow me, we'll get started." He led them around the corner, saying, "King's Lynn, one of the most important seaports in the Middle Ages, used to be known as Bishop's Lynn . . ."

"He seems nice enough," Remi said.

Except for that theft part. Knowing the guy stole Madge Crowley's papers bothered him. He gave a noncommittal response as he held the door open for Remi so that they could look over the brochures that highlighted the various tours. Sam was opening the maritime history tour pamphlet when Remi said, "This one sounds intriguing. 'The Darker Side of Lynn. Tales of murder, treason, hangings, and witchcraft.'" But then she returned it to the rack. "Never mind. They only offer it in the summer."

He handed her his brochure. "Then the maritime walk wins by default."

Instead of following the guided tour as mapped out, they used it to look up points of interest as they walked through the historic sections of King's Lynn. Remi used her cell phone to take a couple of photos of the Town Hall, a stunning, checkerboard-fronted building. They turned down a quaint, cobbled street, with its fifteenth-century brick-and-timber houses. About midway down Nelson Street, Remi pointed to a placard posted on an arched entrance to a narrow street beyond. "Devil's Alley. I'd love to know the story behind that."

Sam tried to find a reference to it in his brochure. "Not here."

"Maybe it's part of the Dark Side tour. The witches and murderers."

They peered beneath the arched entrance to the alley just as a woman emerged, her gnarled hand holding on tight to a cane. Dressed head to toe in black, her shoulders stooped from age, she stopped when she saw them looking at the sign. She pointed at it with her cane. "He was there."

"The Devil?" Remi asked.

"Aye. Came in on a ship one day. But a vicar stopped him with a prayer and holy water. The Devil stamped his foot and left his print in the alley. Or so they say."

Remi loved old legends. "Let's go take a look."

Sam thanked the woman and was about to follow Remi into the alley when the woman said, "Watch out for Black Shuck."

"Black what?" Sam asked.

"Shuck. The red-eyed Hound from Hell. Comes out after dark, it does. Heard tell it's here e'en now. With the Devil." She tottered off, planting her cane with each step, muttering to herself.

Sam glanced back at Remi, who was busy searching the cobblestones for some sign of the Devil's footprint. The sun, well past its zenith, cast long shadows across part of the cobbled lane, accentuating every lump and bump, making it look as if an entire herd of cloven-hoofed creatures had left their mark.

"See anything?" he asked.

"No." She took a photo of the alley anyway, and they continued on through, past the buildings, to a bordered walkway between two empty lots, following it until they reached the water at the South Quay. With time to kill, they strolled along the water's edge until they reached Marriott's Warehouse, where they stopped for a drink. Sam was always up for a Guinness, and they sat at a table overlooking the Great River Ouse. As the late afternoon turned to evening, a light fog swept in from the river, obscuring their view. When it was nearly time to meet their guide, they returned to the Custom House.

Nigel wasn't there when they arrived and so they waited out front, the fog thickening as the evening wore on. Sam looked at his watch, saw Nigel was twenty minutes late. He called Selma, who gave him Nigel's cell phone number. He left a voice mail saying they were waiting at the Custom House. After ten more minutes, he was about to suggest they call it a night when a figure emerged from the mist, walking toward them. Not Nigel.

"Can I help you?" the man asked.

"We're waiting for Nigel Ridgeway."

"Right. He was a bit late on his last tour. He *did* mention he was meeting someone back here, if that helps."

"Thanks," Sam said as the man unlocked the door and let himself into the building.

Remi wrapped her arms close about her. "I hope he gets here soon. It's getting cold out."

Sam pulled her close. A few minutes later, the same man stepped out, locking the office door behind him. He nodded at Sam and Remi as he left.

"Excuse me," Sam said, stopping him. "Do you know which tour he was on last?"

"Pretty sure it was the maritime. That ends on South Quay in front of Marriott's Warehouse. You might check there. A lot of the tourists stop after for dinner."

"Thanks."

"We were just there."

"Let's go back and check," Sam told Remi. "Maybe someone there will know if he actually made it that far."

"And if he didn't?"

"We start looking for him."

By the time they reached the warehouse café, visibility had lessened considerably. The gentle lapping of water on the quay quickened with an approaching boat, invisible in the fog. Diffused auras of light encompassed the street lamps, the glow barely reaching the ground.

They stepped into the café, looking around, but didn't see Nigel. The hostess who'd seated them earlier smiled. "Forget something?"

"Looking for someone," Sam said. "Any chance you're familiar with a tour guide named Nigel Ridgeway?"

"I am, but I haven't seen him tonight. He did have a tour, though. I seated some of the guests." She nodded toward a table near the window where two couples sat, drinking wine. Sam thanked her, then took out his cell phone, telling Remi, "I'll try calling him again."

"I'll check with them," Remi said, walking toward the table.

Sam stepped outside the restaurant and hit redial. The phone rang several times, then someone answered, "Yeah?"

"Mr. Ridgewell?"

"Who—who is this?"

"Sam Fargo. We were supposed to meet. Where are you?"

Several seconds of silence, then, "The silos . . . I'm—I think I've been robbed."

Nigel's voice sounded groggy to Sam, and when he tried to ask *where* these silos were, he heard a soft beep as the phone disconnected. Sam returned inside the restaurant and saw Remi talking to the diners who'd been on Nigel's tour. He started toward her but stopped when he saw the hostess returning to her station. "Where would I find the silos?" he asked her.

"Silos? They're gone."

"Gone?"

"Demolished several years back. Why?"

"If someone said they were at the silos, where would that be?"

"Just down the road." She pointed south. "Can't miss it. The lots are still empty."

He realized she was talking about the vacant lots this side of Devil's Alley. Remi returned just then, and Sam drew her outside. "Something's happened to Nigel," he said as they walked in the direction indicated. "He said he was robbed."

"Has he called the police?"

"Not sure. You find out anything?"

"Not much. He was here but took off in a hurry."

Sam took Remi's arm as he quickened his pace, almost missing the pathway due to the thick fog. He stopped, listened, hearing nothing but the rhythmic splashing of water.

"What are we doing here?" Remi whispered.

"He said he was at the silos."

"There aren't any silos here."

"There used to be." He took her hand and led her down the path. Unfortunately, they couldn't see more than a few yards in front and he stopped. "Nigel?"

No answer.

Sam turned at the sound of footsteps but couldn't see anyone in the thick fog. Whoever it was continued on around the corner, their footsteps fading in the distance.

"Listen," Remi said. "I think I hear something."

Sam heard it, too. Coming from somewhere to their left in the lot. "Wait here," he said, then climbed over the cable barrier that marked the pedestrian path. He took out his phone, turned on the flashlight. Sparse, long weeds and grasses grew on the rocky soil, looking undisturbed as far as he could see. But as he walked a bit farther, he noticed the grass and weeds were trampled, the rocky soil disturbed. Drag marks, he realized. He followed along, reaching a thick growth of shrubs near the adjoining building. Something rattled the branches down low.

He leaned down, shined his flashlight into the bushes, and saw Nigel, blinking against the light. "I found him!"

Nigel struggled to sit, looking confused. He touched the back of his head, then winced.

"You okay?" Sam asked as Remi joined them.

"I think so. Did we just talk?"

"On the phone."

"Right."

Sam held his hand out, and Nigel grabbed on, allowing Sam to help him to his feet. "Think you can walk?"

"Yes." He took a step, then swayed.

Remi reached out at the same time Sam did. "Maybe we should call an ambulance," she said.

"No. I'm fine. Just give me a moment."

"She's right," Sam said. "You need to get checked out."

Nigel smiled, as if to prove he was fine. "What I need is a good stiff drink."

Sam helped him navigate the uneven terrain to the pedestrian path while Remi stood guard on the other side. As far as Sam could tell, he didn't look too injured. No blood, just dirt, leaves, and damp hair from being out in the fog.

After they climbed over the cable barrier, Nigel brushed some of the debris from his gray suit, looking somewhat dazed.

Remi cocked her head at him. "Are you sure you're okay?"

"Going to have quite the headache for a while," he said.

"What happened?" Sam asked.

"Not sure. I ended my tour at the warehouse and was going back to meet up with you. Someone came up and told me there were some shady types on South Quay, so I figured I'd take a shortcut through the alley to avoid them. Don't think I got much farther than this when someone whacked me from behind."

"Sounds like a robbery," Sam said.

He patted his pockets, then gave a slight laugh. "Got my wallet. They're going to be disappointed. Not sure I had more than five pounds on me."

Sam was about to suggest they call the police when he heard a low growl coming from the direction of the quay. The other two heard it as well, and they all turned as a large, dark dog appeared like some apparition in the mist. It stood there, its head low, its teeth bared as it growled.

Sam put his arm out, moving Remi behind him.

Together, the three backed down the path, Sam keeping an eye not only on the dog but on the silhouette of the broad-shouldered man that appeared behind it.

Forty

R emi?" Sam said quietly. "Do you have—"

She handed him a small canister of pepper spray.

"Run," he said.

Remi and Nigel turned and ran. Sam aimed the canister, but the dog, as though sensing trouble, backed off. Instead, Sam sprayed a shot toward the man, then ran after the others, not waiting to see if he hit his mark. The dog started barking just before Sam heard the sound of heavy footfalls as someone chased after them. Either he missed the dog handler or the man had an accomplice.

Remi and Nigel were up ahead, racing beneath the same arch they'd gone under earlier in the day, Devil's Alley.

Aptly named, Sam thought, as he caught up to his wife. He glanced back but couldn't see anyone in the fog.

"This way," Nigel said, turning to the right. "The police station isn't that far."

In less than five minutes, they were pushing through the door of the police station, then reporting the attack. The officer on duty took Nigel back to an interview room while Sam and Remi waited in the lobby.

Remi took a seat in one of the chairs. "A good thing we happened along when we did."

Sam paced the room, keeping an eye out the door. "What are the chances the one man we're waiting to see is robbed?"

"Too much of a coincidence."

"After everything that's happened to us so far? Definitely." He stopped and looked at her. "That whole Black Shuck story from Devil's Alley . . ."

"You think Fisk or Avery wrangled some old lady to stop and tell us some legend about the Devil's dog just to set up this whole robbery? *That* part could be coincidence. But the robbery . . ."

"What good does robbing him do?"

"Stop him from talking to us."

Remi gave a tired sigh. "Who knew associating with us could be so hazardous?"

Eventually the officer came out and took a statement from Sam and Remi as well. When Sam mentioned the man with the dog, the officer shook his head. "Black Shuck and the Devil, right? Can't tell you how many complaints we have anytime anyone walks their dogs on the quay. Last year, it was Rupert Middlefield walking his mastiff. Seemed to think it was funny. Lucky he doesn't get shot, I say." The officer closed his notebook and gave a bland smile. "If there's nothing else?"

They thanked him for his time and left. Outside, after receiving assurances that Nigel did not need medical assistance, Sam offered to buy him that stiff drink. They ended up at a nearby pub, finding a fairly quiet corner to sit and talk.

Sam waited until their drinks were served before moving on to the real purpose of their visit. "About that translation. Have you had a chance to take a look?"

"I have," Nigel said, placing his scotch on the table, then reaching into his inside suit coat pocket. A worried look came over his face and he checked another pocket, then stood, reaching into his pants pockets. "Maybe my wallet wasn't the only thing taken."

Sam and Remi exchanged glances. No doubt in Sam's mind who was behind Nigel's attack. "Were you contacted by anyone else about translating Old English phrases?"

"How did you know?"

"A guess," Sam said. "It's likely the robbery was a cover-up to get to your notebook."

"But it wouldn't take me that long to translate it again. The original text is on the email that Lazlo sent. So why steal it to begin with?"

"Maybe to keep us from getting it."

Remi asked, "Do you remember any of it offhand? The translation?"

"Something about castles, rocks, holes . . . I can't remember exactly what it was. Some of it didn't make any sense. But it seemed harmless enough." He shrugged. "Definitely not something I'd expect to be robbed for. So what exactly is going on? Why me?"

"Are you familiar with Madge Crowley's alternative history on King John's Treasure?"

Nigel reached for his drink, sipped it, then finally met Sam's gaze. "Not my finest moment, taking her papers. Put it this way. I was young and stupid and very arrogant. But, short answer, yes. What's that have to do with what happened to me?"

"Someone else we know believes this alternative history. Enough to go after anyone who has what they want or who gets in their way."

"I'm sorry. You're saying that the translation I was asked to do by your friend—no. That's ridiculous. Madge's theory, though clever, is all wrong. The treasure was lost in the wash. Everyone knows it."

"And what if everyone was wrong?" Remi asked. "What if it was really out there? Hidden somewhere on purpose?"

"That's . . . You can't be serious." He waited for Remi to say something, deny it, and, when she didn't, he turned to Sam. "King John's Treasure?"

Sam nodded. "Bottom line, we have no idea if it's out there. But there seems to be enough evidence on this alternative history that makes it worth looking into. And it seems that your translation of the Old English phrases found on this map could be of value to our search."

The waitress returned, asking if they needed anything. Nigel held up his near-empty glass, and Sam ordered another round for the table. When she left, Sam said, "We'll understand if you'd rather not involve yourself. Obviously, we're dealing with some unsavory characters. But this may be the opportunity of a lifetime."

"*May* be?" Nigel said. "It *is* the opportunity of a lifetime. I'm in. What, exactly, do you need from me?"

"To start with," Sam said, "the translation of what Lazlo sent."

"If you have some paper, I have the original email on my mobile. There were a few words I couldn't get, but several of them I knew right off." He pulled his cell phone from his pocket and started scrolling through his messages while Remi looked through her purse for paper. He glanced up suddenly. "One question. I'm not the only expert in Old English. Definitely not the foremost. And given my history with Madge, what made you pick me?"

Remi handed him pen and paper. "Luck of the draw, mostly. You happened to be in the area."

It didn't take him long. The passage that Lazlo had sent was short. "Something to keep in mind," Nigel said, "is that there's plenty of room for error. We seem to be working with a mix of Old English and Middle English. Spelling varied over the centuries, as did the meanings of words and the order in which they were written. What I'm trying to say is, hand this to someone else, they may come up with something different." He slid the paper across the table toward Sam. "These are the words. The first three are pretty simple. Anyone with an Internet connection could've looked them up and translated them."

Sam read the list. The first three words translated to *hole* or *well*, *castle*, *rock* or *hill*. "No idea about these?" Sam asked, not able to make anything out of them himself. *Wul hol* and *wul eshea od* . . .

"That's the part I had difficulty with. Sorry. No idea."

Remi studied the list for a moment. "So we have a few of the words. Now what?"

"Context," Nigel said, "is everything. It might help to know where they originated, and when they were written, especially regarding any word that might have a dual meaning. Like that last one which could be *rock* or *hill*."

Remi returned the list to Sam, who said, "They were found on an old map that we believe dates from 1696. But the original wording was probably transcribed from something written around the time of King John's death."

Nigel's brows went up. "You're saying *this* list is a key to the missing treasure? That it's here in King's Lynn?"

"That, I don't know. It's taken from a coded message that's not completely deciphered."

Nigel held out his hand. "May I have another look?"

Sam handed the list to him.

He studied it as the waitress brought their drinks. When she left, he said, "When it comes right down to it, any one of these words could be describing a hiding place. The problem arises in narrowing down a location—assuming they've been properly translated."

"Anything around here fit?" Remi asked.

"Yes. But there's nothing around here that hasn't been searched a million times by others looking for the same thing."

"Maybe so," Sam said. "But they're not us. So what's your take on locations?"

"*Hole* or *well* could be a description of King John's Hole. That's about halfway between here and Long Sutton. And, if true, buried beneath about thirty feet of silt. Except—"

"Except what?" Sam asked when Nigel didn't continue.

"Except why have these other indicators with it? *Castle* and *hill*, for instance? Maybe a *well in a castle*? Or a *castle hill*? There are plenty of those about."

"Anything dating from that era in the general vicinity?"

"Castle Rising."

"Looks like we have a bit of exploring to do in the morning."

Remi raised her glass in a toast. "Here's to good hunting."

Forty-one

The following morning, Sam and Remi decided against Castle Acre, which didn't seem to have any connection to King John or the treasure, and settled on Castle Rising. It was the closest out of the three sites Nigel had suggested and had a connection to Queen Isabella. She'd lived there—or was banished there—after her son, Edward III, deposed Isabella and her lover, Roger Mortimer, who had taken control of the throne after Edward's father abdicated. There was even a rumor of a hidden tunnel that Isabella used during her banishment to get in and out of the castle unseen. That, Sam and Remi decided, was definitely worth looking into.

When they called Lazlo and Selma to discuss the possible options, Lazlo felt it was premature to visit anywhere since he hadn't finished with the deciphering of the passage from the map. "I'm working at a disadvantage—what, with the poor photo quality and the worn symbols on the cipher wheel."

"We can't wait forever," Sam said.

"And," Remi added, "we need to stay ahead of Charles Avery."

"Forget them," Lazlo said. "Do you know how many castle ruins there are in Great Britain? You'll be old and gray by the time you finish searching each one."

"Remi's right," Sam said. "Avery and Fisk stole Nigel's notebook with the Old English translations, which means they're looking at the same things we are."

"This area," Remi said, "was where the treasure was last seen. And it does mention something about a castle, so why not there? Maybe we'll find that key piece of information that points us in the right direction."

"I suppose it can't hurt to look," Lazlo replied. "I'll keep working and let you know if anything changes."

He put Selma back on the line, and Sam turned off the speaker, then gave the phone to Remi, who wanted to ask about Bree. When she finished the call, she seemed happy.

"Good news?" Sam asked.

"I think so. No further issues, and Bree seems to be doing well. Selma thinks Bree should stay with them until this is over."

"Probably a good idea. I wouldn't put it past Avery to try to use her and her cousin again."

A knock at their hotel door alerted them to Nigel's arrival. Although they'd been reluctant to include him after last night's robbery, he'd insisted on helping and declared he was well aware of the danger.

Sam drove while Nigel gave directions. Remi was content to ride in the back, taking in the countryside, as they left King's Lynn and drove through the woods. The fog from last night, though thinner, still hung in the air, and Sam turned on the wipers, clearing the windshield.

Nearly a dozen other cars were in the car park when Sam pulled in. He stopped as a few children darted out from between the cars, too eager to wait for their parents before exploring Castle Rising. He pulled into the first space and grabbed his backpack from the trunk.

"Impressive," Remi said as they walked across the lot toward the castle grounds. The mist-filled sky shimmered with silver light as the sun broke through, highlighting the harsh edges of the castle ruins that towered over them. She took out her cell phone and took a photo. "Makes me wish I'd brought a real camera."

The three stood there for a moment, admiring the stone structure, before walking in to start their self-guided tour. Castle Rising was built in the twelfth century, according to the literature. Set on over twelve acres, the stone keep looked like a medieval fortress but had originally been built as an extravagant hunting lodge.

Unfortunately, after spending the next hour walking around, searching every corner, Sam realized that Lazlo was right—at least about this castle. They were wasting their time. "Anywhere else we should be looking?" he asked Nigel as they walked down the stone stairs to the castle grounds.

"The only other place, off the top of my head, is King John's Hole. And that's not an easy place to search."

"Why not?" Sam asked. "We've got time to kill."

"Besides the centuries of silt covering it? No one knows quite where it is. Only a general idea. And, trust me, many have looked."

Nigel, however, wasn't willing to give up on Castle Rising, and when he spotted a fellow tour guide that he knew, he decided to ask about the secret tunnel that Queen Isabella might have used. "He was in our Historical Society . . . Maybe he knows something we don't. Be right back."

Sam and Remi waited for him near the walkway to the car park, not expecting that Nigel would gain any information they didn't already know. As far as Sam could tell, there was nothing here that indicated the ruins were hiding anything more than an old keep.

"That was a bust," Sam said.

He glanced out to the car park, surprised at the number of cars and school buses that now filled it. A blue BMW cruised through the lot, searching for a parking space, catching Sam's attention when a black, boxy head of a massive dog popped up in the backseat. As the vehicle turned into the next row, then pulled into a space, Sam recognized the driver—the white butterfly bandage on his forehead further proof. Right where Ivan was bleeding from the night at the museum. "That's Ivan driving."

"You're sure?" Remi asked.

He pulled Remi back, hoping they hadn't been noticed. "Positive. Jak's riding shotgun. And that dog that we thought was about to attack us last night? I'll lay odds it's in the backseat."

"So much for the legend of Black Shuck," Remi said as Jak hooked a leash to the collar of a dog that if any dog looked like it belonged to the Devil, this one fit the bill.

"I don't see Fisk." No sooner had the words left his mouth than another vehicle, a black Mercedes coming from the opposite direction, stopped behind Ivan's car. Fisk was at the wheel. The passenger door opened, and a blond woman wearing a white parka got out, walking over to Ivan's car as Fisk pulled away. Interesting that Fisk and his crew ended up at this location. Especially considering that he and Remi were dismissing the castle as a possible lead. "What's here that we don't know about?" Sam asked.

"Maybe that rumored tunnel Queen Isabella used is real."

"We better find Nigel."

Remi started to follow him, then stopped, taking a photo of Ivan, Jak, and the woman. "Maybe Selma can find out who she is." As they hurried back toward the tour guide's post, Remi tried to send the photo. "No signal."

"Where is he?" Sam asked, looking around.

Remi looked up from her phone. "He was talking to his friend right there."

But both Nigel and his friend were gone.

Sam took the binoculars from his backpack, searching the grounds. "I don't see him," he said, sweeping his binoculars up the stairs of the castle wall. "This many people and cars, they could be anywhere."

"Maybe we should go up. Get a better view."

"Worth a try," Sam said. They weaved their way through a group of schoolkids coming down the stairs as they went up. On the next level, Sam looked down and saw Ivan talking to someone who looked like a guide, but no sign of Nigel or his friend. "Wish I could read lips. It'd be nice to know what they're talking about."

Remi moved beside Sam. "They've got to be here for a reason. What are we missing?"

"Considering this place made our short list of possible loca-tions, it certainly could've made theirs."

Sam watched a minute longer. Whatever the conversation was, Ivan was in a hurry to leave. He turned and walked quickly in the other direction. "He found out something."

"There's Nigel!" Remi said, pointing down below.

He peered through the binoculars, his relief at finding Nigel short-lived when he realized that Jak and the blond woman were heading straight toward him.

Forty-two

Alexandra Avery looked up to see the tour guide they'd robbed the night before standing just a few yards in front of them. He, at least, didn't appear to see them. "How on earth did *he* get here?"

Jak handed the dog's leash to Alexandra, then drew his gun. "I'll take care of him."

She reached up and pushed his arm down. "Put that away," she said. "At the very least, keep it out of sight. This place is crawling with tourists, never mind we're in Great Britain. They don't do guns here."

"You realize who that is?" Jak asked.

"Of course I do. What you should be asking yourself is *why* he's here." She glanced over at Ivan, glad to see that he'd not over-reacted. Instead, his hand was in his pocket, undoubtedly gripping his handgun. "What'd you find out?"

"No tunnels here," Ivan said.

She turned her attention back to the tour guide. Nigel something or other. Ridgewell. That was it. She smiled at him as she approached. "Mr. Ridgewell. What a surprise."

He stopped in front of her, looking anything but pleased. "You were on my tour last night."

"And found it fascinating. I take it you work here as well?"

"Where is it?"

"Where is what?"

"My notebook."

"I have no idea what you're talking about."

"You, or maybe one of these two," he said, nodding at Jak and Ivan, "stole it."

"I assure you, I had *nothing* to do with it."

"You were asking questions about Old English on my tour. And now here. Why?"

"Sightseeing." She didn't like the way he was grilling her. People were starting to stare. A large group of tourists were heading straight toward them. The place was becoming entirely too crowded. "You, of all people, should know that."

"Were you following me?"

Ivan stepped forward, shoved his pocketed gun in Nigel's side. "I've had enough of your questions."

Great. So much for believing he was the cooler head, Alexandra thought.

She began to wonder if Fisk didn't have his own designs on the treasure. And wouldn't that be ironic? Of course, if that was the case, she was going to have to watch her step.

At this point, it didn't matter. What did was making sure someone didn't call the police. With these two, and their happy trigger fingers, that would be disastrous. She placed her hand on Ivan's arm. "Let's keep it low-key. Maybe take it somewhere else where we don't have the entire countryside acting as witnesses."

He nodded, then leaned in close to Nigel. "My suggestion? If you walk very slowly to the car park, I promise not to pull the trigger."

Ten seconds later, they were jostled by a dozen tourists, trying to squeeze past them. One woman, bundled up like an eskimo, ran straight into Nigel, mumbling an apology as she hurried past. If they weren't careful, they'd lose him in the next group that was headed their way, and so Alexandra handed Jak the dog's leash, then moved to Nigel's other side, linking her arm through his. "Best to cooperate. These two are loose cannons, and I can't guarantee your safety."

The man swallowed, his face turning pale, as he suddenly realized the danger he'd stumbled into. "I won't tell anyone. Just let me go."

"Actually," she said, "we were coming to see you next. But since you've saved us the trouble, this works out fine." She smiled at him, hoping to get him to relax, at least until they were at the car. "I promise you won't be hurt if you come along quietly. We need a few more translations that have come up."

Forty-three

The moment Remi and Sam had seen the blond woman confront Nigel, and then Jak draw a gun on him, they had very little time to put a plan into action.

Remi, armed with a Sig P938, tucked her hair beneath the hood of her jacket, put on her oversized sunglasses, then took Sam's cell phone and hurried down the stairs after them, passed them, and then doubled back until she reached the walkway to the car park. Ivan, Jak, the woman, and Nigel were just a few yards in front of her when she caught up with them.

The four were walking toward her, keeping tight, Ivan on one side of Nigel, the blond woman on the other side. Jak and the dog brought up the rear. Suddenly, the dog pulled to one side and started growling at her. Remi gripped the handgun, ready to draw it from her pocket, when she heard the woman order, "Get that dog under control. That thing's a nuisance. We don't have time for this."

Remi heard the snap of the chain on the dog's collar as Jak yanked the leash, forcing the dog to heel. As they continued on toward the car park, she hung back, waiting until there was enough distance before she followed. She stood behind a tour bus, peering around it to where the blue BMW was parked. They were looking around to see if anyone was watching before forcing Nigel into the trunk of their car. Ivan closed the trunk lid, and they piled into the car with the dog, then took off down the same road they'd driven in on.

Remi hurried toward the street, looking for Sam. A moment later, he pulled up. "Which way?" he asked.

She pointed as she got in. "They just turned left. Nigel's in the trunk."

"And?"

"Worked like a charm."

Sam took off in the same direction. "See if we have a cell signal yet."

She picked up her phone. "Faint," she said, scrolling through the apps until she found the Find My iPhone icon. She opened it. At first, it showed Sam's phone as off-line, and she worried that somehow they'd discovered the phone in Nigel's pocket, then turned it off. But about a mile from the castle, it popped up on her screen. "Got it."

"I have to admit, Remi, your pickpocket skills are a little scary. You sure you weren't some mastermind criminal in a previous life?"

She laughed. "Dropping a phone in someone's pocket is a lot easier than stealing one."

"What about that woman's badge in the museum?"

"It was hanging from a clip on her jacket. Hardly master skills." She eyed the screen on her phone. "They're heading northeast."

"Guess we settle in for the ride and see where they're taking him. Keep an eye out for Fisk in case he shows up again."

They drove north for about forty minutes, finally stopping in a sparsely populated area in the country at a white, half-timbered inn, where a sign out front named it the Pig & Lantern.

Sam stopped down the road, pulling to the side, as the three got out of the blue sedan parked in the small lot in front of the inn. Ivan popped the trunk, then dragged Nigel out by the arm. The poor guy looked scared witless.

"Maybe we should call the police," Remi said.

"If we were in the States? I'd say yes, bring on the SWAT team. Way out here? Who knows how long it would take. Besides," he said, nodding toward the men in the BMW, "you think those two would hesitate before killing an unarmed cop? I don't want that on my conscience."

"We can't just leave Nigel with them."

"We won't. They want him alive. He can't translate if he's dead."

"If only we hadn't let him go back."

There was little he or Remi could do about it now, watching as they escorted Nigel through a side door. Once they were inside, Jak walked around back with the dog. A few minutes later, he returned without the animal, then entered through the same door.

"Sam?"

"I'm thinking." He watched another car pull up, this one with the words *Just Married* spray-painted on the back window. A young couple got out, then pulled two overnight bags from the trunk, before walking inside the front door.

Which gave him an idea . . .

He took Remi's phone from the center console, glad to see that they had a strong signal. "What do you say to a little countryside getaway?"

"Does it include countryside prisoner extraction?"

"I'm not sure it's on the menu," he said, looking up the name of the inn. "But if we're lucky, they take special requests."

The phone rang a few times before it was picked up by a woman. "Pig and Lantern."

"Do you have any rooms available for tonight?"

"One moment . . ." He heard the tapping of computer keys. "Name?"

He then glanced over at Remi, saying, "Longstreet, Mr. and Mrs."

"Longstreet . . ." More typing, then, "How many nights?"

"Just one. It'll be for a late arrival. Sometime after dark."

"And which credit card would you like to hold it under?"

"American Express." He signaled Remi for the card since she still carried one under her maiden name, then read the number to the woman.

"Very good, Mr. Longstreet. We have you booked for one night's stay, checking out tomorrow."

He thanked her, then disconnected. "Now we wait."

Remi's phone buzzed. "It's Selma . . ." She opened the text.

"Didn't see that one coming. That woman with them? Charles Avery's wife Alexandra."

"Seriously? Isn't she a socialite? Parties, fund-raisers—"

Remi made a scoffing noise. "Men are so quick to dismiss women as threats."

"A trait that's definitely come in handy when you've been dismissed as a threat."

"Exactly my point. Remember that if you run into her."

"I don't plan to. Which is why we're waiting for dark."

An hour later, Sam was glad to see that the lighting around the inn was almost nonexistent. That would allow him to get close enough without being seen. "Wait here," he said to Remi. "I want to have a look at the place."

Besides the main entrance at the front, there appeared to be two more exits, one on the north side, the other on the south, where they'd seen Ivan and Jak enter.

Two windows were lit in the downstairs rooms—all the others were dark—at least one belonged to the bad guys.

Sam needed to narrow those odds. He edged his way around the corner, moving close to the building, working his way to the first lit window. The curtains were closed, but light seeped out of a narrow slit in the center, allowing him to see in. The room appeared empty. Alexandra's white parka was tossed over the back of a chair. He moved to the next room. There was a gap in that curtain as well. Just as Sam approached, Ivan walked up and pulled the curtains tight.

But not before Sam caught a glimpse of Nigel seated in a chair, his back to the window, his hands zip-tied behind him.

He knew what he was dealing with, he thought as a third window lit up on the other side of Ivan and Jak's room. The newlyweds. Sam returned to the car. "Ready?"

"So what grand scheme have you planned?"

"Right now, only a half-grand scheme, which we'll be playing by ear."

Forty-four

"Slow night?" Sam asked the desk clerk when they were checking in. He hefted his backpack on his shoulder. Remi called it his just-in-case bag since it contained assorted small tools, knives, as well as a very light but sturdy rope. Other than that, neither of them had any luggage. "Only saw two other cars in the parking lot."

"For us, that's busy."

"Nice and quiet, then. Just how we like it." He leaned against the counter. "If you don't mind my asking, any pets staying in the hotel? My wife is allergic."

"Not belonging to any guests. The owner has a dog, though."

"That wouldn't be a big, black dog, would it?"

"You've seen Teddy, 'ave you? A sweetheart, 'e is. The other party staying 'ere? Taking 'im out for walks the last coupla days. Not to worry. I can put you above stairs, if you like."

"Not necessary." Sam smiled at the clerk and slid a twenty-pound note across the counter toward her. "We'd definitely like a ground-level room. On the east side. We like to watch the sunrise."

The clerk eyed her computer monitor. "We 'ave one room left on the east side ground floor. Right next to the 'appy couple."

She handed him the key. "The rooms are around the corner, past the potted palm. One-oh-one is next to the north staircase. Enjoy your stay."

He and Remi thanked her, then walked toward the palm. Sam peered down the hall, realizing the one big flaw in his plan was getting to their room unobserved if the unthinkable happened and Ivan or Jak walked out their door. At least they knew the dog wasn't as deadly as it seemed.

One less thing to worry about, he thought as they walked past Ivan and Jak's room. Sam paused a moment. Someone was talking. The next door belonged to the newlyweds, then theirs at the end of the hall. The open-beamed room was small, with a double bed, a nightstand, a small dresser with a TV on it and an ice bucket and two glasses. He walked over to the window, pulling the curtains closed. "Wish I had some way to listen in to that room," Sam said. "Any chance we have an app that turns my phone into a listening device?"

"It's called a phone call. Sort of ruins the whole element of surprise, though." Remi picked up a glass, putting the bottom of it to her ear. "Of course, there's also the old-fashioned way."

"Lot of good that does. There's a whole room between us and them."

"We could ask the newlyweds to trade rooms with us."

"I thought of that. But, frankly, I'd feel better if they weren't even in the hotel. What if something goes wrong?"

She looked at the clock on the nightstand by the bed. Just after six. "How far a drive from here to London, do you think?"

"Under three hours."

"We have the room at the Savoy. Paid for and sitting empty."

"That, Remi, is brilliant. As usual."

She smiled. "Let's hope they accept."

"One way to find out. Shall we?"

He knocked softly on their door.

A young man opened it about two inches.

"Next-door neighbors," Sam said. "Heard congratulations are in order."

The man's wife appeared behind him, her young face a mixture of curiosity and excitement. "Who is it?" she asked.

"The people next door."

She reached around him and pulled the door open. "Hi."

Sam didn't give the couple an opportunity to turn them away. He and Remi walked in, Sam closing the door behind them.

"Congratulations," Remi said. "We heard you were just married?"

The woman beamed. "A few days ago."

"On your honeymoon, then?" Sam asked.

The man shrugged. "Taking a few days."

"Ever stayed at the Savoy?"

The man gave a cynical laugh. "You think we'd be here if we could afford that?"

"Tell you what," Sam said. "If you don't mind the drive, there's a free room waiting for you."

The woman's eyes widened.

Her husband, however, crossed his arms, suspicion clouding

his features. He took a threatening step toward Sam. "I think you should leave."

"If you'll just hear me out," Sam said, slipping his wallet from his pocket, "I happen to need *this* particular room. And the suite I have at the Savoy, bought and paid for, is sitting empty." He pulled several hundred pounds from his wallet along with the key card to the room at the Savoy and laid it all onto the bed. "This should cover a few meals, your gas, *and* the price of this room. Even if you choose not to stay at the Savoy, that should more than cover another room somewhere else."

"What sort of scam are you running?"

Remi took her cell phone, found the link Selma had sent for their reservation when they'd first arrived in London, and opened it. "No scam. I'll add you to the reservation. All you need to do is show up. Or take the money and run." When the mobile Internet site came up, she held out her phone and showed them. "Type in your name and email. You should get a confirmation."

He hesitated. His wife, however, grabbed the phone and looked at it. "Looks real."

"It is," Remi said.

The woman typed the info in.

"Are you crazy?" her husband asked, trying to take the phone away from her.

She held it away from him, then turned so he couldn't take it from her. "It's just our name and email. Not like we're giving them our credit card! *I'd* like to go to the Savoy for our honeymoon." She hit send, returned the phone to Remi, then told her husband, "Check your email."

"But they're bringing us a bottle of champagne!"

"Yeah?" she said. "It came with the room that cost us less than sixty pounds. How good can it be? Check. Your. Email."

He pulled his cell phone from his pocket, looking surprised when he opened his email. "This is real?"

Remi nodded.

"But why?"

"Not important," Sam said. "Just know you're doing us a huge favor."

The man looked around the room as though trying to decide if it was worth it. "Fine. Guess it's enough money to go wherever we want if it's not there." They gathered the few things they'd taken out of their suitcases.

"Congratulations again," Remi said as she walked them to the door.

"One thing," Sam said. "Might want to be quiet. They're sleeping." He pointed toward Ivan and Jak's room.

The man nodded, both waved, and then they left.

Remi closed and locked the door after them. Less than thirty seconds later, they heard a soft knock at the neighboring door, followed by Fisk's voice demanding that someone let him in.

Interesting. Fisk didn't seem the type to dirty his hands with anything but the most important matters. So what exactly *did* Nigel know? Remi picked up two empty glasses on a tray next to the ice bucket, then motioned Sam over, whispering, "Time to see what's going on next door."

Forty-five

Fisk walked into the room. Alexandra sat in the chair next to Nigel while Jak and Ivan were sprawled on the bed. "Mr. Ridgewell. Sorry for the inconvenience. I hope you weren't too uncomfortable on your ride over. I understand it was a bit cramped."

Nigel glared at him. "What is it you want?"

"Your translation skills. I understand your specialty is Old English? We're willing to pay."

"And that's why you had me attacked last night, stole my notebook, then kidnapped me?"

"A simple misunderstanding."

Nigel scoffed. "Like being dumped in the trunk or tied to a chair with the circulation cut off in my hands?"

Fisk nodded at Ivan, who got up, then took a knife and cut the zip tie binding Nigel to the chair. Nigel rubbed at his wrists, watching as Ivan returned to the bed.

"The notebook," Fisk said to Alexandra.

"Ivan has it."

He held out his hand, and Ivan tossed it to him. "If you can see it in yourself to forgive my associates for their rough handling, then maybe we can come to some sort of agreement."

"About what?"

"As I said, a simple translation. There's a phrase in your notebook you haven't translated. The person my associates showed it to this afternoon also had difficulty with it. Funny thing, he recommended you as the person to contact."

"That's what you were talking to William about at Castle Rising?"

"You know him. A small world in tourism and academia, I see." He held the notebook out for Nigel, pointing to the words on the last page. Nigel leaned toward it. "Can't tell."

"Why not?"

"Maybe there are letters missing. Or it's completely misspelled. But those aren't words that I can make out. Except the one. *Hole*."

Only then did Fisk realize there were, in fact, letters missing. He'd assumed the list they'd stolen from Nigel was the same as his. Deciphered words taken straight from the map. Then again, he hadn't looked that close at what was written in Nigel's notebook. He'd assumed that the Fargos had somehow managed to get a copy of the cipher wheel—and the words were the same as what he had. How else to explain how the Fargos had made their way this far?

Interesting. The Fargos were working from a flawed copy. He, however, was not, and he took out his phone and found the text from the expert that Charles Avery was using to decipher the map.

There was clearly a letter missing from the words, and he showed the corrected text to Nigel. "What about this?"

"You realize I'm not the only Old English expert in this country?"

"At the moment, you happen to be the most convenient. And the most expendable. So look closely before I decide to find your replacement."

The man studied the text, then gave an exasperated sigh. "I'd say someone mistook an *f* for an *s*. It's not *wulshol*. It's *wulfhol*. As in *wolf's hole*."

"And the other?" he said, pointing to the word listed beneath it: *wulsesheasod*

"It should read *wulfeshéafod*, as in *wolf's head*."

"And what do you think they mean?"

"The den and head of a wolf, if I had to guess."

"You're sure?"

"Of course I'm *not* sure. You'd have to ask the person who wrote it."

"That person's dead. Which is what you'll be if you—"

Alexandra stood. "You have what you need. We, however, haven't eaten since breakfast."

How was it he'd thought bringing her along was going to help him? "Tie him up. We don't want him running off."

"Wait," Nigel said, trying to stand. Ivan and Jak were off the bed in an instant, pushing him back into the chair. Nigel struggled in vain as Jak held him, and Ivan tightened a new zip tie around his wrists. "You can't keep me here."

"As long as you cooperate, you stay alive. Which means you're still needed." He looked at Ivan. "Do *not* leave him unattended if you go out. There's a perfectly good pub across the street. Bring something back."

"And where are you going?" Alexandra asked.

"Picking up two more men to help. The Fargos are more of a problem than we'd anticipated. After that, back to my hotel. Your husband's waiting for an update on the translation. I expect it'll lead us to our next location, where our tour guide will be of use. Of course, *you* could call Charles."

"I'd prefer he didn't know I was here," Alexandra icily replied.

"That's what I thought." He started for the door, then looked back at Nigel. "If he makes a sound, kill him. I'm sure we can always find another translator."

"We are *not* killing anyone right now," Alexandra said. "You realize there are guests right next to us?"

"Then kill them, too. Just don't get caught."

Forty-six

Alexandra followed Fisk from the room. "We need to talk," she said, quickening her pace to keep up with him as he strode down the hallway.

He glanced back at her but didn't stop. "Later. I'm in a hurry."

A maid came around the corner, her attention on the ice bucket with champagne bottle that she was carrying. Fisk barreled into her, knocking the bucket and bottle from her grasp and sending the coat flying from his. He landed against a potted palm, nearly toppling it.

The poor girl's eyes widened as he swore at her. "I'm so sorry, sir. I didn't see you there."

"Apparently," he said as he bent down and swooped up his coat, then stormed off.

Alexandra followed through the lobby, but he stopped her at the door, turning toward her, his voice lowered so that only she could hear. "What part of 'I'm in a hurry' did you not get?"

"You're not going to kill anybody," she whispered. "Not here. The room's in my name."

"You wanted to be part of this. That means you play by my rules. If and when I find it necessary to eliminate someone, *I* make that decision. Not you, not Jak or Ivan. *Me.* Do I make myself clear?"

Shaken by his anger, she nodded, then walked back through the lobby and down the hallway, where the maid was down on the floor, picking up ice cubes from the carpet and dumping them into the bucket.

The young woman looked up at her, her eyes glistening with unshed tears, as she apologized. "I didn't see him."

"It's not your fault," Alexandra said, feeling sorry for her. She started to reach for the champagne bottle that had rolled into the corner by the potted palm. When she bent down to pick it up, she noticed something in the base of the potted palm. The cipher wheel.

She left the bottle where it was. "Let me help," she said as she started scooping some of the ice into a small pile near the palm. "It really was our fault. We were arguing and didn't see you."

"No. You shouldn't trouble yourself. I'll clean this."

Alexandra moved in front of the palm, blocking the maid's view. She shoved the wheel into the dirt and covered it, then picked up the champagne bottle, holding it toward the maid.

"Thank you," the girl said, taking the bottle from her as Fisk rounded the corner.

He stopped, appearing surprised to see Alexandra and the maid still there.

"Forget something?" Alexandra asked.

"Dropped something." He walked around them, his gaze on the floor.

When he reached the palm, pulling back the fronds to look behind it, Alexandra tried to keep her breathing even.

He looked up at her. "You didn't find anything here, did you?"

"No. What is it you're looking for?"

"Maybe it's in the room," he said, then strode that way.

Alexandra smiled at the maid, worried about her safety if she happened to walk past their room at the wrong moment. "Whoever opens this is going to have quite a surprise. Have you ever seen a champagne bottle that's been dropped?"

"I didn't think of that. I should change it out."

She left, and Alexandra returned to the room in time to see Fisk searching under the bed. "Maybe if you told us what you lost, we might be able to help look."

He dropped the bedspread, then stood, looking her over, his gaze lingering on the pockets of her light jacket—making her grateful she'd left the thing in the palm pot. "Maybe it's in the car," he said.

"And if you can't find whatever it is?"

"Doesn't matter." He took one last look around the room. "I have photos."

She glanced over at Nigel. The poor guy was trying to loosen the zip tie binding his wrists, and she wanted to tell him to just stop. They'd kill him in a second if he tried to escape. Which reminded her exactly of what she wanted to talk to Fisk about.

She followed him into the hallway again.

This time, he didn't look back. "I told you, not now."

"I got the message," she said, deciding it wiser to avoid him altogether. "I'm going up front to get a menu from the pub across the street. Thanks to our uninvited guest, we're going to need to get our meal to go."

They turned the corner, and he slowed his pace, undoubtedly searching for that lost wheel. Her gaze lit on the disturbed potting soil in the palm. It seemed so obvious to her, and when he walked up to the plant, she froze as he moved the branches to look behind it.

The fronds rustled as he let them go, and he cursed softly under his breath as he continued out into the lobby. She made a right to the front desk and asked for a menu from the pub, looking it over as he left. When she saw his car drive off, she returned to the hallway, dug her fingers into the potting soil, and pulled out the cipher wheel. She brushed it off, stuffed it into her pocket, then hurried to her own room, where she hid it in the lining of her suitcase.

She had no idea *what* she was going to do with it. She only knew that if the thing was so important that Fisk was carrying it with him, then she wanted it for herself.

Forty-seven

S am parted the curtain in their darkened room, watching the road, until he saw a black Mercedes drive past. Fisk. One down, three to go, he thought, dropping the curtain, then returning to where Remi still sat, listening in with her low-tech glass pressed to the wall.

A knock at the door startled them both until he looked out and saw a maid with the complimentary champagne for the newlyweds. He took the bottle, tipped the maid, then closed the door, grateful she didn't seem to notice he and Remi weren't the couple who should have been in the room.

He put the ice bucket on the dresser. "Anything?" he mouthed.

She held up her finger a moment, then whispered, "Sounds like they're discussing who's going across the street for dinner . . . Alexandra and Jak are going over to pick it up. Ivan's staying behind."

"I like those odds much better."

"Except . . ." She listened a moment, then said, "They're calling their order in."

Which meant they'd have less time than he'd hoped. At least for the plan he was formulating. Definitely a work in progress, as he thought about what could go wrong. No matter. They'd just have to work faster.

Remi was a quick study, and the moment they heard Alexandra and Jak leave, he went over his plan with her. A lot of luck was going to come into play. Although Remi was armed with her Sig Sauer P938, and Sam his Smith & Wesson, neither of them had foreseen anything beyond checking out a castle or two when they'd set out this morning.

Rescuing hostages had never entered their minds.

Couldn't be helped now, he thought, as he gave Remi one of the Buck Knives from his backpack. The ultimate goal was to get in and out without any shots fired. If all worked as planned, he'd have Ivan disarmed while Remi freed Nigel.

He nodded toward Remi, who picked up the phone and called the office. "Room 103, please." She gave him the thumbs-up. "Front desk," she said into the phone a moment later in her best British accent. "Room service should be right there with your champagne . . . No, sir. I believe the woman in your party ordered it on her way out. She said something about bringing it by before dinner . . . It *is* complimentary, sir. You don't have to drink it."

She hung up and shrugged. "He was pretty insistent that they didn't need it."

"It's all we've got. Let's do it."

Remi pulled her hair back into a tight ponytail, figuring that would be more maid-like. Sam grabbed his backpack, then opened the door. "Remember," he whispered. "As soon as you have Nigel free, you both go out the window, get to the car, and meet me out front."

As they left the room, she grabbed the ice bucket with the champagne bottle, stepped out into the hallway, then stood in front of the door. When Sam was in position to the side, she knocked, then looked down so that Ivan would only see the top of her head.

He cracked open the door and peered out. "Yeah?"

"Champagne, sir."

She held up the bucket.

He opened the door wider. "I told you—"

Sam used the weight of the backpack, ramming it into the door. Ivan stumbled back as Sam leaned against the door, holding him tight. The entry to the room was a four-foot hallway. Remi scrambled past Sam, keeping tight to the wall, before running into the room.

Ivan leaned into the door, trying to push Sam out. Sam braced one foot on the doorframe, but Ivan, using his heavier weight, managed to push back. Sam slipped past just as the door slammed shut. He pivoted, kicking out, sending Ivan back into the corner. When Ivan tried to raise the gun, Sam swung the backpack up, slamming it against Ivan's hand. The gun flew from Ivan's grasp as Sam rushed him, using the advantage of his weight and strength in the close quarters of the entry. Ivan swung, hit him in the ribs, knocking the breath from his lungs. Sam was ready. He purposefully fell back against the wall while at the same time bringing his pack up, slamming Ivan in the face.

He ducked as Ivan swung. Ivan's fist smashed through the plaster, his knuckles bloody. He swore, then turned slightly, drawing back, telegraphing his move.

Sam dropped, then darted to the side, as Ivan slammed his shoulder into the wall. The maneuver trapped Sam in the corner by the door. Ivan turned like a mad bull, his eyes narrowed, his mouth grimacing. "I'll kill you."

Before Sam could make a move, Remi cracked the full bottle of champagne on Ivan's head. He hung there a moment, stunned, and Sam slammed his fist into the man's jaw, sending him crashing to the ground.

Remi stood there, holding the champagne bottle, a slight smile on her face. "You looked like you could use a hand."

"Where's Nigel?" he asked.

"Good question."

Except for Ivan, the room was empty.

Remi spied his cell phone on the chair and held it up. "This explains things. They knew we were coming."

"All the more reason to get out of here." Ivan started to stir. Sam grabbed his backpack and Ivan's gun. Sam helped Remi out the window before jumping down after her. They moved around toward the north end.

Sam heard the sound of someone running on gravel. He and Remi ran toward the front of the inn as Ivan jumped into the waiting car. The engine revved and tires screeched as Jak sped out of the car park.

Sam saw four people in the car as it drove off, one of them was Nigel.

He and Remi ran to their car, but by the time they pulled out, the BMW was long gone.

"On the one hand," Remi said, "it was a good rescue operation."

"Too bad Nigel wasn't there."

"We shouldn't have put him in that position in the first place. At the castle . . . with all those people—I never thought they'd kidnap him in broad daylight."

"What's done is done."

She turned toward Sam, saying, "It was about the translation. They were talking about it when Fisk arrived. Something about a letter missing."

"You remember what they said?"

She nodded, her gaze fixed out the windshield. "At least we know where they're going. Once they figure things out, that is."

"Where?" Sam asked.

"Nottingham."

He looked over at her. "How did you come to that conclusion?"

"From the words they asked Nigel to translate," she said. "*Wolf's den* and *wolf's head*. Or, more accurately, *head of an outlaw wolf*."

"How'd you get Nottingham from that?"

"Because *wolf's head* happens to be another name for *Robin Hood*. So it stands to reason that the other words they were asking about, *wolf's den*, would be his home."

"Guess we're going to Nottingham," Sam said.

Forty-eight

R emi is absolutely correct," Lazlo told them the following morning in a Skype call. Outside, the dark gray sky let loose with a sudden downpour, rain beating against the windows. Remi turned up the volume on her tablet, trying to hear what Lazlo was saying. After they'd fled the inn last night, Sam and Remi had driven straight to Nottingham, gotten a hotel suite under a new assumed name, and managed to get a few hours of sleep before making the early-morning call. "Wolf's Head," Lazlo continued, "is a name that Robin Hood has been known by. At least in the very early legends. And the missing *f* fits perfect. Had it been there to begin with, I might have been able to save you the trouble."

"I'm sure you could have," Sam said, steering Lazlo back to the point. "About the map ciphers."

"Right-o. Wolf's den and Nottingham. It's brilliant. I can't believe I didn't think of it."

Selma cleared her throat as she placed her hand on Lazlo's shoulder. "Here's what we found," Selma said. "There *is* a connection between Sir Edmund Herbert and Nottingham. Specifically, the events surrounding his half brother, Roger Mortimer, and Queen Isabella after her husband abdicated the throne to their son. Mortimer was arrested and held in Nottingham Castle while Queen Isabella was banished to Castle Rising."

Remi looked at the map spread out on the table as Sam asked, "So what does this have to do with Robin Hood and King John's Treasure?"

"That," Lazlo said, "is a good question. Especially considering how many legends of Robin Hood exist. Definitely some that place him in the time of King John, though usually at odds with the king. But our research is starting to come together. The key to our map is there."

"Where?" Sam and Remi asked together.

"Nottingham. Or, to be precise, somewhere *within* Nottingham," Lazlo replied. "Something about the 'four chambers' and 'death below.' Still working on that part. And that's assuming that I'm translating this correctly. Since that portion of the wheel was also washed out in the photo, I'm making an educated guess."

Sam's phone buzzed on the table. He looked at the screen, his face registering surprise as he turned on the speaker function. "Nigel?"

"I don't have long. He might come back any second, and my battery's near dead."

"Where are you?"

"No idea except somewhere near Nottingham. Got one hand free and managed to get my phone from the coat pocket of the guy watching me. He's—they were talking about the four chambers. I told them they must mean the four *caverns*. That's where we're going. If they can find it."

"Four caverns?" Sam said.

"I hear them," he whispered. "Go to Professor Aldridge."

The line beeped.

Sam stared at the phone a moment, then looked at Selma on the screen of Remi's tablet. "You catch that?"

"Every word," Selma said. They heard the sound of her clicking away on her computer keyboard. "There's a Professor Aldridge at Nottingham University."

Sam eyed Lazlo, saying, "Could the four chambers be the four caverns Nigel was talking about?"

"Could be. 'Den of the wolf' might indicate caves as long as one overlooks that Robin Hood was known to hide out in Sherwood Forest."

Selma added, "I've got a contact number for Aldridge. I'll see if I can't get ahold of him."

"Perfect," Remi said. "Let's give him a call."

Professor Cedric Aldridge, a white-haired man in his late sixties, met them at his office at the History Department.

Once they were seated, Sam got right down to business. "I hope this doesn't sound odd, but has anyone besides us ever contacted you about King John and his treasure?"

"Funny you should ask," Professor Aldridge said. "I've only ever had one other person ask and that was quite some time ago.

Former student of mine from King's Lynn. Nigel Ridgewell. Wanted to know if it was possible that the story of King John's Treasure being lost in the fens could be a ruse. Protect the treasure from enemy hands or some such. Can't recall what it was for. A book or something, possibly. Never heard from him after that, though."

The professor seemed oblivious to the scandal over Nigel stealing Madge Crowley's papers, which was just as well, Remi thought. "What was your answer?"

"I know I'm in the minority," the professor said, "but why not? I'm the first to admit we don't know everything about history. Piecing it together from this historian or that. Sometimes we're lucky and an event is documented so well, there's no denying what happened. What we do know for certain is that the king died. Whether from dysentery, as believed, or something else altogether, hard to say. We know there are reports he separated from the caravan because of his illness. It's what happened *to* the caravan afterward that is not so well known. Everything after that point is speculation based on stories passed down. So who's to say that someone didn't steal it after making up the story of it being lost in the fens just to throw off suspicion?" He furrowed his brow, pausing for a moment. "Eliminate witnesses, and you can make up any story you want."

"Let's say these rumors are true," Sam said. "That the treasure wasn't lost in the fens . . ." He left it open, to see the professor's reaction.

"You mean as Nigel theorized?"

"Yes."

"It would be the historical find of the century." He gave a slight shrug. "Assuming the treasure was located, that is. An archaeologist's dream."

Remi smiled at the professor. "Not your dream?"

"Mine?" he asked, smiling back at her. "Never gave it much thought. My fascination lies with the students facing me in the classroom. Seeing their expressions and hearing their theories. But you're not here to talk about me. Unless I misunderstood, you're looking for information on the origin of Wolf's Head, or, as we call him around here, Robin Hood. According to some historians, he lived during the same time period as King John. According to others, centuries off—in both directions. Ever since my colleague Professor Percival Wendorf retired, I've added the history of Robin Hood to my syllabus. It's one of my more popular classes. My students walk away with a greater understanding of the Middle Ages, using the hunt for Robin Hood as a backdrop."

Remi had always admired professors who could muster interest with their students. "Definitely a class I would have taken. Was he as heroic as the movies have portrayed him?"

"A good question. This whole rob from the rich to give to the poor is legendary, but with an emphasis on legend. More pirate than hero, according to Percy. Hence the term *Wolf's Head*."

"How disappointing," Remi said.

"Quite. The probable truth is that men like him were nothing more than highway robbers."

"Landlocked pirate?" Sam asked. "Could he, or another like him, have set up the theft of King John's Treasure?"

"An interesting theory, to be sure. That sort of secret would be hard to keep. *Except* the legends that *have* survived the centuries, via ballads or fireside tales, seem to be based on some kernel of truth, even Robin Hood. And the general consensus is that King John's Treasure went down in the fens along with the men who were entrusted with it. It's what became of the treasure afterward that leaves much to the imagination. Why hasn't it been found? In fact, the only account of any physical trace of it was the rumor, several centuries later, that it had been found by Robert Tiptoft, Third Baron Tibetot."

"Tibetot?" Remi asked. "What rumor is that?"

"That the baron is said to have come into a sudden and unexplained fortune quite possibly because he found the king's treasure on his land. Most historians discount that telling."

"Back to Robin Hood," Sam said. "Is it possible that there's some history relating to him that isn't mainstream? Say, if he were to steal the treasure, would there be a place he might hide it? And any experts who might speculate on a location? Something called the four caverns?"

"There are two experts in the area that I know of offhand. The foremost is the retired professor I mentioned, Percy Wendorf. Back in the day, I would have pointed you to him in a heartbeat. Now . . ."

"Now?" Remi asked, wondering what he wasn't saying.

"Just . . ." He gave a slight shrug, before meeting Remi's gaze. "My friend is—*was*—a walking encyclopedia of anything to do with Nottinghamshire and the Middle Ages, including Robin Hood, the castles, King John, and, well, anything else you could think of. Lately, though, Percy's been . . . a bit forgetful. It's why he retired."

Before Remi had a chance to comment, Sam asked, "And this other expert?"

"Malcolm Swift. Knowledgeable, to be sure. Just lacking that obscure knowledge that Percy always seemed to have a handle on. I wouldn't hesitate to recommend either. Being a bit prejudiced in his favor, I invited Percy to join us so that you could meet him yourself. Knowing Percy, I probably should have had someone pick him up. Like I said, his memory is getting a bit spotty."

He looked at his watch, then took out his cell phone. "I'll ring up his wife. He was supposed to meet her first, then walk over here after." He made the call. "Agatha? It's Cedric. Any chance Percy's still there . . . ? I see. What sort of problem . . . ?" His brows went up as he listened. "No. We can drop by . . . It's no trouble . . . Yes. I'll ring you up as soon as I get there."

He disconnected, his expression one of concern. "Apparently he left a message for his wife that he'll have to reschedule. Bit of a problem."

"What sort of problem?" Sam asked.

"That's just it. He didn't say. She hasn't been able to get ahold of him since. Doesn't answer his mobile or his texts."

"We have a car," Sam replied. "We'd be glad to give you a lift."

"Brilliant. Thank you."

Percy Wendorf lived about ten minutes from the university. Professor Aldridge, sitting in the backseat, leaned toward the center, pointing. "Just up there. Next turn."

But when they arrived, a uniformed officer stood at the intersection. "Sorry. Road's closed," he told Sam through the open window. Unfortunately, the road curved, and they couldn't see a thing except a thick cloud of black smoke swirling up above the rooftops before disappearing into the dark clouds that threatened more rain.

"What's going on?"

"House fire."

"We're trying to get ahold of a friend who lives there. Can you tell us how long?"

"No idea. Once they have it under control, they'll open up again."

Which told them nothing. He looked back at the professor. "Sorry. I guess this is the best I can do."

"There's a footpath through the park that should get us closer. I doubt they'll have it closed off. And if they do, we can at least see what's going on from up there." He directed them to the next street up the hill, where they eventually took a paved footpath between two cottages that allowed the area residents access to a small playground situated across the street from Percy's house—which happened to be the one burning. A number of residents had gathered in the park to watch the firefighters in action, and the three joined them. The house, a two-story brick structure, appeared relatively intact from the outside, the rising smoke lighter than it had been when they first arrived. Remi hoped the fire was out.

A tall, bald-headed man with wire-rimmed spectacles stood off to one side, alone, watching the firefighters. Aldridge pointed. "That's Percy."

Forty-nine

S am checked the neighborhood for any sign of Fisk and his men. Only then did he let the others cross over to talk to Percy Wendorf. The man stood, transfixed, as the fire-fighters traipsed through his yard, dragging their heavy hoses back to their firetrucks. "My pansies . . ."

Professor Aldridge clasped his hand on Percy's shoulder. "Flowers will grow back. At least your house is still there."

"I suppose." He turned toward them, eyeing Sam and Remi.

Aldridge introduced them and Sam shook hands with him, saying, "Wish we were meeting under better circumstances."

"Agreed." Percy gave a tired sigh. "Though they tell me it's mostly contained to the kitchen and front parlor."

Sam watched the firefighters rolling up their hoses. "Did they give any indication on what started it?"

"It just blew up. Flames shot out. Lucky I wasn't any closer."

After several minutes, one of the firefighters walked over. "Mr. Wendorf?"

"Yes."

"We'll be finished shortly. A bit of a mess in there. Water and such. Do you have insurance?"

"Yes. Of course."

"Give them a ring. They can recommend who to send for cleanup."

"Very good." He stared at his home, clearly still in shock.

Sam, realizing that Percy wasn't in any frame of mind to ask any important questions, stepped forward to address the firefighter. "Sorry to interrupt, but do you have any idea how the fire started?"

"From what he described when we got here, it looks like a chimney fire. Creosote buildup."

"You're certain?"

The man removed his helmet and then pushed back his hood, running his fingers through his sweat-soaked hair. "Quite."

Definitely good news—as long as they overlooked the damage to his home. Even so, Sam wasn't about to dismiss any involvement from Avery or his men until he saw the evidence himself.

When they finally allowed Percy and the others into his home, Percy stood speechless, eyeing what was left of his parlor. The heavy scent of smoke hung in the air, and Professor Aldridge started opening windows. Sam walked over to the hearth, his feet sloshing in the wet, gray sludge on the floor. The initial burn marks appeared just outside the hearth, the stones blackened, the wooden floor adjacent to it charred. All that remained of an ori-ental rug was a dark, soggy mess beneath a charred upholstered chair, which sat several feet away from the hearth.

The fireman was right, Sam realized. It appeared to have started at the fireplace and worked its way into the room from there. Though possible, he didn't think Avery's men would take such care in an arson to make it look as if it were the result of an accident.

"Sam?" Remi stood in the arched doorway that led to the din-ing room. "There's a to-do list," she said quietly, "on the table. The first thing on there is to call the chimney sweep."

"That seems to be the clincher. Accident over arson."

"We can all breathe a bit easier."

"Except for the part about Nigel still being missing."

Remi glanced at Percy, who stood looking around at the fire damage, refusing to leave when Professor Aldridge tried to lead him from the room toward Sam and Remi. "If we're going to ask him to help, he certainly can't stay here," Remi said.

"No," Sam replied. "We could put him and his wife up at our hotel. At least until this place is cleaned."

They posed the idea to Aldridge, who immediately declined the offer. "As generous as it is, I'm not sure that's the best course of action for him."

Before he had a chance to explain, a woman, mid-sixties, walked into the house, then stopped just a few feet in as she looked around. Undoubtedly Percy's wife, Agatha. "Oh no . . ." She held her hand to her mouth as she took in the damage. "Percy. You didn't light a fire, did you?"

"Of course I did. Why wouldn't I?"

"I left a note to call the chimney sweep. I told—" She gave a deep sigh. "Never mind," she said, her gaze lighting on Sam, Remi, then Professor Aldridge. "I see you have guests." She walked over, took Percy by the arm, and Sam was certain the sparkle in her eyes was from being near tears. "Let's all go into the kitchen where it's cleaner, shall we?"

"Yes," Percy said. "Good idea."

The look that passed between Agatha and Professor Aldridge told Sam that today's fire was not totally unexpected. Aldridge eyed the wet floor. "I'll go see if I can find a mop and broom and start sweeping out some of this water. First, I'll introduce you to Percy's wife."

They followed him into the kitchen. Percy was seated at the table. Agatha smiled at them as they walked in. "How frightfully rude of me for leaving you standing there. And with guests. I'm not normally this inconsiderate."

"Nonsense, Agatha," Aldridge said. He turned toward Sam and Remi. "Percy's wife Agatha." As they shook hands with her, he said, "Agatha, this is Sam and Remi Fargo. They're here looking for information on some archaeological artifacts, and, well, Percy was supposed to meet us. He never made it."

"Understandable," she said, glancing toward her husband. "Normally, Percy's very good with lists. Perhaps I should have written 'Don't light the fire' and called the chimney sweep myself."

"I simply forgot," Percy said.

Agatha gave a tired smile. "I know."

"Maybe," Aldridge said in a quiet voice, "it's time for live-in help?"

Agatha's eyes glistened and she turned away, busying herself with the dishes in the sink. Eventually she took a seat at the table, giving another tired smile. "Rather like sitting around a campfire, what with the smoky scent all about."

Percy looked at his wife. "I forgot to call the chimney sweep."

"I see," Agatha said, patting his hand and smiling at him. "So what sort of artifacts are you discussing, Percy?"

"Artifacts?" Percy eyed Sam and Remi. "I . . . Aldridge? Are these the people?"

"The couple I told you about."

"Right . . . We were supposed to meet. Slipped my mind. Almost burning down one's house will do that."

"Indeed," Aldridge replied. "But they're here now."

"Yes," Percy said to Sam and Remi. "I expect you'll want to have a look for yourself."

Sam felt Remi tapping his foot with her own. "Maybe," he said, "we should reschedule."

Remi gave a sympathetic smile. "You probably have enough on your plate right now."

"Actually," Agatha said, "it'll be best if he's out from underfoot. I expect I'll have a lot of calls to make while you're all off doing whatever it is you're doing."

"Very good," Aldridge said. "It's settled, then."

As they left the house and walked through the park toward their car, Sam told Remi quietly, "We'll catch up to you," then slowed his pace, signaling for Professor Aldridge to follow suit. Sam waited until Remi and Percy were out of earshot. "In light of Percy's memory issues, maybe we should go with this other expert?"

"Normally, I'd say yes," Aldridge replied. "This is beyond his usual forgetfulness. But he seems to have more trouble when he is out of his element. When something happens to throw him off his game. Like starting a chimney fire."

"But if this other expert is willing to help . . ."

"Maybe give Percy a chance. He lives for this sort of thing. And I know Agatha agrees with me. I ran it by her first. She's the one who insisted. He's happiest when he's in his element, and the tunnels below Nottingham, well, are definitely his element."

"Is it possible he can just point us to the cavern entrance?"

"I suppose so. Though he does enjoy walking through them. I'm sure that'll be fine. In fact, I believe he's mapped most of them out on some chart, if that'll work."

"That'll work perfectly." Sam watched as Percy pointed something out to Remi in the hedge, some bird, as both started laughing when it flew off. He hoped he wasn't making a mistake. "Let's go find this chart."

Fifty

S am expected that Percy and Aldridge would be returning
to Percy's home, not to a shopping district in town.

Percy directed Sam where to park. "The entrance is
about a five-minute walk from here," he said, leading them down
a cobbled street past several storefronts. He stopped before a tailor's shop. "The map's in here."

Remi looked up at the sign. "You're kidding."

Percy's face lit up as he held open the door. "Quite unexpected, wouldn't you say?"

Remi then glanced around the shop. "I guess I was expecting
something . . . different."

"The entire city is sitting on tunnels and caves. A lot to look
through."

Apparently Percy was related to the owner, a second cousin,
who was used to Percy's unexpected visits. He walked them to
the back of the store, then opened a door. A stone staircase led

down to darkness, and Percy stood there a moment, eyeing it. "Don't forget the electric torch on your way down."

Aldridge opened a nearby cabinet. Several flashlights stood on the shelf, and he handed one to each of them.

They started down the stone steps, the temperature cooling as they descended. "This is my favorite," Percy said, "the first I'd ever been in. I knew, from that moment on, I wanted to explore every one of them."

Sam brought up the rear, wondering exactly where it was Percy stored this map. "How many caves are there?" he asked.

"Over seventy-five, and counting. Most have been lost due to building and garden encroachments. Others have slowly collapsed after eight hundred years. Sadly, few people even know they exist outside of those opened as an historic attraction."

"And this cave?" Sam asked, shining his light on the fairly smooth walls, noting that shelves had been carved into the side where things had been stored. "What was it used for?"

"The previous shop owners used it as a wine cellar." He led them through the cavern into a tunnel that opened into another wider space. "Hand-carved. Sandstone. Centuries before that, people lived in here. Actually, in caves all over the city. The entrances were carved aboveground to prevent flooding when the river overflowed. It's all quite fascinating."

"One question," Sam said when he realized this last cavern was a dead end. "What does this have to do with Robin Hood and your map?"

"Robin Hood?" Percy turned a confused glance toward Aldridge. "I thought they wanted to see this one. Did I tell you it was the first one I'd ever been in?"

"You did," Aldridge said.

Sam looked at Remi, who kept a bland smile on her face as she ran her hands along the cavern walls. He should have insisted they contact the other expert, especially after the incident with the fire. "We appreciate your bringing us here," Sam said, "but we were hoping to learn about any caverns that have some connection to Robin Hood, King John, William the Marshal, and the four chambers."

"You mean the four *caverns*?" Percy asked.

"I believe so," Sam said. Percy's recognition of the name had to mean they were on the right track. "Do you know where it is?"

"It's been a while, but I believe I can find it again. Don't recommend it, though. Very dangerous. Places to fall. Wrong turns. There are so many better places to explore."

"But we love exploring," Remi said slyly. "Maybe you could tell us how to get there?"

"Getting toward midday, don't you think? Haven't had lunch." He turned and started walking toward the outer cavern and the stairs that led up to the shop. "I feel as if I'm forgetting something but, for the life of me, can't remember. Why do they want to go there?" he asked Aldridge.

"They're looking for historical artifacts."

"Ah, yes. Now I remember. Won't find much there. A lot of tunnels to get lost in. And some Celtic carvings on the wall. That's about it. Any artifacts are long gone."

As they followed him up the stairs, Sam asked Aldridge, "You're sure this is a good idea?"

"Don't forget, Percy's off his game today. The fire definitely rattled him. Naturally, if you'd rather go with that other expert, I'd be glad to call him for you."

"In this case, we'd better." He didn't want to count on the failing memory of a retired professor when it came to saving Nigel's life and he pulled Remi aside and told her who Aldridge was calling.

"I have to agree with you. Except . . ."

"Except what?" Sam asked.

"He did mention the four caverns and Celtic carvings. That fits right in with the four chambers that Lazlo mentioned and the Celtic knot on the cipher wheel. Which means he knows what he's talking about."

"When he *remembers* what he's talking about."

"It seemed to me he has more of a problem with his short-term memory. Since the caves are something he's been visiting since he was a boy . . ."

"It's not so much that, Remi. We came here for a map and got a tour of a wine cellar. What if something else happens to him and we end up on another wild-goose chase? Bad enough we've gotten Nigel mixed up in all this. And, right now, our priority is to rescue him—never mind Percy has no idea of the danger. Which brings me back to my original concern."

"I didn't think of it that way. Let's hope Professor Aldridge gets in touch with this other expert."

Aldridge stepped outside of the shop to make the call, then returned shortly after. "Sorry, but Swift's wife said he's not due back until later this afternoon. Business trip. She'll call me as soon as he gets in. But I do think you'll be fine using Percy. He'd want to do this. Especially if there was a chance that it led to something of historical significance."

If they were on a simple expedition, sure. Sam looked at his watch. Just past noon. It was looking like they didn't have a choice. Nigel was out there, and Percy was their only option. If he couldn't find this map, then maybe he could remember the location and point them to it. Sam explained everything to Aldridge, including why he didn't want the police involved.

"That certainly changes things," Aldridge said. "Let me see if I can settle him down long enough to figure out where this chart is. I'm fairly certain he keeps it in the shop, which is probably why he led us here to begin with. He does get distracted by the caverns."

"Thanks," Sam said. "We appreciate your help."

Sam and Remi waited outside while Aldridge spoke with Percy.

They looked in through the window, discussing what to do if Percy couldn't find the chart. "Maybe," Remi said, "he'll remember the general vicinity of the four caverns. We could have Aldridge drive him there while we follow. He won't even have to get out of the car. Just point to the location, then Aldridge could take him home."

"That might be our only option," he said as Aldridge called them back inside.

"Good news," Aldridge said. "Percy and I had a little chat about those caverns."

Percy was holding a cardboard tube. "My friend tells me you're interested in the Nottingham caves. Some of my favorites. Been visiting them since I was a boy."

Aldridge tapped Percy on the shoulder. "Show them the map, Percy."

"Right." He walked over to the table and pulled the top off the tube. Tipping it over, he slid out a large printed map of Nottingham, which he spread out on the counter. Thick red pencil lines were drawn all over it, with notations scrawled in various places. "Been mapping the things as long as I can remember. These are my favorite," he said, tapping the spot where they were now standing.

Sam eyed the map, noting a cloverleaf pattern drawn near the grounds of Nottingham Castle and the notation *Four Caverns* written above it. "Tell us about this place," he said.

Fifty-one

It's the four caverns," Percy said. "Dangerous place, that. Lots of twists and turns. Some of the chambers drop right down. Too easy to fall. These, though," he pointed toward the tailor's shop again. "Much easier to get in. First ones I ever went into. Used to be wine cellars."

Remi put her hand on Percy's shoulder. "Definitely my favorite. But these," she said, pointing to the clover, indicating the four caverns. "Where do we find them?"

"Behind the ivy. Lot of those caves were hidden when the houses were built. There's an ancient stone wall in the park. The ivy grows right over it. See the X?"

Sam leaned in close and saw the entrance was actually marked. "Would you mind if I took a photograph?"

"Not at all," Percy said.

Sam took a few photos with his phone while Remi asked, "When's the last time you were there?"

"Years ago. Used to take some of my students on tours down there. It's still there. You came with me, remember?" he said to Aldridge.

"Vaguely. We've traipsed through a lot of caves."

Percy nodded. "This one I like because it's right there, but no one even knows. Through the ivy. That's how a lot of them are. Lost. But right there in their own backyards."

Sam and Remi left for Nottingham Park, a neighborhood that had once been the deer park for Nottingham Castle. The area they were looking for—from what Percy had described to them—had a greenbelt running between some of the grand houses set on large parcels. Unfortunately, what he didn't have was an exact address, and as Sam drove around, they realized the description fit several areas.

It wasn't until Selma called with a piece of information that allowed them to fit a puzzle piece into place. He pulled over. "Can you repeat that?" Sam said as he put her on speakerphone. "I want to make sure we heard you right."

"Grace Herbert-Miller's cousin," Selma said. "The one who inherited the estate in Nottingham?"

"Something McGregor, wasn't it?" Sam said.

"Henry McGregor. I did some checking. This estate he inherited is in that very neighborhood." She read off the address. "The property's up for sale, and nobody's living there at the moment. But we called and Mr. McGregor said you're welcome to go anywhere on the property that you want."

Remi plugged it into the GPS on her phone. When it came up,

she and Sam compared it to the map that Percy had given them. Almost in the middle of his red clover marking the four caverns he'd talked about.

"X marks the spot," she said.

Sam dug out his backpack, pulling out what they needed for their initial foray into the cave—should they be lucky enough to find it. He and Remi each took a compact Stinger flashlight and case, a four-inch Buck Knife, and a magnetic compass. Sam carried his gun in the hidden holster of his fishing vest and his knife in its case on his belt. Remi wore a pancake holster with her P938 nine-millimeter, pushing it toward the small of her back so it wouldn't be readily visible.

They drove to the address given for the McGregor property. Other than the sign out front listing the estate for sale, there was nothing to indicate that there was anything unusual about the place. It was Remi who pointed out that the property lines could've changed over the centuries. "Who knows if the Herbert or McGregor ancestors parceled any of this out, way back when. The entrance might be on someone else's property by now. Never mind that there's no ivy here. Percy mentioned something about ivy."

Sam let his foot off the gas as he looked at the McGregor property.

"Now what?" she asked.

"Drive around and see if we can't find some ivy." He glanced in his rearview mirror and saw a car pull onto the street behind.

"There!" Remi pointed to the right of the McGregor estate. "A lot of ivy in that park."

Not quite a park, it was a greenbelt running between the two homes with a graveled footpath. Right now, though, Sam was more worried about the car behind him—until he saw it pull into the drive at the corner and caught a glimpse of the woman driving and the young boy sitting in the front passenger seat.

He continued past the greenbelt, when Aldridge called. "Bit of a problem," he said after Remi put him on speakerphone. "I just got off the phone with Swift's wife. He's just returned from meeting with someone about the caves. I'm assuming these are the men you're worried about."

There was no doubt in Sam's mind who Swift met with, which meant Fisk and company were probably on their way to the caves. "Thanks for the update."

Remi shifted in her seat to get a better look as Sam continued down the street. "I don't see any other ivy in the area. Maybe that's really the entrance."

"It certainly looks like it. Right now, I'd like to find a place to park without being seen."

"You think it's really there?"

"The treasure?" Sam said. "Wouldn't Percy have found it in all his wanderings? Or someone else during the last eight hundred years?"

"I was thinking more of a clue." She gave a faint smile. "Who knows? Maybe we'll get lucky."

Sam drove a bit farther, making a U-turn as the rain started up again. "A lot of other treasures out there waiting to be found. If we don't find this one, it isn't the end of the world."

Remi picked up her phone. "Slow down. I'll take a few pictures on our way out."

He let his foot off the gas while Remi took a few photos of the ivy vines cascading down the stone wall. Now that he had a better look at it, he realized the crumbling, ivy-covered wall against the side of that low hill didn't really seem to belong to anything—maybe left over from some other time before the current houses had been built in the area.

That had to be it, he thought, when he saw a blue BMW turn the corner up ahead. He threw the car in reverse and backed into the drive across from the park.

"What's wrong?" Remi asked.

"Company."

Fifty-two

Rain splattered down on the windshield, blurring their vision, but Sam wasn't about to turn the wipers on and risk being seen. Not after seeing the BMW pull up to the park. Ivan and Alexandra were in the front, Jak and Nigel in the back. Ivan got out of the driver's seat, opened the back door, pulling Nigel out by his arm. Jak and Alexandra followed close behind, the four walking into the park.

A moment later, Fisk's black Mercedes pulled up behind the BMW. He and two stocky, dark-haired men got out. Sam saw the bulk of handguns beneath their matching brown leather coats. "Fisk's brought reinforcements."

Sam and Remi watched as they entered the park, walking toward the wall of ivy. Apparently Alexandra was left to guard Nigel while Jak and Ivan picked up a couple of sticks, poking them into the thick ivy vines, searching for the entrance. Ivan turned toward Nigel, saying something, and Nigel nodded at the ivy as though he had some knowledge of the location. Jak moved to the opposite end, poking his stick in and out of the vines.

"We have to do something, Sam. We can't let them take Nigel down there."

"I wasn't expecting so many men. We rush in now, we might as well be stepping into a viper's nest."

"At least they're not golden lancehead vipers."

Fisk said something to Alexandra, who moved closer to Nigel as he and his new henchmen started exploring the greenbelt. Right now, the odds of a rescue didn't look good. They'd be seen the moment they left the car and started walking down the drive to the park.

"So what's the plan?" Remi asked.

"You mean, miracle?" Trying to rescue Nigel while avoiding five armed men and possibly one armed woman—with very little cover other than a few hedges—was going to be a lot harder than they'd anticipated.

"There's always Bree," Remi said.

Sam glanced over at her. "What about her?"

"She's passed on information to her cousin before. Why not now? Why not make them think they're in the wrong location? They leave, we follow, and find a better place to get to Nigel."

Sam weighed the risks. Lazlo and Selma had gone to great pains to make sure that the only information Bree passed on to her cousin was that she hadn't been in touch with Sam and Remi. They had the perfect setup, Bree passing info on to Larayne, Larayne passing it on to Jak or Ivan. If it worked, Avery's henchmen would soon be racing off to explore some other tunnels.

If it didn't and those men found the tunnel entrance and took Nigel down there, he doubted he'd get the man out alive. "Looks like Bree's our only option."

Remi made the call, giving Selma a quick rundown on what they needed. She held out the phone for Sam. "Selma said that Lazlo finished the translation."

Whatever Lazlo had found could wait. They needed to get Nigel out of there, and he got right to the point. "Remi told you what we need. Will it work?"

"It should," Selma told him. "We've monitored every call between Bree and her cousin since Snake Island. As far as Larayne knows, we don't know where you are."

"Which plays into this perfectly." The wind gusted and rain poured down, but none of them moved from the park. "Try to get it so Larayne asks Bree if she's heard from us first. If Bree offers up the information, her cousin might become suspicious."

"Understood. And if Larayne does ask? What disinformation are we passing on to her?"

"Anything that will move them away from the cave entrance. They know it's in the vicinity, but they haven't found it yet. We need them out of the area or we'll never get Nigel out."

"We could use the priory where Robin Hood was buried."

"I think we need a better connection to King John—and something closer."

"There's Nottingham Castle," Selma said. "Documented caves and tunnels, some of which even fit the names on the map."

"Let's go with the castle. If we can get them out of this area, we might have a better opportunity to get Nigel."

"You're not going to search it?"

"There's no reason to. Even if we did get in, we don't know what we're looking for."

"That's what I was trying to tell you. Lazlo finished the translation. It's a riddle. Above death, below death, with my last meal."

"Which means what?"

"Lazlo thinks the Celtic knot engraved on the center of the cipher might have something to do with the riddle. That type of pattern is called interlacing. Sort of like basket weaving. *Above* and *below*, like in the riddle. The Celts were known to hide things in the pattern. Pull off layers of the interlacing to see the pattern below. Maybe it's a pattern of the tunnels that leads to the treasure. We haven't quite figured out the answer to the riddle, but we're working on it."

The riddle could wait. "Have Bree make the call to her cousin," he said.

Fifty-three

A few minutes later, Selma called back, saying the conversation went as expected. "Hopefully, you should see some action on your end once the information's passed on. Assuming they *believe* the information."

They did. Just as Jak poked his stick into the ivy, his arm nearly disappearing through the vines, he backed up, reached into his pocket, and pulled out his cell phone. After a brief conversation, he called Fisk over.

"Look at Nigel," Remi said. "I think he's trying to make a break for it."

Alexandra's attention was fixed on Fisk and Jak. Nigel edged away from her toward the ivy, then bolted through the vines, disappearing from view.

"I don't know if that was brilliant or idiotic," Sam said, one hand on his gun, the other on the door.

"Can't be any more brilliant and idiotic than our plan trying to get them to move."

They watched as Jak and Ivan seemed to balk at entering the cave, until Fisk pulled a gun on them. Alexandra shook her head as though exasperated, walked up to the ivy, parted the vines, and followed them in. Fisk lifted the vines, then stepped back, and Sam wondered if he was trying to decide if the phone call about Nottingham Castle was worth following up. He turned, tossing something to one of the new guys, probably the keys, since they both walked toward the Mercedes. And then Fisk followed the others into the cave.

"Guess our plan worked after all," Sam said as the Mercedes drove off.

"Not quite how we wanted."

"We got rid of two of them. That's a start. Text Selma that we're going into the caves to get Nigel."

"So she knows where to send the cavalry?"

"Gotta have a backup plan."

They waited a minute to make sure no one was popping out of the ivy before making their way down the long drive and across the street to the park.

Remi followed Sam through the heavy, gnarled ivy vines into the dark passageway. They stood there a moment, guns drawn, acclimating themselves to the dim passage. The rain fell harder, splattering against the ivy leaves behind them, covering any noise they made as they started down the steep passage. They had to walk single file, following the twisting path down, the tunnel floor gritty beneath their feet. Sam gripped his flashlight in his hand, covering up most of it so that only a sliver of light escaped to illuminate their path.

The floor dipped sharply, then raised again. Eventually the tunnel widened into a chamber, much like the one they'd been in with Percy. They stopped, and Sam peered out, then backed quickly and held up his hand.

They heard the scrape of footsteps, then someone saying, "Down this way."

They waited until the echo of footsteps faded from the chamber before stepping out.

Sam shined his muted light across the sandstone walls and saw several rough-hewn tunnels leading off from the main chamber. Something caught Remi's eye at the top and she pointed. The Celtic knot Percy had mentioned, carved in the sandstone above the opening. She checked each of the other tunnels that led off the cavern. Five tunnels in total, four with an identical Celtic knot carved above it. The fifth, with no marking at all, was the upper tunnel that led up to the park.

Sam eyed the symbols again. They must lead to the four chambers Lazlo had told them about. He flicked his light at the opening of each passageway, then pointed to the third. Footprints in the sandstone floor. The other passageways had none.

The space was wide enough for two to walk abreast, but took even more twists as it descended. Unlike the tunnel that led in from the park, this one had several smaller passages breaking away on each side.

The main passage started narrowing as it made a steep slope downward, then curved to the right about twenty yards ahead.

They hit a dip, and their feet scraped against the ground. The sound carried.

Sam shut off the light, and they stopped.

"What was that?" It sounded like Jak. "Someone's coming down from that main chamber."

"It's Victor and Rogen," Fisk said. "Hopefully, back with flashlights since you idiots only brought cell phones."

Their plan didn't work, a fact confirmed when Ivan asked, "What about that call from Larayne? Why isn't anyone going to the castle?"

"Because the cipher is for the four caverns."

"You mean chambers," Alexandra corrected. "That could be a completely different place."

"You want the treasure?" Fisk sounded annoyed. "Find the tour guide. If it's not here like he says it is, I'll break every bone in his body right before I kill him."

The sound of their footsteps faded as the group continued down the tunnel.

Sam and Remi started to follow when they heard the heavy scuff of boots coming from the main chamber.

Victor and Rogen were back.

And Sam and Remi were trapped.

Fifty-four

S am took Remi by the arm, leading her back toward the upper chamber, running one hand on the wall to feel their way in the dark, until they reached one of the side passages off the main tunnel. He and Remi stepped in, Sam taking up a position closer to the opening, with Remi right behind him.

A moment later, the bright beam of a flashlight flickered across the stone walls and the ground. Sam noticed the very obvious footprints they'd left that led right to them. He aimed toward the tunnel entrance.

There was only one man, and Sam relaxed his trigger finger as he continued on and the passageway grew dark once more.

They were about to step out when a soft scrape alerted Sam that whoever it was—Victor or Rogen—had probably doubled back and was now standing just outside the tunnel entrance. Sam felt the slightest movement of air as the man brought his gun upward, then turned on his flashlight, calling out, "Vic—"

Sam grabbed the guy's collar and swung him around, ramming his head against the cave wall. The flashlight went flying.

Gripping his Smith & Wesson like brass knuckles, Sam smashed him in the face. Rogen staggered, grabbing at Sam's shirt with his left hand, swinging his gun toward Sam. Sam grabbed the semiauto by its slide, the metal cutting into his hand as Rogen tried to pull the trigger. Sam dropped his Smith & Wesson and grabbed the gun with both hands to keep Rogen from firing. He leaned in, twisting the gun with all his strength. Bones snapped and Rogen's grip suddenly gave way. Sam freed the gun, crashed it down on his skull, stepped behind him as he swept his arm around his neck, squeezing in a chokehold to finish him off.

Remi picked up both guns while Sam dragged the body into the side tunnel. One down, five to go.

"If he was calling for Victor," Remi whispered, giving both guns to Sam, "where is he?"

"Good question." There was only one reason Sam could think of as to why Victor wouldn't have come down with Rogen.

Someone had to stand guard in the main cavern.

Sam pointed in that direction, and Remi nodded. They started up, turning the light off before they reached the cavern. A light, its glow reflecting into the tunnel. Remi waited as Sam continued to the end of the tunnel.

Not only was Victor standing guard, he had one arm around Nigel's neck, his flashlight pointed toward Sam, and, in the other hand, his gun to Nigel's head.

"How'd you get past my brother?"

"Oh. *That* was your brother down there?" Sam kept his gun

pointed at the guy, sidestepping around the circumference of the cavern. Victor turned with him, careful to keep Nigel between him and Sam.

"What'd you do to Rogen?"

Sam didn't answer. Just kept moving so that Victor followed until his flashlight was no longer pointed Remi's direction.

"Where is he?"

Just as Sam saw the barrel of Victor's gun edging from Nigel toward him, Remi stepped out of the tunnel, took a deep breath, then threw her knife.

Victor cried out as the knife hit him square in the back. His gun and flashlight flew from his hands. His head dropped back as he crumpled to the ground, dragging Nigel with him. Nigel scrambled away, his gaze fixed on Victor's body.

"Nicely done, Mrs. Fargo. Let me guess—you thought I could use a hand?"

"It crossed my mind."

"I had it under control," he said as Nigel moved closer to Remi.

"Is—is he dead?" Nigel asked, his face pale.

"Or paralyzed," Sam said. Remi's Buck Knife was imbedded up to the hilt against his spine. The man wasn't going anywhere. Nigel, however, looked about ready to faint as he gave wide berth around the body. "Exactly how *did* he get you?" Sam asked, more to take Nigel's mind off the body than anything else.

"I was hiding in one of those side tunnels. I think they saw my footprints."

Sam eyed Remi's knife. "Don't suppose you want that thing back."

"Not really. But I'll take his gun." She reached down, picked it up, then shoved it into the back of her waistband.

"What do you say we get out of here?"

"Splendid idea, Fargo."

As luck would have it, Fisk and his crew raced into the chamber at that exact moment.

Fifty-five

Sam fired several rounds, forcing Fisk, Ivan, and Jak back into the tunnel. Bits of sandstone flew up from the ground. "New plan," Sam said, pointing at the first tunnel.

Remi nodded, shut off her Stinger flashlight, pulling Nigel with her.

The only light now was coming from the third tunnel where Fisk and company were holed up.

Fisk realized the disadvantage. The cavern went dark.

Sam kept his aim in that direction as he backed toward the fourth passage. He hadn't gone more than a few feet when someone stumbled from the tunnel and the chamber lit up with the dim blue beam of a cell phone that tumbled out, then landed light side up. Sam aimed his gun, only to find Alexandra standing there, unarmed, a sacrificial lamb to light up the chamber more. And Sam was right in the middle of it.

"I'll kill the both of you, Fargo!" Fisk said. "The moment you or that woman moves."

Alexandra froze, her hands in the air, as she looked at Sam's gun.

So much for any advantage. "What is it you want, Fisk?"

"My cipher wheel. You were at the inn— Victor!" Fisk said, seeing the body. "What happened to him?"

"Ran into the wrong end of a knife," Sam said.

"Guns on the ground. Now!"

Sam lowered his gun to the ground.

"Kick it away from you."

Sam gave it a tepid push.

"Now Victor's and Rogen's guns."

Sam tossed the gun in his waistband.

"The other."

"Only one I found." Remi had the other, not that he was about to mention it.

"Your wife. Where is she?"

"Good question."

"Get her out here or you're dead."

Sam remained silent.

"Get her out here or I'll kill you."

"I'm here," Remi said from just inside the first tunnel entrance. She turned on her flashlight, held up both hands, and stepped out into the cavern toward Sam. Nigel at least stayed safely hidden.

"Toss your gun."

Remi started to lower her Sig.

"I said toss it."

She did, closer to Sam.

Fisk turned on his light and stepped out of the tunnel, his gun aimed at Sam and Remi. Ivan and Jak flanked him. "Your flashlight," he said to Remi. "Turn it off."

She lowered the Stinger to the ground, aiming the beam of light at the Night Sights of her Sig in front of Sam, taking her time before switching it off.

"The cell phone light," Fisk said, motioning with his gun. Alexandra picked up her phone, turned off the light, and shoved it into her pocket.

The only illumination now came from the flashlight that Fisk aimed at them. "Keep your hands up," he said.

Suddenly, Alexandra glared at Fisk. "Aren't you at all interested in the cipher wheel? Turns out, it wasn't the Fargos who took it."

Fisk looked at her. "What're you talking about?"

She reached into her pocket and pulled it out. "The tour guide said it's a map to the treasure. Go and get it." She flung it like a Frisbee toward the farthest passage on their left.

Fisk followed it with the beam of light, his attention diverted as it landed with a clatter, then rolled off into the darkness. "Get it!"

Ivan ran toward the tunnel.

Sam dove, scooping both his hands across the ground, grabbing two of the guns. Remi's Night Sights were still glowing. He zeroed in on Ivan and fired twice.

Fisk turned off his flashlight, plunging them into darkness. He shot once, the muzzle flash lighting his face.

Sam fired at the light, then rolled in the direction of Victor's body, using it as cover.

Several sharp blasts came from his right, echoing across the chamber. He glimpsed Jak in the muzzle blast. Remi snapped off a couple of rounds from the upper tunnel, taking him down.

Fisk returned fire.

Sam aimed over Victor's body and fired back.

Remi's gun was empty. He dropped it and used his Smith & Wesson.

He heard Fisk down the tunnel in front of him. What he wouldn't give for a light. As if Remi had read his mind, she rolled the Stinger toward him, the aluminum casing rattling as it bounced across the floor. He felt around until he found the flashlight, his fingers grasping the cold metal. If not for Victor's body, any lucky ricocheted round off the ground would take Sam out. Not exactly the best cover, but it would do.

He took the flashlight, reaching as far to his left as he could, shoving it under Victor's outstretched arm. He kept his finger on the button, waiting to turn it on at the right moment. Then, raising his gun just enough to clear Victor's body, he aimed toward the tunnel where he'd heard Fisk.

A risky plan, but they were running out of ammo. He flashed the light on, then off.

Ivan fired at it.

Sam aimed at the muzzle blast and double-tapped. A thump, then silence. Not who he was looking for, but the next-best thing.

Where are you, Fisk?

How to draw him out? He felt around for Remi's empty Sig, found it, calling out, "Remi! Get out of here. I'm out of ammo." He threw the gun so that it clattered across the uneven ground.

A lengthy pause, then Remi saying, "So am I. I'm going for help."

Someone ran up the tunnel as Sam kept his aim on the lower tunnel, listening for any sound of Fisk.

Just when he wondered if the man was ever coming up, a bluish light lit up on the right side of the cavern. Alexandra holding her cell phone as she walked along the circumference.

"Get out here, you coward," she shouted. *"I'm* the one you need to deal with."

Sam watched, stunned, as she approached the tunnel Fisk had disappeared in. He glanced toward it, the darkness absolute. But then, surprising him, Fisk stepped out, saying, "You think you can steal my cipher wheel and get away with it?"

He leveled his gun at her.

Sam fired.

Fisk jerked back. He looked at Sam, shocked, as he staggered to one side, his gun falling from his hand. "You were out of ammo."

"I lied."

Fifty-six

I hope you haven't gone to too much trouble searching for those caverns," Lazlo said after Sam and Remi called to check in. "We may have sent you on a bit of a wild-goose chase."

"No trouble at all," Sam said, watching the multitude of cops on the premises, many of them from the firearms unit—the only officers in Great Britain authorized to carry guns. "Why?"

"Turns out, we were wrong. Definitely a fourth *chamber*, not cavern. In fact, we're fairly certain the treasure can't possibly be anywhere *near* Nottingham Park. I'm not sure why Nigel would have sent you there. It just doesn't fit."

Sam and Remi exchanged glances as they ended their call home, then looked at Nigel. "Why did you send us there?" Remi asked.

He drew his gaze from Alexandra, who was giving her statement to one of the investigators. "It was the only thing I could think of that might convince them they needed me. I'd been to the four caverns on a tour years ago during one of my university classes." He shrugged, giving a faint smile. "I figured if I could make them believe the treasure was there and that I could take them to it . . ."

"It worked," Sam said. Fisk was in custody. Ivan and Jak were dead. Alexandra had a small cut on her forehead from shrapnel but was otherwise unhurt.

Remi gave him a tired smile. "It was a good run. Getting that close to possibly solving the mystery of King John and his treasure."

"It was. But, on the bright side, our schedule's wide open. So where do you want to go on vacation?"

"I thought you had that all planned out?"

"I did, sort of. Where did we leave off?"

"Carmel."

One of the investigators poked his head out of the tunnel entrance. The ivy had been pulled back and tied with a cord, giving them easy access. The investigator looked over, calling out to the two officers standing guard. They walked over, conversing quietly.

Remi leaned her head against Sam's shoulder, watching them. "Nice shooting down there, by the way."

"Likewise."

One of the officers walked over, taking out his notebook. "About your pistols . . ."

"We have visitor permits for them," Sam said. Handguns

were prohibited in Great Britain. They'd confiscate theirs in a heartbeat, and Sam liked his Smith & Wesson. "They should be on file in London."

"Very good, sir. I'll pass on the information." He walked back to inform the investigator.

Sam waited until he was out of earshot, telling Remi, "Remind me to call Rube as soon as we get out of here." If anyone could pull strings to make permits magically appear in the files, Rube Hayward could.

Alexandra, finished with her statement, returned to the wall, sitting on the other side of Sam.

He looked over at her, curious. "You turned on Fisk. Why?"

She gave a cynical laugh as she reached up, touching the small bandage on her forehead that one of the paramedics had put there. "I never wanted anyone hurt. Ever. I only wanted to find this treasure to get back at Charles. And then . . ." She glanced at Remi. "I knew that once Fisk got what he wanted, they were going to kill me like I was nothing. And dump my body down there." Her eyes teared up, and she brushed them with the back of her hand. "He was going to do the same to you. I just felt I had to take a stand. I wanted my two kids to know I finally did something right." She gave a ragged sigh. "It doesn't matter. Charles might not have the treasure, but he'll get away with trying to kill us like he does everything else."

"That," Sam said, "we can probably do something about."

"How?"

"Trust me," he replied, thinking about the security reports Archer had been forwarding to him on Charles Avery. "I've got an entire team gathering evidence on him as we speak."

"If you do find it—the treasure—do me a favor and send me a picture? I'd like to forward it to Charles."

"Doesn't seem likely now," Sam said. "The map's completely deciphered, and this was our best hope. We seem to be at a dead end."

"Or a better location," Remi added.

Eventually they were all escorted to the police station, where formal statements were made. Hours later, they were released, and by the time that Sam and Remi got back to their hotel room, they fell into bed, exhausted, not even bothering with dinner.

"We did it!"

The excitement in Lazlo's voice was enough to bring Sam fully awake.

"Did what?" Remi asked.

"Finished the cipher." Lazlo announced. *"In the castle rock. Beyond the den of the wolf's head. The fourth chamber. Above death. Below death. With the last meal."*

Sam and Remi looked at each other, then turned back to the tablet and Lazlo's beaming face. "Great," Sam said. "Exactly what does it mean?"

"The location of the treasure," Lazlo replied. "Except that first part."

"First part?"

"We're fairly sure it's telling us it's *not* at Robin Hood's lair."

"Would have been nice to know yesterday," Sam said.

"So," Remi said, "eliminating the Robin Hood connection, where does that leave us?"

"As vague as it is," Selma replied, "we believe it means Newark Castle."

"Newark Castle?" Remi glanced at Sam, then back at the tablet. "Why there?"

"The talk of *death*, *chambers*, and *the last meal*, it's got to be talking about where King John died."

"Sorry," Sam said to Remi. "Looks like that vacation's going to have to wait."

Fifty-seven

The next day, Sam, Remi, and Nigel drove out to Newark under a dark sky that threatened more rain. They parked in the lot across the River Trent, the wind gusting as they walked across the bridge toward the imposing fortress. From this side, the castle appeared whole, but when they passed through to the other side, it was apparent that little remained of the once-impressive structure beyond the near-intact curtain wall along the riverbank, the gatehouse, a large hexagonal tower at the northwest corner, and a lower tower at the southwest end where King John was said to have died.

"Not much left," Sam said as they looked around at the park-like grounds in what had at one time been the castle keep.

The wind whistled through the crumbling ruins, whipping at Remi's hair. She nodded toward the lower, southeast tower. "My money's where King John died. The riddle's clearly talking about his death."

"Isn't that a little obvious?" Sam asked.

"Hide in plain sight. Why not?"

Sam picked up a few pamphlets so that they'd look more like visiting tourists instead of burglars who planned to sneak into the parts of the castle closed to the public. "As many times as this place has been occupied and remodeled since King John's death, where would they hide it?"

"The point of our visit, isn't it?" Remi asked.

He pulled out his phone and accessed the text with the ciphered riddle that Selma had sent.

The fourth chamber. Above death. Below death. With the last meal.

Remi tapped the screen. "*Chamber* is another word for *room*. That could be the room where he died."

"The *last meal* could mean a *dining hall*."

"Which is long gone."

"The tour's starting," Nigel said, pointing to the small crowd near the south tower.

They followed the others into the tower, climbing up the stone steps, as the guide gave a running commentary on the originations of the castle. "In 1646, after the civil war, Parliament ordered the castle destroyed. Had an outbreak of plague in Newark town *not* halted the destruction, there'd be nothing left."

As they filed down the hall into one of the rooms, a gust of wind swept through the castle ruins, sounding much like a person moaning. "Ghost!" someone said, followed by soft laughter from several in the crowd.

"Actually," the guide told them, "the castle is said to be haunted by those murdered here over the centuries. In fact, this room is where King John died, some say poisoned by his enemies. And there's the dungeons far below where hundreds of poor souls were tortured and left to die, starved, their bodies eaten by armies of rats until they were nothing but a pile of bones."

Sam pulled Nigel and Remi back as the group moved on. Nigel stood guard in the hall while Sam and Remi examined the room where King John breathed his last, looking for any hidden doors, loose floorboards, or passages. After twenty minutes, they found nothing encouraging.

"Looks like old King John took the secret of his treasure with him," said Sam.

"We still have several chambers in the main part of the castle to search," Remi countered.

They hurried out and caught the group as the guide finished another lecture on the castle kitchen. Then he led them down a narrow circular staircase, quoting his spiel about the castle being haunted by the ghosts of those who died here. They passed the level containing the castle sewer and the root cellar. Next, he lectured the group about the gruesome torture of political prisoners as he stopped at an opening in the floor with a ladder that led straight down into the dismal dungeons.

"For those of you brave enough to climb down, you can see some of the graffiti carved, they say, by the Templar Knights who were imprisoned here."

Of course, Sam, Remi, and Nigel made the descent, with a moaning greeting them that sounded much like a chorus of ghosts. All three knew it was a recording coming from one of the cells.

Remi studied the graffiti on the stone walls while Sam and

Nigel studied the walls themselves, pushing and tapping for any suspicious movement or the hollow sound of a tunnel.

"Any rumors of King John hiding his treasure here?" Sam asked once they left the dungeons.

The guide's brow went up. "Here? That would be an interesting twist on the legend of his treasure being lost in the mud of the fens. Now, if you will follow me."

"One question," Remi said. "It concerns an old riddle from centuries past. Something to do with King John."

The guide looked at her, waiting.

"*The fourth chamber. Above death. Below death. With the last meal.* Any idea where that location might be if it meant somewhere in this Newark Castle?"

"Easy." The guide grinned. "The root cellar. It's the fourth level above the lowest dungeon, and below the tower where King John died."

"And where would that be?"

"The root cellar? We passed it on our way here." He pointed up. "You're welcome to take a look, since Mr. Ridgewell is with you."

That they did, but like the other locations, there didn't seem to be anything that appeared as though it might contain a hidden chamber. The ancient stone walls looked solid after eight hundred years of mold, dust, and dampness.

Just as they were about to leave, Sam stopped and stared at a arch in one wall, about the size of a window but bricked in solid. Considering how barren and dreary the rest of the cellar was, it didn't seem likely that some twelfth-century contractor decided to put a decorative touch in an underground room designed to hold potatoes for the winter.

"Remi, look at this. Odd, don't you think?"

She aimed her flashlight beam at the faux window and studied it for a few moments. "Looks like whoever dug the chamber had an artistic streak."

Sam didn't reply. Using the butt of his flashlight, he tapped on the bricks inside the border arch and heard only a hollow clink, giving evidence that the bricks were either loosely stacked or shielding a hollow area behind them.

He started pressing and kicking the bricks. Finally, one came loose. It took a minute to work it free. Then he used it to strike and remove the other bricks until he stopped to aim his flashlight into the darkness beyond.

"What do you see?" Remi asked anxiously.

Sam shrugged. "I guess we don't have to waste our time looking for King John's Treasure anymore."

"The chamber is empty?" Nigel muttered with deep disappointment in his voice.

"No," Sam spoke with a broad smile. "You can reach out and touch it."

Fifty-eight

Remi, her heart pounding twice its normal pace, crawled through the narrow opening, followed by Nigel, then Sam.

At first, it looked like nothing more than dust-covered stones, as their lights darted about the walls and ceiling of the chamber. On closer inspection, it soon became obvious dozens of ancient metal chests littered the area, floor to ceiling, in at least thirty stacks, deeply coated with sandstone dust.

"They all have locks," said Nigel. "How are we going to open them?"

Without a word, Sam picked up a brick he'd knocked to the floor and beat it against the lock on a rusty chest. The ancient latch easily broke apart.

Sam lifted the lid, and they were stunned at seeing it was filled with hundreds of tarnished silver coins, depicting the heads of

King Henry I, King Harold II, and King William I. The next three chests were loaded with gold coins. Then came a mixture of pearls, silver plates, gold goblets, swords and their scabbards, inlaid with precious jewels.

History recorded that King John had a passion for rubies, emeralds, and diamonds, and had a large cache of semi-rare gems.

"Amazing," Sam said, suddenly leaning down and picking up something none of them had noticed. "Look at this." A golden arrow—or, rather, a gold-leafed arrow. He passed it to Remi.

She stared in awe. "Robin Hood?"

"No one in Nottingham I can think of," said Nigel, "would have a golden arrow. Maybe the legends were true after all."

"Jackpot," Sam gasped, staring into another open chest. "This one holds the crown jewels, scepter, and orb." He held up the golden crown encrusted with pearls and rubies.

"You should see what goes with them," said Remi. She showed them three large chests filled with King John's wardrobe. Most had survived inside the chests, some had rotted away, but there were many robes in magnificent colors and gold thread.

"Can I put one on?" asked Sam with a broad smile.

"Don't you dare," said Remi. "It's been eight hundred years since King John wore the crown and royal clothing. They're historic relics."

"He's been dead a long time." Sam grinned. "He won't mind."

"You're looking at and touching artifacts worth a hundred million pounds," said Nigel. "If the authorities knew what you want to do, you'd be locked up in Nottingham Prison for the rest of your life."

"I don't think I'd like that," said Remi with a note of sarcasm.

"Better we clean this place up before the next tour comes through," Nigel warned.

Sam nodded as he checked his watch. "Nigel's right. We only have another ten minutes before our jolly guide shows up."

Remi took several photographs from different angles for their own records, then swiveled back into the chamber so Sam and Nigel could replace the bricks.

Their tour guide and his followers came along just as Sam, Remi, and Nigel reached the opening to the root cellar. "Find the treasure?" he asked teasingly.

"Wrong chamber," replied Sam.

"Wrong castle," added Remi.

The guide simply smiled and said, "I told you so."

Sam and Remi fought to keep straight faces.

Once outside, they breathed clean, crisp air again. Sam stared at Nigel and said, "Well, Nigel, it's all yours."

Nigel looked at Sam with a lost expression. "I don't understand."

Remi gave him a light kiss on the cheek. "We're leaving before the mob floods through the front gate."

Fifty-nine

In the morning, Sam and Remi checked out of their hotel and decided to stop by Newark Castle and see the turmoil from a company of security guards and an army of archaeologists over the discovery of the largest treasure in a hundred years. They parked as close as possible and approached the front gate, guarded by the Nottinghamshire police. A guard stopped them as they approached.

"Your name, sir?" asked the guard.

"Longstreet," announced Sam. "Lord and Lady Longstreet."

"That name is wearing a little thin, don't you think," said Remi.

The guard scanned a notebook and shook his head. "I'm sorry, sir, your name is not among those who are allowed to pass."

"Could you contact Mr. Nigel Ridgeway," asked Remi, "and let him know we're here?"

"Yes, milady, I can do that for you," the guard said politely.

Ten minutes later, Nigel, with Percy Wendorf and Professor Cedric Aldridge tagging along behind, walked briskly across the keep.

"Thank heavens, you came," said Nigel. "We have government officials driving us crazy, from the Ministry of Culture to the British Museum, and many others claiming jurisdiction, all crawling over each other to glimpse a piece of history that had been frozen in time."

"Remi and I are foreigners," said Sam. "I don't see how we can help."

"I don't understand," said Aldridge. "The treasure never would have been discovered without the two of you.

"Because of your contribution to the British Realm, you could achieve the honor of knighthood," added Aldridge.

"Sir Sam," said Remi with a wide smile. "I couldn't live with him."

Sam gave Remi a dark look. "Spread the word that it was the three of you, working as a team, who found and deciphered the key to the cipher that led to the hidden trove."

"And don't forget to mention Madge Crowley and her theory about the king's riches secretly hidden by William the Marshal, Earl of Pembroke," added Remi.

"Because of him," said Nigel, "the king's treasure never left Castle Newark, while William spread the story that it was lost in the fens during a storm. Unfortunately, a week later he was killed in battle with the French and the secret of the treasure's location died with him."

"I wish we could stay while the treasure is studied and restored, but we have a plane to catch at Heathrow."

"Can't you stay for a few days?" asked Percy.

Sam gave a slight shake of his head. "We're truly sorry, but we have important business at home that can't wait."

"But you will come back?" pleaded Nigel.

"We promise to return," said Remi. She kissed all three on the cheek as Sam gave each a warm, masculine hug.

Sam and Remi climbed into the car, waved, and drove away.

Remi waved until they were out of sight. "I could have sworn Percy and Nigel had tears in their eyes as we left them."

"They weren't the only ones," said Sam.

"Me too," said Remi, dabbing her cheeks with a Kleenex.

For the first time in two weeks, Sam looked relaxed. He glanced at Remi, who was absorbed with something on her cell phone that made her laugh.

"What's so amusing?"

"This." She showed him a photo of the treasure taken after the three of them opened at least twelve chests, revealing much of the gold, gemstones, and King John's crown jewels. "I sent it to Alexandra, who emailed it to Charles. Apparently right after he opened it, the police arrived and arrested him."

"That's got to hurt." He took one final look at Newark Castle in the rearview mirror. "Now that our work here is done, how about that vacation I promised you?"

"Forget it, Fargo. You're never going to top this," she said as she gave his knee a tight squeeze. "Best vacation. Ever."

T. M.